THE R.

AND

THE PIPE

Simon Catterel

24 December 2021

—

HOB HOLE

THE RAVEN
AND
THE PIPE

S A Catterall

Published by Skid Publishing

DISCLAIMER

A CIP catalogue record for this book is available from the British Library.

 Find us on Facebook

ISBN 978-0-9933431-3-1 (Paperback)
ISBN 978-0-9933431-4-8 (epub)
ISBN 978-0-9933431-5-5 (mobi)

Book layout and cover design by Clare Brayshaw

Cover images   8223761 © William Perry | Dreamstime.com
            18227703 © Kari Høglund | Dreamstime.com

Prepared and printed by:

York Publishing Services Ltd
64 Hallfield Road
Layerthorpe
York YO31 7ZQ

Tel: 01904 431213

Website: www.yps-publishing.co.uk

ACKNOWLEDGEMENTS

I would like to thank Tim Catterall, David Chadwick, Hilary Duncan, Deborah Gilbert, Andrew Kelly, Olivia Skeoch and Rob Turnbull for their proof reading and advice, everyone at YPS for their management and professionalism, Lucy, without whose encouragement I would still be talking about one day writing a novel and finally, you, the reader, for taking the time and trouble to share my tale.

ABOUT THE AUTHOR

Simon Catterall is a criminal defence solicitor from North Yorkshire. *The Raven and The Pipe* is the sequel to *Hob Hole*, his debut novel.

He can be contacted at **simon.catterall@mail.com**

FOREWORD

This is the sequel to *Hob Hole,* my debut novel published in 2016.

In the event any reader is wondering how Edmund Bullick arrived at the opening chapter of *Raven,* I have annexed a second edition of *Hob Hole* as a prequel to his continuing adventures.

Thank you so much for reading this duology. I hope you enjoy it.

HOB HOLE

*And all things, whatsoever ye shall ask in prayer,
believing, ye shall receive.*

Mathew 21:22

CHAPTER ONE

I have to begin this account with the silent memories that creep up and stab me when I'm lying awake. You will know the feeling, I'm sure; you're so tired and it's so late but sleep passes you over and the mind wanders strangely. Old friends and lovers. The sins and the regrets. The ghosts on your shoulder. The draining penance of staring at luminous hands as they crawl through the digits. If the clock would just lie flat for a moment, I could clear up the mistakes at the back instead of having to live with them. If only, hey?

Cursed sleep. How do you break the spell? I've asked many people this question and it seems we all have our different ways. There's the obvious, of course, and tallying sheep over a farm gate is popular although my brother imagines he's up on the old railway line at Sandsend counting breakers as they rush over the slate flats at the turn of tide. Tom employs a quite novel approach. He says when it happens to him, he applies the *length x breadth x height* formula to try and work out the number of blocks in Hadrian's Wall until slain by the mental arithmetic. Each to their own, I guess. If we were all the same, it would be a very boring world.

When I can't sleep, I scramble the pillows in search of cool linen, like you do, and then flopping back into the covers I start tracing the contours of my own little life. It usually begins with that first memory on my father's shoulders in the unsaddling enclosure at Thirsk, marvelling at the steam rising off the washed down horses, either that or I drift fondly to endless blue summers digging holes in Scarborough beach. I'll recall my first impressions of Ampleforth, the distress of small boys abandoned by their parents, the strange looking Benedictines in their cassocks and above all the beautiful canticles that used to drift through the corridors and tell me that somehow, everything would be all right in the end.

These moonlit hours sketching my youth have diminished with the years and nowadays, I'm usually asleep long before a virtual stroll carries me from the college chapel and into the lecture theatre. However, if I go on to take my old seat in there, I might as well start counting waves or Roman blocks myself because if I don't, I know I'll go back to that muggy autumn afternoon when my life changed forever. There is a delicious irony it should all have begun in the lecture theatre, a place of learning. It was to be an education for sure and with the rest of my life so inextricably tied to that dreadful afternoon, I do not see how I could begin this narrative at any other interval.

It was late in the fall of 1914, and I was boarding an extra term to sit the Oxbridge exams. It remains with me now, the scent of smouldering leaves floating through the window together with the shouts and whistles from a distant rugby match and the *Angelus* chime of St Lawrence's. To my left we are walled in by layer upon layer of books stacked up to the medieval beams, the dusty rows criss-crossed by a pair of sliding staircases giving the whole the appearance of a giant *Snakes and Ladders* board. On the other side of the theatre an enormous pair of curtains hold back the Scorpion sun although a few tiny shafts burst through the moth holes to skewer a billion particles of dust. Then down there in the middle, beyond the creaking benches and their fresh-faced occupants, right in the bowl of the auditorium, just there behind the black marble island stands the hapless figure of Brother Wallace wrestling with a city of bottles and tripods as he endeavours to illustrate the combustion of ethanol.

'Now pay attention class: this is a weally important expewiment and in the final examination you will be expected to wemember how it is conducted.'

Wallace was not a young man and should have been retired long before he scrutinised one of my equations. He was the ultimate academic, but he'd been Head of Science since at least the second Boer conflict and maybe even the first. No one seemed to know. It wouldn't have surprised me if he had been teaching chemistry since the Crimea for there was something quite ageless about him. I often studied the crablike manner he used to slide his thin, humid form around the theatre with that signature sprinkling of dandruff upon the shoulders of his black gown. I swear he'd been doing it for so long his tracks were worn in the flags.

'Now, first we place the thermometer in this beaker of water then we light the ethanol spiwit burner…'

'This is boring. How long until supper?' sighed a voice to my left with such an exaggerated yawn that everyone in the seminar appeared to hear it apart from the old monk in the pit. Tommy Brentnall was also sitting Oxbridge although it was common knowledge he spent more time boxing and chasing women from the village than he did in his books. I gave him a sharp elbow.

'Tom, don't, you'll get us turfed out.'

'What if we are? Mother Earth is burning around us Edmund, burning I tell you. We are living through the most extraordinary passage of world history with civilization itself ablaze, and yet you and I are destined to loiter on the sidelines, trapped in this time warp of cassocks and Latin.'

'Do you mind? I've just about had it with your endless commentary Brentnall. Some of us are trying to pay attention to this'.

So spoke Conway, the head boy who unfortunately for us was seated in the next row down. *One-way Conway* as he was better known because he was always in chapel and did everything by the book, fawning and crawling to the staff on his way up. He actually came from my hometown too where his family ran a taxi business, but the bloke was a stiff and there were poles between us.

At Tom's exchange with the head boy Brother Wallace looked up and glowered in our general direction before returning to the array of implements before him.

'Now we give the spiwit burner half a minute or so to settle then using gloves on both hands we lower the beaker of water onto the appawatus so it sits diwectly on top of the flame...'

'Psst- Edmund, *Blue*' mumbles Tom. 'I've fixed up a session of *Three Old Maids* behind the 1st XI pavilion tomorrow after supper. I've persuaded big Hilda and two of her friends from the kitchens to come along – you up for it?'

Someone snorted at the end of our row. I gritted my teeth and carried on taking notes.

'I warn you, I'll be filing a report with the headmaster' snapped Conway.

'Hey, don't look at me,' I retorted. 'I didn't say anything.'

Wallace glared at the back row where we were sitting, a little longer and more deliberately this time before returning to his spiel.

'Note please that the mass of ethanol in the spiwit burner and the tempwiture of water must be measured before and after the expewiment. In theory, the heat generated by the combustion of the ethanol should be twansferred to the water…'

'Surely you remember big Hilda don't you *Blue*?' quipped Tom. 'You should do having salivated over the size of her hooters these last twelve months.'

Several students burst out laughing and it was too much for Wallace who put down his chalk and turned to the class.

'Would the young man at the back pwactising his elocution please make himself known. Come come, don't be shy, who is it?

Conway, unable to pass any occasion to increase his stock pointed an arm out in our direction, not that there was any need for Tom was already on his feet.

'Bwentnall. I might have guessed it would be you. Well then, Bwentnall, I deduce the only weeson you have time for tittle tattle in lectures is because you know all about this expewiment.'

'I wouldn't go so far as to say that …'

'No, no Bwentnall don't be coy,' interrupted Wallace before adding darkly 'we are all quite *intweeged* to ascertain if your knowledge of the syllabus is diwectly pwoportionate to your capacity to excite disorderly tittle tattle. Down here now if you would Bwentnall, come come, that's wight, to the front of the class'

All eyes were fixed on Tom as he shuffled his stocky frame to the end of the row and down the steps to join Wallace in the bowl of the theatre.

'That's wight, come this way. Good. Now Bwentnall, since you already know so much about this expewiment you will doubtless be able to complete it for the benefit of the class. And be sure to acquit yourself Bwentnall for if you fail, you will answer for this most weecent exhibition of diswuptive behaviour to the headmaster, who after last time will take a gweat deal of persuading that you should not be sent down from college stwait away.'

Tom shuffled round the island where to sarcastic jeers he inspected various bottles holding some to the light and sniffing the contents of others before carefully replacing the stoppers and setting them down again.

'Well, Bwentnall? We are all on the edge of our seats.'

Tom cleared his throat then gathering some yellow chalk turned to the blackboard and began to scribble enthusiastically.

'First of all, we need to weigh the spirit burner and various fluids and record the information in a table. Next, we ignite the alcohol then using the glass rod to stir the water, we wait until the temperature rises to 40°C at which point we immediately replace the cap on the spirit burner to extinguish the flame. We then record the final temperature of the water using the thermometer.'

Wallace looked surprised. We all were.

'Yes, yes, that's all well and good Bwentnall, but what is the *purpose* of the expewiment?'

Tom twisted to the board and continued in that familiar, easy manner.

'Well sir, that's simple because from the information provided, we can establish the amount of energy transferred from the burning alcohol to the surrounding water utilising the equation $q = mc\Delta T$ where q is the energy transferred, m represents the mass of water and c is its specific heat capacity.'

Wallace furred his brow while Tom continued, fluent and assured, occasionally tapping the board with his chalk as he underlined various sections of the equation.

'...and so it is through the application of *this* formula that we can identify which alcohol – or rather which *fuel* – provides the most energy per ounce of liquid burned, which when considered on a commercial scale has obvious implications for the industrial consumer. Tarra! I thank myself!' at which my friend gave a small bow and tossed the chalk into the box leaving the assembly focussed back on our tutor who was still glaring at the board. After what seemed like an age, but was probably no more than a few seconds, Wallace turned back to the class.

'Well, well, Bwentnall' said he 'quite contwawee to my expectations it appears you shall live to fight another day. You may weturn to your seat.'

'Thank you very much sir,' beamed Tom who was already striding back up the causeway, chopping the air in acknowledgement of the raucous applause that had broken out upon Wallace's capitulation.

'That will do class. That will do!' bayed Wallace waiting for the clamour to die down before continuing. 'Bwentnall is wight, the purpose of this expewiment is not only to assess the combustion of various fuels but also to measure their *efficiency* against one another…'

Tom settled back in his place.

'How on earth did you know that?' I whispered.

'Piece of cake. My family are chemists in York, remember. Here now, watch closely, this should be a good laugh…'

'Watch what?'

Conway span round again. 'That's it Brentnall, I shall report your behaviour to the headmaster at the next captain's meeting.'

Tom screwed his face at Conway then dipped his head to the front where I followed the cue back to Wallace still beavering away over his city of tripods and burners.

'Now class, I want you to note the manner diffewent alcohols burn at diffewent wates, let us take this second example of methylated spiwit…'

Wallace picked up a large green bottle and pouring the contents into a fresh flask, carefully balanced the combination over the tripod where it began to simmer on the indigo spike of a Bunsen burner. Within seconds one or two students at the front began to splutter, followed by others behind them, and then still others as if some invisible force was scaling the bank of desks.

'Dear me. Who was *that*?' wailed a voice from below.

'Who was what?' thought I until a revolting smell of rotten eggs hit the back row. Tom's face was deadpan.

'Switched a few bottles when I was down there didn't I?'

Within seconds the cries and accusations multiplied, some students amplifying their distress with contorted faces and theatrically clenched throats. As he frantically dismantled the apparatus Wallace shouted to a bucktoothed lad in the front row to open the window.

'Who me sir?' replied the youth as if butter wouldn't melt in his mouth.

'Yes, you boy, open that window, in fact open all the windows! Quickly man, get on with it.'

The lad did as he was told and with a roar like gravel sliding down corrugated iron, the curtains tore open filling the hall with sunlight.

'What do you mean it's stuck? Lift it up boy, don't pull! Lift! Lift! Here, move over' at which Wallace and a couple of others puffed and heaved at the base until with an appalling shriek the window finally gave way. All the while the coughing and spluttering rose to a crescendo as even the meeker scholars made hay in the unexpected crisis.

All of a sudden, the air was cut by the rattle of the latch as the towering profile of Father Mathews appeared in the doorway. Immediately, the coughing ceased and everyone jumped to their feet as the headmaster scowled at the assembly before turning his attention to Wallace shuffling anxiously by the window.

'Good grief Brother Wallace, what on earth's going on? And what's that disgusting smell?'

Wallace looked crestfallen.

'Good afternoon Father Headmaster. The students are conducting an ethanol expewiment but there appears to be a pwoblem with some of the labelling.'

Mathews picked up a few bottles then turned and raked the bank of students as if daring anyone to even blink. No one of course did and the tension was only broken when having murmured something in Wallace's ear to make the latter nod like a penguin, he looked up and fixed his steely gaze on the rest of the class.

'I would like to speak with Edmund Bullick in my office now.'

A sea of faces turned and stared in my direction. Who, *me*? What could the head possibly want with *me*? I exchanged a nervous glance with Tom then disregarding Conway's gesture of cutting his throat, edged to the walkway. I sensed the worried stare of the assembly. Something was horribly wrong. Mathews addressed the remainder of the class.

'I formed the impression on my way in here that some students are suffering from a respiratory ailment, the condition no doubt triggered by a lack of fresh air. I therefore direct the whole of upper sixth including the Oxbridge scholars rise at 6.00am tomorrow for a cross country to Byland Abbey and back. That's 6.00am tomorrow morning and I shall expect everybody to be up, dressed in sports kit and assembled in the courtyard before the clock chimes. Carry on please Brother Wallace.'

Without another word Mathews turned and with a swish of his gown, he was off leaving the theatre in stunned silence and me to trail anxiously in his wake.

We fell into step under the gaze of a thousand eyes from the old team photographs that lined the corridor. There was real purpose in the headmaster's stride but other than to admonish some juniors for slouching with their hands in their pockets he remained silent, and it was only when we reached his office and he was fishing for his keys that the icicle was plunged into my breast.

'Bullick, you must prepare yourself for some bad news. Your father has been killed in an accident and you are needed at home.'

He'd no sooner spoken when I heard footsteps and turned to meet the distressed gaze of my younger brother

Alfie and Spangle, his line master. Alfie and I looked at each other in disbelief as the head marched to the far side of his desk and reached for the top draw.

'Gentlemen, I received a telegram this afternoon from Mr Barnaby, chief steward of the Craven estate. It seems that yesterday afternoon, Lord William and your father were involved in an accident while riding out on the moors. I am sorry to tell you your father was killed while Lord William remains in a critical condition. I am afraid I have no further details other than you are both to return home immediately. Please accept my profound condolences.'

For a while Mathews remained quite still, eyes peering up at us over his half-moon glasses as he allowed the dreadful news to sink in. Alfie began to tremble and sob uncontrollably. I was too shocked to say anything. The headmaster closed the draw and picked up the threads of his matter-of-fact address.

'It's too late to set off this afternoon so Mr Spangle will take you to the village station first thing tomorrow. I would like you to pack all your things before you depart but take with you only what you require for the immediate journey, as your books and trunks will follow in due course. Edmund, I shall expect you to return for your Oxbridge examinations in two weeks' time. Alfie, as it is nearly December, we shall not expect you back until after the Christmas holidays. Please go now and make your arrangements. Look after them will you Mr Spangle'.

Mathews picked up a Latin textbook and began to thumb through the pages. Was that it? Was there anything more to say? It appeared not. We waited for a second then Spangle nodded and the three of us turned to go and pack. I screwed my eyes in disbelief. Had I really just heard Mathews tell me my father was dead? Spangle's grim expression and the tears running down my brother's cheeks told me it must be so.

Alfie was billeted with the other new boys, and it was to his dormitory in Bolton House that our sad little party trudged first. When we reached the top of the creaking staircase Spangle paused by the washbasins and surveyed the line of crisply made beds.

'Edmund, I'm going to leave you to help your brother gather his belongings. Let me know when you're done, and I'll arrange for everything to be taken down to the stables where Robinson can send them on later. In view of what has occurred, you are obviously both excused benediction.'

We stood in silence for a moment before Spangle added in a low voice 'I will go now. The milk train passes through the village at six thirty so I'll wake you both at quarter to. I'll also wire Mr Barnaby to ensure there is someone to meet you when you get into Durham tomorrow. The Abbot has arranged for High Mass on Sunday to be offered for the soul of your father but otherwise I don't think there is anything else I can usefully say at the present time – only that I am so terribly sorry boys about what has happened.'

I muttered some garbled appreciation. Spangle nodded and slipped away leaving Alfie and I alone in the dormitory. A flock of pigeons clattered on a nearby roof while somewhere in the distance a hand bell generated a rush of footsteps across the courtyard. Alfie began to cry, warm tears falling from his little face onto the bedspread as he manfully tried to dab them away with the back of his cuff.

'Edmund, what are we going to do? Please tell me this isn't happening, and we are in the middle of a terrible dream?'

The eight years that separated us had never appeared more of a gulf than at that moment. I folded a comforting arm around him.

'I'm afraid neither of us is dreaming. There can be no mistake about something so awful.'

'I don't want to go home. Not anymore. Not ever. If father is dead I feel like I just want to die as well.'

'Alfie, look at me. Look at me. Now listen. When Mum died I made a promise that I would always take care of you. And haven't I always looked after you?'

My brother spluttered in agreement.

'That's right. I always have and I always will. Now while we don't know what's happened at Craven – at least not yet – whatever it is we shall go home tomorrow and face it together. Right?'

Alfie nodded at the floor.

'Good lad. Now come on, wipe those eyes and let's get started with this packing. Which locker over there is yours?'

CHAPTER TWO

I barely slept that night, my sorrow tossed through each quarterly chime of St Lawrence's, and even when I finally succumbed, it was to emerge in a troubling dream where my father was calling out to me from the clock tower at Craven Castle. I woke with a start and believing in my confusion that the voice was emanating from the courtyard, I leaped out of bed and raced to the window. The abbey church stood graceful in the moonlight but other than a trickle of water from the broken pump in the corner, there was no sound at all.

I lay awake for a long time anticipating the trials of the next few days. I was at a loss to understand how the two of them could have been riding on the moor when they spent so little time together. Dad took care of Lord William's horses, but their relationship was strictly master and servant and apart from race days and when his Lordship inspected the yard, they barely saw each other.

The hours passed. Midnight. One o clock. My thoughts turned to Lady Alanna and the household as I tried to picture what sort of an evening they would be having in the wake of the accident. No doubt this depended upon the extent of the master's injuries but with the telegram describing them as 'critical', I perceived the castle would be in turmoil and that word of events would have already reached Oxford from where, no doubt, Lord William's heir would also be making plans to return.

Although I was two years younger than Julian, we had grown up with the other children on the Craven estate and I have fond memories of us building tree houses in the park and playing in the quarries or down on the banks of the Wear. As we grew older, we would pick up the threads in the holidays and help Barnaby around the estate or ride the novices out with the *Braes* where we were often accompanied by Julian's sister, Jane, and Alfie when he was old enough. These were such happy times which made the cracks that began to appear in Julian's character later all the more perplexing. Oh, the changes were barely noticeable at first like he would inexplicably turn sharp in conversation or peer rudely over your shoulder as you were talking to him, but when he returned from his first term at Oxford equipped with a cane and speaking with an unbearably contrived twang, I obviously asked him if there was anything the matter. I mean he sounded so ridiculous what else was I supposed to do? Julian, of course, promptly dismissed the notion that he had changed but if any confirmation were needed, it arrived at Craven that summer in the form of his university friend Lord Johnny Clifford.

I had grown up with most of Julian's friends who were from the Durham area but Clifford was something quite different making it obvious when we were introduced that the son of a horse trainer was not a suitable companion for the heir of the estate. *Horse Boy* he had called me, not that I needed any snub to keep out of his way because the fellow was trouble and having spent barely a minute in his company, I was under no illusions from where Julian had been taking his cue.

Lord Johnny Clifford appeared to have it all. At least, at first sight he did. His father was an hereditary peer, the family seemed to own half of Arundel and apart from appearing as rich as Croesus with a dash of blue blood in his veins, Julian's friend was a handsome, powerful man with a deep booming voice and it wasn't difficult to see how he cast his spell. However what Julian failed to notice, or more likely chose to overlook, was that Clifford was proud and needlessly unpleasant and if after our first meeting I had any reservations that I might have misjudged his character, these were swiftly dissipated over the following months.

When Clifford's party arrived at Craven that autumn, everyone assumed it was a brief call to look up Julian on their way to the Percy shoot. Perhaps that was the original intention although as soon it was discovered that Lord William and Lady Alanna were in Brighton for the season, the guests promptly weighed anchor and started eating and drinking the family out of house and home. On their last night the party bestowed their patronage upon the *Black Horse* from where, having caused a large amount of damage, they went on to gate-crash a stable lads' boxing tournament that was taking place in the village hall. Needless to say, their appearance was not welcomed and in the fracas that followed, Clifford proceeded to knock the front teeth out of an apprentice jockey half his size. If the incident had not already alienated the community to breaking point, the situation was compounded the following morning when the guests departed for Northumberland crowing about 'grockles' and the appalling excesses of the night before. Neither did there appear to be the faintest trace of remorse from the heir to Craven. At least at first there wasn't. It was all 'high spirits' wasn't it? The villagers, however, thought very differently and in the end it was left for Barnaby to persuade Julian that with his friends off the scene, he should compensate the lad and while he was at it cram in enough humble pie that the incident could yet be swept under the carpet before Lord William returned.

After the fracas with the jockeys, I resolved to speak to Julian about the kind of company he was keeping, and a few days later I tackled him outside the village post office. We had been friends for a long time so I cut straight to the quick suggesting that *the Merton crowd* (as they were known on the estate) were a bunch of parasites and that Clifford, in particular, was seriously bad news. Julian, though, was having none of it stating blandly that these were his companions now and that my comments were spawned by jealousy on account that they were all wealthy and titled, and that being of humbler stock, I could not be expected to understand their ways.

'Oh, come off it Julian there's nothing elite or even remotely admirable about Johnny Clifford. The fellow is a complete arse.'

'You don't understand him as I do Edmund. Just know that he is my best friend and I will not hear a word spoken against him.'

'Your friend? The only friends these people have are themselves. Look at the mayhem he brought to the village the other night? The fellow is nothing more than a self-centred, stuck-up, loud mouthed thug.'

Julian coloured at these words and to my surprise began to tremble as if fighting to master his emotions.

'You should be wary what you say about my friends in future Edmund. It is not your place to lecture me.'

'Look, there's no need to be so defensive. I'm just trying to give you the kind of advice I would expect from you if our positions were reversed.'

Julian turned the colour of beetroot.

'Reversed? Reversed you say? Our positions could never be reversed. There is a gulf between our respective stations in society or hadn't you noticed?'

'Julian, can't you see what's happening? These people are *using* you and you need to ditch them.'

Julian drew a sharp breath before spitting out his response.

'How dare you lecture me on how I should lead my life? Do you know something Edmund? I could never understand what induced my father to provide the Bullicks with such a generous living, when at the drop of a hat he could secure his pick of trainers from Malton or Middleham. Yes, that's right. Calvert, Elsey, Budgett, Wainwright; any one of them would jump at the opportunity to manage Craven but oh no, father won't hear of it, he has to persevere with a family of bogtrotters he met all those years ago. Your old man hasn't achieved anything like the level of success that would even begin to justify the estate's investment in him. Yes, that's the reality of the situation Edmund, my father has been carrying your father for years, it's a standing joke in racing circles and I'm not the only one who's been urging him to recruit someone who can make a better fist of their potential. Fred Molyneux for one would leap at the prospect of taking the string to Sherriff Hutton. You would do well to remember this because one day, the inexplicably good fortune that reposes with your family will be dependent upon my goodwill, which I can tell you at this precise moment is in extremely short measure.'

I felt a surge of anger and rounded on him.

'My father is the finest trainer in the region. It's only because of his sheer hard work Lord William has been among the top northern owners for the last decade....'

He cut me short.

'Enough! No, I said enough! How dare you answer me back?'

'What do you expect when you insult my father? You should hear yourself. You're talking rubbish.'

'I tell you now Edmund, it is you who forgets his place. You ought to remember I am the heir to Craven while you are nothing more than the son of an estate employee. First you try to lecture me about the company I keep and then you have the gall to tell *me* that I don't know what I am talking about when I bring home a few truths about your father? Consistently one of the top owners you say? I suggest that with all the investment poured into the yard my father should be head and shoulders above any other owner north of Leicester. Yes, that's right, head and shoulders. The finest trainer in the region you say? I don't think so. Your father is a show pony, Edmund. He fawns and makes all the right noises but when it comes to cutting the mustard at the highest level anyone can see he is near enough useless. *Useless!*'

Julian's face was right up against my own. At the final insult I struck him as hard as I could and we wrestled to the ground, clutching and clawing at one another. Julian was stronger and I felt his nails go down the side of my face but I was so incensed that I managed to hold my own until a giant hand suddenly grabbed his collar pulled him away. I sprang to my feet and was about to charge in when the gigantic figure of Harry Sample, the village blacksmith, stepped between us.

'Lads, what the fuck d'ye think you're doing scrapping in the street like a pair of yobs? Come on; enough's enough, shake hands.'

I wiped the blood trickling down the side of my face. Sample was right. What were we thinking of? I held out my hand but Julian would not take it.

'No be still' he cried wiping his brow. 'You have greatly insulted me Bullick and from this moment on I consider any association that previously existed between us to be at an end.'

His voice was raised and half the village must have heard it.

'Julian, please, don't be like this…'

'Don't you 'oh please Julian' me. You *dare* to strike me? You can keep your 'pleases'; keep them and save them for the gods that they postpone the hour that the lot of your family should fall from my father's gift into my own.'

Julian spat on the ground then ignoring further supplication turned on his heel. At Sample's behest the crowd of spectators quickly dispersed although I knew tales of what they had witnessed would spread like wildfire.

'You all right son?'

I assured him I was and tried to play down the disagreement, but Sample had seen it for what it was.

'He's not like his father young 'un. I blame those so-called friends he brought back from Oxford. You only told him what everyone in the village thinks, much good it will do because he doesn't want to listen.'

Sample was right although I would have been better holding my tongue. I left for the stables where I didn't dare confide in my father but put the injury to my face down to play fighting with one of Lord William's lurchers. Whether he suspected the truth I never knew although the incident troubled me greatly. Julian's acid dialogue had come so easily it was as if he had long since chosen his words waiting only for the kind of opportunity that was presented by our disagreement. I was at a loss how someone I considered as my friend could turn so quickly. It was as if the prospect of his inheritance was starting to corrupt him.

Our quarrel had taken place in August, since which time we had not spoken. The holidays were concluded without further episode and Julian returned to Merton College and my brother and I to Ampleforth. However, as I lay there in my room that night listening to the broken pump, the manner in which Julian would respond to the events that had overtaken our respective fathers was not the least of my concerns.

CHAPTER THREE

I woke to the crashing of a handbell making its way down the corridor. It was still pitch dark and flapping for the top of the locker I found my wristwatch and squinted at its' luminous face. 5:40 am. I opened the door on Spangle who from the look of the rain twinkling on the shoulders of his coat had been up for some time.

'Ah, good morning Edmund, I see you're already out of bed'.

'Out of bed?' I replied through a muzzle of mint before turning to spit in the basin. 'I know Father Mathews promised to get everyone up at crack of dawn, but that bell of his would wake the bloomin' dead.'

Spangle laughed. 'Quite so, quite so. I don't doubt the whole College is in turmoil wondering if the Germans have landed. Alas, I bring you the less remarkable news that I have just loaded your cases and will bring the trap to the front in twenty minutes.'

'Where's Alfie?'

'Your brother is in the refectory tucking into one of Mrs Parson's cooked breakfasts. If you're quick you might just catch her.'

Our attention was diverted by some tuneless wailing in the corridor as Tom trotted by in his crumpled vest and shorts.

'Good grief Brentnall you look as if you have been dragged through a hedge backwards and the run hasn't even started yet.'

Tom was bouncing up and down on the spot.

'Indeed Mr Spangle, indeed, although a man in pursuit of excellence should not be judged on appearance alone. Wait until we get going. None of the others will see me for dust. Hoo! Ha! Hoo! Ha!'

Spangle surveyed my friend's peculiar karate-type stance.

'Dust? I think you mean mud, don't you Brentnall, or have you not seen the weather outside?'

Tom performed a few star jumps.

'Dust or mud, it makes no difference to the human arrow. Is it a bird? Is it an 'plane? No, it's Tommy Brentnall, the Rosedale Express; blink and you'll miss it! Choo! Choo!'

'Brentnall, the only time you rush anywhere is to get to the front of the queue at mealtimes.'

'I shall ignore the slight Mr Spangle. This is the day where through the sheer power of my engine, I shall roar to the Abbey and back with my opponents trailing far behind! Choo Choo!'

Spangle shook his head as he set off down the corridor before calling back over his shoulder. 'Twenty minutes Edmund, twenty minutes.'

The words had scarcely left his lips before Tom was in my room pressing his substantial frame against the closed door.

'Edmund my dear fellow, I'm so sorry about your father. We were only given the news late last night otherwise I'd have been along sooner. Everyone is devastated. What happened?'

'That's the thing, I don't know. The telegram from the estate simply said that father and Lord William had been involved in an accident and that my father had died from his injuries. If the headmaster was told any more, which I doubt, then he's not letting on. At the moment my only concern is to look after Alfie and get back home as quickly as possible.'

Tom remained silent for a while, deep in thought.

'How long do you think you'll be away?'

'I'm not sure. I'll obviously stay for my father's funeral and make some kind of start with his affairs, but after that I don't know. At some point I'm going to have to discuss the future with Lord William and Lady Alanna and hope they'll stand by us because as you know, my last meeting with Julian was not a happy one.'

Tom frowned. 'Yes, I recall you telling me, but surely Lord William won't throw you out? From what you say he appears to be a man of honour and hardly the type to abandon you in your hour of need.'

'I hope you're right because Craven is everything to me; Alfie and I were born on the estate, the stable lodge has always been our home and I cannot imagine living anywhere else. Lord William *is* a good man but I shudder when I recall my quarrel with Julian and his threat to evict us. I can only pray that his father's injuries are not severe enough to accelerate the promised day of reckoning, for at the time it was given I have no doubt that Julian meant every word.'

I went to the window. The cross-country runners had assembled in the courtyard with some of them stamping around to keep warm. We walked into the corridor,

Tom's gaze following the last of the stragglers as they were swallowed up by the staircase.

'Look, I have to go. Take care of yourself, be brave and we'll talk some more when you return.'

We shook hands at which Tom galloped off in the direction of the others, bellowing some weird chant about being mowed down by the Brentnall Express. I gathered my belongings and passing through the kitchens to pick up my brother and a handful of Mrs Parson's egg sandwiches, made it round to the front just as Spangle was drawing up in the school trap.

CHAPTER FOUR

The tiny village station was almost deserted with just the three of us and a farmer with a couple of cattle at the far end of the platform. It was a bitterly cold morning and as I spared a thought for Tom and the others bobbing up and down Jerry Carr Bank, I wondered what they would have given for a minute by the coal fire in the waiting room. A tell-tale column of steam suddenly pierced the trees and I stepped from the warmth to see the murky face of the engine round the corner and grind to a halt in front of us. A ramp on one of the trucks at the back crashed down as the cows we had seen earlier clattered aboard. Spangle raised his voice over the hiss of the engine.

'Right lads, good luck. I'll wire Mr Barnaby to expect you at Durham sometime after midday. You've just the one change at York but it's frantic on the railways at the moment so keep your wits about you and be careful you don't leave anything behind.'

'Thank you very much for the lift.'

'Not at all' yelled Spangle tossing his head towards the village. 'I'd far sooner do this than take the cross country' then adding with a thin smile 'seriously though boys, take care.'

An unscheduled stop at Tollerton to pick up some sheep meant it was after nine when we shuffled into York and our progress wasn't helped when even before the train stopped, an enormous wall of people closed in and began pulling at the smoky bronze handles of the doors. I could see that if we didn't act quickly, we would be trapped in the carriage so I yelled to Alfie to hang on behind as I battered our way to the exit. At the far end of the coach a guard blew his whistle and shouted for order, but no one was taking any notice and neither did I as the scrum carried us closer to the door until we burst out onto the platform.

The station was absolutely heaving. It had been our intention to pick up a northern connection but there were so many people milling about we couldn't even see the track. It was like the streets near Roker Park on Boxing Day, only instead of an ocean of red and white, we were in a sea of khaki with hundreds of soldiers swarming around like ants, climbing in and out of the carriages, hanging onto the walls, some running alongside the trains as they swept in and out while others wandered about aimlessly or gathered in large mounds next to their packs. There must have been battalions from all over the country, hordes and hordes of Scots and Irish Guards while up on the overhead walkway a detachment of Welsh Fusiliers were giving an impromptu choral recital. On the cold grey platforms, the mothers and fathers, the brothers and sisters and the sweethearts swayed and wept against a backdrop of magazine sellers, porters and trolleys, a Salvation Army soup kitchen and at the far end of the station a solitary porter desperately trying to clear a path through the mayhem for a small horse and trap. Above everything there was the ear-splitting discord of noise; the squealing and screeching of locomotives, the heavy sigh of steam, the slamming of doors and whistles of guards constantly mingling with the shouts of the paperboys, the calls and songs from the khaki multitude and the soft cries of women. Spangle had been a master of understatement when he predicted the terminal might be busy; every nook and cranny, every delve and covert in and around those sooty brick walls was the roost of mankind in rapture or distress and while I had expected the war to have impacted the rail network, I was totally unprepared for the Tower of Babel that greeted us at York station that morning.

It was quickly apparent that all of the trains were heading south and as we washed about in that rudderless mass, I began to despair that we would ever find something travelling in the other direction. When a harried looking porter confirmed there was a points failure at Selby and the wait would be a long one, I looked to the skies suddenly noticing the unusual moon and star holes punched into the girders supporting the roof. Moon and stars! Would we ever get out of this place?

It occurred to me that news of my father's death might have made the papers so I grabbed a copy of *The Yorkshire Chronicle* from one of boys howling next to a sandwich board that Britain was now at war with Turkey as well as the German empire. I scanned the first few pages but other than casualty lists and reports of a battle somewhere near the Marne there was little domestic news and nothing at all about Craven. I quartered the paper and tucked it away in my pocket just as we were approached by a young lieutenant from the Durham Light Infantry.

'Hello, it's Edmund Bullick isn't it? *Blue* Bullick?'

I looked into a familiar countenance I couldn't quite place.

'It's me, Fergus Vaughan, I played front row when you broke into the first team. I saw the uniform from the other side of the platform and had to come over and investigate.'

'Fergus! I didn't recognise you with the moustache. How's life treating you?'

'When I left Ampleforth in the summer of '12 the old man put me to work in the accounts department of the family mill, and I was halfway through my training when the war broke out. I said to him 'father, I want to be released from my pupillage so I can join the army'. When he realised I meant what I said there were tears in his eyes but he embraced me just the same and gave me his blessing. The next day myself and a few others went down to the Market Place and signed up for the 18th *Pals* and lo and behold here we are! How about you? It can't be the end of term yet so what are you doing in York?'

I introduced him to Alfie and explained the reason for our journey and the problems we were having getting back home.

'Well, I think I might just be able to help you there. Our battalion has just completed training in the Brecon Beacons and we're actually on our way to Chester-Le-Street now. The train is drawing water in one of the sidings but what say I have a word with the CO and see if we can give you a lift? We'll be at Durham in a couple of hours if you don't mind a bit of a squash'.

I had always liked Vaughan but never more so than when for the last time that day, I stood on my tiptoes and squinted down the line. Nothing. I turned to our rescuer.

'That would be brilliant. Thank you so much.'

'Excellent. Come on Alfie, you too. Follow me' and with that Vaughan led the way over the east-west footbridge where we slipped through the Welsh chorus and dropped down onto the far platform.

The CO turned out to be a larger-than-life colonel from Bishop Auckland called Rowley who was surprisingly engaging as he chattered away, pipe bobbing up and down in the corner of his mouth.

'My subaltern here has told me about your pickle, boys, and while giving lifts to civilians is probably against the rules *heh heh* there is a war on and we have to help one another so we won't say anything about it if you don't *heh heh* – carry on Vaughan' and with that he wheeled away and started *heh hehing* at some NCOS gathered by the salvation army cafe.

Alfie and I followed Vaughan and his batman to the end of the north bound platform. The line was empty so we jumped down and crossed the tracks to a far siding where two scruffy black locomotives were drawing water from an enormous iron tank. I felt for the solitary operative who had to scale the ladder and swing round the hose because it looked as if the slightest gust of wind would bring the whole lot crashing down, operative, hose and all. I was watching the fellow beavering away when at three sharp blasts from Vaughan's whistle, scores of soldiers poured off the platform and scrambled towards a long line of carriages parked up further down the siding. I say 'carriages' but they looked more like the stubby boxcars we used for transporting horses. Each was about 20 feet by 10, there were no benches or furniture, the boards were covered in straw and the trucks were fully enclosed, except for a small window at each end latticed with barbed wire. As we drew nearer, I noticed that stencilled in large white letters on the side of each wagon were the words *8 horses 40 men*. I didn't know whether this meant eight horses *or* forty men or eight horses *and* forty men but I assumed it was the former, at least I hoped so because when Alfie and I were hauled into the second wagon reserved for junior officers and batmen, there wasn't enough room left for one horse let alone eight.

The clanging of buffers announced the two dirty black engines had recoupled and we were ready to go. I made my way to the door and peered down the carriages. A real sense of excitement was in the air as a pair of NCOs ran along the track slamming the doors and sealing protruding heads and arms that right to the last were gesticulating obscenities down the long arc of the train. It seemed unlikely the two engines could cope with such a huge load but movement began with an abrupt jolt on the front buffers that whipped along the wagons, followed by another brief jar forwards, a stop, a longer jolt, another stop and then, with a piercing groan of iron, we began to shudder forward. I looked at Alfie who smiled and gave me the thumbs up. At last we were on our way.

The train gathered momentum surprisingly quickly and very soon we had left the pale blocks of York behind and were steaming through open countryside. From my vantage point at the door, I surveyed the patched landscape of North Yorkshire as the lengthening shadows of the wagons chopped alongside the track. It was late autumn; the trees were stripped and in the charred fields, clouds of gulls trailed lonely teams of oxen as they strove to turn the soil before the first frosts of winter. In the distance the sloping chalk horse of Kilburn stole into view, its usual white profile turned salmon pink as the evening light fell on Sutton Ridge. It would be dark by the time we reached Durham. I only hoped that whoever had been sent to meet us would still be there when we arrived.

A tap on my shoulder brought me back to the present and I turned to meet the friendly eye of a lean young corporal with cropped hair and glasses who had a kitbag on his shoulders that was so disproportionately large for his frame that it gave him the appearance of a human snail.

'Edmund, isn't it? The name's Alix Liddle from Darlington. I just wanted to say how sorry we all were to hear about your father. I did some riding out at Catterick before the war and always followed the Craven horses, especially the two-year-old *Stornoway*. Please accept my profound condolences.'

The man had been a jockey all right. His grip was like iron.

"Ah *Stornoway*' I sighed. 'That horse is, or rather he was the apple of my father's eye. When he won the *Gimcrack* last August, it was the most wonderful day ever.'

'I was there with some pals' replied Liddle drawing on his pipe. 'We all backed Captain Elsey's *Greenwood* but he didn't stay the six furlongs. It was such a different world then: now there is talk of racing being suspended for the duration of the conflict. I hope it doesn't happen but if hostilities extend into 1915 there'll likely be a call on horses for the war effort. When the fighting is over, racing will need people like your father to get it back on its feet. Do you have any plans to follow him?'

'It's too soon to say. Dad's accident is such a shock that I still haven't taken it in. My mother died when I was little and apart from some distant relatives in Ireland, who I hardly know, there is only Alfie and me left.'

Liddle struck a match and catching a ripple of discomfort across his face I berated myself for my self-pity.

'I'm sorry Alix, it's just the shock and uncertainty over the future.'

The train rattled through Northallerton. Alix drew on his pipe and I followed the smoke from his nostrils as it was snatched up by the draught and pulled out the door.

'You must be strong for your brother.'

'The thing that gets me most is I know so little. The telegram to college simply notified us of father's death. I'm desperate to get home and find out what happened.'

Liddle's eyes narrowed and he pulled out his pipe.

'Have you not seen today's papers? There were a couple of lines in *The Yorkshire Chronicle*. I assumed you'd seen it.'

I pulled out the quartered newspaper I'd bought at the station and shook my head up and down the pages. Nothing.

'Try the sports section'.

I jumped to the back cover and there it was, a small paragraph tucked away below the racing results.

Horse trainer perishes in freak accident

James 'Jimmy' Bullick the well-known Durham trainer has died while riding with the Derwent of Braes Hunt. It is reported that Mr Bullick, 49, was killed on the moor after his horse took fright in a thunderstorm. Mr Bullick, originally from County Cork Ireland, has been one of the leading trainers on the northern circuit, his notable horses including Dinsdale Boy, Farid Filsouth and the unbeaten 2-y-o

Stornoway, winner of the 1913 York Gimcrack Stakes.
Mr. Lewis Priestman, Master of the Hunt, said it was
a freak accident and they had never known a death
caused in this manner. Unconfirmed reports suggest
Mr Bullick was accompanied by leading owner Lord
William Cavendish who has been injured although no
one from the estate has been available to comment.

I read the passage several times before turning back to Alix who was chewing away on his pipe.

'This doesn't make sense. My father never went hunting.'

'According to the Master of the *Braes* it seems he did' replied Liddle as he cupped his hands and relit the bowl. I looked around for my brother who was talking to a few NCO's on the other side of the carriage. As if he sensed something was up Alfie turned and meeting my eye excused himself and crossed over to join us.

'Alfie, this is Corporal Alix Liddle who used to do some riding out in Civvy Street. Alix has uncovered some information about father's accident.'

My brother tilted his head quizzically.

'What information?'

I passed him the newspaper. Alfie read the passage several times then looked at me blankly.

'I don't understand – it says here Dad was killed while out with the *Braes* but he never went hunting. As for being thrown in a storm he would never saddle up if there was a risk of thunder. This cannot be right'

'My thoughts exactly' I replied. 'And out on the moor? What on earth were they doing up there? Father would never go out on the moor in the rain. There must be more to it.'

Alix blew out a match. 'I expect a more detailed account will appear tomorrow'.

I kicked the wall in frustration.

'It's tomorrow's news today that we want.'

A thunderstorm raged over the industrial landscape of Durham as we spent the rest of the journey discussing the conflict. Alix and the *18th Pals* were being sent to the coast in case there was an invasion across the North Sea. The notion seemed a bit farfetched to me, but Alix assured me they had intelligence that the Germans might try something. I was so wrapped up in our conversation I hadn't noticed the miles slipping by and it was only when the train began to slow that I realised we must be approaching our destination. I strained my eyes into the deluge beneath the railway viaduct. Sure enough, the jagged streets of Durham ghosted into view, the houses a jumble of shadow in the smog and the rain while up on the top, the castle and cathedral silently looked down. Alix slapped a paw on my shoulder.

'Well Edmund, this is where we say farewell. When you get to Craven do tell the lads we ran into each other and that I shall look forward to catching up on the gallops soon.'

CHAPTER FIVE

The tall, unmistakable profile of Barnaby was waiting on the platform.

I took his outstretched hand and peered into that familiar, wrinkled face. Barnaby was soaked; the downpour had trodden his curly, black hair and darkened the shoulders of his long, felt coat. I traced his features for a window into what lay ahead. It was the eyes that gave him away. They were so sad I could only guess what hostages he was keeping behind them.

We jumped into the car and set off down Station Approach. The weather was now closing in, the rain hammering onto the canvas roof completely drowning out the purr of the engine and splashing of tyres. Barnaby twisted round to break the silence.

'Lads, I'm glad you're home.'

'What on earth happened?'

'I'm sorry *Blue*, but I'm under instructions from Lady Alanna not to discuss your father's accident as she intends to speak to you herself when we reach the castle.'

'Is there nothing you can tell us? The paper claims father was thrown from his horse while out with the *Braes*. Dad never went hunting. What was he doing on the moor?'

'I wish I could say but I don't know, none of us do. What I can tell you is when the huntsmen found him, he was taken in a horsebox to Dryburn Hospital where he died a short time later. Once the dreadful news reached Craven, Lady Alanna arranged for the body to be given over to Seaton Maley to prepare for the funeral. Mr Seaton is attending the castle tomorrow morning to discuss the arrangements. We put back the appointment until then so yourself and Alfie can be involved.'

'Thank you for that although the meeting is not one I shall relish. Who else was there when the accident happened? Have you spoken to any of the huntsmen yet?'

'No. I'm as much in the dark as you are although the police are taking statements.'

'Why are the police involved?'

'Their interest is routine, just as it is routine for the Coroner to be notified where there is an unexplained death. It is believed your father was unhorsed in a thunderstorm but as I say I wasn't there and I haven't been able to speak to anyone yet who was.'

'What about Lord William? What's he said about the accident?'

'His Lordship has not been in a position to say anything. He was carried from the moor with serious head injuries and remains at the castle where he has yet to regain consciousness. Dr Addison thinks he's fractured his skull. A specialist neurosurgeon has been sent for but the signs are not good and we are all extremely worried.'

'Good grief this is dreadful. What of Julian? I assume he knows of the situation?'

'I sent a telegram to Merton College yesterday. Julian was apparently in London with Lord Clifford and will not have received word of events until a few hours ago. I anticipate he'll leave St Pancras first thing in the morning and we can expect him at Craven tomorrow night. Lady Alanna may have received further information in our absence. We will know soon enough because as I say, I am instructed to take you to her when we get back.'

We left the cobbles of Durham behind and picked up the old Howden Road. The night was as black as jet while all the time the rain lashed down pitilessly, choking the tiny brooks and drenching the livestock in their flooded fields. I focussed on the *Spirit of Ecstasy* perched at the end of the bonnet like Boudicca, defiant to the elements as the front lamps cut a path through the night. I suddenly remembered Jane and realised that with the shock of what had just been imparted by Barnaby, I had completely overlooked Julian's sister.

'And Jane? How is she coping with the situation?'

'In a word, badly. She sits hour after hour wiping her father's brow constantly talking to him in the hope that somewhere deep inside his broken body, he can still hear her. Unfortunately, there's not the slightest flicker of recognition and we must face the possibility that he may not recover at all. I'm afraid it's that serious.'

At the northern entrance to the estate a few blasts on the horn brought old Amos out of the lodge.

'Welcome back Mr Barnaby sir' he shouted through the driver's window. 'I'd given up and assumed you had decided to remain in Durham.'

'We nearly did Amos. I don't believe I've seen a worse storm in all my years at Craven. Lock up when we're through will you? There'll not be anyone else on the roads tonight'.

Amos loosened the enormous chain and slowly lugged the gates open. Barnaby cranked the Rolls into gear and with a light touch of the throttle we slipped beneath the old sandstone arch and into the grounds of the estate. The castle was another mile; we had to pass through some woods first where with each twist of the lane, the *Ghost* headlights swept eerily across the face of those once familiar thickets. In the shifting shadows a line of rhododendrons stood silent guard at our arrival. Julian and I used to play hide and seek amongst these bushes when we were children and I thought how much smaller they looked now. We emerged from the trees into open parkland where the rain lashed us with a fresh vengeance and I felt no little sympathy for all the deer that would be huddled in clumps under the sparsely dotted oaks.

The old tower was the first part of the castle to peek over the brow as if its medieval stones had sensed our approach. There were few lights burning in welcome. The hall and library were clearly engaged but above the neatly clipped yews the upper rooms merged into the night, all, that is, except for one window high over the entrance where a solitary candle flickered behind the diamond panes. Alfie stirred as the rattle of a grid under the wheels heralded our approach. Outside the storm was approaching its zenith with the rain hammering down at near right angles, thrashing the gardens and weathering the sandstone blocks of the boundary walls. Barnaby swung across the gravel and halted at the steps leading up to the giant oak door.

'Looks like it's time to get wet lads. One, two....'

CHAPTER SIX

The unflappable figure of Monmouth the butler paused until everyone was stamping around in the foyer then bolted the storm behind us.

'Good evening gentlemen, her ladyship is waiting in the library. If you would care to hang your coats and follow me?'

We shook off the rain and followed Monmouth across the chequered tiles of the Great Hall, our footsteps ringing off the stones and suits of armour while high on the whitewashed walls the previous occupants of the castle exchanged their knowing glances. In the library we were met by a wave of heat and I instinctively looked to the hearth where three leather armchairs formed a semi-circle around an enormous log fire. A large Irish wolfhound stretched out on the carpet briefly raised its head while the occupant of the closest chair, Lady Alanna herself, now rose and crossed the room to greet us.

'You're here boys, thank goodness for that. I can only imagine what you must have gone through on the roads this evening. Mr Barnaby, have they eaten yet? I wonder if you would be good enough to go to the kitchens and fix them some supper? You may want to grab a hot drink yourself; you look as though you could do with a rest and anyway, I'd like to speak alone with the boys. Monmouth, can you go with him? I'll ring when I need you'

'As you wish ma'am' replied the butler at which he and Barnaby left the room, their footsteps echoing across the Hall before fading away down a distant corridor.

Lady Alanna must have been about forty and although her hands and neck were creased and her fine strawberry hair was beginning to wane, she was tall and slender with high cheekbones and long pale arms that protruded regally from her velvet gown. It was said she hailed from a clan of Irish landlords where she was considered the beauty of her generation and there was no question that in her youth, she must have been an extremely attractive woman. Lord William had certainly thought so because he proposed to her at a ball in Tralee on the first evening they were introduced. Lady Alanna was only eighteen and her Catholic family were utterly opposed to the match but she went ahead anyway and it was said they married in secret before she followed Lord William back to Durham. The absence of a society wedding and the faint whiff of scandal was fertile ground for gossip, and almost from the day Alanna arrived at Craven, rumours about the couple caught fire in the county drawing rooms. Some said there had been no marriage at all and that Alanna had appeared unaccompanied and penniless on a Liverpool steamer, disowned by her family and disgraced by the obvious conception of Julian. Others claimed stories about her noble blood were a myth and that she had been taken in from a family of itinerant horse dealers. One Irish apprentice holding court in the *Black Horse* swore blind that

Alanna had been given her looks by the devil himself, and that when she refused Lord William, he had resorted to the occult to win her over. This was too much for Barnaby and my father who were in the pub at the time, but while the jockey was promptly sent packing, the tale he left behind sprouted wings only adding to the conjecture.

In the end I heard so many conflicting accounts about the lady of the house that it was impossible to know what to believe. The subject had cropped up but once in conversation with my father and I always remembered his reaction because it was one of the few occasions he was ever short with me. I was about fourteen at the time and had asked him if it was true that Lady Alanna was descended from Irish gypsies to which my father responded that I was playing with fire involving myself in scandalous tittle tattle and would do well to remember that our family depended upon Lord William for our livelihood. It was a severe dressing down but I had deserved it and from that day on, while I could not steer completely away from the gossip, I brought no more of it to his ears. We *did* rely upon Lord William for our livelihood quite apart from which the lady of the house had always treated our family with kindness and respect, and for this alone she deserved our loyalty. It was also true that irrespective of the intrigue that surrounded her, Lady Alanna was palpably well educated with the kind of elegance and style that made her a most worthy mistress of Craven. She and Lord William were an illustrious couple and in their early years no fashionable ball or house party was complete without them. Even when the seasons passed and her beauty began to fade, Alanna was never short of admirers, the irony being that many of these were the husbands of the gossipmongers whose brittle industry had only enhanced her allure.

As I grew older I, too, had observed her from a distance and in the dreamy meadows of youth would sometimes imagine what it must be like to be master of the castle with Lady Alanna at my side. It wouldn't have bothered me that she hailed from a family of drifters, any more than in my salad way I could see no obstacle in the seasons that lay between us, believing that the love of this woman could have held any man forever. In the real world though my father was right. Whatever people said or thought of Lady Alanna behind closed doors, only a fool would talk about her in public because Lord William had sharp eyes and ears and he was ruthless when it came to protecting the reputation of his family. Not that his wife's Achilles heel lay in the circumstances of her birth, although society was not to know it. Lady Alanna's weakness was that she drank to excess, particularly when Lord William was absent from the estate. Neither had she succumbed to intemperance overnight, with the seed of youthful excess flowering in lonely middle age.

Boarding at Ampleforth I was oblivious to the condition creeping up on her but by the time Julian left for Oxford, alcoholism had taken hold and the servants were already adept at covering it up. Lord William, having failed to recognise the early signs, now sought to manage the problem by restricting his wife's access to funds and keeping all liquor in the castle under lock and key, but Lady Alanna was nothing if not resourceful and employing all the deceit that serves the condition invariably found a way round the embargo. When I first learned she was an alcoholic I used to study her closely for some tell-tale sign of distress, but Lady

Alanna's demeanour gave very little away, and as she seldom left Craven these days it was unlikely that anyone beyond her immediate society was aware of the addiction. However, an addiction there certainly was and the unpredictability of her routine together with inexplicable confinements only underlined the helplessness and misery of it. And now, as I stood in Lord William's library and measured those fine features that had once so captivated me, I saw only grief and wondered if she had been drinking on this particular evening. She could scarce be faulted if it were so.

I was brought back to reality by Dr Addison climbing from the farthest armchair to acknowledge us with all the bonhomie of a Shetland undertaker. A tall, thin man about sixty, Addison was regarded as the foremost practitioner in Durham and the grim expression told me all I needed to know about the condition of the patient upstairs. Lady Alanna seemed to pick up on this too and after a brief exchange about Lord William's treatment, Addison was despatched to check on his well-being leaving the three of us standing alone by the fireplace. Lady Alanna waited until Addison was out of earshot then addressed us in that beautiful soft Irish voice.

'Please boys, sit down and let us talk for a while. We have a hectic few days coming and there are some things I have to say to you.'

Alfie and I exchanged a nervous glance but did as we were asked and settled in the two empty chairs as the mistress of the house stood for a while longer holding the palms of her hands to the fire. I had never been alone or virtually alone with Lady Alanna before, our only previous conversations being routine and always in passing, and yet here we were, just Alfie, me and the mistress of the house among the flickering shadows of Lord William's library. The scene about to play out before me would have been unthinkable when I was home a few weeks ago yet as Lady Alanna threw another log on the flames and sat down in her chair, her vulnerability was real enough.

'The first thing I want to say to you both is how dreadfully sorry I am about what has happened to your father. He was not only a most trustworthy servant to the estate but also a much-valued friend of Lord William and myself and I offer my sincerest condolences. I realise the news about his accident will have come as the most frightful shock, and I am so sorry it had to be communicated by telegram, but information travels so quickly these days and I did not want you finding out from anybody else.'

Alfie and I listened in silence as Lady Alanna drew her hands from the sides of the chair so they were resting on her lap and then looking first to the door and then straight at us continued in a low whisper.

'The second thing I want you to know is that whatever changes follow in the yard, there will always be a place for you both here at Craven. It may not be in the stables because I cannot say at the moment what we are going to do with the string, however all that is in the future and for the time being you will continue to live in your father's house.'

Although I hadn't expected to be turned out I thanked Lady Alanna just the same. Alfie also piped up appreciatively.

'Please, there's no need to thank me, it is in my gift and the least I can do. What becomes of the horses will depend upon his lordship when he recovers, or if he does not... in the event that he fails to recover at all...' at this point

Lady Alanna drew her hands to her face and began sobbing uncontrollably. It was a most awkward moment and for a while Alfie and I sat looking helplessly at each other not knowing what to do. The wolfhound sensing her distress pricked its ears and began to whimper and it crossed my mind to reach out and console her until I remembered this was the mistress of the house in her husband's library and abruptly dismissed the idea. Instead, I motioned to Alfie that we should leave but just as we stood up to make our excuses, Lady Alanna regained sufficient composure to carry on albeit her words came and went in small tracks.

'No, please, don't go, I am fine, or I shall be in a minute. I just ask that you bear with me for I do not know when I will get the opportunity to speak with you again on these matters.'

I exchanged another uneasy look with Alfie but we sat apprehensively, while Lady Alanna retrieved a small lace handkerchief from her cuff and began to wipe her eyes. It was a most embarrassing interlude for us all but particularly for her and I cursed my inability to find something to say that would ease the tension but what *could* I say? Nothing. Words were inappropriate and all Alfie and I could do was sit it out until Lady Alanna felt able to continue which after an interval that seemed much longer than it probably was, she finally did.

'I'm so sorry you bear witness to my grief boys. It shames me to break down before you but there are some things I have to say before we are overtaken by events. The decision whether we keep the horses and appoint a new trainer or dispose of the string altogether will be made by my husband once he recovers. You will know Lord William has been seriously injured and we have sent for a specialist neurosurgeon from Edinburgh, but until I am advised differently, I must work on the basis he is going to pull through. In the event that my husband is permanently incapacitated or dies, and I appreciate I must face that possibility, the future of the training establishment will be decided by Julian. Nevertheless, I am acutely aware that Craven has always been your home and as long as it is mine, I give you my word now that there will always be a place here for you.'

We sat through another silence while Lady Alanna blew her nose. Her grief was distressing and when a spark suddenly jumped out of the fire, Alfie and I followed it across the hearth thankful that we did not have to meet her gaze. I stared into the flames and wondered if the promise she had just made was beyond her power? I had to know.

'Does Julian know this?'

At first Lady Alanna said nothing as if thinking the question through in her mind before making a response. At length she brushed down the arms of her chair then looked straight at me, her long curls and soft skin glowing in the firelight.

'Julian has views that do not always accord with my own. I know from talk in the village that the two of you do not see eye to eye, but whatever his sentiments on this particular issue, my son will bow to the will of his parents and there will be an end to it.'

'When do you expect his return?'

Lady Alanna leaned forward and stretched her hands out towards the fire. She was still an attractive woman, but I suddenly noticed how thin she had become.

'I received a telegram this afternoon from the principal of Merton College. Julian will arrive on the Pullman tomorrow evening. However, you should not fret at his homecoming. My son might be impulsive, but he will not see you displaced.'

'I am relieved to hear it; we have been friends for many years.'

That much of course was true. We *had* been close once although Julian's dark promises were real enough when he made them, and I found myself hoping rather than believing his mother was right.

Lady Alanna stopped crying and slipping her handkerchief into her sleeve reached for the cut glass tumbler on a small hexagon table to the side of her chair. In the firelight the contents looked like rosewater, but whatever was in there appeared to fortify her and I took my chance.

'Lady Alanna, do you know anything at all about our father's accident? The newspapers claim he was hunting with the *Braes* but he detested the sport.'

Lady Alanna held her glass up to the light before taking another sip and replacing it back on the table.

'I honestly cannot say. That your father had little time for hunting was common knowledge but the *Braes* were on the fells that afternoon and it appears that for whatever reason, he decided to go up there. I only spoke briefly to the huntsmen when they carried Lord William in and as you will appreciate, our conversation did not extend beyond my husband's immediate condition.'

'I apologise ma'am, but I am anxious to find out how our father died.'

Lady Alanna gathered the poker and stabbed at the flames.

'I quite understand Edmund and if I was sitting in your place I would ask the same. Alas, I can tell you very little other than I don't believe your father was riding with the hunt because he saddled up some time after Lord William and the others left, and I can only assume their meeting was either a coincidence or because your father went to look for them. I don't doubt he will have had his reasons for being on the moor and knowing your father, I expect they were sound, but more than that I cannot say. The Coroner has instructed the police to look into the accident so I expect they will get to the bottom of it soon enough.'

With that Lady Alanna rose out of her chair and pressed a small button by the side of the hearth. As she did so the wolfhound which had been stretched out at her feet sprang up and waited expectantly beside her.

'Now it's been a long day and I expect you are both very tired. Mr Seaton is attending the castle at ten tomorrow morning to discuss your father's funeral arrangements so I recommend you get a good night's sleep, and we shall meet in the library then.'

I turned to the sound of footsteps entering the room.

'Ah, Monmouth?' said her Ladyship 'what news from the kitchens?'

'Mrs Pearce has made up some dinner and taken it down to the house as you ordered ma'am.'

'In that case gentlemen I bid you good night. Monmouth, please see the boys down to the house and then lock everything up on your return. I will not be requiring you again this evening'

'Very good ma'am.'

'Thank you. Gentlemen, until tomorrow' and with that Lady Alanna picked up her glass and clacked her tongue at the wolfhound which followed her dutifully into the hall and up the magnificent Jacobean staircase.

My father's house lay next to the stables about two hundred yards to the rear of the castle. It was a modest building of sandstone block constructed in the early 1800's by Lord William's grandfather to house the then resident trainer, a purpose it had served ever since. Our family were its most recent tenants; my father moving in some twenty-five years previously when Lord William brought him back from Ireland to look after the horses. Three seasons later he was joined by my mother, Derina, a young veterinary assistant he'd met in the steward's room at York races. It seems one of Lord William's horses had interfered with the runner up and Derina who was on duty that day gave evidence to the stewards that led to its disqualification. My father was furious but love must have blossomed because by the *Gimcrack* the following year they were married and settled on the estate. Alfie and I had been born at this place but our mother had died in childbirth here and as we raced over in the pouring rain, I saw only too well how the house must have held bitter-sweet memories for him.

Monmouth turned the key and we entered the hall to the familiar aroma of saddlery and an enthusiastic welcome from Domino, my father's aging black lab. The dog was actually mine; he had been given to me as a Christmas present many years before although Dad looked after him when I was away at College. Domino hobbled around, tail thrashing. That's the great thing about keeping a dog. They never forget and are always pleased to see you.

'Now then old fella, how are you doing? Get down now, down, good boy.'

Domino fell obediently to heel as I made my way through the hall where the scattered boots, general clutter and pegs groaning with coats testified to the lack of order in my father's house. In the kitchen Monmouth had laid two places on the table together with some cold meats and a loaf of bread, while a bright copper pan simmered away on top of the stove. Monmouth ladled out the soup then announced he would leave us. I saw him to the porch then slid the bolts on the storm. On the way back to the kitchen I poked my head into the front office where the crackling fire and my father's print in the cushion of his favourite chair tricked me into thinking he was somewhere in the building, and for a moment I half expected to hear him call down the stairs. This spooked me and pulling myself together, I quickly joined Alfie in the kitchen where we started on our supper, glad to be home but unsettled by the circumstances that had brought us into the unspoken presence of our father. Alfie cut a slice of bread and dipped it in his soup.

'Lady Alanna promised she would look after us but how long do you suppose we can stay here?'

'Not long, I fear. The family will need to appoint another trainer.'

'Well, if father was alive, I'm certain he would want us to stay on. Is there no way you can ask Lord William if you can take over the string?'

'It's a grand idea but I'm in the middle of my studies and I don't have enough experience. In a few years maybe but it's out of the question at the moment. Look, it's been a long day, let's go to bed and get a good night's sleep like Lady Alanna suggested. Everything might look a bit grim right now but take heart, things can only improve and whatever lies in store we'll face it together. Okay?'

Alfie put down his spoon and looked at me.

'If only Dad was here, he'd know what to do. I can't believe he's gone and never coming back.'

I walked round the table and held out my arms. Alfie stood up and gave me an enormous hug at which we both burst into tears.

'I'll take care of you, I promise.'

It was now after midnight. We grabbed a candle each and went upstairs. The door to my father's bedroom was closed and for a moment I thought to look in but instead, Alfie and I parted on the landing and I went into my own room and lay on the bed staring at the ceiling. Outside the rain pattered on the windows but the rolls of thunder were becoming fewer and more distant. I thought about what Lady Alanna had said in the library and hoped she was right about Julian not wishing to see us displaced. In retrospect she had spoken surprisingly freely about his being headstrong. It was true enough of course – Julian was worse than that – but for his mother to acknowledge any weakness in his character was something of a revelation. As I mused on this, I suddenly felt very tired and without changing into my pyjamas rolled over and snuffed out the candle.

CHAPTER SEVEN

I hadn't been asleep very long when I was woken by Domino howling at the foot of the stairs. It was still dark and at first, I didn't know where I was. I felt my way onto the landing where I met Alfie coming out of his room with an oil lamp. There were shouts in the yard and someone was hammering on the door. I told Alfie to stay where he was and grabbing a poker from my room, raced down to the hall and called through the letterbox.

'Who's there?'

'Master Edmund, Master Edmund you must come at once, you are needed at the castle'

'Who is this?'

'It's me, Monmouth. I've been sent by Mr Barnaby. Quickly, you must hurry. You have to come with me at once.'

I drew back the bolts and opened the door on the butler who stood awkwardly in his dressing gown seemingly oblivious to the drenching he had sustained on the way over.

'Monmouth, what the devil is going on?'

'You have to come with me now Master Edmund. I have instructions to bring you to the castle at once.'

'What on earth for?'

'There's no time to explain Mr Edmund, you are to come over immediately.'

There was a resolve in his voice that unnerved me.

'Wait there' I said and ran back upstairs to Alfie who was leaning over the banister trying to figure out what was going on.

'Alfie, I have to go to the castle. Heavens knows what this is about but when I leave the house, I want you to bolt the door after me and let no one, absolutely no one, pass until I return. Do you understand?'

Alfie nodded. I handed him the poker then, grabbing one of my father's coats, raced after Monmouth who was already halfway down the flag path that led to the servants' wing of the castle. We were met at the door by Barnaby who ushered us into the kitchen.

'What happening?' I cried.

'It's Lord William. He's regained consciousness and insists on speaking to you.'

'To me? Whatever for? Can't this wait until morning?'

'No, it cannot' replied Barnaby abruptly. 'His Lordship is delirious; he's making no sense at all and we are unable to calm him down. What's more, he is refusing any further treatment until you are brought to him and Doctor Addison fears if you do not go directly, it may not just be Lord William's sanity at stake but his very life'.

Barnaby was leaning forward as he said this, the palms of his hands spread over the table, his eyes burning. Monmouth, usually so unflappable was prowling around the kitchen like an expectant father. My mind was racing but the anxiety written across the faces of them both left me in no doubt as to the gravity of the situation.

'I don't understand what this has to do with me but if you think it will help, then I'd better go. Where is he?'

Monmouth gathered a candelabrum from the sideboard and shielding the flame from the draught, led the way as we chased our shadows through the narrow corridors. The Great Hall was empty but the fire still blazed away, its light dancing on the richly polished spindles of the staircase. I was suddenly aware of raised voices coming from the next floor including that of a young woman and, realising this was Julian's sister, I forged ahead of the others and sprinted to the top. I had not previously ventured into this part of the castle and on the landing, I was forced to check and gauge my surroundings. The staircase had met a long, east west passageway and there was a labyrinth of doors to either side. Ahead of me was another, shorter corridor and at the end of that another staircase. Which way? I spun to the left but could see nothing other than Lady Alanna's wolfhound which growled at me from outside one of the rooms at the bottom. Monmouth and Barnaby reached the top of the stairs.

'Quickly, Edmund. Follow me.'

I trailed them down the eastern corridor where Jane emerged from one of the rooms at the end with her head in her hands. She looked up at our approach and ran straight to me.

'Oh Edmund, thank goodness you're here. I knew you would come.'

'What on earth's the matter?'

'It's father, he's wild with fever.'

Monmouth and Barnaby went into the bedroom while I stood with Jane, her little body trembling with grief as she wept on my shoulder. We had always been close, she was the younger sister I'd never had and while her brother scoffed at our friendship, he had never been able to turn her kind heart.

'It's alright. Really it is. Now tell me, what's happened and what can I do to help?'

We were joined on the landing by Addison who had his sleeves rolled up and was drying his hands on a rusty-stained towel. He spoke quietly so as not to be heard in the bedroom.

'There is a blood clot under Lord William's skull. So long as he was unconscious, we could at least stabilize him but an hour ago he suddenly came round and began lashing out wildly and screaming. It's mostly drivel but the one recurring theme appears to be an urgent desire to speak with you. We've repeatedly told him that you're not here but he won't listen and having tried everything else to calm him down, we had no choice but to send for you. I'm sorry young man, it was a last resort.'

'I'll obviously help if I can. What do you want me to do?'

Addison replaced his cufflinks and drained a glass of water.

'The priority is to get him settled before he aggravates his injuries further. Hopefully, your presence will achieve this and we can take it from there.'

'I'll do what I can. Shall I go in now?'

I felt Addison's hand on my sleeve.

'A word of caution before you do; Lord William may appear lucid but he doesn't know his mind and speaks of strange and outrageous things. You should be prepared for this.'

I stepped into the dimly lit chamber hardly knowing what to expect. The first thing that struck me was the closeness of the air and a smell of sour vomit that stopped me in my tracks, and it was all I could do not to wretch myself. On the table by the bed a solitary candle illuminated a large jug of water, a silver kidney dish and an assortment of glass bottles. Over on the far side of the room a second candle lit the wall near the window and I wondered if this was the light I had noticed when we drove into the courtyard earlier that evening. I made my way forward to where the master of the house was propped up in a large four poster bed swatting away at a nurse who was trying to dab his brow. Lord William was always such an impeccably well-presented man and as I stared at the dribbling wreck before me, I was taken aback, even on this night of shocks. The first thing that hit my eye was a large, jagged cut that ran down the forehead to the bridge of his nose. The wound was freshly sewn and still weeping and while the patient appeared oblivious to its existence, I grimaced to think of the scar that would be its legacy. As I moved closer, I saw how under the mask of stubble, one side of the face was covered by a shocking purple and yellow bruise, the sight only exacerbated by a gory orange stain on the pillow next to his ear. I then saw how Lord William's fine silver hair had become tangled in a braid of sweat and bile. The Lord William of old would never have allowed himself to get in this state let alone admit people to his presence to see it. Perhaps he didn't know or care because he had taken leave of his senses like Addison had said. I reasoned I would find out soon enough.

Jane spoke first.

'Father, Edmund is here to see you.'

At the sound of her voice Lord William pushed the nurse away and struggled to sit upright.

'Edmund? Edmund? Where are you boy? Come into the light so I can see you.'

I approached the bed as the nurse gathered up her things and hurried out of the door.

'Hello sir, it's Edmund. I heard about your accident and thought I would drop by to see if you needed anything.'

It was a ludicrous remark, but I had to start somewhere.

'Edmund? Is it really you? Come and pull up a chair and talk with me for a while. I've waited so long for you to arrive. Everyone else out – I want you to leave now.'

'I don't think that would be wise my Lord' said Addison. 'I should remain in case…'

'Did you not hear what I said?' interrupted Lord William. 'Out now the lot of you! Jane my dear, I would like you to leave as well.'

Barnaby approached the bed.

'My lord, I can ask one of the servants to remain and tend to you if you wish?'

At this Lord William began to yell at them thrashing his arms about as he emphasised every word.

'Did you not hear what I said? I want you all to leave now. Get out. Get out, out of my sight. I said out! Out!'

The others looked uneasily at each other but did as they were told, the men muttering to themselves while Jane gesticulated that she would be in the corridor if I needed her. When they had left, Lord William crumpled back in his bed and screwed up his eyes.

'They think I am mad Edmund, but I tell you I am not, I have never seen things so clearly.'

'Mr Barnaby said you wished to speak to me, sir.'

'And so I do Edmund, and so I do. They told me you were away at college, but I knew they were lying. I could sense your presence in the castle from the moment you arrived. It woke me from my dreams and I would not be denied this interview.'

Lord William sounded confused, and I thought he misunderstood who he was addressing.

'It's me Edmund, Jimmy the trainer's son my Lord. Julian your own son is still in Oxford but will be home to see you tomorrow.'

'Julian?' he whispered. 'Julian is no son of mine. He never was and to think I raised him from nothing, nothing at all to be my successor. I gave that boy the finest education, wealth in abundance and a position in society; I gave him my name, the revered title that comes with this estate and see how he repays his mother and me …'

At this Lord William began to gasp and I instinctively placed an arm around his shoulder and settled him back onto the pillow. His eyes were streaming and a trickle of mucous seeped from the corner of his mouth.

'My Lord, please, let me go and fetch some help.'

'No. No, I do not…' said he coughing again and seizing both of my wrists '…I do not want you to bring anyone, I do not need them, there may not be time. I have no interest in any of the others except Jane. Now tell me you will stay here and listen to what I have to say. Promise me. You have to promise me this.'

I looked down at the haggard face on the bed, gaunt and sickly except the eyes which were burning and pleading with me.

'I promise sir' I whispered. 'Please don't vex yourself. I will remain if it is your wish.'

The tension in Lord William eased. I picked up a towel and dabbed the slime from his chin. The contorted face looked up appreciatively and I thought how its owner seemed to have aged twenty years since August when we had all been together in the paddock at York.

'Thank you, thank you my boy. You always had a kind heart and you are right, I am sick, yes lad, sick, but confused I am not. You speak to me of Julian? That quarrelsome youth is no son of mine, he never was, he was dropped into this estate like a cuckoo's egg and being the blinded fool that I was, I took him in. You look surprised? Why are you surprised? Did you never wonder that the apple had fallen so far from the tree?'

'I hadn't given it any thought my Lord. Julian and I grew up together, he is my oldest friend.'

'Your attempt to cloak the truth is to your credit Edmund, but you well know what kind of man Julian is, or rather what he has become. That boy was brought up to aspire to the finest values: respect, decency, compassion and yet now on the verge of his majority I find the devil himself is my heir…' at this Lord William broke off into another bought of coughing.

'My lord, you are ill. You don't know what you are saying. You must rest for a while.'

'Oh I am ill, indeed I am ill, the truth has made me so, I see it only too clearly. Too clearly and too late. I am so drained but time is short and there are some things you must know. You must hear me out. Will you promise it lad?'

Lord William was fraught with emotion as he said this, his little brown eyes burning into me as every muscle in his body tensed up waiting on my response.

'Will you promise it lad?' he repeated.

I wondered if I should call for help but I was impatient to know more. Perhaps he would tell me something about my father's accident.

'You have my word.'

Lord William heaved a sigh and relaxing his grip on my wrists motioned to the entrance to make sure no one was listening. I crept to the door. Monmouth and Addison were dawdling in the passage and when they saw me moved as if to enter the room but I waved them away.

'How do you find him?' whispered Addison.

'Confused, as you say, but he is settled and I expect he will shortly be asleep.'

'I am thankful to hear it. I will wait in the library but I wish to be notified the moment there is any change in his condition.'

'Of course' I replied before turning to Jane.

'Where's Lady Alanna?'

'Mother is indisposed. I've not been able to rouse her and I fear I shall not get a response until the morning. Why does my father wish to speak to you?'

'I've no idea. He's talking nonsense but has asked that I sit with him a while longer and as he appears calmer than before, I am happy to do so. I'll call if I need anything but, in the meantime, can you go back to your mother and see if you can wake her? Your father is very ill and your mother will want to be with him.'

Jane nodded and headed off in the direction of the wolfhound at the other end of the corridor. Barnaby sent Monmouth to make cocoa for everyone then threw his hands in the air and slumped across a chaise lounge.

'I'm going to get my head down for a while. This could be a long night. Call me if you need me. I'm not going anywhere.'

Closing the door behind me, I pulled a stool up to the bed and took Lord William's outstretched hand. He spoke to me with the urgency of a child.

'Have they gone?' he whispered.

'They have. We are unlikely to be disturbed.'

'Are you quite certain?'

I assured him it was so.

'Very well then lad. What I have to tell you goes back to the autumn of '92 not long after my own father died and I came into the estate. I was a young man in those days and having inherited the family passion for racing, I accepted an invitation from my father's cousin, Lord Derrymore, to travel to Ireland and purchase some yearlings at the sales. I found the society over there agreeable and quickly embraced the way of life; everyone was so informal and with Derrymore parading me as the new Lord Craven we were lionised wherever we went. In the end I lingered in Ireland several weeks longer than I had intended until realising I was neglecting my responsibilities in Durham, I told Derrymore I had to leave. On our last evening we attended a ball in Tralee where I first set eyes on Lady Alanna. I had heard much talk about her beauty and wit but without wishing to appear conceited, that fact is many handsome women were placed in my path and I'd always had their measure. It was not so with Alanna.

When I first saw her it was love at first sight and from the moment Derrymore introduced us I was totally captivated. I was twenty-seven at the time, she was seventeen.'

Now this much even I knew, because for all the intrigue surrounding Lady Alanna, the setting of her introduction to Lord William was not one of them.

'We danced together for the rest of the evening and I found I came alive in her company while she for her own part teased and played me with a skill that was astonishing for one so young, not that I could see it at the time. By the end of the night, I was utterly enchanted and when we parted I asked her if she would marry me. I expect this will seem bewildering to you in view of the length of time I had known her, but Alanna appeared to be everything a young woman should be, and from the first touch of her hand I was so consumed with desire that nothing else mattered other than I should make her mine. Edmund, my throat is burning. Will you pass me some water?'

I reached for the jug and poured a glass. Lord William sat forward and took a sip then continued.

'She would not have me. She said she would give her answer on the 'morrow then sent a note to say that she was betrothed to another. As you can imagine I was devastated. I went immediately to her father, but I was informed she would not see me and eventually I had no choice but to return to England alone and disconsolate. I wrote to her repeatedly from Durham telling her I would never give up and beseeching her to allow me at least to have hope, but she ignored all of my letters. In the end, the more she rejected and rebuffed me, the more I wanted her until I was driven half mad. Have you ever felt this way about a woman Edmund?'

I confessed I had not. My understanding of the misery of unrequited love was restricted to what I had glimpsed between the lines of Shakespeare's sonnets.

'Not yet hey lad? Well one day Edmund it will happen to you, and when it does you will not know what has hit you and you will recall this conversation. Can you pass the water again please?'

Lord William took several large gulps then banged the glass on the bedside cabinet cracking it. I looked to the door half expecting someone to come and investigate but nobody did. I turned back to the patient. He had been perspiring heavily and his nightshirt was drenched. I reached for the towel and wiped his brow.

'You say she would not have you, but you must have won her over in the end.'

'I did, but I blench at the means I used. I was so obsessed with the girl to the extent that nothing else, nothing at all mattered and I was prepared to do anything to have her. My opportunity arrived most unexpectedly when I was riding out one day with the *Braes*.'

'With the *Braes*? You mean the hunt?' .

'Please, please do not interrupt. You said you would hear me out lad and I must hold you to your word. I am so weary and already feel my time ebbing away.'

I raised a hand in acknowledgment. Lord William continued.

'A few weeks after I returned to Durham I was out hunting with the *Braes*. We were drawing cover on top of Hamsterley Fell when my horse went lame and rather than hold the others up, I opted to dismount and walk him back to the road. The path led me by the ruined abbey, and

I remember I had to keep clear of the old mine workings there. I had just stopped by the brook to water the horse when suddenly this figure climbed out of the boulders and began walking towards me. I tell you Edmund, I almost died with fright because it was starting to get dark and I remembered all the tales about the fell being haunted by monks. Foolish of me really. In the end it transpired that my companion wasn't a ghost at all but merely an old vagrant who used to drift around up there. He seemed harmless enough and when he asked if I had any liquor, I felt sorry for him and readily shared my hipflask, glad of the company to be honest. For all his misfortune this tramp turned out to be an educated man and we quickly fell into conversation during which I confided in him about Alanna. Ah. I see what you are thinking. You are asking yourself how it was that I allowed myself to share such intimacies with a stranger, and yet life itself is blessed with such opportunities if only we recognised them when they came along. His response, surprisingly unequivocal in the circumstances, was that if I was certain she was what I wanted I should take my burden to the Galilee Chapel and pray at the tomb of the holy man of Jarrow. Well, what do you say to that? I had never been a religious man and thought the tale was drivel – beautiful drivel mind – and told the old tramp as much. He said I was entitled to my opinion but as I had nothing to lose, I might at least try.'

Lord William paused for a moment and reached for the jug.

'I never saw the old vagrant again and at first I didn't give much thought to what he had said, but as the weeks slipped by with no word from Ireland, I became more and more desperate. One day, when a matter of business took me into Durham, I decided I would seek out the holy man of Jarrow and do you know what I did Edmund? I recalled what the old tramp had told me and I fell down on my knees and I prayed. That's what I did. I prayed. I prayed that afternoon like I had never prayed before, pleading with him to make this girl love me, to ask the Lord to change her heart so she would sail from Ireland and bring an end to my misery. Of course, deep inside I didn't believe it would make the slightest bit of difference, but even as I strolled back to my horse, I felt lighter. The following week a cable arrived from Derrymore to say Alanna had broken her engagement and then shortly afterwards, I received a letter from the girl herself begging me to return to Ireland. As you can imagine I required no second invitation and the following week she and I were reunited at Derrymore's at which interview I learned she was in child to a former lover, a young officer in the Irish Guards who had died in Ceylon. It was a crushing discovery, but I was so consumed with desire that the child and disapproval of her family were nothing if she would only consent to be mine. The following Sunday we were married at St John's in Tralee with Derrymore and the church organist standing as witnesses because her kin and mine refused to attend the service. We remained in Ireland for a few weeks then returned to Craven where in the months ahead we presented the child as our own. It was not difficult. We saw little of society in those early days and the furtive nature of the wedding together with frequent trips to Europe muddied the waters sufficiently to allay any conjecture about the child's paternity.'

Now here Lord William was wrong because the oldest rumour circulating was that Lady Alanna had come to Durham when she discovered she was pregnant. Lord William fitted the last few pieces of the jigsaw.

'I expect you have already guessed that the child was Julian and that I embraced him as my own on account of the love I had for his mother. And so it was. Of course, it was our intention to have more children but with no others arriving after Jane and with Craven rigidly entailed, Julian assumed the mantle of heir as Lady Alanna and I came to an understanding that he would succeed to the estate.'

This was such an astonishing revelation that I instinctively looked around to see if anyone else had witnessed what had just been imparted. Needless to say, no one had as there were just the two of us in the room. I turned back to Lord William.

'Forgive me sir but this is absolutely incredible. Does Julian know anything of it?'

'It was never our intention to tell him because we saw no reason. However, two things changed my mind. Firstly, I saw the dissolute traits Julian developed in his youth and it troubled me greatly. You will know he was given the finest possible education and that his mother and I brought him up to recognise the difference between right and wrong, yet from an early age Julian ascribed to values that were alien to us. I was particularly concerned at his treatment of the servants, the way he spoke to them and bullied them. I pulled him up on it many times and prayed it was just a stage he was going through, but as the years passed, he only became more arrogant and offensive. I hoped that Oxford would be the making of him but my fears for the future were only compounded when he fell under the spell of Clifford and the others. I was deeply concerned after the *Black Horse* fiasco and that dreadful incident with the stable lads, but it was only when Sample told me of your own disagreement in the summer that I decided to act.'

'You knew about that? I thought the incident was closed although I am sorry for my part in it.'

Lord William spoke in little more than a whisper.

'There is no need to be, it was not your fault. I heard about the disdain Julian poured on your father's reputation and his threats to evict you and am surprised you managed to answer with any kind of poise.'

At this Lord William's voice cut short as he was overtaken by another ferocious bout of coughing.

'Edmund, quickly; can you pass me the bowl, under the bed lad, hurry?'

I knelt on the floor and reached for the chamber pot which was already half full and still warm. It was all I could do not to be sick myself but somehow I confined the urge and managed to position the receptacle on his lap just as Lord William leant forward spewing a mixture of blood and gastric juices. It was a terrible sight; he was so ill and distressed and the wretchedness of it all melted my heart with pity.

'Sir, you must allow me to fetch someone.'

'No. No Edmund, please. I do not want any help; Addison and the others would only waste what precious time is left. There is so much unsaid lad, please, you must permit me to finish and then by all means bring to my bedside whoever you care. Please, my boy, please you must hear me out, I beg you.'

I was at a loss what to do. I knew Addison and the others would be in like a shot if they saw how he was deteriorating yet such was the sorrow in those brown eyes that instead of calling for assistance, I found myself settling him back down in the crease of the pillows where I gently wiped his face and pulled the sheets forward so they covered his soiled nightshirt. Lord William recovered his speech and continued.

'I said there were two reasons that caused me to act over the estate and so there were. The first I have already explained, the second was because I fell in love with another woman. Again, you look surprised and you have every reason to be because after all I went through to secure Alanna, you might take some persuading there was capacity in my affections for anyone else, and for a time this was so. Nonetheless after a few years at Craven I began to tire of Alanna. I have no doubt that she loved me in the beginning as I loved her but after Jane was born, we began to drift apart and somewhere along the way we lost sight of what we had once meant to each other. I mostly blame myself because I allowed the business of the estate to take me away from Craven more frequently than it might have done leaving Alanna on her own. Craven is a beautiful home when it is ringing with voices Edmund, but it can also be a forlorn place if you are here on your own. Looking back, Alanna did not make friends easily and having forsaken her family in Ireland I should have realised she would be lonely, however these things passed me by, and before I knew it, she had begun to drink to disguise her unhappiness. Let me tell you lad how soul destroying it is to live with an alcoholic, because having experienced it for many years with Alanna I can vouch there are few worse ailments. I would I had read the tell-tale signs at the beginning; the consumption of alcohol at dinner, an increasing lack of propriety at social gatherings together with inexplicable periods of confinement followed by startling recovery but they all passed me by. When I eventually supposed she might have a problem and could have done something about it, instead of acting I was only too ready to accept the vehement denials which in retrospect was the biggest mistake of them all. In the end the disease gripped her like a vice, and I have no one to blame but myself for the unhappiness it brought to us both.'

I did not reply nor attempt to feign surprise at what Lord William had imparted because his wife's addiction to alcohol had been an open secret in the castle for many years.

'It was about this time another woman came into my life, or rather I should say back into my life. Unlike Lady Alanna who battered down the door to my heart this other girl crept so softly into my affections that at first, I barely noticed it. You will remember me saying how, when I first went to visit Derrymore, that various attractive women were placed in my path?'

'You said you always had their measure.'

'Indeed, and so it was. Edmund, I am not proud of the fact but before I met Alanna, I was an unashamed rake and when women virtually threw themselves at me, I had no qualms in taking advantage of them. In retrospect it was an abominable way to behave, using my wealth and position to entice them into bed although in my defence most of these girls were seasoned campaigners and all they were looking for was a good time and a gold necklace at the end of the affair. However, there was one, a beautiful young veterinary assistant I met at the Gorsebridge sales who was unlike the others in that she was green and showed no interest in me whatsoever until I audaciously pursued her. It was easy enough to convince her family that my intentions were honourable – although they were anything but – and to my eternal discredit I employed trickery and false promises on the road to seduction before dropping her like a stone. I knew I had broken the poor girl's heart and her reputation, not that I cared at the time because once I met Lady Alanna it was a simple exercise to draw a line under my previous conquests. Nevertheless, as the years passed, I found myself thinking more and more about this girl wondering what became of her and I began to regret the way I had behaved. It was her sweetness that haunted me as much as anything else, that and my wish to make amends although I knew it could never be so. Her name was Derina Colburn; she was your mother, Edmund.'

I nearly fainted.

'My *mother*?'

'Your mother Edmund. I never thought we would meet again but several years later in one of those bizarre twists of fate she befriended your father at York races and the rest you know. I was shocked to see her again after all that time, it cannot have been easy for her either but we managed as best we could. I don't know if your father had knowledge of our affair, I certainly never raised it with him and unless your mother spoke of it, he would not have known. Lady Alanna, though, suspected the truth from the moment Derina came onto the estate. Women are very perceptive in this way, and while I dismissed the suggestion that we had been previously associated, I took great care to keep a distance between our families. It was not always easy because I loved your mother very much Edmund. I always did.'

'This is incredible' I said burning with shock. 'You loved my mother all those years?'

Lord William's voice was barely a whisper now, and I could see every word was becoming a struggle.

'I'm not proud of the way I treated her, Edmund. I loved your mother and if I could turn back the clock there are so many things I would change. However, what was done was done and all I could do was try and put right some of the harm I had caused. When I saw the kind of person Julian had become and measured this against the inherent decency of your family, a few weeks ago I instructed my solicitors to alter the succession. I never told a soul but word has somehow reached Julian and his mother. Your father discovered this and rode up to warn me'

'Is that why he was on the moor?'

He did not hear me. The tiny voice was already trailing away. I gripped his fingers and shook them. The glassy eyes slowly opened, each tortured syllable parting from his lips through bubbles of slaver.

'Your father came to warn me, but he was unhorsed in the storm. There were monks, ghosts…'

'Ghosts? What ghosts?'

'I thought it was Julian.'

'What? Are you certain?'

'No, I did not see their faces. They were in monks clothing…'

Lord William continued in tiny whispers, his breathing heavy and intermittent between each flurry of words.

'What do you want me to do?'

'I have instructed Crake to treat with you Edmund, he knows how to act. I should have done it years ago but at least it is settled now. He has the Will and birth certificate. When you see him tell him I gave you my blessing and he…'

Lord William sank into the pillow, his eyes vacant and staring.

'Lord William?'

Nothing. I raced into the corridor and bellowed for help. Barnaby sprang up from the settee as Monmouth tumbled down the stairs to fetch Addison. Jane rushed over to the bed and cried into her father's ear.

'Oh no, not this, not now, please speak to me'

Lord William reached for her hand.

'Jane' he whispered.

'Oh Daddy, no, please don't leave me.'

Addison cleared everyone away from the bed and placed a thermometer into Lord William's mouth.

'Quickly. Pass me my case, hurry man. Hurry!'

We scrambled around for his bag. Barnaby was closest and bundled it over. Addison pulled out a brass syringe and injected the contents into Lord William's neck. The patient's breathing, light and erratic sounded as if he was blowing through water.

Jane started to cry.

'You have to do something doctor, you must, *please*'.

'I'm trying, dammit' replied Addison as he placed both palms on Lord William's chest and pushed down violently.

'Come on man' he shouted. 'Hang on damn it, hang on.'

'Look' whispered Barnaby. 'He's changing colour.'

I looked and it was true. Lord William had turned white.

Addison ceased pumping and climbed to his feet shaking his head.

Jane was distraught.

'Don't leave me Daddy' she wailed. 'Please don't leave me'

Lord William did not hear her but stretching himself out, took one or two very deep breaths and then passed quietly away.

CHAPTER EIGHT

Jane wanted me to stay at the castle but having left Alfie on his own, I was anxious to get back which turned out to be the right decision because he was waiting up. As he unbolted the door I explained that sadly, Lord William had died and that we would talk about it in the morning, although when I stuck my head round his door he was still asleep, so I dressed and went across to meet Seaton on my own.

It was a beautiful dawn. The courtyard and grounds were strewn with debris but the tempest of the previous evening was gone and as I made my way down the connecting path the air was simmering with birdsong. Mrs Pearce answered the door in tears, she was pale and drawn and it was clear she'd had little rest. I walked through to the kitchen and sat at the table while she filled a large copper kettle and placed it on top of the stove with a hiss. Monmouth was hovering about but for once his all-encompassing gaze was vacant, and it looked as though he had been crying as well. The sound of voices in the corridor heralded the arrival of Barnaby and Dr Addison, both grim faced and still attired in the clothes of the previous evening. We exchanged a token greeting but a veil had fallen over the castle and the tea was poured in silence.

'What is there to be done?' I asked.

'A message has been sent to the cathedral for Handley Moule to anoint Lord William's body. We are expecting him shortly although the upmost secrecy prevails around the undertaking because Lady Alanna does not wish Julian to hear of his father's death before he returns. His lordship is catching the Edinburgh Pullman and should reach Durham about eight o'clock. It's too soon to make any further arrangements and no reports of Lord William's death will leave the estate until after Julian arrives.'

I mulled over the deceased's revelation that Julian was adopted. Could it be true? That would make Jane the rightful heir. Addison had warned me to be on my guard and yet Lord William had appeared perfectly lucid. In the end, there was so much whirling around my head that I didn't know what to believe apart from one thing: the key to it all was Crake, the solicitor. I had never heard of the fellow, but I was going to seek him out. The doorbell rang. Barnaby looked at his watch.

'This will be Seaton; you're probably best discussing matters in the library. Monmouth will show him through.'

The undertaker was a short stout man about sixty who attended the castle with a teenage boy who he introduced as his grandson. Having entered a profession surrounded by constant reminders of his own mortality, I had expected someone dour, but Seaton was a surprisingly jocular fellow with a refreshing attitude to the job in hand.

'Ah good morning, you must be Edmund Bullick, I am honoured to meet you sir, indeed I am, notwithstanding the circumstances. My partner Mr Maley and I are avid disciples of the turf and have always tracked the fortunes of the Craven stable. I used to ride out for his Lordship's father in my youth; indeed, I would have liked to have been a professional but grew up the wrong shape. I always hoped young Nathaniel here might have more success but as you can see, he's already too tall to be a jockey, isn't that right Nathaniel?'

His grandson, who had been gazing around the library snapped to attention and began to take notes.

'I knew your father well' continued Seaton. 'I often ran into him at the races; excellent fellow, always found the time to stop and chat. I was so sorry to hear about his accident. Please accept my condolences and those of Mr Maley and our respective families.'

Having braced myself for a difficult interview it was heartening to learn of Seaton's connection to the stable for I had not supposed horseracing would interest a funeral director.

'Why on earth not?' he replied. 'Life can be so dull sometimes, especially in this profession, and we all need a splash of excitement every now and then to cheer us up. Some find it in science, others in the arts, I get mine at the racecourse; you cannot beat the thrill of having a wager and then waiting for the roar from the grandstand at the furlong pole, or the sight of all those beautiful ladies in their brightly coloured hats and dresses.'

He wasn't wrong but it was time to get down to business.

'If you were expecting a delegation from the family, I'm afraid you will be disappointed Mr Seaton as there is only myself here to make the arrangements. Lady Alanna who summonsed you is presently indisposed while my younger brother is still asleep. However, I am ready to discuss what I believe my father would have wanted and if you are agreeable, we will determine what is to be done between us.'

Seaton was surprisingly accommodating; at times his words gushed out so quickly that he tripped over them like a music hall act and while it might not have been his intention to cause mirth, his approach added a welcome lightness to the proceedings.

'An excellent idea. Like they say, life goes on or rather it doesn't, well not for the deceased it doesn't but it does for the bereaved and for we undertakers if you see what I mean?'

I think I understood but nodded anyhow as Seaton continued to flap his arms as his excitable little voice rose up and down the scales.

'Of course, the most important thing' he continued 'is that whatever the instructions, they must be followed to the letter and we will only ask questions if they are appropriate but without interrupting at inappropriate times. Believe me Mr Bullick, it can be a minefield keeping to these rules especially when relatives don't see eye to eye. It happens more often than it should, the enmities of a generation coming to roost in the arrangements where families have been ready to trade blows over the slightest detail. I find it is usually the ladies who are the worst offenders. I always try and remind them of the solemnity of the occasion and invite them to consider the deceased's wishes instead of their own, but it can be a thankless business, isn't that right Nathaniel?'

The boy looked up from his notes.

'Indeed grandfather, most volatile most definitely thankless'.

'Well, you will not find it so with the Bullicks' I replied.

I warmed to Seaton; he was a delightful mixture of eccentricity and down to earth humility. He talked like an old woman, but his manner was engaging and it was straightforward to do business with him. We settled upon a requiem mass at St Cuthbert's in Old Elvet the following Monday followed by internment at St Oswald's cemetery up at the top of the hill. It was not a difficult choice; my father used to worship at St Cuthbert's and often spoke of the fine view from the Oswald burial ground to the cathedral and gardens on the other side of the valley. Seaton would provide a hearse drawn by two black ponies to carry my father on his last journey and would see that appropriate notices went in *The Northern Echo* and *Yorkshire Post* so anyone who wished to attend the service would get to know about it. At the conclusion of our meeting, it only remained to choose the hymns and readings and to source half a dozen lads from the stable to act as pall bearers. This would not be a problem as I was planning to go down there later and catch up with Fenoughty, the head lad. When we had finished, I turned to Seaton and broached the one subject we had not discussed.

'I would like to see my father a final time. How do I go about this?'

The undertaker's sheen dimmed for a moment as he put his hands on his hips and slightly cocked his head.

'What is it Mr Seaton? Is there a problem?'

'I do not recommend it Mr Bullick' said he. 'Many people find the experience distressing and have told me afterwards they would they had remembered the deceased as they were in life.'

'That may be so but the police have asked a member of the family to formally identify his body and there is no one else. Where can I view him?'

'Your father is in the morgue at Dryburn Hospital awaiting a post-mortem. If you still feel the same tomorrow, I suggest you attend my office at noon and we will go and collect him together?'

I thanked Seaton for the offer and it was agreed; I would meet him at the parlour. We fell into some general conversation about progress of the war, he told me his youngest son was in the BEF* and he and his wife were worried because they'd had no news. He then moved on to the Turkish entry on the side of the Kaiser but wary of getting caught in another loop of his ramblings, I pressed the bell for Monmouth who took Seaton and his grandson to their carriage outside the front porch. As they climbed into the cab I reached up and shook hands.

'Tomorrow at noon then Mr Seaton'

'I shall look forward to it Mr Bullick, I shall look forward to it. Well I don't mean I shall look forward to it like I look forward to happy events but I shall look forward to seeing you again then.'

The fellow was as mad as a hatter.

'Good day Mr Seaton.'

I watched their carriage rattle away then ambled back to the house where I found Alfie in the kitchen making breakfast. Not surprisingly he wanted to know more about Lord William's death and why I had been summoned to the castle, but I played everything down explaining they needed a witness for a business document. Alfie appeared satisfied with this and the conversation quickly moved on to our father's funeral where after much discussion we settled on the hymns *Lord of all hopefulness* and *All things bright*

---

* British Expeditionary Force

and beautiful. The last choice was particularly apt because apart from caring for animals all his life my father was a keen gardener and very accomplished at growing roses. I recalled the summer evenings he spent in the walled shrubbery to the side of the house nurturing the flowers and tending the vegetable patch. Someone else would have to look after them now. The image saddened me greatly although I tried my best not to show it.

We moved on to the readings; Alfie chose the extract from St Mathew's gospel about 'many mansions' while I settled on the 'clanging bell' passage from *Corinthians*. Although I was only a boy when my mother had died, I remember my father had chosen the same reading for her funeral since when the words had always moved me.

'Alfie, I know Father Williams was happy for you to remain here until after Christmas but I want you to go back to school. The next few weeks will be difficult but at least you have a routine there and your friends will be around you, to say nothing about your studies.'

Alfie looked at me unhappily.

'I thought we were going to stick together?'

'And so we shall, don't worry; I'll not be far behind you. It's the Oxbridge exams at the end of the month and whatever happens I won't be missing those. However, I need to deal with father's affairs; They're not complicated but I'd sooner get on with it now while I'm in the mood than have to face the task in the Christmas holidays.'

'Are you sure you can manage on your own? I can catch up with my studies any time and I promise I won't get in the way.'

It was tempting because as long as Alfie remained at Craven I could keep an eye on him, however I was greatly troubled by Lord William's revelations and having resolved to get to the heart of the matter, my instincts told me it was a road I should go down on my own.

'Look; why don't we leave it until after the funeral and then go back together on Tuesday morning? I need to speak with Father Williams and pick up a few books and it'll be good to catch up with Tom and the others.'

'Well, if you're sure you can manage on your own?'

At that moment the doorbell rang. I rose from the table still talking to Alfie over my shoulder as I started for the hall.

'Quite sure. It's only a few weeks then you'll be back home again for Christmas.'

Jane was rocking on the step in her riding clothes. We looked wretchedly at each other.

'Edmund has just told me about your father' said Alfie. 'I'm so sorry. Is there anything we can do?'

'Oh Alfie, thank you but no, you and your brother have enough on your plate without shedding any tears for me. I've dropped round to see if anyone fancies a trip over to Willington because I know if I stay in the castle another minute, I'll go mad. You boys up for it?'

'You can count me in' said Alfie. 'You don't mind do you *Blue*?'

'Not at all although I'll pass as I've a few things to deal with here. When you're saddling up can you ask Fenoughty to drop round?'

''Course' said Alfie 'I'll just go and fetch my coat' at which he tore upstairs leaving Jane and me alone on the step.

'The ride will do him a world of good. How far are you going?'

'I thought we'd cross the park to East Lodge then pick up the towpath. The rector at St Stephens is a cousin of

Monmouth's so we'll call in and see if we can scrounge a cup of tea. Edmund, why did my father insist on speaking to you last night?'

I looked into Jane's pretty freckled face, her eyebrows knitted as she waited on my response. She was as honest as the day was long, and I wished I could have told her.

'It was nothing, at least nothing I could understand. You heard Addison warn me what to expect before I went in.'

'But you sat with him for nearly an hour. Surely he said something?'

'Not really, just mumbo jumbo.'

'How very strange.'

I was rescued by my brother clattering back down the stairs.

'What's very strange?'

'Nothing' said Jane as she swished her crop to the side of her jodhpurs.

'Come on then, let's get going,' said Alfie eagerly, at which they gathered a saddle each from the tack room and headed off to the stables. I watched them from the door as they crossed the yard. About halfway over Alfie ran on ahead at which Jane, sensing my gaze on her turned around and shook her head, miming the words 'very strange.'

As soon as they were gone, I decided to try and get a handle on my father's affairs. He had always been a private man and the prospect of going through his possessions made me uneasy but his affairs had to be tackled and with Alfie out of the way for a few hours, now seemed as good a time as any to make a start. I gathered my thoughts. I would begin with his office in the front room. I stared at the door for a moment and hesitated. I did not relish the prospect of rummaging through his things, it seemed almost as if I was going behind his back. I told myself not to be so ridiculous but the moment I touched the latch my heart jumped as I imagined my father about to swing round in his chair with that huge smile he used to give me when I was little. The image was so profound it really shook me and it was all I could do to hold myself together and step into the room. In the event my mind had been playing tricks on me. The door creaked open on a cold office with a cold stone floor and by the large oak desk, my father's cold and empty chair. The racing watercolours and bright rosettes still hung on the walls and the yellow eyes of the fox above the fireplace still glared into eternity but my father was not there and in that moment I understood that he was never coming back. I sank to my knees under the weight of the memories and suddenly all the tears I had held back came at once. Oh Dad, I loved you so much and I never told you. I so wish you were here with me now.

I cast my sorrow aside and fished for the little silver key that lived at the bottom of the Gimcrack Cup awarded to *Stornoway* the previous year. It was still there. I took it to the safe in the far corner of the office and at the first turn of the lock, the heavy door swung open to reveal a cashbox containing various mixed notes and coins, a leather purse of 32 gold sovereigns, an old tattered post office savings book together with my father's last will and testament, a pile of old books and some faded photographs. Everything was in its place just as I expected. At the last count there was just over £800 in his savings account which together with his other possessions represented the sum of his estate to which Alfie and I were the sole beneficiaries. I put everything back, locked the safe then switched my attention to a pile of papers and documents scattered over the desk.

My father had been diligent and highly organised in his affairs. His systems were easy to follow and I quickly filed the assorted race entries and Weatherby's certificates into their respective folders, setting aside the urgent correspondence and overdue invoices (including a few from Sample and the local vet) for process. As I worked through the ledgers, I found myself agreeably distracted by the intermittent rattle of hooves outside and realised that my father had arranged the furniture so he could monitor events in the yard as he dealt with the paperwork. In forty minutes, I had caught up with the correspondence and reached for the journal I knew he kept in the top right-hand drawer.

It was an absorbing read. Every day without fail my father had recorded information about the welfare and progress of the various horses together with his plans for them and any general gossip about the stable. I skipped through the pages noting the feeding schedules and comments about medicines, bloodstock and weights. The journal and others that preceded it were thoroughly comprehensive manuals that would prove invaluable to my father's successor. The further I read into his methods, the more I began to understand the disciplined and dedicated approach required to flourish in the profession and wondered if the opening might not be beyond me after all? I had my university examinations in a couple of weeks but then what? Suppose I did not make Cambridge? Why should I not take a post in the stable as, say, assistant trainer? I was my father's son after all and with Lady Alanna's support and the lads behind me I was sure I could make a good fist of it. There was, of course, the small matter of Julian who made clear in the summer that when it came to appointing my father's successor, I wouldn't even make the shortlist. However, for all the disappointments he would relish in bestowing upon me, I might yet prevail if Lord William had spoken the truth on his deathbed. Again, the key to it all was Crake, the Hartlepool solicitor and as soon as my brother was safely back at College, I was going to seek him out.

The entries in my father's journal ceased abruptly at the foot of the left-hand page of Monday 9 November 1914, the day before he died. I leaned back in his chair surrounded by his memories. It was comforting to learn about his work, and this in but one journal; there were another twenty or so epistles neatly arranged on the bookshelf for me to go through later. I was just about to snap the 1914 chronicle shut and place it with the others when I suddenly noticed the ribbon in the crease of the bind was loose. The dislocation was so fine it was barely discernible but the date of 12 November in the top right-hand corner confirmed my suspicion. It should have been the 10th which meant someone had been into the office and removed a page. I was staggered. I looked at the bind again but there was no mistake. A page was missing and the only plausible explanation was that my father had made another entry which had been removed. I looked to the fireplace and seeing a curl of lilac dust on the dead coals, would have bet a pound to a penny that these were the remnants of the missing leaf. I knelt down to see if a negative image of the print had survived combustion, but at my touch the ash fragmented, and the page was no more.

I returned to the desk and holding the journal up to the light, squinted at the surface to see if any trace of the missing

10th had imprinted below. Nothing there. I reached for the drawer where Dad kept his stamp collection and taking out a magnifying glass, held the diary up like a telescope and this time I saw it, the faintest impression of the nib had passed through to the page below which while too frail to decipher, betrayed enough in its silhouette to discount it being a cast of anything else. I stared through the curved lens until my eyes watered. There was no mistake. An image of my father's last words was there, they had survived; all I needed was the time and expertise to unlock what he had written.

Suddenly, there were voices in the yard and I looked out of the window to see Fenoughty roaring at one of the grooms who was loitering by the horse trough. Parked on a stool next to him changing a shoe was Sample, the village smith and the two fell into conversation. I had not spoken with Sample since my very public fall out with Julian in the summer, but I supposed our acquaintance was about to be renewed when Fenoughty wafted an arm towards the house and they began to make their way over. I placed a ruler in the fold to protect the imprint then carefully closing the journal, had just enough time to shut the draw when the knocker clattered. I dropped the key back into the Gimcrack Cup then went down the hall to open the door on Sample, the man mountain with his dark leather britches and dusty face towering like a Colossus over Fenoughty, the craggy old ex-jockey. For a while they swayed awkwardly on the step, Fenoughty, poker faced, with Sample switching the weight of his massive frame from one foot to the other. Fenoughty spoke first.

'Miss Jane said you needed to speak with me sir. I would have called sooner to express our condolences but my good lady figured you and your brother would prefer to be alone at the present time. If we misjudged the situation then please don't think we was being disrespectful, it's just that I'm not good with words at the best of times.'

'Won't you come in?'

'That's very kind of you sir but if it's all the same to you, the string will be back shortly and I need to be there to meet 'em.'

'Of course. How are things in the yard?'

'Stable is fine, the 'orses are fine and the lads are well enough too although I wish I knew for how long. Truth is Master Edmund, we're all up in the air with the accident to your father and Lord William. The lads were talking about it at supper last night. Proper worried they are, worried about the future, and I don't blame them. Has anyone said 'owt to you about what's going to happen?'

'I'm afraid not' I replied truthfully. 'Julian is expected home this evening, so we'll know soon enough. However, while that can wait, there is another matter that cannot.'

'What's the problem?'

'My father's funeral is at St Cuthbert's on Monday and we don't have any pallbearers. I was wondering, could you muster up some of the lads?'

''Nuff said sir. Indeed, I would be honoured to be one of the bearers myself; I knew your father better than most. He would have expected anything less of me.'

'And I too' added Sample, his booming voice chiming up for the first time.

'You're too tall 'arry' whispered Fenoughty.

'No, I'm not, I can adjust my posture.'

'You're joking aren't you?' said Fenoughty dryly. 'How are me and the lads going to carry the boss with you tilting up one of the corners?'

There was a short silence as they looked at one another and then back at me waiting for my response.

'Well that's settled then. I'm sure I can leave you to sort the details between yourselves.'

The two of them laughed before Sample suddenly came over all serious and frowned at me.

'What about you, Edmund sir? I have to be careful what I say but we're very worried what Julian will do if he succeeds his father.'

It was a moot point but I batted it away.

'Julian can be a decent enough bloke when he wants to be.'

Sample looked around cautiously.

'I wish I could share your optimism,' he whispered 'but I believe it is misplaced. If Lord William dies Julian will succeed before his time which would be a sorry situation for us all.'

'I'm worried too,' added Fenoughty shaking his head. 'I know every one of these horses inside out and I believe if we all pull together, we could manage. All we want is the chance to carry on into next season but there's a change in the wind and I dread what's coming.'

We turned at the clatter of hooves to see a line of about sixty horses file through the arch. Alfie and Jane had met up with the rest of the string and were trotting their mounts in at the back. Alfie saw me and waved as he slid down from the saddle.

'Look, my brother's back so we'd best leave it. These *are* worrying times but there's not a lot we can do at the moment. If I don't hear anything I'll see you on Elvet Bridge Monday morning 11:45 sharp.'

Fenoughty tapped my shoulder and they headed back to the stables. In the middle of the courtyard, they met my brother and the three exchanged a brief word before Alfie came and stood next to me.

'Where's Jane?'

'She's gone straight back to the castle. She said Julian was arriving this evening and she needed to get herself and Lady Alanna ready. She thinks they could be in for a long night.'

'I don't doubt it,' I replied. 'Come on then, let's go in and light the fire. You can tell me more about your trip while I bring you up to date with Dad's affairs.'

CHAPTER NINE

Seaton's premises were in Allergate, the business operating from a stable and workshop that were accessed down a passage that ran to the side of one of the terraced houses. I entered the small parlour that served as a reception area and rang the bell on the counter. At first there was no response but just as I was about to shout through to the back, the door behind me swung open and Seaton himself stepped in from outside.

'Ah good morning, good morning Mr Bullick,' he said breezily 'I assume you've decided to accompany me to Dryburn after all?'

'The police have been to the castle again chasing the formal identification statement. It needs to be done today so they can release the body and I'd rather get it over with.'

'Very good, very good. You're just in time as we'll be setting off as soon as Nathaniel brings the box wagon to the front.'

'You mean you're not collecting him in one of the hearses?'

The undertaker scribbled a note on his clipboard before tucking it under his arm and jamming the pencil behind his ear.

'No, not this morning. We have several pick-ups to make and we always use the wagon when there's more than one.'

I followed him to the entrance where he twisted the *Open* sign to *Closed*.

'Are all your collections from the hospital?'

'They are indeed. The mortuary there serves as a holding room for the district and it's been a busy week even by their standards.'

'How do you mean?'

'It's the weather Mr Bullick' he replied turning the key and dropping the bunch into his suit pocket.

'At this time of year when the nights are long, the cold starts to pick off the elderly and infirm. We had two funerals on the books even before we were contacted by Lady Alanna about your father. Then yesterday we received another set of instructions making four in all, hence the box wagon.'

'Who are the others?'

'I don't have the names because we've only just been notified. One is an apprentice shifter who died on Wednesday following an accident at Littleton Colliery. It seems he was crushed between two bogies, poor lad, and survived the journey to Dryburn only to perish on the operating table. Then late last evening Nathaniel was contacted by the family of a young lass who died in childbirth, and then this morning we were instructed by the Coroner to look after a tramp who expired in the castle grounds. So we have four people to make ready over the next few days which is more than enough work in progress for a small business like ours.

If we took the hearse it would involve several trips for which we can spare neither the time nor the horses.'

There was a jingle of harnesses as Nathaniel led the box wagon onto the road.

'Are arrangements in place for the others?'

'There are plans for them all. The funerals of the apprentice and the young girl will take place on the morning and afternoon of Thursday next week, although the tramp has no known relatives and will receive a pauper's burial.'

'A pauper's burial?'

'If someone passes away and there's no money for a burial, funds are available from the Coroner's office to provide a pauper's funeral, although this is very basic as the description infers. We supply a cheap coffin and transport to the service and churchyard but there are no frills and the deceased is buried in a communal grave with no memorial or headstone. Society regards paupers' funerals as something shameful which is why many people contribute to burial clubs so when the time comes, they have the funds for a decent send off. Pauper's funerals are such sad and lonely events, although more common than people realise. Come now. Let's be on our way.'

Dryburn Hospital was a sorry spectacle with many of the walls subsided out of alignment and the whole blackened by railway soot. The blistered windows had not been painted in years while beneath the cracked tiles, long grey-green smears down the brickwork told of congealed gutters and general decline. My father said the hospital had been built on the site of the old gallows where many of the town's unfortunates had met a gruesome end. It was said these included a Jesuit priest who was hung, drawn and butchered following which event the local stream expired never to flow again, thus giving rise to the name. It was a grim résumé and even before we entered the building, as far as I was concerned this aspect of the day's business could not be over quickly enough.

I trailed Seaton up the fractured steps to the reception area where we were met by a short stocky man in a dusty navy coat who I took to be one of the porters. He and Seaton clearly knew one another and following a brief word, the porter went around the back and returned with a police officer who came through clasping a mug of tea.

'Morning Seaton,' said he addressing the undertaker over the rim of his drink but flicking his eyes to me. 'I take it the gentleman accompanying you is here to identify one of the deceased?'

I stepped forward and held out my hand.

'Good morning Sergeant, my name's Edmund Bullick. We're here to collect my father who died earlier this week following an accident.'

The policeman rested his drink on the counter and looked at me oddly, as if weighing me up.

'That would be James Bullick, the racehorse trainer?'

I nodded. 'I would have come sooner but I was away at College when he died.'

The police officer shook hands, his palm still warm from the mug he'd been clutching.

'The name's Tench, Sergeant Tench, first officer to the Coroner. We've been waiting days for someone to come forward and identify your father's remains. I'm so pleased you've decided to drop by.'

Unsure if he was being sarcastic, I said nothing as Tench drained the remainder of his tea before switching his attention to the undertaker.

'Mr Seaton, if you would be good enough to wait here while I take this young man through to the back? We won't be long. If you talk nicely to Judy in the kitchens, I expect she'll make you a cuppa. Mr Bullick, if you'd like to come with me please?'

I followed the policeman as he bumped through a pair of double doors into a long stone passage that served the ground floor of the infirmary. We passed by several treatment rooms although with enough worries of my own, I shut out the groans and quickened my step to keep up with Tench who was already bounding ahead. At the end of the corridor the policeman came to a halt and thumped on a large oak door that led off to one side.

'Tench,' he shouted.

I looked at him inquisitively as he brayed on the door a second time.

'We're almost there but I need to get the file. Tench!'

His entreaty excited a rattle of keys and the entrance swung open on a large bespectacled nurse of middle age wearing a soiled green apron.

'Come in' she said flatly.

I followed the policeman down the steps into some kind of secure ward. A second more beefy nurse joined us, and as my eyes adjusted to the light, I noticed that what little there was came from three grated windows high up in the wall. I stared down the corridor in front of us. A string of semi-secure chambers lay to either side of the corridor before this expired into a large office at the end. It was more like a prison than a hospital. The only thing missing was the bars.

We walked through a line of patients staring out vacuously from their beds. They had been silent when we

95

entered but as soon as we started down the passageway a discord of tortured voices turned the atmosphere to one of menace.

'Repent or face eternal damnation! You must repent of your sins now!' screamed one.

'It is the soldiers, they have arrived. It can only mean death!' cried another. 'I don't want to die! I don't want to die!'

'Have you come to take me home?' came the pitiful sob of an old woman somewhere in the gloom. 'I have to go home, my mother is waiting by the fire, and she'll be worried where I am.'

In another cell a wiry youth began to twist and contort on his mattress, the springs wailing in protest as the frame of his bed jumped up and down.

I froze in my tracks.

'Good grief sergeant, who are these wretched people?'

Tench put his arm across my path to prevent me moving closer to the beds. He had to shout to make himself heard above the din.

'I'm sorry sir, I should have warned you before we came in. This is where we treat the city's mental patients. We house them in the protected environment here because they pose a threat to society and frankly, there is nowhere else for them to go. We must pass this way to the mortuary. It's the most secure area in the hospital which is why the files are kept in the office at the end there.'

I was in a mental ward. I had heard of such places but not in my wildest dreams had I imagined the desperate conditions in which the inmates were held captive. It was such a wretched scene, the foul air thickened with misery and the stench of decay. That the patients were unhinged was obvious, but when I listened to the pathetic entreaties of the old woman, I suggested that she at least could be as much misunderstood as ill.

'You must never let yourself be taken in by these people,' yelled Tench over his shoulder as he reached for the office door, 'because you've no idea what they're really like. They may seem harmless now, but that's because they're secured to their beds. Believe me; if the chains were undone, they would fall upon you like a pack of dogs.'

'But this place is utterly dreadful' I shouted. 'Can some of them not be transferred to the asylum at Winterton?'

'I'm afraid it's impossible,' yelled the bespectacled nurse joining the conversation for the first time. 'Two of these men are killers who only escaped hanging by reason of insanity, the young man there is a cannibal, and the women are lunatics who have been detained for years.'

The shouting and screaming became louder. I shook my head.

'What hope can they ever have in a place like this?'

The second nurse who had been standing next to me looked up from her clipboard.

'We do what we can for them. The patients are given drugs and subjected to moral guidance although it is more a case of managing their disorders than treating them. Only last week one of them crammed excreta into all the locks so the soiled keys were back in our pockets before we realised what they were up to. Would you invite any of them to come and live with you? No, you would not, and neither would anyone. We are not without compassion within these walls sir, but our first duty is to the people outside.'

Through the glass windows of the office I could see Tench rummaging among the cabinets and wished he would make haste. The screaming was approaching a level where it was impossible to hold a conversation however just as the cacophony reached its atrocious crescendo, the nurse who had been addressing me fished a tin whistle from her apron and blew the first few notes of *Twinkle, Twinkle Little Star*. The effect was extraordinary. In an instant the shrieks fell away and the unit was in silence.

'Sweety, sweety, sweety time...' she trilled to the melody.

An excited murmur rippled through the patients.

'...sweety time, sweety time,' she continued in a voice of saccharine and honey.

'Sweety time! Sweety time!' they echoed, the howls and racket nearing the previous intensity until a second toot from the whistle cut it dead.

'You must be quiet for matron,' chanted her colleague as the two of them systematically went to each patient with a small glass of medicine, one nurse to minister while the other watched over only too ready to access the truncheon clipped to her waist. The effect on the patients was astonishing. Only a minute ago they could have been possessed by Beelzebub himself yet now they sat and waited by their beds as obedient as Spaniels.

'What on earth are you giving them?' I asked.

'*Mrs Winslow's Soothing Syrup*,' replied the matron. 'Each serving contains sixty-five milligrams of morphine. We try to administer it frugally, but the patients get upset when they see strangers and sometimes it is the only way we can calm them down.'

'This is terrible.'

'I'm afraid life's terrible sir,' said Tench emerging from the office with a sheath of files. 'Terrible, terrible, terrible but we have to get on with it. Your father is this way sir. Walk slowly towards me and mind you keep clear of the last few beds on your way down.'

The policeman's office was dominated by a large portrait of the king in full coronation regalia. At one end was a hefty oak desk covered in files and books while at the other, a large station-type wall clock marked time over a row of battered filing cabinets. Tench reached for a thick velvet curtain behind which was a riveted iron door. I was so engrossed in the rest of the office it hadn't occurred to me there might be another way out, but there was no mistaking the notice on the cold façade:

Mortuary

Authorised persons only.

The policeman looked over his shoulder.

'Are you ready lad?'

'I think so,' I replied, but he was already turning the handle.

CHAPTER TEN

We entered a long tunnel shaped chamber about eighty feet by thirty, the whole enclosed in a wall of glazed avocado and cream bricks that met in an arch overhead, and even as my eyes adjusted to the gloom, I was struck by the coldness of the air and the unpleasant smell of what I supposed to be embalming fluid. The chamber was totally enclosed, the only natural light entering through a large skylight in the middle of the ceiling, the frame of which was rotting and caked in moss and algae. I swept the walls for exits and saw one other at the far side which probably led to the yard at the back, the double-doors well secured with vertical bolts and a massive horizontal bar.

'This way sir.'

I followed Tench down the steps where laid out in neat order were nine granite tables, each connected to the flags by a solitary iron stalk. The unit closest to us was vacant but the remainder were all taken, the bodies concealed under dark green cotton although the feet were poking out and the measure between some of the occupants was apparent from even a cursory glance. I stared with incredulity at the line.

I had never seen a dead person and shuddered at the task ahead. Tench looked up from his files.

'You all right young 'un?'

'I don't know. I've not been to a mortuary before and it's just all these, well, dead people.'

'You don't need to worry about them son,' he replied. 'I've been doing this job for fifteen years and none of 'em have said a word to me yet.'

I swallowed my fear.

'Which one is my father?'

'I've no idea,' he replied without looking up from his papers, 'but those who have been formerly identified have a label on the big toe. Your father will be among those that do not. Take your time. We're in no hurry.'

The feet sticking out from the three nearest tables were tagged so I made my way over to the fourth and slowly drew back the cover. It was an old man with silver hair and skin as white as marble. His eyes were closed and several days' beard grew against a number of cuts and abrasions scattered across the whiteness. There was a rupture running down the side of the head and into the ear.

The silhouette on the adjacent table was that of a child so I passed it by and drew back the cover of the next under which lay the body of a striking young woman who looked as if she was asleep. I gazed down at her china face and blue lips. Is this what people look like when they die? She seemed so peaceful I expected her to suddenly open her eyes and ask me what time it was, but then I inadvertently brushed her arm. It felt like ice.

There were two more benches. The first was occupied by a young miner who had such atrocious injuries that I supposed he must be the casualty from Littleton Colliery Seaton had mentioned earlier. As I took a closer look, I noticed the scalp was partially detached from the head like the lid of a boiled egg and a dark jelly-like substance had gathered on the surface below. It was an appalling sight made all the more distressing because the poor lad couldn't have been much older than Alfie. I promptly replaced the sheet and turned to the final mound behind me, although any expectation that I was about to discover my father immediately dissolved when I pulled back the sheet on a heavily whiskered tramp with chains of matted hair that spilled over the back of the table. He couldn't have been in the morgue for long as the body was covered in tiny maggots and wreaked of unspeakable fluids that had seeped through his clothes. It was a pitiful sight, the head lying with the mouth open exposing two yellow teeth, like you sometimes see on a dead rodent. I imagined I half recognised the fellow from the stairwells in Castle Street, although there was probably little to distinguish him from the tramps of a hundred city markets. Poor bloke. His boots were falling apart with the flap of one so badly detached that you could see the crusted toes beneath. He had probably died of exposure all alone in the churchyard. He could have been there for days before he was discovered. I wondered if he had a name and whether anyone would claim him as he must have been some mother's son? I replaced the sheet and turned to Tench who was still scribbling by the door.

'He's not here'.

'Are you sure you've checked them all?'

'I'm sure. He's not here.'

Tench sighed wearily and put down his clipboard. 'You must have passed him over. You have to remember that at the moment of death the muscles in the face relax and rigor mortis often causes people to look different. Here, I'll go through them with you. Who've we got?'

'I didn't check the benches that are ticketed but as for the rest we have an old man, a young woman, a child, a miner's lad and a tramp. There are no more tables and unless there is another room somewhere my father isn't here.'

Tench heaved another sigh and crossed over to the first untagged body. I did not relish starting all over again and it probably told in my voice.

'I've checked that bench officer; it's the remains of an old man'.

Tench pulled back the sheet exposing the body to the cold air.

'Can I ask you to look again sir, but more carefully. Take your time.'

I measured the old gentleman with his silver hair and marble skin. There was not the faintest trace. It wasn't him. I turned to Tench and shook my head.

'Look again. Look *closely* sir. Can you see any birthmarks, any at all or any other distinguishing features?'

I twisted back to the body. My father had a semi-circular scar above his right eyebrow where he had been kicked by a horse. I stared at his forehead. There was nothing. I was about to report this to the sergeant but hang on, what's that? I leaned right down to make sure. Oh my God, the scar was there. It was there. My heart pounded wildly. I began searching for other familiar marks, many of which I remembered and some that I had not. They were all there. The tiny mole under the chin, the fine eyebrows, the small hairs growing out of the side of his ears. All there. I looked back at Tench who was scribbling away with the indifference of a reporter at a council meeting. It was all in a day's work for him but I needed to be certain. When my father was at school, he had been struck in the face by a cricket ball which permanently damaged the left iris making it appear as though he had different coloured pupils. I reached down and settled my thumbs over the lids but even before I looked into those eyes for the last time, I knew the answer and was asking for his forgiveness.

'It's my father.'

'Are you quite certain?'

'Yes. I'm certain. It's my father.'

There was a short pause broken by Tench turning a sheet of paper over his clipboard.

'Very well. In that case can I ask you to complete the blanks and sign this statement so the body can be released?'

I gazed at my father's broken remains.

'Mr Bullick? Did you hear me?'

'I'm sorry officer. What did you say?'

He passed his clipboard.

'Here young man, complete the blanks then sign at the bottom.'

I read through the statement. Tench must have been drawing it up as I moved from bench to bench;

I am Edmund James Bullick. I am 19 years of age and I live with my father James Michael Bullick and my younger brother Alfred Michael Bullick at The Stable Lodge at Craven Park County Durham.

On Friday 13 November 1914 I attended the mortuary at Dryburn Hospital with Sergeant Tench of the Durham Coroner's Office where I was shown the body of my father James Michael Bullick aged 49. I can positively say it was my father because I was able to recognise him from his features including the scars and marks on his face and the distinctive colouring of his eyes.

I last saw my father alive on Sunday 20 September 1914 when he accompanied my brother Alfie and me to Durham Station to catch a train back to college. My father had always enjoyed good health and he appeared quite well when I last saw him.

Signed.............................

Dated Friday 13 November 1914

I scribbled my name at the bottom and returned the clipboard.

'Thank you, young man, I'll take this through to the office and fetch the interim death certificate so you can be on your way. I shan't be long. If you like I can call for a mortuary attendant to sit with you while you say your farewells, or if you prefer you can wait in reception.'

I looked at my father. His face, once weathered by the seasons, was like marble and as those familiar features drifted in and out of focus, I thought my mind was playing tricks on me. His hair had never been white. It was not the same man lying on the slab and yet there could be no mistake. Is this what happens to people when they die? That they change so much you have to trawl your memory to recalibrate the senses? The opportunity to say farewell was in my grasp but for a moment. It would not return.

'If it's all the same with you Sergeant I'd like a few minutes alone.'

'So be it. I'll let Mr Seaton know you're here. He'll be along soon anyway with the hospital porters.'

Tench gathered up his notes and disappeared into the mental wing clunking the heavy iron door behind him. I traced his progress down the corridor from the pathetic cries percolating through the wall until eventually these fell away leaving the mortuary in silence. I was alone with my father for the last time. I folded my arms and looked down at him.

What were you doing on the moor?

My father did not reply.

What were you writing about in your journal just before you rushed out? What were you trying to tell me and why would anyone wish to destroy it?

I noticed the tip of a wound just below the oesophagus. As his hands were at his side, I was able to lift the shroud and trace the incision down the trunk to just above the navel where it ended. The opening was long and deep and the trough it had made was clumsily sewn back with fishing wire in the usual legacy of a post-mortem.

And mother? I know you can hear me. Did she really court the master in Ireland all those years ago?

The expression did not change. It never would. Cold, still, silent. I began to pace around the mortuary.

Lord William told me he had altered his will and changed the succession. How did you learn about that? I suppose I'll discover more when I meet Mr Crake. What do you suggest I say to him?

Someone hammered on the outside door. I nearly jumped out of my skin.

'Mr Bullick, are you in there? It's me, Seaton; can you open the doors?'

I replaced the sheet over my father and crossed to the other side of the mortuary. One of the vertical bolts was jammed and I had to take off my shoe and use the heel to dislodge it, but after a couple of whacks it gave way and I shouted through that it was clear. Almost at once the heavy doors groaned open flooding the morgue with sunlight.

'Nathaniel is bringing the box wagon round now,' panted Seaton as he kicked a pair of wedging chocks in place. 'Did you identify your father?'

I confirmed it was so and that Sergeant Tench had gone to fetch the interim death certificate.

'Excellent. The porters are on their way round so we'll get started with the loading. We should be away in twenty minutes.'

Even as he spoke the jingle of harnesses announced the arrival of Nathaniel in the yard.

'Whoa, whoa there,' he cried softly as the horses were eased to a standstill and he jumped down from the plate. Seaton took the bridle and stroked the animals while his grandson loosened the canvas cover of the hold to reveal a stack of wooden coffins. Two porters entered the yard wheeling a trolley.

'Good afternoon gentlemen. If you could bring numbers six, eight and nine in that order please,' said Nathaniel sliding out one of the coffins. 'We'll leave number five until last.'

The porters did as they were instructed and one by one the bodies were loaded up. As the second casket was slotted into position Sergeant Tench reappeared clutching the death certificate in one hand and a file and large carton in the other.

'These are the clothes your father was wearing when he was brought in. I'm afraid the hospital staff had to cut off his riding boots but they're included anyway together with the rest of his attire and the contents of his pockets.'

He passed over the carton. There wasn't much; boots, trousers, a felt shirt, tweed jacket, underclothes, socks, riding crop, a leather pouch containing some loose coins, his silver cross and chain and gold wedding ring.

'Is that it? Where's his watch?'

'It appears he wasn't wearing one,' replied Tench scanning down some kind of register.

'My father had a gold wristwatch that used to belong to my grandfather. He never went anywhere without it. Here, could I look at that please?'

'I'm sorry' replied Tench wafting the document away, 'but your father's records are government property and I'm not authorised to let you have access to them.'

'Sergeant, if you're holding an inventory of my father's belongings when he was brought into Dryburn I should like to see it please.'

'I'm afraid that's not possible. The schedule is part of the hospital file and the contents are classified.'

'Classified? What exactly have you got there sergeant?'

'An inventory of your father's possessions together with any notes made by the staff when he was brought in. These include the date and time of his admission, details of witnesses in his company, records of any conversations your father had with the doctors, the notes of his initial examination together with a summary of his injuries. However, the file is the property of the Coroner's office and I cannot allow you to inspect it.'

'For goodness sake why not? It's not as if it will be of interest to anyone else.'

'That's not the point sir. Your father's file is the property of the Coroner and I shall require his written authority before you or anyone else outside this office can inspect it.'

It was with some difficulty that I kept a degree of measure in my response.

'This is absurd. James Bullick was my father and as his eldest son and next of kin I insist that you show me his file.'

The policeman, however, was entrenched and brought down the portcullis by tucking the folder under his arm.

'I regret that will not be possible sir. We have strict instructions from Mr Lockwood not to let anyone have access to your father's papers. If you have a problem with this, I suggest you go to his office and take the matter up with him. In the meantime, unless or until I receive directions to the contrary, I cannot allow you to view the file and that is the end of the matter.'

By now I was starting to get annoyed and had to bite my tongue before I said something to Tench we would both regret.

'I certainly shall take the matter up with him,' I replied angrily 'in fact, I shall go and see Mr Lockwood right now. Whereabouts can I find him?'

'His office is in Old Elvet' replied Tench nonchalantly. 'It's about twenty minutes' walk from here or ten on horseback, that's if he'll see you without an appointment.'

Seaton who had been listening cut in.

'Old Elvet is only a few streets from the parlour Mr Bullick. Why don't you come back with us and we can drop you off on the way?'

A squeak of trolley wheels announced the arrival of the last coffin which the porters slid into the back of the wagon so it rested on top of the others. I did not have to read the chalk scrawl to know it held the remains of my father.

'Thank you, Mr Seaton, I'm most grateful' and then turning to Tench, 'You haven't heard the last of this Sergeant.'

Tench shrugged his shoulders.

'I'm just following orders sir. If you don't like it, take it up with the Coroner' said he and disappeared back into his office.

I kicked the ground in frustration. 'What a prat.'

'It's difficult for me to comment,' replied Seaton. 'It's not that I don't have a view'.

'Don't worry about it Mr Seaton. It's not your fault.'

We stood in silence while his grandson clambered into the back of the hold and wafted the canvass sheet over his sorry cargo. For a while, the cover flapped awkwardly in the breeze until Nathaniel brought it under control as he went round the wagon tying down the ropes. Seaton drew a little closer so as not to be overheard.

'While I'm not at liberty to discuss my business relationship with Sergeant Tench, there's something I don't mind telling you and it is this; I've been doing this run for over twenty years and...'

His words stalled at the approach of one of the porters who required a signature to acknowledge receipt of the bodies. Seaton took the clipboard and having read it through, signed at the bottom and handed it back. The porter nodded an acknowledgement then re-joined his colleague at the empty trolley which duly squeaked away. I looked at Seaton.

'You were saying?'

'What I was saying Mr Bullick,' he whispered in a low voice, 'and I'd sooner you didn't quote me on this, but I've been doing the Dryburn pick up every week for nigh on twenty years and this is the first time I've ever heard anything about a patient's file being classified.'

'Are you sure?'

'Oh yes, quite certain. It's never happened before.'

'Well that's extraordinary. What can be so different about my father's case?'

'I haven't the faintest idea,' replied Seaton climbing up onto the wagon. 'The hospital file is the first thing we usually look at to cross reference the deceased's' possessions against the inventory. Property has been going missing recently and it's our job to ensure that everything on the list is passed to the next of kin. Until this afternoon I'd never known Tench reserve the file although he clearly had his instructions. Perhaps the Coroner will be able to explain.'

'I'd like to think so,' I replied as I hauled myself up on the bench, 'although, as you say, it's very strange.'

Nathaniel waited until I was settled then with a small crack of the whip we were away.

I did not get to meet Lockwood that afternoon. Seaton dropped me at Framwellgate Bridge from where I walked up to his office but when I stated my name and business the receptionist made it clear that the Coroner did not see anyone without an appointment. I asked if I could wait but having been informed he was not expected back that day, I left my details and said I would call again. It crossed my mind that Lockwood might have been in but had chosen not to see me, especially when I heard the receptionist trot up and down the back staircase before confirming his unavailability, but at the time I was prepared to give him the benefit of the doubt. I would be in Durham again soon enough.

I walked back across the river to the undertakers where Barnaby was waiting as arranged. He told me news of Lord William's death was on the streets and there had already been a flurry of visitors to the castle.

'I've been tooing and froing from town all day,' he sighed wearily. 'First the bishop then the solicitor, then you and I'm due back again in just over an hour to collect some friends of Lord Julian from the station.'

'The solicitor you say? Who was that?'

'There were two actually. I drove Mr Lockwood to the castle this morning then returned for his partner Mr Crake who arrived on the Hartlepool train a couple of hours ago.'

'Are they still at Craven?'

'Mr Crake is. I took Mr Lockwood back to Old Elvet a couple of hours ago.'

So he had been there all along. I could understand him declining to see anyone without an appointment but why instruct his staff to lie about it?

It was dusk when we arrived back at the stables. A pair of muddy boots in the hall told me Alfie had been out riding again and I could hear him splashing around in the bath.

'That you *Blue*?' he called down the stairs.

'Yes, just back from town.'

'How did it go?'

'Pretty much as expected,' I replied hanging up my coat. 'I met Seaton as arranged and sorted what needed to be done.'

There was the sound of splashing water and the soft pad of feet. Alfie appeared at the top of the stairs in his dressing gown.

'Did you get to see father?' he asked quietly.

'I did. There was not a great deal to it in the end. I was able to view his body and signed a statement confirming it was him. Everyone was most helpful.'

Alfie had tears in his eyes.

'What did he look like?'

'Pretty much the same as he always did. It was extraordinary. Like he was asleep.'

'Really?'

'Really, and that's how you and I should always remember him.'

The grandfather clock at the foot of the stairs chimed half past the hour.

'Anyhow, the important thing is Dad has been formally identified and Seaton will be looking after him until Monday. What about you?'

'I've been at the stables most of the day. Fenoughty took the string into the park and I tagged along on one of the hacks. It was a bit hairy and I'm absolutely exhausted.'

'Is the water still hot?'

'Yes, I filled it to the brim. Took me absolutely ages as well, lugging buckets up from the back fire.'

I kicked off my boots. I had just slipped into the water when Alfie called up the stairs.

'Oh, I meant to say a telegram came for you about an hour ago.'

'Who's it from?'

'Haven't a clue,' came the barely audible reply from my brother as he wandered in and out of the downstairs rooms, 'but it looks like it was stamped at Ampleforth first thing this morning. Hang on, I'll bring it up.'

I closed my eyes floundering in the warmth as Alfie scurried up the stairs and dropped a coffee-coloured envelope into my hand. 'I'll get the supper ready. See you in the kitchen when you come back down.'

I opened the envelope, taking care to waft the contents away from the bath to keep the print from running. When the steam cleared I saw the message was from Tom, typically brief and to the point.

Ampleforth Post Office 0830 hrs 13 November 1914
HANG ON IN THERE STOP TOM

I smiled wryly. The last time I had seen my friend he was shivering in his sports kit. It was only a few mornings previous but it could have been an age, so much had occurred. Tom would know exactly how to tackle Lockwood, Tench and the others however his counsel could wait until I took Alfie back to Ampleforth.

We spent the remainder of the evening with chairs drawn to the kitchen stove sorting out the funeral, then, after the pots were washed and cleared, Alfie announced he was tired and went off to bed. I was planning to stay up a while and tackle some more of my father's paperwork but after a few minutes I found I couldn't keep my eyes open and also decided to call it a day. I whistled Domino for his last walk and in our usual routine we went to the far end of the orchard. It was a cold, clear night and the flush of a new moon spilled over the frost covered pasture. I felt Domino nudge my leg to tell me he was ready to go back in. As we reached the door, I turned to the sound of yet another taxi rattling up the drive. It was late for visitors, but this was no ordinary evening and as I locked up, I tried to picture the scene inside the castle library. There would be servants, lawyers and other bureaucrats milling around, Julian would no doubt be swinging the lead, his poor mother was probably drunk while Jane and Barnaby would be trying to keep the peace.

I climbed into bed and having struggled through half a page of a novel reached over and pinched out the wick.

CHAPTER ELEVEN

The next two days passed surprisingly quickly not least because on the Saturday morning while we were having breakfast, a huge wad of mail arrived at the house, so much that it wouldn't go through the letterbox and the postman had to bang on the door.

To my surprise, only three of the letters were addressed to my father, one being an invitation for us both to a ball at the castle to celebrate Julian's 21st at the end of the month. The remainder of the correspondence was addressed to myself and Alfie (or 'to the family of..' or 'to whom it may concern') and while the letters varied in presentation and style, they were all from my father's friends and colleagues in the racing industry expressing shock and sorrow at what had happened. Oh, there was the usual unctuous standard from the local bank manager but the rest were written by people in the industry warmly reminiscing on times past, together with some amusing compositions from owners and punters alike including an anonymous note from an illegal betting syndicate to say they were sorry that the trainer of *Stornoway* had passed away and hoped that the animal that had been so good to them would quickly get over the bereavement and his form would not suffer. That gave us a laugh, in fact many of the letters did and it was a touching exercise ploughing through the mound because we could sense my father's spirit in the room enjoying the moment. The practical consequence of receiving so many letters was that they all needed to be answered before we went back to College otherwise we would never get round to it so that's how I spent the weekend, writing, writing, writing, trying to think of an original response to each one until shortage of time forced my hand into automatic ten-line mode.

There were over a hundred letters to compose but it wasn't too difficult. Alfie addressed all the envelopes and on the Sunday afternoon, and when Jane dropped by we seconded her as chief envelope and stamp licker.

'How are things at home?' I asked scribbling furiously.

Jane was hammering stamps and didn't even look up. 'It's mad, absolutely mad. If you think you're rushed here, you should see how frantic it is at the castle.'

'Is there anything Alfie and I can do to help?'

'No, not at all. It's just a bit crazy with so many people coming and going. Mother and Julian are beside themselves, it's like they have twenty balls in the air and are trying to land them all at the same time. Barnaby too, backwards and forwards to the town on various errands. I'm so relieved to be out for a while'

'Has anything been decided about Lord William's funeral? Alfie and I would like to attend if we can.'

'Strange you should mention it as Bishop Moule was just finalising the arrangements as I came down. It's been decided father will have a private funeral and interment next Tuesday with a memorial service the following week.'

'You say lawyers have been at the castle. Would that be Mr Crake?'

'Both Mr Crake from Hartlepool and his partner have been constant visitors, Crake in his capacity as the family solicitor and his partner because he is the Coroner for the County. There's to be a reading of the Will in the library on Tuesday morning and one of the reasons I came over is because Mr Crake has requested that you delay your return to College so you can attend. Why do you suppose he wants you there when everyone else is staff or family?'

I was electrified by this information because the only plausible explanation for being invited to the reading of the Will was that I would benefit under its terms. Lord William had said as much on his deathbed. Could it be true? I suppressed my excitement.

'I expect it's a formality because I was present when your father died. I could certainly do without it because we're booked on the York train and now we're going to have to put everything back.'

Jane held my gaze as she detached another portrait of the king from the block of penny reds.

'Did father say anything during your interview that would account for Mr Crake wanting you there?'

I pressed the blotting paper and did my best to appear uninterested.

'Not a thing. I can only guess it's something to do with the Coroner's rules because I was with him at the end.'

I hated misleading Jane and my brother, but Crake held the key to the future of us all and until he showed his hand, I had little choice but to play my own very closely.

CHAPTER TWELVE

The clock tower had just struck eleven when Barnaby, Alfie and I convened in the courtyard for my father's funeral. A watery sun hung over the city but there was a snap in the air which made us embrace the warmth of the Rolls which Barnaby brought round to the front once he had scraped the frost off the windows. For a while we jolted along the country roads until Barnaby broke the silence.

'It'll not be an easy day for you lads but it will pass,' he said. 'Just remember to keep your heads up as your father would expect and take comfort that he had many friends who will be there to support you.'

No sooner had we drawn up in front of the parlour than Seaton scuttled out into the road to greet us, his coat and tails flapping in the breeze as he danced over the cobbles.

'Ah good morning, good morning to you Mr Bullick, and good morning to you too gentlemen,' he gushed as he hopped around the vehicle shaking everyone's hand. 'Now for goodness sake do come on in out of the cold. Nathaniel is round the back scrubbing down the horses so we have a little time and the kettle has just boiled.'

We trailed Seaton into the parlour where a petite softly spoken lady he introduced as his wife ghosted in with a tray of tea and biscuits.

'Gentlemen it is such a fine morning for a funeral,' enthused the undertaker sipping from his cup, 'just like an excellent pot of *Earl Grey*, not too warm, not too cold but just right (thank you so much my dear). The weather is so important on a day like this you know. I remember years ago managing a funeral at St Andrews at Aycliffe when there was the most terrific thunderstorm. Dreadful it was, one of the worst I had ever known, the deluge hammering down on the roof so loud you could barely hear the eulogy. When it was time to carry the deceased out everyone wanted to remain in the church until the storm had subsided but the parson, a fellow named Eade, I recall, had to be off for a shooting party and insisted the burial took place straight away. Frightful business it was but when we protested, he shamelessly retorted that the weather was down to the Lord and *thy will be done* and all that. Needless to say the interment proceeded with indecent haste but everyone still ended up drenched and covered in mud.'

We all looked at each other. If I hadn't met him before I would have supposed Seaton was some kind of comedy hall act. He took another sip from his China cup and began again.

'No, I'll never forget that day,' he sighed running his fingers through his grey mane, 'such a cold-blooded fellow that Eade, evidently was going shooting which is why he couldn't wait to be off and down the hill but he might have said. Oh, don't get me wrong, he was an excellent man but not quite my cup of tea. My cup of tea? Do you see? Oh there,

I've done it again, I'm so sorry gentlemen, I don't mean to make quips on solemn occasions like today, forgive me, I don't know what I'm saying sometimes.'

At that moment, the door opened on Nathaniel looking as polished as a groom on the way to his wedding.

'The hearse and carriage are at the front. We're ready when you are grandfather.'

Seaton checked his watch. 'Gentlemen, the hour approaches. I will drive the hearse; Nathaniel, you will follow behind in the carriage. Mr Barnaby I would like you to accompany me on the bench please. Mr Bullick, you sit in the second coach with young Alfie here and my two lads. If we need to stop for any reason, I shall raise my right arm although St Cuthbert's is not far and I don't propose to halt the cortege until we reach Old Elvet. When the service is over, we will resume our positions for the short drive to St Oswald's cemetery. After the interment we will proceed directly to the County Hotel. Does anyone have any questions?'

Hearing none, Seaton opened the door on the cobbles where two of his men waited at the side of a magnificent glass carriage behind which stood an open black Landau. Alfie and I stared at our father's coffin, beautifully arranged within the crystal facade. I felt my brother's touch on my arm.

'Is that him *Blue*?' was as much as he could say.

'It's only a casket. It's just his remains. Dad's not really here, if he's not here then he must be in heaven and at this moment he'll be looking down expecting us to be strong.'

'Do you really think so?'

'Absolutely.'

It might have been true and I hoped it was but at that moment I felt as if I didn't really know anything.

'The horses are very smart,' said Alfie.

I liked the sleek shape of my father's coffin, the cherry wood buffed and polished like one of Lord William's drinks cabinets. I smiled inwardly wondering what Dad would have made of the comparison before quickly rebuking myself for entertaining such blithe thoughts at his funeral.

Seaton checked his watch a final time then nodded to his men. As if sensing the development, one of the horses whinnied and a jangle of buckles and brasses ran along the cortege.

'To your places everyone and good luck.'

Alfie and I moved through the silent crowd gathered on the pavement. As we climbed into the carriage the women curtsied and the men touched their hats.

'This is it Alfie,' I whispered. 'Remember, he'll be looking down expecting us to be strong.'

CHAPTER THIRTEEN

As our sorry little party wound through the streets of Durham it was extraordinary how the people fell silent and shuffled to the edge of the road to let us pass, each one no doubt speculating who was in the casket before turning their gaze to Alfie and me in the second carriage. When we reached North Road, progress was in startling contrast to when Seaton and I had collected my father from Dryburn a few days previously. Transporting our precious cargo in a covered box wagon had been like wading through treacle, but today, from the way the flags opened ahead of us you would have thought we were carrying the plague.

On Framwellgate Bridge we were whipped by an icy breeze coming off the river and sensing the clouds groaning with winter, I turned my collar and prayed Seaton was right and that the weather would hold. In Market Square the clatter of hooves made the traders look up from their stalls, hands on hips, while small children stood and pointed before rushing to their mothers' aprons. In the crescent at the top, little white faces peered down from the upstairs windows, each one wrestling with their own mortality as they hurriedly crossed themselves and drew the curtains. What is it about a funeral procession? It was the same at the fork between Saddler Street and Elvet, the great and good of the town frozen to the pavement, repelled, and yet fascinated by our sad little convoy.

The cathedral bells chimed quarter to the hour as the cortege made its way onto Elvet Bridge where stood the giant figure of Harry Sample, top hat and gloves drawn across his ample chest. Fenoughty was at his side reverently holding my father's binoculars and going stick, the giant and the dwarf standing to attention with six stable lads in matching coat and tails.

'I wish he were here to see this,' said Alfie.

'He will have known lad,' replied Fenoughty quietly, his gentle words almost lost on the breeze.

Seaton jumped down from the hearse.

'You must be Mr Sample? Can I suggest that you and your men lead the way and we'll follow behind in the carriages? Edmund, perhaps you and Alfie would go back and join Nathaniel in the Landau? We don't want to be late.'

'Just a minute,' said Barnaby drawing a pewter flask from the inside of his jacket. 'You might want a quick nip of this. I find it helps steady the nerves.'

I took a deep swig of a warm fluid that tasted like a mixture of port and brandy. Whatever its constituents a delightful glow settled in the pit of my stomach and I was ready for anything.

'Here, let me have some of that,' said Alfie.

'Perhaps later,' replied Barnaby wafting the flask beyond my brother's reach before taking a quick draw himself and burying it inside his jacket. 'You have a reading to do.'

My brother moaned something about it not being fair but Nathaniel who was swigging from his own flask cut him off.

'Don't worry young 'un, you can have nip of mine later. Let's get the service over first.'

Alfie was still muttering as he, Nathaniel and I retraced our steps and jumped back into the carriage. Seaton, who was already astride the hearse twisted round and seeing we were in position rattled the reins and with a jolt and a jangle of harnesses, the cortege was on its way again.

A policeman held back the traffic as we swept over Elvet junction and clip clopped up the hill to St Cuthbert's where a large crowd was already gathered on the green, their number stretching across to the court building.

'Looks like a full house,' said Nathaniel as we pulled up behind the hearse. I gazed down the footpath leading to the vestibule. He was right. They were queuing to get in. Scores of them. Alfie and I jumped down and stood by the railings as Nathaniel shepherded the stable lads into order.

'Right lads, I want you to form up between the carriages. That's right, three sets of two, tallest at the back with a corridor down the middle. No, not like that cloth head! Now pretend the person next to you is your girlfriend and you're at the local ceilidh stripping the willow. That's right. Now put your arms over each other's shoulders and link up. Don't be shy man. Good. Now link up'.

When everyone was in position, Nathaniel and his assistants reached into the glass case and drawing on the experience of generations, carefully extricated my father's casket and lowered it on not a few anxious shoulders.

'Steady lads, steady,' said Nathaniel softly. 'We're in no hurry. Mr Seaton will not give the signal until each one of you is comfortable'.

For an anxious minute or so the coffin bobbled and wobbled as the stable lads adjusted to the unfamiliar burden and Seaton went round straightening backs and uttering words of reassurance.

'Gentlemen, after the deceased has been securely positioned at the altar you will withdraw and wait by the carriages until the end of the service. I would remind you to look straight to the front at all times and remember we are in no hurry. Gentlemen, on the count of three you will place your left foot forward. One, two, three…'

Sample was first into the churchyard, the blacksmith's head bowed with top hat drawn tightly across his barrel chest. Immediately behind him shuffled the stable boys caterpillar-like with my father's remains balanced on their shoulders, then Barnaby and Fenoughty and finally Alfie and myself. As we approached the porch a solemn faced Cannon Brown hovered out to greet us but seeing we were already in step, promptly withdrew back into the foyer leaving the rest of us to bump in after him. The organist, observing events through his mirror, immediately struck into *Nimrod* generating such a scraping of chairs I did not have to look up to see the church was packed. When we reached the top of the aisle Brown started to sprinkle holy water over the congregation, occasionally wheeling round to ensure the coffin and pallbearers received their share. It was a profound moment.

'Man, that is born of a woman, hath but a short time to live, and is full of misery. He cometh up, and is cut

*down, like a flower; he fleeth as it were a shadow, and
never continueth in one stay'*

A wall of uneasy faces twisted round to stare at us. I recognised a handful from the village but most of them were strangers.

*'In the midst of life we are in death: of whom may we
seek for succour, but of thee, O Lord, who for our sins
art justly displeased? Yet, O Lord God most holy, O
Lord most mighty, O holy and most merciful Saviour,
deliver us not into the bitter pains of eternal death.'*

When we reached the altar my father's coffin was lowered onto a brass bier and the pallbearers melted away leaving Alfie, myself, Barnaby, Sample and Fenoughty to occupy the vacant front bench. From the half empty pew immediately behind us Lady Alanna and Jane smiled nervously but we had no sooner taken our place when it was all eyes to the front as Cannon Brown started to address the congregation in that familiar rich baritone.

'A very good afternoon ladies and gentlemen. On behalf of Edmund and Alfred and their family and the ministers and parishioners I would like to extend a very warm welcome to you all to St Cuthbert's. There has been a church on this site for more than a thousand years and ever since Anglo-Saxon times the people of this town have gathered here to offer their prayers and thanks to Almighty God. This has been a place of joy and happiness such as weddings and baptisms, but it is also a place of reflection when on occasions like today we remember that life is but a temporary arrangement within which nothing is constant but change. This requiem mass is offered for the repose of the soul of James Michael Bullick who was a regular worshipper here and while our hearts are heavy with sorrow at his untimely passing, we can take comfort that he died, as indeed he had lived, under the careful watch of the Lord Jesus in the one true Christian faith.'

There was a short silence and a few coughs as Brown flicked through the pages of his missal.

'After the service, the family would be honoured if you would join them for some refreshment at *The County Hotel* and share some memories of James and all the good times you had with him.'

There was another short pause while Brown stepped behind the altar before continuing in the semi sing-song voice that most clerics seem to adopt before a packed house.

'And so, my brothers and sisters in Christ, we will commence our offering to almighty God by singing together our first hymn, *Lord of all Hopefulness* which you will find at page 204 of the green book in front of you.'

It is said that the nearer one is to the coalface of a wedding or funeral, the quicker the day passes and my father's requiem was no exception. Cannon Brown, familiar with the contours of the occasion galloped through the liturgy and before I knew it, we were filing back out into the churchyard. However, there was one event that took place in St Cuthbert's that winter's afternoon which I shall never forget, and where just for a moment time stood still. It happened during my brother's reading when he began to choke with grief and it looked as though he might not make it to the end. The interval lasted no more than a few seconds but within the stillness of those walls it seemed like an age and the tension was agonizing. I was about to intervene when the spell was broken by the rattle of a latch followed by some kind of commotion near the doorway. I instinctively turned round with everyone else to be greeted by the sight of Julian and Lord Clifford jostling through a wall of mourners hemmed in at the back. I knew Julian had returned from Oxford but assumed he'd far too much on his plate to be bothered about consoling any of us. Clifford, though, I had not expected to see and was just mulling this over when I saw they were accompanied by another who was the last of the trio to squeeze through the gathering. I had no idea who this girl was but even from the other end of the church I could see she was striking. There was something about her form, the way she carried herself, indeed in her very presence that seized the attention and would not let it go. Neither was mine the only gaze resting upon her willowy frame as the latecomers swept down the aisle to take their place next to Jane and Lady Alanna. I surrendered to propriety and switched my attention back to the front but that fleeting glimpse had quickened my heart and I was aching to steal another look even before I caught the whisper of her skirts as she moved in the pew behind me. The opportunity presented itself a few minutes later when I stood at the lectern and opened the pages of *Corinthians*.

Though I speak with the tongues of men and of angels, and have not love, I am become as a sounding brass, or a tinkling cymbal.

And though I have the gift of prophecy, and understand all mysteries, and all knowledge; and though I have all faith, so that I could remove mountains, and have not love, I am nothing...

The attention of the whole congregation was fixed upon me but as I looked up, I saw only one person and that my first impression of her loveliness was not misplaced.

Love is patient, love is kind. It does not envy, it does not boast, it is not proud. It is not rude, it is not self-seeking, it is not easily angered, it keeps no record of wrongs…

She surveyed me with an unnerving intensity, her delicate chin resting upon gloved fingers intertwined as if in prayer.

Love does not delight in evil but rejoices with the truth. It always protects, always trusts, always hopes, always perseveres. Love never fails…

Over the rim of the manuscript, I caught the swirl of her long dark hair as she leaned back and whispered something into Julian's ear. The new Lord Craven tossed his head then muttered something through cupped hands that made her smile as she passed the remark on to Clifford who was seated to her other side.

When I was a child, I talked like a child, I thought like a child, I reasoned like a child. Now I know in part; then I shall know fully, even as I am fully known. And now these three remain: faith, hope and love. But the greatest of these is love…

I closed the heavy cover of the bible and glanced up at the congregation. She was watching me closely, her head slightly cocked with eyes fixed upon my own as she squeezed Julian's arm and mouthed, 'the greatest of these is love'. Her beauty and poise were awesome, and I could barely take my eyes off her. I had not previously believed in love at first sight, but this girl was the most stunning creature I had ever seen and from that moment onwards I was utterly captivated.

CHAPTER FOURTEEN

During the service snow had begun to fall over the city, stifling the pavements and muffling the hooves of the horses as the cortege whispered up the hill on my father's last journey. When we reached St Oswald's we dismounted and shuffled in silence to a far corner of the churchyard where through a swirl of blue flakes we found the large bank of glazed soil that marked my father's final resting place.

'So this is it,' I thought as we rocked in the cold, waiting for the others to catch up. I wondered if Julian and his party would be among them but as I scanned the crescent of sombre faces there was no sign. After what seemed an age the ropes were slipped beneath the coffin which was duly lowered into the waiting hole. I would never see my father again. I noticed how the old priest's white cassock stood out against the dark apparel of the mourners and screwing my eyes to a rush of tears I willed the contrast had been a sign from the Lord. Cannon Brown began the final prayers, his words hushed in the snowfall.

Forasmuch as it hath pleased Almighty God of his
great mercy to take unto himself the soul of our dear

brother James here departed, we therefore commit his
body to the ground;
earth to earth, ashes to ashes, dust to dust …

Brown reached for the pile of soil but finding it frozen could only dislodge a single lump which he threw into the hole where it crashed onto the lid of the unseen casket. I felt for my brother's hand as we followed suit then watched while others stepped forward to do the same, then others after them, and then still others, each clod of earth beating its shocking lament until the drumming gradually subsided and we peeled away. It was as grim an occasion as anything I had ever known but I took solace from Nathaniel who, sensing our misery, whispered that my brother and I would come back to this place on happier occasions, perhaps in the spring when the birds were singing and the churchyard was in flower.

The atmosphere at the *County* was in startling contrast to events at the top of the hill when in the normal manner of funerals, the tension gave way to release and the surge of bottled-up conversation. As our party stepped in from the dusk the first thing that hit me was the surprising level of noise as old friends caught up with one another, many hailing a lost connection from across the room as they struggled to make their way over. There must have been close on two hundred mourners packed into the ground floor of the hotel, although goodness knows who they all were. I relieved a schooner of sherry from a passing attendant and turned to Barnaby.

'This is astonishing. I never thought so many people would turn out to see father off, particularly on a day like this.'

'I agree,' replied Barnaby, eyes darting as he lit his pipe. 'I expected a few from the racing fraternity but not this many. I've been stood here a while tuning into the accents. Most folk sound like they're from York and Ripon way.'

I recognised a couple of the Middleham jockeys, and then over by the fireplace I could see the Malton trainers Lambton and Budgett deep in conversation. I had known Budgett since I was little and he must have sensed my gaze upon him for at that moment he looked up and gave a strange kind of salute.

'Barnaby, did you catch the arrival of Julian and his friends in the middle my brother's reading?'

'How could I not?' he replied through a cloud of smoke. 'The whole church saw what went on. You'd think anyone else arriving late would have slipped in quietly and stood at the back but not them.'

'I tell you Barnaby, the way they shoved through was awful, it showed a complete lack of respect but when I saw that arse Clifford was with them, I suppose I shouldn't have expected anything less.'

Barnaby waved to a small wiry man who was thrashing his way over.

'Julian's memory is short. He doesn't realise how much his friend is loathed in these parts, or maybe he does and couldn't care less which is even more worrying.'

'There was a girl with them. Have you any idea who she is?'

In my attempt to appear nonchalant I had left the question until last, but Barnaby saw though the ruse.

'Ah, that will be the Lady Victoria, Clifford's sister. She's quite a looker don't you think?'

'She's certainly that. To own the truth when she was sat there a few feet from the lectern I found it hard to concentrate on my reading.'

Barnaby struck another match and cupped it over the bowl of his pipe.

'It seems she has that effect on most people although word is she's destined for Julian in a match that would enhance the stock of both families. And why not, hey? Julian's brains are in his trousers – and who can blame him with someone like her – and the Cliffords need the cash I shouldn't wonder. Who says love is blind? Oh, don't look so disheartened Edmund. If it's any consolation my spies tell me the lady is a right cow which would make her and Julian extremely well suited don't you think?'

I grabbed another glass of sherry.

'She's far too beautiful to be with someone like him.'

The wiry man had almost reached us and was extending his hand.

'Money talks or didn't you know?' said Barnaby.

'She's the most stunning creature I have ever seen.'

'Mark my words, she's a bad 'un and if you want some friendly advice, steer clear…. Fergus you old dog! Fergus, I want you to meet Edmund, Jimmy's eldest lad. Fergus grew up with your father in Ireland you know?'

As it was, I did know.

'So you're the legendry Fergus O'Hare? Delighted to meet you Fergus. Dad often spoke about your times as apprentices together.'

'Ha. Don't believe a word of it. Anyway lad, I just wanted to tell you how sorry we all are. Jimmy was my oldest friend and I'll never get used to the fact he's gone. Nowhen, I've a lot of people to catch up with so I'll get straight to the point. Judy- my wife- and I, well we can't bear the thought of you and Alfie being on yer own at Christmas and wondered if you'd like to join us in Ireland?'

Ireland? I'd always wanted to go to Ireland. In fact, if my father had lived, we were going to the Kilkenny sales the following spring. It was tempting but probably a bit soon.

'Oh, I don't know Fergus. Its very kind of you but I have my Oxbridge entrance in a couple of weeks and there's Dad's estate to sort out.'

'Never say never lad. Look, it's an open invitation. You can leave it to the last minute if you want to, just promise me you'll think about it, that's all.'

I said I would and after a few tales about when he and my father were lads, Fergus wheeled away to engage some of the other mourners. It had been my intention to try and get round everybody as well but there were so many, I passed most of the time hemmed in by the door as some cut across to share a few words, while others stopped to shake hands on the way out.

If a funeral could be remembered in that way, I have to say that my father's turned into an agreeable afternoon, especially when measured against what had gone before. Sustenance at the hotel was in no short measure and as the hard-core weighed anchor, off came the jackets and the party like atmosphere that settled over the day was only enhanced when one of the stable lads produced a fiddle and some of the others began to jig. There was some memorable singing too, with renditions of *Early One Morning* and *Widecombe Fair* sticking in the mind, the latter especially because of the raucous struggle most people had trying to remember who came after *Peter Davy* and *Harry Hawk*. My brother seemed to know all the words; he must have learned the song at school although I inferred from the way he was marshalling the chorus that Nathaniel had been true to his word about the flask.

It was early evening and the ranks had noticeably thinned when I felt a tap on my shoulder and turned to face Julian. I was caught completely off guard because I hadn't seen him arrive and at the back of my mind assumed he must have gone straight back to the castle.

'Julian, I'm so pleased you could make it, we were just…'

Julian swotted away my hand.

'What did my father say to you?' he demanded.

'I'm so sorry about Lord William,' I replied. 'He was such a good person and we're all numb over what happened. I don't know what else to say.'

'You can start by telling me what you were doing in his room when he was dying. That's right, on his deathbed.'

'How do you mean?'

'Oh don't stand there all mealy mouthed pretending you've no idea what I'm talking about, although God knows what mother and Addison were thinking of letting you anywhere near him. What did you think you were doing?'

At the sound of Julian's raised voice, a number of people glanced uneasily in our direction.

'Julian,' I replied steering him to a corner, 'this is hardly the time or place. If you like I can come to the library tomorrow morning and we'll talk about it then but not now, not here in front of everyone.'

'And why not here?' growled Julian wafting his arm about the room. 'I couldn't give a stuff about any of these people, they were your father's friends not mine and most of them are only here for the free drink so don't give me your 'not here' patter. I want to know what my father said to you as he lay dying, the poor sod. Now. Here in this lounge. Do you understand what I'm saying?'

The fiddle immediately stopped playing and the room fell silent. Julian's squat face was inches from my own. He stank of booze. I don't think I had ever been so embarrassed in my life.

'For heaven's sake Julian,' I whispered, 'Where's your dignity let alone the respect you owe to my father's memory? If we really must talk about this now all I can tell you is that when I saw him, your father was so poorly he barely said a word, at least not to me he didn't. If I knew any more, if he said any more, I would tell you but he didn't and I can't and that's it. There's nothing else. Now can we leave it?'

Julian fixed his cold grey eyes on me as he gathered his thoughts. His expression was unforgiving, the contours of his plump face totally devoid of warmth or sincerity

'I don't believe you,' he said at length. 'You're lying. What were you doing over there in the first place?'

The fiddle cranked up again as the room slipped back into conversation.

'Look, it was in the middle of the night. I was asleep when I received the call. By the time I had dressed and was shown to his room your father had deteriorated and unfortunately he slipped away without regaining consciousness.'

I could almost hear the whir of cogs clicking away in his nasty mind as he tried to figure out if I were telling the truth. Eventually he spoke.

'I still don't believe you, but it is of no matter, no consequence. My father will not be coming back and neither will yours, more's the pity for you.'

'What do you mean?'

Julian took a deep drag on his cigarette, exhaling as he spoke.

'What I mean Edmund old man is the untimely demise of our respective fathers heralds the establishment of a new era at Craven where one of the first things I'm going to do is run the estate like a proper business and address the blight that your family and others like you have been on it all these years.'

'Blight?' I repeated searing with anger. 'My father's only been in his grave a couple of hours, and you come here to his funeral and talk to me like that? What has happened to you Julian? You're supposed to be my friend.'

Julian grabbed a glass from a passing tray.

'Your friend?' he said draining the contents in one before replacing it and seizing another. 'Friends? What, as in equals? You and me? Don't make me laugh. The occasion or the drinks have gone to your head Edmund. We were never 'friends' as you put it and we certainly never shall be. Very shortly when I'm in charge around here there's going to be a few alterations. With the advent of war it's a tough old world and if the estate is to remain solvent there's going to be some changes. Looking through the accounts one of the biggest drains on our resources is maintaining the stables. It wouldn't be so bad if we ever won anything, but the enterprise has been going backwards for years and I'm not prepared to subsidise what was in effect the old man's hobby. The stables and stud farm must either make a profit or we wind them up. If it were down to me, I would close them both tomorrow, but mother says I'm being too hasty and should give it another year.'

'I think you should listen to your mother. If it weren't for your parent's enterprise, you wouldn't have your doll's house to play with.'

'A doll's house? Very good Edmund. A doll's house. I like it. That just about sums up the way the stables have been run, like an expensive toy. Well, not for much longer. You might as well know I've asked Harry Budgett to take over and he'll be moving into the lodge at the end of January.'

Julian swigged the contents of his glass and watched for my reaction. So that's why Budgett had looked uncomfortable when our eyes met earlier. So much for my own pipedreams. The words came with a rush.

'The end of January? But that's only a few weeks away. I have to sit my Oxbridge entrance, Alfie is too young, Julian you cannot mean it, this is our home, we've more than twenty year's possessions in the house and I haven't even begun to sort out my father's affairs.'

'Oh, I mean what I say Edmund. How does the expression go 'the needs of the many' and all that? Craven is or should be a working estate that makes a profit and not some kind of charitable trust for my father's old pals. I need to run the estate as a business, you know old lad, a bit like the days of the hunter-gatherer – those who don't go hunting don't get nothing to eat? Simple as that. Don't worry; you won't be on the street. Mother can house you in one of the cottages if she must but in a couple of weeks when I come of age, it will be with a new broom and one of the first things I'll be doing is clearing out you, your brother and that sick dog of yours.'

I was so absorbed in what I was hearing that I hadn't clocked much else in the room until suddenly she was there in front of me tucking her hand under Julian's arm.

'Now then darling, are you going to introduce me to your friend?'

Julian who was in the middle of his tirade suddenly stopped and stared at her, then looked at me for a moment and then back to the girl again before wrinkling his nose.

'Oh, there you are Victoria. This is Bullick, one of the workers from the estate. He's the son of my late father's late trainer and will shortly be moving on.'

The girl turned and, in that moment, when she set her gaze upon me, I was so overwhelmed by her loveliness that I almost froze to the spot. She was utterly striking with high cheekbones and a porcelain complexion set against violet lips that parted on a row of perfect teeth when she smiled, although she wasn't smiling now as she looked me up and down.

'Moving on are we?' she said as her long dark hair caught the light. However, it was the eyes that transfixed me; they were black and beautiful, I had never seen anything like them. She held my gaze but her words were addressed to Julian.

'Who did you say this was? Bullick your trainer? I thought we'd just been to his funeral."

Julian rolled his eyes. The girl considered him quizzically for a moment then the penny dropped.

'Oh, I see! *That* Bullick, young Bullick the son of the other one whose funeral it was?'

Julian rolled his eyes again. She threw her hands in the air with inappropriate elation.

'So *that's* why he was doing the reading. I see now. You're such a tease darling, really you are.'

Julian grinned piously and stooped while she hoisted her slim frame on tiptoes to peck his cheek before turning her attention back to me.

'So you're *Horse Boy,*' said she with a slope of the head. 'I've heard a great deal about you *Horse Boy.*'

'Nothing favourable I assure you,' exhaled Julian wearily as he lit another cigarette and stared aimlessly about the room. I ignored the slight and bowed graciously to the girl, the manners my father taught me instinctively kicking in.

'The name's actually Edmund m'lady. Edmund Bullick. How do you do Miss? I'm honoured to make your acquaintance.'

If I thought I had gone over the top I was wrong as just for a moment her cutting manner subsided and she took my outstretched hand, all the time sweeping my face with those bewitching eyes.

'Quite the little charmer aren't we *Horse Boy?*' she said softly.

I savoured the brush of her fingers as she turned to address Julian whose back was to her shoulder.

'My brother sent me to hurry you along darling. He's outside in the automobile. Don't forget we're dining with Lord Lambton this evening. If we don't make a move we're going to be late.'

'Why, what time is it?' asked Julian through a cloud of tobacco.

She withdrew her hand and checked the Cartier on her wrist. It was exquisite like its owner.

'Six fifty.'

'What, already?' replied Julian irritably. 'I thought time only passed quickly when you're enjoying yourself.'

I wondered why he had bothered coming at all. At least Johnny Clifford had kept away although after his performance at the stable boxing match it would have been a brave call to show his face again among this lot. Julian downed his drink then taking a final pull from his cigarette, flicked the butt in the general direction of the fireplace where it struck the log basket and bounced out onto the carpet. Julian, who was already making for the door paid no attention and it was left for one of the guests to intervene and discard it into the flames. Halfway across the floor he suddenly stopped and turned to address me a final time.

'Edmund, we'll talk again next week but my decision about Budgett taking over is final. And as for the rest of you, take note because from now on I'll be watching you closely and if I find anyone not pulling their weight, believe me, your feet won't touch the ground on the way out.'

With these words he scanned the room daring any of the guests to say anything before calling to the girl.

'Come on Victoria; we've done our duty as mother requested. Now let's get out of this dump.'

Victoria switched on her smile for a last time.

'Hail and farewell *Horse Boy*. Have a good life.'

I bowed my head but she was already away. I called after her.

'The name's Edmund ma'am and the pleasure's all mine.'

Victoria looked back over her shoulder.

'You wish,' she mouthed sweetly as taking leave of no other, they gathered their coats and marched out into the snowstorm, the crash of the door sealing a room of perplexed faces that instinctively turned towards Alfie and me.

It was Barnaby who broke the tension.

'Take no notice anybody, really, pay no attention. His lordship is in shock following the death of his father and he doesn't know what he's saying. Now come on, tomorrow will take care of itself. For now let's all raise a glass to the memory of our good friend James Michael Bullick. Landlord, another round of punch if you please, and have a glass yourself sir!'

Barnaby's call to arms sliced through the tension and with yet more drink circulating, Julian's extortions were put aside, and the party resumed as before.

'I hate funerals,' said Barnaby. 'They reek of my own mortality. As for Julian, I've seen this kind of thing before; people say stupid things when they're drunk and upset. I expect he'll apologise when he wakes up tomorrow. Don't let it bother you, Edmund; really. He didn't mean it.'

'Of course he meant it. People speak the truth when they're drunk although whether he can carry out any of his threats is another matter entirely.'

Barnaby struck a match and cupped hands over his pipe. 'How's that?'

'What I mean is that for all his bluster, Julian may not be the man he thinks he is – in every sense of the word.'

Barnaby stiffened and immediately I knew I had said too much.

'How do you mean 'not the man he thinks he is?'

'Nothing. Look Barnaby, forget it. I've already talked too freely which was not my intention.'

'You *do* know something don't you? What is it? Did Lord William speak to you after all?'

I cursed my loose tongue. Fool Bullick, fool.

'I can't say any more, really I cannot. I know nothing that could change anything at this time and I must ask you not to press me further.'

We watched the stable lads construct a human pyramid that collapsed amid a tangle of limbs, profanities and beer. Eventually he spoke.

'If that's your wish, so be it but remember this Edmund: you have no greater friend at Craven and when the time comes you need to talk to someone, and it will, my door is open.'

I looked into Barnaby's weathered face. He plainly knew a great deal more than he was letting on but that much had been obvious when he picked us up from the station. It was so tempting to confide in him and I don't think I had ever been more in need of a friend than at that moment, but I managed to hold back because I knew Barnaby was not the key. Crake was. Everything came down to him and I was more determined than ever to confront him.

CHAPTER FIFTEEN

On Tuesday morning Lord William's family and the various beneficiaries gathered in the library for the reading of the Will. Alfie and I had spent the early part of the day packing our trunks for college and I was one of the last to arrive. I surveyed the room. There were thin smiles from Jane and Mrs Pearce but everyone else was on edge and you could cut the atmosphere with a knife.

The library had been cleared for the event and in place of the usual furniture, a large wooden table had been set up by the window which was positioned in such a way that it was slightly (and I suspect deliberately) raised to give its occupants the appearance of looking down upon the crescent of wooden chairs that were facing it. The room bore little semblance to the ruddy stage of Lady Alanna's distress but a few evenings before. The arrangements were now such that were it not for the air of gravitas hanging over the proceedings, the uninformed observer could easily have mistaken the venue for some kind of recital.

From my seat at the end of the first row I scanned the long faces around me. Barnaby, Fenoughty, Monmouth, Cannon

Brown, Bishop Moule, the elusive Lockwood – who wouldn't look me in the eye – they were all sitting together among the estate tenants with the domestic staff lining the walls at the back. There were others present who were not known to me; foremen from the local mines, an assortment of tweeds and bowlers and others in military uniform whose association with the estate was a matter of conjecture. I particularly remember one old boy with a chain of office around his neck slumped in a wheelchair near the front, listening trumpet pressed to his ear tuning into the background conversation which was growing with the tension as the hour approached. Friendly faces were thin on the ground. When I'd sat down Barnaby came across to shake my hand and there'd been reassuring smiles from Fenoughty and Monmouth, but the others were far too preoccupied with their own expectations to take notice of anyone else. The atmosphere, though, was simply electric; there was no other word for it; the very air in the room a bilious mixture of anticipation, suppressed excitement and dread.

As we all sat there waiting for the lawyers, I thought about the consequences if I were to be a major beneficiary of the estate as Lord William had implied. I remembered the awful scene as he lay dying, the revelation about my mother, his obvious distress, how he had been so appalled by his son's behaviour that he had instructed his solicitor to change the succession. That's if Julian was his son in the first place. This had been the most astonishing revelation of all, yet there was something so earnest, so utterly compelling in his address. 'Treat with Crake' he had said, 'he knows what to do'. His very last words; 'treat with Crake'. Over the last few days I had gone through our conversation time and time again, I had thought of little else. This was it. I sensed we were in for a morning of high drama and that a number of people in the room were about to be seriously disappointed.

As soon as the clock on the mantelpiece pinged eleven, the door behind us opened and everyone rose to their feet as if we were in church. Monmouth entered the room with Lady Alanna, Julian and Jane and led them to the table by the window. The family were accompanied by two grave looking individuals who were not known to me but as they also took their place, I figured they had to be the solicitor, Crake, and one of his clerks. There was no mistaking the tall, imposing figure of Crake in his immaculate dark suit and stiff white collar. I was instantly drawn to the thick silver mane brushed back over his brow, that and a heavy gold chain that swung from his pinstriped waistcoat as he marched across the carpet. The man had an unnerving air of self-assurance, he simply oozed confidence and even before a word was spoken, it was apparent to everyone that we were in the presence of a class act.

The person who trailed him in was much shorter and almost buried under a tower of documents which he promptly collapsed onto the table. He was not so much scruffy as slightly dishevelled with oily red hair combed over from the sides in a futile attempt to conceal his bald crown. He wore curious bottle-bottom spectacles of a type I had not seen before which tended to distract from the rest of his attire which was not dissimilar to his colleague's. I figured this must be Crake's clerk and when everyone was settled, it was he who opened the proceedings in a distinctive and rather irksome nasal tenor.

'Good morning ladies and gentlemen. My name is Glyder and I'm the chief probate clerk at *Baxter, Crake and Lockwood*. In a few moments Mr Crake will read the Will but first I would like to address some housekeeping rules. Each one of you has been invited this morning because the provisions of the Will concern you in some way. It is expected that at all times everyone present will conduct themselves with the decorum the occasion warrants, and refrain from talking or interrupting while the reading is in place. Secondly, to facilitate the smooth running of proceedings and to circumvent any unnecessary distraction, it is requested that until the reading is completed no one leaves the room unless this cannot be avoided. Lastly, I am instructed to thank you all for attending Craven Castle this morning, the family are aware that many of you have travelled some distance. I will now defer to Mr Crake.'

His master, who had sat motionless throughout the preliminaries now reached over the table and selecting a large brown packet, carefully loosened the pink ribbon surround and unfolded the document inside. The tension was unbearable. All eyes in the room were upon him with only the anxious shuffling of feet and creaking of chairs feathering the silence. Crake spread the document before him and adjusting his glasses addressed the room in a deep, rich voice that was in marked contrast to the nasal ramble of Glyder who had preceded him.

'Good morning ladies and gentlemen.

This is the last will and testament of me, Lieutenant-Colonel William Surtees Fitzroy-Cavendish, 6th Marquis of Craven, CVO OBE TD DL of Craven Park in the country of Durham.

*I hereby revoke all former wills and testamentary
dispositions made by me...*

*He'd revoked his previous Will. I knew this was
a standard clause at the beginning of every Will
to eliminate the capacity of any previous real or
imagined instrument, but it already sounded exciting.
I sat forward lest I should miss a single word. Crake
swept the assembly over the rim of his glasses then
continued in that grave, gravel rhythm.*

*I appoint my wife Lady Alanna Jane Fitzroy-
Cavendish and Thomas Edward Crake solicitor of the
Hartlepool practice of Baxter Crake and Lockwood to
be the executors and trustees of this my will.*

*I make the following specific cash legacies free of death
duty or associated taxes*

*To the parish of St Oswald's, Old Elvet in the city of
Durham I bequeath the sum of one thousand pounds
for the upkeep of the church building and to be
applied for continued Sunday school instruction for
the benefit of the young people of the community.*

*To the Durham Miners Association I bequeath the
sum of one thousand pounds to be applied at their
discretion to the purchase of musical instruments
for the colliery bands in the county with any sum
in remainder to be used for the maintenance and
replacement of colliery banners and the general
expenses of the annual Durham Miners' Gala.*

*To the trustees of the Union Workhouse at 37
Crossgate, Durham I bequeath the sum of one*

*thousand pounds for the upkeep of the building
and provision of books and facilities to enhance the
academic and spiritual welfare of the orphans of the
city.*

*To the members of the York Racecourse Company
I bequeath the sum of one thousand pounds to hold
in trust for the sponsorship of a two year old colt
classic trial to be held annually in the second week of
May together with the sourcing of a suitable trophy,
such race to be named in honour and memory of my
family.*

*I direct my trustees to invest the sum of three
thousand pounds in ten year Treasury stock the
interest thereof to be applied to the continued full
time school and university education of Edmund
Bullick and Alfie Bullick, the sons of the said James
Michael Bullick, the capital sum thereof to be divided
absolutely and equally between the said Edmund
Bullick and Alfie Bullick at the time both of them
have completed their full time education or when
the last of them has attained the age of twenty-five
whichever event first occurs.*

On hearing this last disposition Julian shook his head
muttering to himself so that no one in the room was left in
any doubt what he thought of the bequest. Glyder, who was
clearly embarrassed, shot him a nervous look although I was
too stunned and excited to care what either of them thought.

'What? This cannot be right. There must be a mistake!'

'Julian,' whispered his mother. '*Please!*'

'No mother. We're not having this. Father would never have left them so much money. They're not even employees.'

Crake paused for a moment and laying the will down on his lap peered at Julian over his glasses and gently shook his head.

'There can be no mistake sir,' he answered coolly. 'I personally attended your late father in this matter and drew up the will myself. The dispositions are precisely in accordance with his instructions and as to their integrity I can, if you insist, defer to the testimony of my partner Mr Lockwood and Mr Glyder here who were both present at the time.'

Julian exhaled loudly mumbling and cursing in the face of sustained entreaties from his mother and sister, although curiously no one else was taking much notice of him. Instead, all eyes in the room had turned and were staring me. If I was in any doubt as to what had just been imparted its reality was confirmed by a warm smile and thumbs-up from Barnaby. I had been so worried how we were going to pay our school fees out of my father's modest legacy when all along the Craven estate had been footing the bill and would continue to do so. I was truly astonished. There was never the slightest hint of the arrangement and yet in a few words from the grave, Lord William had confirmed it was so and made Alfie and I financially secure for the next few years. I could only sit in bewildered silence as the rumpus died down and Crake was finally able to continue.

To my estate steward Cornelius Barnaby and my head stable lad Paul Fenoughty in recognition of their loyalty and service to myself and my family I bequeath the sum of five hundred pounds each.

*To the domestic, household and estate employees in
the service of my family at the time of my death I
bequeath to each the sum of five guineas to be paid by
my executors on the first quarter day after the reading
of this will, together with a further five guineas to be
paid on the Christmas Eve first following my demise.*

And so it went on, a long and detailed schedule of specific cash gifts to organisations and people that would be in need of them, the awards bearing testimony to the munificence of the deceased. While no one had been permitted to speak during the reading, with every charitable disposition murmurs of approval had rippled through the beneficiaries until the bequest to the staff which almost brought down the house.

'Ladies and gentlemen. Ladies and gentlemen. If you please' cried Glyder raising his little voice to try and make himself heard over the din.

'Ladies and gentlemen. Please. *Please.* I would remind you of the request for decorum that was made at the commencement of this reading. Thank you.'

The rapturous mood on the floor was in marked contrast to the disposition of the deceased's family. Julian's outburst at the bequests to the Bullick family gave way to a general surliness although his mother and sister remained dignified throughout. I felt so sorry for Lady Alanna who sat wretchedly with her hands on her lap, eyes watering as she gazed into oblivion, but a public reading of Lord William's intentions could not be avoided and there was little anyone could do to help her through it. My feelings towards Julian slouching in his chair next to Crake were quite different. It was not in my nature to dislike anyone but as I watched him there aloof and prickly, and recalled how he had spoken and behaved at the funeral it was difficult to resist a feeling of loathing. I switched to the end of the table where I caught Jane's eye. She smiled back thinly but looked totally worn-out which in view of the events of the previous few days, was hardly a surprise. Crake's calm voice moved on to the specific donations. Lord William had been an extremely wealthy man. There were numerous disposals of money and specific personal possessions together with provision for local charities, all of which were greeted with enthusiasm. The Will then addressed provisions for tax and so forth which mostly went over my head, although I picked up on the creation of substantial portions for Lady Alana and Jane which would see them financially secure for the remainder of their lives. Eventually, after what seemed an age but was probably no more than a few minutes, the document reached the non-fiduciary clauses dealing with the destination of the residuary estate and ultimately the succession. At this point Crake, who had been speaking virtually non-stop paused and taking off his glasses reached over the table and decanted himself a tumbler of water. The unexpected recess made Julian shuffle irritably in his chair and he whispered something to his mother which I couldn't make out, but supposed it was caustic because Lady Alanna grimaced. Thomas Mathias Crake, the consummate professional, appeared to ignore the remark but as he took another sip of his water, he flashed Julian a quick look before replacing his spectacles and once more picking up the threads of the document.

Clause thirty-six. I direct that the administration of the Craven Racing Stables and Equine Stud Company will be managed after my death by the said James Michael Bullick or in the event that he shall predecease me or otherwise be unable to accept the appointment then I direct that the administration of the said Company shall vest in such person, persons or organisation as my trustees in their absolute discretion shall direct.

Clause thirty-seven. The remainder of my estate including all land, livestock, buildings, shares and all other investments in the United Kingdom and overseas, and all other property, possessions and personal chattels, whatsoever and wheresoever together with the hereditary seat and grounds of Craven Castle, and title of Marquis I devise and bequeath to my son Julian Dacre Fitzroy-Cavendish upon trust in the event of any minority but otherwise to take the bequest absolutely.

IN WITNESS WHEREOF, I have hereunto set my hand this 16th day of April in the year of our Lord nineteen hundred and five signed William Surtees Fitzroy-Cavendish, 6th Marquis of Craven.

Ladies and gentlemen, there ends the last will and testimony of the late Marquis. The instrument concludes with the standard clause of attestation by the two prescribed witnesses, these being my partner William Lockwood and myself. I shall now defer you to my clerk Mr Glyder who will remain in the building to verify your personal details and answer any enquiries. Ladies and gentlemen, thank you again for attending. I bid you good day.'

At this Crake folded the Will and replacing it in the brown package, carefully retied the ribbon and promptly left the room with Lady Alana, Jane and Julian trailing behind. I remember hearing raised voices as they disappeared into the hall, but I was too stunned to take much notice. The reality was that Alfie and I were in a position to complete our studies. Several of the assembly came over to congratulate me on my good fortune but I was in too much of a daze to take in what they were saying. The legacy was very generous yet at the same time it wasn't so much what had been said but what had not. The Will was drawn nine years ago which meant Lord William had not changed the succession after all, and yet on his deathbed he had been adamant it was so. I exchanged a few words with Barnaby and one or two of the others but there wasn't time to hang about. The York train was leaving within the hour and I was anxious to find my brother and tell him the news before he heard it from someone else.

CHAPTER SIXTEEN

'Lord William said *what*?'

'I know it sounds farfetched, but he was adamant he'd disinherited Julian -who wasn't his natural son in the first place- and changed the Craven succession. He also insisted he saw monks on the moor,.'

Tom paced up and down shaking his head.

'This is incredible. Are you quite certain?'

'Regarding the exact words he used no, but as to the substance of what was imparted, absolutely. The poor guy may have been on his deathbed but in those last few moments there was an intensity about him that left me in no doubt he was speaking the truth.'

'I assume you didn't get to see Crake after the reading?'

'I had to rush for the train.'

'That was unfortunate although from Crake's point of view, I don't suppose it was the time or place either.'

'How do you mean?'

'I mean your Mr Crake sounds like a bit of a show-off, the kind who revels in the drama of these occasions. Many lawyers are like that you know, they forget what they're actually there for fancying themselves as lead actors playing out some Greek tragedy. Your man Crake is obviously one. I expect he was in his element this morning seeing his own performance rather than Lord William's intentions as the focus of the occasion. It's as well you didn't speak to him. Any suggestion that the Will had been superseded by another would have been met with very short shrift.'

'Perhaps you're right. It wasn't the time or place. It all points to a disturbing inference though. If Lord William was speaking the truth, and I've no doubt in my own mind that he was, then Crake must be holding something back. You don't suppose he's bent do you?'

Tom lit a cigarette and waved out the match.

'I certainly do. Twisted as a barrel of hooks.'

I bit my lip trying to think a way round the obvious conclusion.

'That's one heck of a call, you know. It would explain the paradox but you should see the fellow, he's awesome and frankly, he just doesn't look the type. There's another thing. If Crake is dishonest, Julian would have to be in on it, in which case how do you explain him kicking off at some of the legacies? He went mad over the trust for Alfie and me and it took the others some time to calm him down. He couldn't have put that on.'

'On the contrary, I suggest that's exactly what he did. I would also venture the whole reading was little more than a carefully scripted charade in which the two main actors played their part. Look Edmund, it's a question of logic. Either Lord William was telling you the truth, or he wasn't. Think about it. He calls you to his deathbed – which in itself is incredible considering the gulf between your positions –

he sends everyone else away and then uses his last breath to tell you he's changed his Will. You were there my friend; I was not but you seem to have no doubt he was speaking the truth.'

'None whatsoever. I didn't doubt it then and I don't doubt it now.'

Tom moved over to the window where he pressed his forehead and hands to the glass. I watched in silence until he drew away again leaving tiny shivers of frost melting down the pane where his breath had been. Presently he turned.

'Then it's simple,' he said. 'Our default position is that Lord William was speaking the truth, which means Crake is a villain and we plan our next move accordingly.'

I recalled the way Lord William looked at me as he was dying. Tom was right. There was something up and Crake was in on it.

'It's the only sensible conclusion but where do we go from here? Do we report what we know to the authorities and leave it to them? I have to say I'm reluctant. I don't want to appear neurotic but after the way Lockwood blanked me at his office, I wouldn't be surprised if they were all in cahoots.'

Tom twisted from the window and blew into his cupped hands.

'No, we must keep the law out of it for now. We can't accuse anybody of anything without evidence. Instead, you are going to have to seek Crake out, let him know you're on to him and measure his reaction. I'll come along as well if you like. If there's an innocent explanation to all this no doubt he'll tell us although I cannot imagine what it might be.'

'I'll wire his office tomorrow,' I replied, 'and as soon as the Oxbridge exams are over, we'll go down to Hartlepool together. I've reason enough to make an appointment. I was supposed to wait in the library to discuss the mechanics of the trust with Glyder, so they'll be half expecting me.'

'Right, it's decided then; we'll confront the wolf in his den and see what he has to say. In the meantime, what else can you tell me about this other fellow, what's he called, that policeman at the hospital?'

'His name's Tench, Sergeant Tench of Durham Constabulary and as he was at constant pains to remind me, he's the first officer to William Lockwood OBE, his majesty's Coroner.'

'Lockwood who pretended he wasn't in the office that afternoon?'

'The very same, who also happens to be Crake's partner.'

As we sat there in my room, I went on to describe everything else that had occurred since I left Ampleforth on the morning of the cross country. The fractious journey home, Lady Alanna's firelight misery, the tramp in the stones, the Galilee chapel, the jovial Seaton, the wretched wing of mental patients, discovering my father's body in the mortuary, the behaviour of Julian and his party at the funeral, the riddle of Barnaby, I related it all, exactly as it had happened. Tom, who was slumped in the other armchair with his feet across the table, threw in the occasional question but otherwise listened intently and it was late into the night when the rush of words finally ebbed away and I realised I was done.

Tom exhaled a slow whistle.

'Sheesh Edmund, what have you got yourself into?'

'I would I knew. When I listen to myself setting everything out like that it makes me question my own sanity, but that's exactly how it happened. Oh, and there's another thing. When I arrived home I discovered someone had been into my father's office and removed a page from his journal.'

'What journal?'

'Dad used to keep a log where he recorded day-to-day events at the stables. There's nothing remarkable about it, just training programs for the horses, medicines, section times that sort of thing. I'd often seen him at his desk scribbling away and the volumes were one of the first things I came across when I started going through his papers. It seems he was making an entry on the day he died when he was suddenly called away. I've brought it back with me. Hang on; I'll get it out of my case.'

I retrieved the 1914 chronicle and magnifying glass from my luggage and opened the cover at the missing page. Tom skimmed over the last few entries then brought the final leaf to the oil lamp where he floated the book to and from the light.

'You're right. There's a page missing. You have to look closely but you can just make out where the bind has been undone and retied. I suspect whoever did this was no novice.'

'Maybe,' I replied, 'but novice or not, they can't have been that competent because they've overlooked the impression my father's last words made on the next page. Look...'

I pointed to where the words had traced through. Tom ran a forefinger over the leaf.

'It's not exactly braille but there's definitely something,' he replied, 'which is perfectly logical if you think about it. When writing is fashioned on a sheet of paper resting upon other pages, which is what we have here, the surface indentations or impressions are automatically transferred to the page below. This appears to be the case with your father's last entry and, if I'm not mistaken, we should be able to uncover it with a bit of iodine fuming.'

'Never heard of it.'

'Yes, you have. Brother Wallace mentioned the procedure last year. It's not complicated. All we need are a few iodine crystals and a round-bottom flask and then blow on the contents in such a way that the breath moisture generates iodine fumes. When the fumes meet the surface area of the page, *voila,* the hidden message will hopefully appear. I've actually got some crystals in a chemistry set back in my room. Hang on; I'll go and get them.'

Tom clattered down the corridor and promptly returned with a small test tube of purple crystals in one hand and an empty lab beaker in the other.

'Now when I say the word I want you to lightly blow into the flask, do it like a soft whistle,' he said, 'but be careful you only blow and don't inhale, this stuff's toxic.'

Tom unscrewed the test tube lid and having emptied out the crystals slowly tilted the flask above the blank page at an angle that would have dispersed the contents had they been fluid.

'Now keep it soft and be careful you don't breathe anything in.'

I crouched down to the table while my friend held the flask in position with one hand and brought the flame of the oil lamp beneath the bowl with the other. I leaned forward and began to blow in the spout.

'Slowly, slowly. You're doing great. Now, take a few paces back, fill your lungs again as much as you can and repeat and remember whatever you do don't breathe any of this stuff in.'

I did exactly as he asked; carefully blowing out, slowly, softly and steadily until there was nothing left and I span away gulping for air. Tom held the flask in position for another minute or so then having vanquished the contents in the sink dried his hands and came back to the table.

'That should be enough,' he said. 'All we do now is wait.'

An unpleasant odour filled the room, like a kind of mixture of burning metal, nail varnish and pear drops all rolled into one. It made our eyes water so I moved to the window and unfastened the top segment until an icy blast reminded me how cold it was outside and I promptly slammed it shut again.

'Look,' said Tom, 'look, it's working.'

'What? Here, move back a bit, let me see.'

I crouched by the table and stared at the blank page only it wasn't blank like before as slowly but surely a few letters began to materialise, then a few words until a small paragraph of about a half a dozen lines ghosted into view. It reminded me of when we were children and played with invisible ink. I reached for the magnifying glass and raised it up and down over the page until the twinkling message came into focus. Tom and I stared at the page utterly transfixed.

Edmund, there's no time to explain but Lord William is in terrible danger. Julian and his mother know he's changed the succession and are resolved to act. I am riding to the moor now to warn him. You will only see this note if I fail to return.

With my love as always.

Dad

I read the lines again barely taking in the words. Oh my God. Lord William had changed the succession like he told me, and Julian knew about it.

'This is incredible,' whispered Tom.

'It's not only incredible,' I replied, 'it's rock-hard evidence that the Will was changed. No wonder the original page was destroyed. Thing is, I don't trust the authorities. I can't help it. If we took this to the police what's the betting the whole journal wouldn't go the same way as the top copy?'

Tom lit another cigarette.

'I agree. It's too risky. We need to hang on to the diary while we gather more evidence and then take the lot to someone out of the area who we can trust.'

I moved to the window. It was deathly quiet outside; even the drip on the pump was silenced in the cold.

'If we're looking for evidence the starting place has to be Dryburn after the carry on with my father's papers. Like the undertaker said, a patient's admission notes are hardly the stuff of official secrets so why keep them back unless there's something they don't want anyone to see? We need to get our hands on that file.'

'I agree,' replied Tom. 'I've been racking my brains to think of a way to do it ever since you told me about your disagreement with Tench; thing is how? There's no point going through official channels and I don't suppose you know anyone at the hospital who can help?'

'I don't. Everyone I met was miserable and the place is more like a prison than a hospital.'

Tom joined me at the window.

'Could we not gain access on the pretext of visiting a sick relative and then slink off and have a good rummage through the cabinets? Or how about disguising ourselves as doctors or clergymen and get in that way?'

'It would never work. The office where the files are kept is at the end of the mental ward and the whole wing is locked down.'

'There must be a way. Suppose I feign lunacy and get myself detained in the ward and then have a snoop around?'

'Tom, until you see and hear these patients and the conditions in which they're kept you have no idea just how wretched they are. We're not talking about a few cranks here; these people are dangerous; many are possessed or believe they are possessed by demons and some of them are killers. I understand where you're coming from but take it from me; anyone volunteering to join them would have no need to feign madness.'

Tom flopped back into the armchair.

'Then we're left with no choice,' he said. 'We're going to have to break in.'

'What? Burgle the place?'

'If you choose to put it that way, then, yes.'

'You're joking. We'd never pull it off. The mental wing is in the heart of the building, all the windows are barred and the only access is through a locked steel door.'

Tom climbed out of his chair and began to pace up and down.

'There must be a way in. There has to be. What about the foundations? Did you see any trapdoors or stairs in the floor? What about the roof? Were there any skylights?'

'No. The wing is built into a basement; the floor is solid flag and the ceiling props up another two storeys of the hospital. The only skylight was in the mortuary.'

Tom mulled things over for a while then gave me a look.

'Where's the mortuary in relation to the mental ward?'

'Oh no you don't. Oh no. You have to be kidding me.'

'Where is it in relation to the ward?' he repeated.

I recalled the layout of Tench's dusty office at the end of the wing.

'It's actually next door. There's an entrance behind a curtain that leads straight through but Tom, it's the bloody mortuary. The place freaked me out in the daylight and I had Tench with me then. There's no way I'm going back.'

'Do you want to see what's in that file or not?'

'Of course I do but there has to be another way.'

Tom took a drag from his cigarette and blew a perfect smoke ring which rolled steadily towards the window until he exhaled again and shot it down.

'There is no other way. You're going to have to go back, only this time I'll be with you. Oh come on Edmund don't look so horrified, you know we can pull it off, they'd never dream anyone would sneak in through the morgue.'

'I don't like it.'

'I don't particularly like it either but that's not the point. Think about it Edmund. We can do this. You know we can'

I did think about it. The whole concept was totally outrageous but once I discarded images of the undead and focused on the mechanics, I realised it was not without prospects. I remembered the mortuary skylight had moss growing around the edges and how water leaked down the sides. The frame was also rotten and probably less than secure. The arched ceiling wasn't very high either which meant a soft landing and reasonably straight forward exit, assuming we could get that far. The only fly in the ointment

166

was the iron dividing door which I knew was fitted with a bolt on the other side. It wasn't drawn when Tench took me through but if they locked it at night, our adventure would end right there on the wrong side of the dividing wall.

'It's a risk we have to take,' said Tom, 'because this is the only way we'll get our hands on your father's file and what's more, if we don't go in now, the information could soon be lost forever.'

Tom was looking at me intently, he was clearly excited at the prospect and his enthusiasm was infectious.

'It pains me to say it but you're right. It *is* the only way although I shudder at the idea. I don't like it. All those dead people. The very thought gives me the creeps.'

'Oh, never mind all that supernatural nonsense. It's the spooks in this world we have to look out for. I say we go in as soon as possible and at night, preferably when there's no moon. Agreed?'

'I can't vouch for the moon,' I replied, 'but I think I know the time'.

'Go on'.

'It's Julian's coming of age ball at the castle a week Saturday and there'll be hundreds there. I was invited with my father but I don't suppose anyone would mind if you went along with me instead. It would be the perfect opportunity with the perfect alibi; we could go to the party, sneak away, do the deed and be back again before anyone misses us. It will be a cracking bash too. The County set will be out in force and with Julian out to impress there'll be no expense spared. What do you reckon?'

'I think it's a brilliant idea,' replied Tom. 'I've always dreamed of going to a society thrash. The champagne, the

167

orchestra and the girls! Oh, the girls! Come on Edmund; let's take a twirl around the floor. *Oh if you were the only girl in the world, and I was the only boy…*'

'Whaaa…'

Tom drew a forefinger up to his lips and pointed to the door. There was someone on the other side. He ghosted across the room. For a large man he was surprisingly light on his feet.

'… *nothing else would matter in the world today… come on Blue*, you must know the words…'

'… *nothing else would matter in the world today, we would go on loving in the same old way…*'

Tom lunged at the handle and wrenched back the door. The solitary figure on the other side didn't stand a chance and promptly crumpled in a heap before us.

'Bloody hell Conway, what do you think you're doing?'

The head boy jumped to his feet as Tom and I scowled over him.

'What do I think *I'm* doing?' he said, colouring as he brushed down his jacket. 'What do you think *you're* doing more like? Planning a burglary by the sound of it. Have you taken leave of your senses? I've a good mind to report this to the headmaster only I didn't come down here to eavesdrop.'

'Really? Then what were you doing with your ear against my door?' I demanded. 'Checking for woodworm?'

'I heard you were back at College and wanted you to know how sorry I am about your father. Truly I am. Having lost my grandfather a few weeks ago I know something of what you must be going through and I wanted to see if there's anything I could do to help.'

Tom was unimpressed.

'That's all very well but it doesn't explain why you were glued to the keyhole' he snarled.

'Look Brentnall, I didn't come here to spy on you and certainly not to argue. I just wanted to express my condolences to Edmund. It was only when I entered the corridor and heard raised voices that I was curious to discover what all the fuss was about.'

'And now you know our business, are you disappointed? You bloody creep,' growled Tom.

Conway ignored the insult.

'Please believe me *Blue*. When the Head called you out that afternoon, I'd no idea what it was for and I've felt awful about my throat gesture ever since. I'm truly sorry. As for anything I might have heard just now, well I didn't catch that much and whatever you're getting yourselves involved in, it's your business and I swear what little I heard won't go any further.'

'How can you expect me to believe that?' I replied. 'You're always hob knobbing with the masters.'

'I promise you; your secret is safe with me. I give you my word.'

A look of candour washed over Conway's face as he spoke. He certainly sounded as if he meant it. Thing is, could we take the chance?

'What do you reckon Tommy? Do we trust him?'

Tom circled Conway like a farmer inspecting a bull at the market.

'It seems we have little choice. We must take him at his word. But I tell you this *One-Way*, if the slightest whiff of what we were just discussing leaves these four walls, I'll personally remove your testicles and feed them to the hamsters in the junior's pet club. Do you understand?'

'I'll not tell a soul. I give you my word,' then turning to me, 'will you shake on it Edmund?'

I looked at Conway with his small green eyes strangely magnified behind the bulbous lenses of his glasses. He'd always been too standoffish to make friends and he'd never been one of mine but I appreciated the gesture and was prepared to give him the benefit of the doubt. I took his outstretched hand.

'Guess all's well that ends well then,' muttered Tom cynically 'although if you ask me it's a damn shame.'

'What do you mean?' replied Conway.

'I mean it's a shame about you not wanting to know what we're getting ourselves into. We could just do with a getaway driver Conway, and you'd fit the bill perfectly.'

'Tom, let it go. I'm happy to take him at his word not that we have much choice. Just ignore him Conway.'

'No, no that's fine; I brought it upon myself by listening at the door. Mind you, if you want my opinion, it's not a getaway driver you need at the hospital but rather a chauffeur, or better still a taxi.'

'A taxi?' I repeated.

'A taxi.'

'How's that then?' asked Tom suddenly interested.

'Look at it this way,' said Conway lowering his voice. 'Somehow the two of you need to get from the castle to Dryburn and back again before anyone notices you've gone. Have you given any thought how you're going to manage it? How far is the trip? About six miles each way I'll bet. You could just about make it on horseback but it's asking for trouble on the lanes that time of night, and you'd need someone to mind them while you go in. You'd also have a problem explaining yourselves at the stables.'

'So, what's your point?' I asked.

'Well, if horseback's out of the question, and it's clearly too far to walk, there's only one thing left. You're going to need some proper transport are you not gentlemen?'

'And I suppose you're about to tell us this is where you come in?'

'I see you're ahead of me,' said Conway dryly.

'What?' cried Tom. 'Are you going to get your old man to lend us an automobile?'

'No, we won't be lending you anything, but I'm happy to drive for you. Not so much of a car though, I was thinking more of a taxi. You see there'll be that many of them coming and going from the party one more isn't going to attract any attention and I know from the office diary that most of ours are already booked. I frequently drive for my father when I'm at home and could easily arrange to be working that night. What do you think Ed? Are you interested?'

Tom and I exchanged glances.

'It sounds a marvellous plan.'

Tom was silent.

'Tom?'

'Forgive me for being wary Conway but in situations like this I tend to rely upon my instincts because they don't often let me down. Edmund's correct, it's a good idea and I agree it could work. The thing I don't understand is why you should be willing to put yourself at risk by helping us, because if anyone gets caught in there, we're all in deep shit. It would involve the police; we'd be expelled from college and could even go to jail. I'm standing by Edmund because he's my closest friend and we've always looked after one another, but what's in it for you?'

'What's in it for me?' repeated Conway, shrugging his shoulders, 'the short answer is 'nothing at all' but then I'd not be risking anything would I?'

'How do you figure that out?' I asked. 'Just driving the vehicle makes you part of the enterprise.'

'Not at all. Look fellahs, let me make it clear at the outset I want no part of any burglary or break in. Not a bar of it. As far as I'm concerned, you'd just be a couple of punters I'm dropping off in town. What you do when you get out of the cab is your own business. I'll happily take you there and when you're through I might accidentally-on-purpose be passing along the road outside, but as far as anything else is concerned, well I don't know and I don't want to know anything about anything else if you get my drift?'

I saw his drift very clearly.

'So, if we get caught it's nothing to do with you?'

'You must promise to leave me out completely'.

There was a brief silence while we considered the proposition.

'Seems fair enough to me,' said Tom eventually. 'Looks like we're going to have to trust each other.'

'I agree,' I replied. 'You're a star Conway. I don't know how to thank you'.

'Nor me' said Tom 'although I still don't understand why you're helping us. It's just so unlike you.'

'Please, you don't have to say anything,' he replied. 'Although I haven't a clue what this is about, I suspect there must be good reason for the enterprise which is why I'll lend a hand. It's the sort of thing my father would have done when he was younger, and he didn't get where he is today following all of the rules all of the time. There's something else.'

'What's that?' I asked.

'Well contrary to what you two might think, I'm not a complete bore and a spot of adventure rather appeals to me.'

It was settled. We discussed the strategy into the night, everything falling into place with surprising ease. Tom and I would go to the party as intended, make sure we were seen by as many people as possible then at the appointed hour we would slip away and meet Conway's taxi in the courtyard. He'd take us straight to the hospital, cruise around until the deed had been done and then pick us up again on the North Road. Like all the best plans it was simple and we believed it could work. The only drawback was not letting the agonising wait for the party distract us from revision. We managed it though. After ten days furious study the Oxbridge exams were behind us and having said farewell to my brother, the three of us caught the train to Durham.

CHAPTER SEVENTEEN

The castle looked magnificent on the night of Julian's twenty-first party and no expense was spared. Neither was it a small affair. It seemed that anyone who was anyone in the County and beyond had been invited and in expectation of the event, a host of trucks and carts had spent days toing and froing from the city with provisions.

It was the first ever society outing for Tom and me and notwithstanding the grim business of the later evening, we were determined to make the most of it. Half the fun was getting dressed up and with the invitation specifying white tie, we raced into Durham to secure the necessary garb which my father's outfitter assured us was tails, formal striped trousers with white waistcoat and a piqué stiff fronted shirt with detachable wing collar. I'd never worn anything like it and having returned with arms full of boxes, we spent an absolute age getting ready in the way that young men do, bathing and shaving in the early afternoon before spending an inordinate amount of time meticulously pressing shirts, brushing down jackets and polishing our shoes. Eventually, when all studs and cufflinks were in place and our hair was combed for the umpteenth time, we stood in front of my father's tall dressing mirror.

'Ha! This is brilliant!' said Tom twisting from side to side. 'I look like one of those society models in *Men's Fashion Magazine*.'

'Society rake more like.'

Tom picked a speck of fluff from his collar.

'There's nothing wrong with being a rake, at least that's what my father told me, 'just don't fornicate with friends of the family' he used to say.'

We burst out laughing. He was right though. He did look great. We both did. It was wonderful how simply dressing up transformed the mood even before we stepped out of the house. For the first time since my father's funeral, I began to feel alive again, not only alive but strangely self-confident and positive about the future. I studied myself in the glass and thought of Victoria Clifford. I wondered if she'd be at the party. Of course she'd be there. I wondered if she would remember who I was or even care. Or even notice me. I recalled our conversation at the hotel and those beautiful black eyes. My heart skipped a beat as I imagined what it must be like to hold her. 'You wish' she had said. How the words haunted me. Little did she know, or maybe she knew all too well which was why she said it. She probably said the same to all her admirers. Tom snapped a finger.

'Wake up Narcissus. There'll be enough girls for us both.'

I sprang out of my daydream. It was time to go across.

'Right, check watches. What do you make it?'

Tom rolled up his sleeve.

'By mine it'll be exactly eight seventeen in… four, three, two and one. Agreed?'

'Agreed.'

It had stopped snowing. We gathered our scarves and locking the door made our way through the yard and into the castle grounds. In the middle of the gardens where the gravel paths converged, the Lion's Fountain was strangely silent, the familiar plane of water reduced to an ugly blob of ice that hung like mucus from the creature's stone muzzle. I went through the itinerary a final time.

'Conway will meet us outside the tradesman's entrance at eleven forty so we've a few hours yet. If for any reason we get separated, I'll see you in the Great Hall at half past.'

'Eleven thirty it is' replied Tom waving out a match. 'The important thing is we get around as many people as possible and establish the alibi. Also watch the booze. A bloke can only get drunk once in a day and there'll be time enough when we get back.'

'That's assuming we get back at all' I laughed nervously.

Tom cupped a hand and took a deep drag, his face briefly lit up in the glow.

'Indeed,' he exhaled 'assuming we get back at all. But seriously Ed, failure is not an option here because if we get caught, we've absolutely had it – we're history. The only thing keeping me focussed is to look at this like a military exercise, namely we go in and grab what we came for then get the hell out and back to the party before anyone notices we've gone.'

We fine-tuned our strategy as we crunched over the snow. In the distance the drop off area was churning with traffic like Elvet Bridge on market day. Tom bent down and scooped up a handful of snow.

'Did you give him the holdall?'

'It's all there'

Tom lobbed his snowball into the air and booted it to smithereens.

'Excellent. Let the party commence.'

We slipped through the gardens and joined the long queue of guests snaking their way under the keep. The setting was awesome. Although the night was as black as pitch, down in the valley dozens of torches flared on either side of the driveway, their auburn light fashioning strange shadows that raced across the virgin snow of the surrounding parkland. The castle itself looked superb; the ancient blocks illuminated by a further line of torches that crackled on the ridge of the dried-up moat turning the windows into molten gold and bringing life to the wicked faces of the gargoyles scowling down from the battlements. In the courtyard, it was like York races as everyone shuffled forward in a hullabaloo of flush and anticipation, the gentlemen in their mess jackets and tails, the ladies oscillating in a sea of colour and fur coats, everybody hollering and laughing, everyone happy and excited.

Just inside the doorway I caught sight of the reception line, Lady Alanna at the front, then Julian, then Jane, the three of them bobbing and pecking like a row of pullets. At the top of the steps we were challenged by the master of ceremonies, an ex-military type looking resplendent and not a little self-satisfied with his bright red coat and medal ribbons. There were another two doormen standing quietly in the shadows, no doubt hard as nails and more than ready to deal with any gate-crashes or troublemakers.

'Good evening gentleman, my name is Sparks. May I see your invitations please?'

I passed him mine and explained that Tom had been invited in place of my late father. Sparks raised an eyebrow and flashed a quick glance towards Lady Alanna who was engrossed in conversation with the local vicar. Fortunately, Jane had been watching from the door and gave a little wave at which Sparks nodded and cleared his throat.

'Mr Edmund Bullick and Mr Thomas Brentnall.'

Lady Alanna turned to greet us. It was a pleasure to see her looking so well because she must have had a great deal on her mind, but then I supposed an attractive woman who was the centre of attention at her own party could be expected to light up like a beacon.

'Edmund, you look wonderful, your father would have been so proud. How did the examinations go?'

'Very well thank you ma'am. Lady Alanna may I introduce my friend and fellow scholar, Thomas Brentnall.'

Tom took a step forward and bowed. Lady Alanna greeted him warmly.

'Welcome to Craven Castle Mr Brentnall. We've heard a great deal about you from Edmund and are delighted you could join us. Please now, go on in, both of you and have a wonderful evening.'

Julian's welcome was predictably cooler.

'Edmund' he said curtly. 'Who's this?'

'Thomas Brentnall, a friend from College.'

Tom bowed as he shook Julian's hand.

'How d'ye do Lord Craven. Thank you so much for including me. It's an honour to be here.'

Julian seemed pleased to be addressed as 'Lord Craven' although his response was typically caustic.

'It's not me you have to thank Brentnall but my mother. I

assure you I had nothing to do with it. However, since you're here I suppose you'd better come in.'

All the while Jane had been standing at the end of the line hopping up and down, waiting her turn. She looked so grown up I had to do a double take. It was a remarkable transformation for someone who spent half her time shifting muck in the stables.

'Edmund, I'm so pleased you're home, I've really missed you' she said excitedly. 'Tell me, how were the Oxbridge exams? Do you think you've done enough to get in?'

'I hope so' I replied. 'If not, it won't be for want of trying. But never mind me, what about you? Where did you get that dress? You look stunning Jane.'

'Oh, do you like it?' she replied with a little flourish. 'It's one of Mama's, it didn't fit me at first but I had Mrs Johnson take in the seam. She's such a sweetie. She said she had to do the same for Mama when she first wore it and it was no trouble. Mind you I had to stand still for ages with all these beastly pins holding it together but I'm so pleased we made the effort. I feel like a London debutante …'

Her voice trailed away as she suddenly noticed Tom.

'Jane, I'm so sorry, may I introduce Tom Brentnall, my best friend from College.'

Tom gave a small bow.

'How do you do Lady Jane. Delighted to make your acquaintance.'

Jane gave a shy curtsy.

'Pleased to meet you too Mr Brentnall'.

'Please, call me Tom.'

The spell was broken by the Master of Ceremonies hollering down from the doorway.

'Ladies and gentlemen, please, you're holding up the queue, at the end there, move along please…'

I gave Tom a nudge.

'Look, we'd better do as the man says. Jane, come and find us when you can get away'.

'You can count on it' she cried after me. 'I shall insist on at least three dances so you'd better get loosened up.'

A magnificent Christmas tree stood in the centre of the Great Hall, every branch groaning with clusters of sweetmeats, almonds and raisins in papers. Tom eyed the silver star at the top as he addressed me from the side of his mouth.

'She's gorgeous.'

'Who is?'

We peered back at the line where Jane was giggling with a group of young officers who had just arrived.

'I thought you said she was just a kid.'

'She is.'

'You're nuts' said Tom.

'Look, never mind that, we've got an alibi to sort. What say we have a nosey around?'

The party was well organised and considerable care had been taken to ensure everyone was spread over the ground floor. To avoid congestion in the Great Hall, the guests were quickly relieved of their coats and shown through to the drawing room where three large trestle tables had been set up in the middle, each supporting an enormous pyramid of crystal glasses. Alongside the first pyramid was a large pair of stepladders at the top of which Johnny Clifford was wrestling with a gigantic flagon of champagne. The bottle was so large he had to grip it in a headlock and as he leaned forwards to pour, the steps were wobbling so much it looked as if the whole lot would come crashing down. It was an exact and skilful performance well worthy of all the roars of encouragement and acclaim.

'Methuselah!' shouted Tom.

'What?'

'The champagne, it's a *Methuselah* Edmund. Eight bottles in one named after the biblical patriarch who lived to the age of 969. Who's the show-off?'

'Guess.'

'Really?'

'Yep.'

At the foot of the steps Clifford held his arms aloft to milk the acclaim while two or three beaming waiters dismantled the pyramid for further distribution.

'So that's Johnny Clifford. Well, give the guy his due, that was some party trick.'

'Certainly was, although he has other tricks in the box that you may find less agreeable.'

'How so?' replied Tom without taking his eyes away from the action.

'Well apart from beating up stable lads, he's the most horrible, terrible drunk. Truly he is. In fact, if he runs to form, we might get a demonstration later on.'

Somewhere in the distance a band was tuning up so we trailed the source into the ballroom and merged with a host of others lining the wall. It was no ordinary turn. Instead of the expected orchestra there was a large jazz ensemble fronted by a dapper male in Eton boating costume with three African girls in national dress. I'd always loved my music and knew about the *ragtime* craze sweeping America, however the closest I'd been to the real thing was straining

181

my ears to a twisted gramophone record I'd borrowed off Spangle. There had been a whisper in the village we were in for something special, but it never occurred to me that one of the top ragtime bands would venture this far north. Yet here they were, *Billy Murray and the Haydn Boys* in the Craven ballroom thrashing out this fabulous wall of noise.

I'd read in the columns the band had docked for a whirlwind tour of London and Brighton and that tickets to their performances were like gold dust. They must have been persuaded to break off their schedule especially although goodness knows what it had cost the family to lure them all the way up to Durham. As entertainers they were sensational, I'd never heard or seen anything like it and it would have been worth all the dressing up and preening to be within earshot let alone have a grandstand pitch. I remember as we leaned against the wall, they suddenly struck up a rendition of *Alexandra's Ragtime Band,* a melody I would come to know very well later in life. The effect on the guests was electric and within seconds the floor was packed with youngsters whooping and spinning round.

As I gazed into the melee, I was suddenly aware of Victoria. She was easily the most handsome woman in the room and knew it as she took to the floor with a group of young men vying with each other for her attention. She wore a strapless black sequin dress with a daringly short hem that showed off every sinew of her beautiful long legs. Her pale arms were exposed to the shoulders and her hair was tied up at the back and sparkled with studs of diamond. I watched her laughing and singing as she danced without inhibition or care. She looked so fabulously beautiful, she moved as if the devil himself was in her step and I could not take my eyes from her.

'That's the girl isn't it?' shouted Tom.

I could barely hear myself think above the noise.

'She haunts me' I yelled.

'What?'

'She HAUNTS ME!'

There was a tap on my shoulder. Jane was there hands on her hips.

'Who's hunting?'

'What?'

'Hunting. I asked who's hunting? We're out tomorrow …oh, look never mind. Are you going to dance with me Edmund Bullick?'

'Here Tom, take my glass?'

Now my father always told me never mind shirking around the borders, if you're going to dance with a girl, you take them smack bang right into the middle of the action. It was always sound advice although that evening I had another reason for being particular where we surfaced.

'Tell me about your friend' shouted Jane.

'Tom? He lives in York. His family are chemists there.'

'He's very handsome don't you think?'

'No. He's a moose.'

Jane laughed.

'Well, I like the look of him very much.'

We turned to the window where Tom was arm-wrestling with a group of lads I didn't know. He was always at ease with strangers. He must have seen us out the corner of his eye because he suddenly turned and pulled a face. Jane smiled and waved back as we danced on to the infectious refrain.

Oh let me take you by the hand,
Up to the man, up to the man,

Who's the leader of the band!
Who's the leader of the band!

It had been my intention to engage Victoria at the end of the first dance but I didn't get the opportunity as the band played through and the numbers came thick and fast. Eventually she saw us, or rather she noticed Jane and shuffled over with her little group.

'Darling, I love the dress. Where did you get it?'

'It's one of Mama's' yelled Jane although she was cut off mid-sentence as the song ended abruptly and everyone burst into applause.

'Lord, I need a rest' she said clapping her hands. 'Edmund, do you mind if we take a break? These shoes are killing me.'

'Of course not. Go check on moose face and see if he's behaving himself.'

Jane laughed then peeled away leaving me standing next to Victoria. It was now or never.

'Lady Clifford. It appears I have been abandoned. Will you dance the next number with me?'

Victoria looked surprised.

'What, with you?' said she, still catching her breath.

'With me.'

In the corner Billy Murray was introducing the band.

'You know you want to' I said quietly.

Victoria burst out laughing bringing her hand to her face. A few people turned and glared before switching their attention back to Murray.

'Well?'

Victoria addressed the others she had been with.

'Would you excuse us for a moment? Would you mind awfully? This gentleman and I have some unfinished business.'

Her little troupe of followers didn't like it but had no option but to trudge away.

'Well *Horse Boy*, looks like it's just you and me.'

'Indeed it does Miss. And the name's Edmund.'

Victoria smiled and mouthed the words *Horse Boy*. I was struggling for something droll to say back when Bill Murray came to the rescue.

'Ladies and gentlemen, we're going to slow things down with a little number written by my old friend, Gus Edwards. If you'd take your partners please for *By the Light of the Silvery Moon*. Ok fellahs, two three and in…'

Victoria reached for my hand and suddenly I was holding her as we moved in time to the music. I felt half the eyes in the room upon me and flushed with rapture and desire. Victoria spoke first.

'Jane tells me you're famed for your party trick of leaping onto the mantelpiece from a standing jump. Will you show me later?'

'I don't think so Miss'.

'Oh, come on. Whyever not?'

'It's not my party. Look Miss, I'm not very good at this kind of thing but I have to tell you I think you are the most beautiful girl I have ever seen.'

Victoria tossed back her head and laughed.

'Oh no, not you as well'.

'Put me down if you must but you are beautiful, and if I don't say this to you now, I may never get another chance.'

We swayed for a minute or so until Victoria broke the silence.

'Look, I'll cut to the quick. You're wasting your time. I only danced with you to get rid of those Oxford creeps. If there's one thing I abhor, it's hangers on with two left feet. Yak.'

'Charmed, I'm sure'.

Victoria leaned forward. I caught the scent of her perfume; it was as fragrant as May blossom.

'Charmed or not I'm just saying how it is so you know where you stand. Let me tell you something. There's a young Guards officer over there in the red mess suit. You'll catch him on the next turn staring at us. That's Roland, or rather the Right Honourable Roland, a cousin of the Earl of Faversham and heir to half of Bilsdale. He's madly in love with me and would propose this evening if I gave him any encouragement. There are other illustrious young men in this room and believe me, I could have any one of them, any single one if I wanted to but instead, I'm dancing with you *Horse Boy*. Do you want to know why?'

I looked at my partner for a moment, her beautiful dark eyes mocking me in the candlelight.

'I would like to think it is because you want to.'

'I do want to; you seem a nice boy even if you're too poor for me to take seriously. Oh, come on, don't look so crestfallen, you know it's the truth. You had the nerve to ask me to dance and to tell me I'm beautiful and I like that, I really do. I appreciate men who say what's on their mind which is why you will find me just as candid. I'm dancing with you because I want to make the rich boys jealous. Word has it you're one of the finest horsemen on the estate, you certainly move well and that you allow me to use you in this way is because you find me utterly irresistible, and you cannot help yourself. Please, you don't need to try and answer that because we both know it's true.'

We sailed on in silence. What a cow. She had it all worked out, or at least she had me worked out to a tee. I was stung but damned if I was going to show it.

'If you ever scratched the surface, you would discover more in me than movement, I assure you.'

Victoria smiled amiably.

'Perhaps,' she said, 'but I never shall. I saw the way you looked at me in church and later at the hotel, but I'm not interested. There's a social gulf between us and more to the point, you cannot afford me.'

At this she pressed her cheek against my own and closed her arms around my neck. An enormous pit opened in my stomach, and I was helpless.

'Now dance with me' she whispered. 'Come now. I won't bite.'

Looking back, I should have stood her up but I was intoxicated by her beauty and couldn't bring myself to walk away, as well she knew. Instead, I surrendered to the bitch and placing my hands around her slim waist drew her closer as her sweet little voice chimed into my ear.

By the light,
Of the silvery moon,
I want to spoon,
To my honey I'll croon love's tune.
Honeymoon,
Your Silvery beams will bring love dreams,
We'll be cuddling soon,
By the silvery moon.

The thrill of holding Victoria was inexpressible as for several minutes we glided in and out of the other couples, all the while her beautiful voice singing into my ear. I didn't bother to look for the host of hungry eyes upon her because I knew they were all out there, exactly as she had predicted. I just felt nauseous with longing and frustration until the end of the dance when there was nothing for it but to disengage and politely join in the applause, even though every sinew was already craving her embrace. The feeling of loss that rushed through me was overpowering; it made me want to tear off her little black dress and ravish her there and then and the devil with the consequences. Instead, I had to linger at her side struggling for something to say.

Victoria gave a mock curtsy.

'Much obliged to you *Horse Boy*' she supposed as if she were addressing the Gas Board.

'I think you are wonderful Miss. Will you dance again with me later?'

'I don't think so. I'm counting on Julian or my brother to rescue me long before then. Have you seen them anywhere?'

'In the bar.'

'Of course' said she 'although Julian will find his way for he cannot help himself either.'

I took her hand and kissed it gallantly.

'In that case, thank you for your company Lady Clifford. It was a pleasure to dance with you.'

'I don't doubt it' she answered coolly.

'Your humility does you no justice Miss.'

Faversham was hovering in the distance. Victoria crooked a finger towards him and smiled.

'Love will conquer many things *Horse Boy* but the commercial aspirations of a beautiful woman is not one of them.'

'You really do fancy yourself, don't you?'

Silence.

'Please, Victoria. Just give me a chance.'

'You're not listening *Horse Boy*. Your family are minions, or hadn't you noticed? End of, I'm afraid.'

I felt the blood rush into my cheeks.

'Well screw you.'

'You wish' said she sweetly, then turned her gaze on Faversham who was striding over.

I did wish it. I desired it above all things but before I could say anything else she discharged me with a wave of the hand.

'Goodbye *Horse Boy*. Off you go.'

I felt a surge of rage welling up inside me, but we were no longer alone. I faltered for a moment exhaling in frustration as Victoria slipped her fingers under Faversham's arm and whispered something in his ear that caused him to look me up and down and laugh. It made me want to smack him in the teeth, the prat. Another time maybe. For now, however, there was nothing I could do but walk away smoking with anger, exactly as she intended.

Tom and Jane were still bouncing across the floor. I tried to catch his eye but they were oblivious to anyone else so I left them to it and went for a wander. Under the tree in the Great Hall I found Barnaby, Sample and Fenoughty surrounded by stable lads, all of them well into their cups.

'Whoa Edmund, you look quite the dapper young man' said Barnaby with a huge grin. 'Have you broken any hearts yet?'

'Not exactly'.

'But you're working on it hey lad?' boomed Sample which made the others holler even more.

'You could say that'.

'Did you hear that fellahs?' said Barnaby. 'We saw you in there dancing with Lady Victoria. Do you reckon you're in?'

They howled with laughter. His words were in such startling contrast to the warning I had received at the *County* I figured he must be drunk and resisted the temptation to say anything.

'Actually *Blue* boy, I'm glad you've come over' said Fenoughty draining his glass 'we're taking the string out with the *Braes* tomorrow. The snow's a bit thick, but the horses are all whinnying in their boxes and kicking at the doors and I can't keep them in any longer. You up for it lad?'

At that precise moment I didn't really feel up for anything, but I guess it would blow away the cobwebs.

'Sure. What time?'

'Come over about eight. That's if you can haul yourself out of bed. Hah! The young 'uns today, they don't make them like they used to hey Barnaby?'

'They don't Henry' he replied jovially. 'When you and I were bucks we worked hard and played hard and ne'er would the twain meet unless it were a night with the milk maids.'

The others roared with approval.

'That's settled then. I'll come straight on from the party.'

Everyone burst out laughing.

'Love it, love it, he talks a good talk this one' cried Sample slapping me across the shoulder.

'Aw don't be so hard on him man' bawled Fenoughty covering everyone with spittle. 'Hey young fellah, young fellah, you enjoy yourself while you can, and we'll see you if we see you.'

Good grief Fenoughty. For a man who hardly ever spoke the transition was remarkable. I wondered what they'd been giving him. I opened my arms in supplication.

'Eight bells it is then gentlemen, white tie optional.'

This provoked yet more hilarity and another shower of spittle from Fenoughty.

'He wouldn't be the first jockey heading out in coat and tails would he lads? Remember the Zetland Ball in '98 when young Willie Manners and that friend of his Bertie -what was he called- Straker, that's it, Bertie Straker, when young Willie Manners and Bertie Straker raced to the moor and back at midnight?'

They were plainly inebriated and not being on the same frequency I mumbled an excuse about getting something to eat and drifted through to the library. The room was just as we had left it, absolutely heaving with Julian and Johnny Clifford still holding court at the champagne bar. I grabbed a drink and passed the time with one or two of the servants as they zipped about like hornets in their black and gold tunics.

'Hello Edmund, I trust you're enjoying yourself?'

I turned to find Lady Alanna smiling behind me, her skin radiant in the candlelight.

'This is an excellent party. The band are terrific.'

'They're causing quite a stir by the sound of it but no one has asked me to dance, at least not yet, and it's my party. Would you do me the honour and take me through?'

'I'd be delighted.'

Lady Alanna gripped my arm and we headed back to the ballroom crossing through the Great Hall where Sample, Fenoughty and the others were still laughing and carrying on by the tree. From the crook of my eye I fancied I caught

Barnaby watching us a bit strangely although I didn't think anything of it at the time. Back inside the ballroom it was now roasting, the atmosphere charged with the slog and sweat that was ever the hallmark of a good party.

Lady Alanna danced gracefully and it was not difficult to imagine the allure that captured Lord William all those years ago. All the while Victoria was strutting up and down in the background, laughing and teasing. I tried my best to look away, but my partner was nothing if not astute.

'She's very beautiful don't you think?'

'Who is?'

'Can you not guess?' she answered gesturing to the girl in question. 'I so wish Julian would get a move on. It's time we secured the succession.'

So it was true. They were earmarked for one another.

'You're too young to be a grandmother.'

Alanna burst out laughing.

'Do you know, you're such a charmer Edmund' said she with a slur.

'I wouldn't say that my lady.'

'No, really, it's true. You're so like your father. We were very close, you know.'

What on earth did she mean by that? Alanna was not finished.

'Here, let me give you some advice.'

'What might that be my lady?' I wasn't sure where this was heading.

Alanna stopped dancing and clutched my shoulders. It happened so quickly there was no time to feel uncomfortable.

'Learn when to speak out and when to stay silent' she said rocking me. 'I should never have told your father. Don't make the same mistake.'

This was getting heavy. One or two people were looking in our direction.

'You're starting to embarrass me my lady'.

'You're just like your father' said Alanna with tears in her eyes. 'I loved him so much.'

Yikes. I hoped no one else heard that. She didn't look especially drunk but then the wiliest drunks never do; it's only in conversation that the mask slips. I was rescued by a tap on my shoulder. I hadn't noticed Barnaby enter the room, but I saw the expression on Lady Alanna's face soften and was happy to stand aside as she reached for the hand of her new partner.

'Thank you for the dance, Edmund. And remember what I said.'

I left them to it. I hadn't expected her company to be so intense and it was a relief to get away. What did she mean she 'shouldn't have told my father'? Shouldn't have told my father what? And telling me she loved him? I put it down to the drink. Was everyone at the ball hammered? It certainly looked that way. Or perhaps I noticed it more because I was sober. Same thing really. I checked my watch. Ten to eleven. I made a beeline for the buffet. I was not hungry but I wanted to dislodge a stack of plates so people would remember me being there. I even assisted with the clearing up in the knowledge that the servants would be the first port of call if anyone started asking questions. Eleven twenty-six. I excused myself and headed for the Christmas tree where I found Tom smoking a cigarette.

'All ready?'

'Conway's at the back.'

'Meet you in five.'

Tom stubbed the bucket and made for the entrance. I waited until he disappeared then headed for the cloakroom before veering off into the staff wing. There was some yelling coming from the kitchens, but the passageway was deserted. I opened the door at the end and slipped into the courtyard. A dark green hackney cab was ticking over in front of me. I recognised Tom's silhouette in the back and jumped in. Conway twisted around.

'All aboard?'

'Where's the holdall?'

'Under the seat.'

I reached down. It was there.

'Right. Let's go.'

CHAPTER EIGHTEEN

Tom and I ducked out of sight as the taxi slipped into gear and munched across the gravel. I heard Conway squeeze the hooter and swear at a couple of drunks staggering about but we were soon over the cattle grid and into the park.

'All clear.'

We sprang back up. In the rear window the castle was rapidly disappearing. In front of us there was nothing but darkness. I tipped out the contents of the holdall. A large *Ever Ready* flashlight. Six-inch nail. Two black sweaters. Two army balaclavas. Tom started to remove his jacket then noticed the tin whistle.

'What on earth do you want with that?'

'Let's just call it insurance.'

We hit the outskirts of Durham at a quarter to midnight. The roads were empty and there were few people about. When we reached Dryburn, Conway slowed and made a pass of the hospital. The building was in complete darkness, the only sheen coming from the frosted slates glowing eerily in the moonlight. Conway drove on for half a minute then pulled up under a large beech tree.

'Ok fellahs, meet back here at twenty past. If you're not around, I'll do a sweep every five minutes. If there's no show by twelve forty, I'll assume the worst and you're not coming. Good luck.'

We watched from the shadows as Conway trundled off into the night, the taxi climbing through the gears until the drone of the engine faded altogether. Suddenly, we were very alone. Tom handed me a balaclava, the coldness of the night riding on his breath.

'You ready?'

'If it were to be done, then 'twere well it were done quickly.'

'Macbeth?'

'Aye.'

We crossed the road in single file keeping clear of the flickering streetlamps. The tall iron gates at the hospital entrance were closed but surprisingly, there was no chain or lock and we slipped quietly through the grounds until we reached the milky stone wall that marked the boundary of the mortuary yard. Tom scrambled to the ridge and hauled me alongside. Not a soul in sight. We dropped silently down and made our way to the far end of the yard where the mortuary building waited in the shadows. We scrambled onto the roof then paused for a moment to take stock of the position. The asphalt was obscured by a blanket of frozen snow that sparkled like mother of pearl and crunched to the touch. In the middle was the unmistakable hump of the skylight. I looked around warily. Somewhere far off a dog was barking but otherwise it was deathly quiet. Heck, it was cold. We clambered on all fours to the skylight and wiped away the snow. The bulbous glass frame was thick with ice and the unit looked worryingly secure. I bent down and gave it a shunt just the same. Nothing. I looked at Tom who was pointing to his feet. Immediately I understood and we squatted on our backs with our soles against the rim and pressed against the wooden frame for all we were worth. Nothing. I took my feet away and paused for breath.

'We can't stop now,' panted Tom. 'Again, come on, *harder*. Come on. Three, two, one…'

We repeated the process, this time consumed by an urgency that harnessed every bone, every tendon and muscle to the task. Suddenly there was an ear-splitting crack as the skylight flew off its mountings and jumped several feet across the roof. I almost died with fright. Crikey, that was loud. We held our breath steeling ourselves for the inevitable commotion but there was none. I scanned the facade of the hospital and the neighbouring houses expecting all the lights to come on, but not a curtain rippled. We were riding the devil's luck. I stared at our handiwork. A dark vortex had opened in the roof where the skylight had been. It was no time for faint hearts. Oh God, don't let my courage fail me now. I shuffled to the edge and dropped into the void.

CHAPTER NINETEEN

I landed with a crash against a trolley and instinctively assumed the foetal position as various pathologists' tools and kidney dishes went sailing across the floor. The noise was horrific in the stillness but thankfully, it was short-lived. I reached into my pocket and fumbled for the torch as Tom landed beside me in a shower of ice crystal.

'What the hell was that?' he whispered.

I placed a finger to my lips as I fought the noxious reek of embalming fluid and decay. This ghastly place was every bit as grisly as I had remembered it. I passed the flashlight to Tom who mowed our surroundings. It was a harrowing spectacle, the beam darting from one silhouette to the next, each sweep casting wicked shadows that rose and fell on the greasy tiled walls. We were in the company of the dead; they were laid out all around us, the projecting feet confirming that all the slabs were taken, all, that is, apart from one at the far end of the chamber where the dark green sheet was as flat as a millpond.

'Where's the office?'

I pointed on the back wall. Tom followed with the flashlight then turned and swept the tables.

'Now, don't go away you lot.'

How could he make a quip at a time like this?

We tiptoed to the dividing door. It was the moment of truth. If this were bolted, we would go no further. I turned the handle and pushed. It held fast. Damn. I tried again this time with my shoulder against the iron bulkhead. I sensed a slight movement. I tried again, more weight now. The heavy door swayed open an inch or so then slammed shut almost trapping my fingers.

'It's not locked but there's something on the other side holding us back,'

Tom gave it a push with the same result.

'The curtain. You said there was a curtain. This must be what's stopping it. Here, try again but do it slowly, gradually build the pressure then give it everything you've got.'

It worked. The door suddenly burst open bringing down the curtain, the rail and several pieces of plaster.

A hum of alarm rippled down the cells.

'Who's there?'

In the distance the Cathedral bells chimed midnight as with a whir of cogs the clock on the office wall followed suit.

'Who's there?' wailed a little voice in the darkness.

I made a 'shhh' noise. It dampened the appeals but not for long.

'Who's there? Who is it?'

'Have you come to take me home?'

'You out there in the dark. Show yourself.'

Suddenly the whole wing resonated with the rattle of chains and springs as the patients began to climb out of their cells. Somewhere in the darkness the tortured youth thrashed about on his mattress.

It was no time for stealth.

'Tom, get to the end of the passage and fix that bloody door.'

Tom raced off as I frantically pulled at the cabinets. Where was it? Where? I flew from draw to draw ignoring a large pile of documents that fell on top of me from an overhanging shelf. Come on you bugger, where are you?

'There's no bolt!' yelled Tom.

'The nail,' I shouted. 'Use the nail and wedge the keyhole.'

I clawed away furiously running the torch over the files with one hand as I flicked through the names with the thumb and forefinger of the other. There were many folders to get through but everything was filed chronologically, and I made sharp work of it. In the top draw of the third cabinet, I found what I was looking for and bellowed to Tom who was crouching by the door.

'Let's go!'

Tom raced towards me but had only covered a few feet when someone tripped him and he measured his length in the corridor. Immediately, several figures leaped out of the shadows and a violent struggle ensued.

'Edmund!'

I raced down the passage and neutralised the first attacker with a boot in the stomach but as I reached for the second, someone sank their teeth into the top of my leg. I lashed out with my feet, yelling in shock and pain as Tom grabbed my assailant around the neck and pulled her away. As we struggled, more patients came out of their cubicles blocking the way out. I couldn't understand it. Everyone was supposed to be secured with some type of galley chain. They must have broken the shackles in their desperation to get at us and now we were surrounded. I ran my torch over the screaming faces of the filth encrusted wretches and cursed Tench. If only he'd let me see the file. But it was all too late now. The patients' obscenities rose to a crescendo as if Beelzebub himself was scoring them and they began to close in.

In desperation I reached for my pocket and took out Alfie's tin whistle. I was no maestro, but I knew Middle C and earlier that week I'd made a point of learning the first seven notes of *Twinkle Twinkle Little Star*. The effect was extraordinary. Immediately all the screaming stopped, it didn't just die down, it ceased altogether as the patients suddenly looked at each other then pathetically at Tom and I.

'Sweety time?' asked a young woman excitedly. A one-eyed man repeated the phrase, then someone else until the chanting was embraced by all as if it was the overture of some ghastly opera.

Swee-tee time! Swee-tee time! Swee-tee time!

'It is sweety time,' I yelled 'but you must go back to your cells and wait. Go on now. Back to your cells.'

Incredibly, the patients started to go back to their cells.

Suddenly, there were voices in the corridor.

'We've got company,' said Tom.

Even as he spoke there was the sound of a key in the lock.

'Run!'

We tore through the office and into the mortuary. As I closed the connecting door the ward entrance swung open and three people tumbled into the wing. Two were night porters. The third was Tench in his dressing gown.

I slammed the door and raced to the skylight. Tom climbed on my shoulders and hauled himself up.

'Quick, gimee your hand.'

There was shouting in the office. Any moment they'd be through.

'There's no time,' I whispered. 'Pull the skylight back. Hurry man. I'll give three flashes when it's clear.'

I raced to the far end of the morgue desperately looking for somewhere to hide. The voices in the office grew more animated. Think Bullick think. I could hear Tom stamping about on the roof and winced as the skylight was dragged back into place. Someone fumbled the handle of the connecting door. There was nothing else for it. I dived onto the empty slab opening a tiny crevice in the shroud so I could see out.

I was just in time. Seconds later the connecting door opened on Sergeant Tench, flashlight in one hand, truncheon in the other. Now I was for it. I dissolved into the table. Got to keep still. Tench took a few steps forward then ran his beam in a slow arc across the chamber. I pressed my cheek into the cold marble. A shiver ran down the back of my neck. Don't move Edmund. You have to keep still.

'Come on you bastard. I know you're in here.'

I remained completely motionless, hardly daring to draw breath. The policeman's torch was powerful and as it flashed over the enamel walls, the mortuary filled with an eerie glow.

'This is your last chance. Come out now,' he ordered.

I cursed all the bravado back in Tom's room when we decided upon such a perilous venture. If I were discovered in this awful place, I would never be able to explain myself because no one would understand or believe me. Instead, I would pay for my sacrilege with a prison sentence, vilified by everyone who knew me; it would destroy my Oxbridge aspirations and bring shame to the College and above all disgrace to my younger brother and the family name. No wonder Conway had been so meticulous in keeping himself out. I thought of the party back at Craven and wished to hell we had never left it.

Tench took a pace forward, slowly probing each ghastly figure as he swept down the line. There was nothing I could do but melt under the shroud and keep as still as a church mouse. Suddenly, the beam was on the floor below and when it danced over me, I almost vomited with fear. Had I been seen? Silence. Was he about to charge across? It appeared not, although any sense of relief abruptly turned to horror as Tench marched to the nearest table and threw back the cover. In the half-light it looked as though he was standing over the body of a middle-aged woman. Tench brought the torch to the bleached face then after a few seconds, suddenly raised his truncheon and slammed it down on the torso of the corpse. I was appalled. What was he thinking of? Making sure they were dead? The hobnailed boots grinded down to the next table where the bone crunching process was repeated, and then on to the third and then the fourth. It would be my turn next. I couldn't even make a run for it. There was nowhere to go. Oh, please God, please help me.

A head suddenly poked through the connecting door.

'Hey Sarge?'

Tench nearly jumped out of his skin.

'Whooaahh! For *fuck's* sake man! What d'ye think you're doing creeping up on me like that!'

'Sorry Sarge. Just letting you know the patients are all accounted for and we're locking them back in their cubicles. You couldn't give us a hand, could you?'

'All of them? Are you sure? I could have sworn I heard someone rattling around in here a couple of minutes ago.'

The other laughed nervously.

'Don't be daft man.'

Tench scratched his head.

'But I heard something. I know I did.'

'What, as in *ghoulies and ghosties* and things that go bump in the night? If you ask me, you need a holiday.'

Tench swept the morgue a final time then switched off the beam.

'Aye lad, perhaps you're right. Anyhow what happened back there?'

'I've no idea. They don't usually kick off like that.'

'Anyone hurt?'

'One or two were scrapping but nowt serious. Mind you, they've wrecked the office and torn the chain out the wall so we're having to lock individual grates. I'll send for the mason tomorrow to fix the rings…'

The voices trailed away as the heavy iron door clanged shut leaving the morgue in darkness. This time the bolt on the far side was drawn and the second it clicked into place I leaped from under the shroud and raced to the skylight. At the agreed signal, the giant dome growled to one side leaving Tom peering down from the gap.

'Shit mate, I thought you were done for.'

'Just get me out of here.'

I passed up the file then Tom dragged me onto the roof where I almost burst into tears with relief. The air was so fresh, so clear; I felt like the condemned man who had been reprieved on the scaffold.

We were not yet out of the woods but having come this far I was damned if anyone was going to catch us now. We heaved back the skylight and within a minute or so had traversed the courtyard and vaulted back over the wall. Five more and we were crouched in the shadow of the tree back where we'd started. Had we been followed? I stared down the road. A few lights were on in the hospital but the street between us was clear. Against all the odds it looked like we might have got away with it.

'Someone's coming,' whispered Tom.

I strained my eyes to the bottom of the hill where the goggle lamps of a motor vehicle loomed out of the mist. A Taxi! It had to be him. We walked towards the city pretending to take no notice until the vehicle ground to a halt on the other side of the road. Conway pulled back the window.

'Taxi to Craven gentlemen?'

We scampered over the road as fast as whippets and jumped into the back. Oh sanctuary, blessed sanctuary. I locked the doors as Conway chewed through the gears and Tom lit a couple of cigarettes.

For a while no one said anything until our driver spoke into the mirror.

'Well chaps. How did we get on?'

Tom and I looked impishly at each other then bringing our faces together let out a tremendous scream.

CHAPTER TWENTY

Conway lost no time getting back and as he flew through the gates, Tom and I hunched down again to keep out of sight. I felt the shudder of the grid and familiar munch of gravel.

'Anyone about?'

'Loads. Somebody just tried to wave me down - probably my fare,' said Conway checking his watch. 'I'm late but that's too bad. Believe me, it's normally the other way round with us trying to shoehorn people out.'

Conway swung into the stables and yanked on the brake.

'You can sit up now guys; this is the end of the line. I hope it was worth it.'

'Amen to that,' I said. 'What do we owe you?'

'Don't be ridiculous.'

'I insist. You can't drive all that way for nothing.'

'I don't want anything. Really. I was just pleased to atone for that day in the theatre.'

'Well, I'm not going to argue. Let me just say I can't thank you enough, I really can't.'

Conway laughed.

'Glad I could help. Perhaps one day you'll tell me about it although from what I saw in that bag I'm not sure I want to know. Anyhow can't dally, there's an angry punter at the front wanting a lift home. Enjoy your evening!'

We banged the roof and went into the house. As ever Domino was pleased to see us and while Tom took him for a wander in the garden, I locked the file in the safe then rammed the holdall and contents into the kitchen stove topping the flames with a large shovel of coke. That should do the trick. I checked my watch. Twelve forty. We'd been gone just over the hour. I dropped the key back into the Gimcrack Cup then after a quick conference by the Lion's Fountain, Tom and I slipped back into the castle the same way we had left.

We reconvened at the Christmas tree. The party was in full swing. A few of the older guests had retired but there were still hordes of people stumbling around with most of the gentlemen in shirtsleeves. I poked my head into the ballroom where the band were still playing. There was no sign of Jane but Victoria was dancing as evocatively as ever, this time with Julian who was shuffling awkwardly beside her. Victoria looked incredible even though her skin was drenched and her long hair tangled from exertion. Suddenly she opened her eyes and catching me staring at her, blew a sarcastic kiss. Damn it. I was about to go across and say something when I felt a paw on my shoulder and turned to see Tom pointing to the ceiling.

'Drink?'

We made straight for the library where we fought our way to front of the queue and demolished a couple of mugs of ale. We then ordered a couple more and set up camp by the trestle tables where the champagne glasses had been. Two of the towers had completely disappeared but the third was virtually intact. I checked our surroundings. The room was chock-a-block, the men, as ever, congregated by the supply of alcohol while the ladies blathered in the background. In the far corner a mound of people were flocked around a grand piano murdering *I'm Henry the Eighth I am I am*. It was a dreadful noise; it really was but a few more drinks and I'd have been straight in there. Tom removed his jacket and hung it on the back of the chair.

'You're trembling. Are you all right?'

'I think so. But shit mate, when Tench was belting those corpses I nearly died. Talk about saved by the bell.'

'What would you have done if he'd pulled back your cover?'

'Filled my pants probably. Who knows, if I'd sat up, he might have filled his own – you should have seen him jump when his mate yelled from the door!'

We laughed like hyenas at the picture. When it came down to it, Tench had shown himself to be just as vulnerable as anyone else although it had been an incredibly close shave and we knew it.

'What now?'

I reached for my tankard and took a slug.

'We'll inspect the file when we get back and take a view. Judging by the thickness there's not a lot there. I just hope after all we've been through it was worth it.'

Tom moved closer so no one could hear.

'We're going to piece this together you know. We've already recovered your father's diary entry and there's your testimony about Lord William's last words.'

'True, but who's going to believe *that*?'

'You shouldn't underestimate yourself. I believe you and there's many others out there who will. The fact that he called you to his deathbed is irrefutable and while no one else heard what he said, what possible reason can he have had for doing that?'

'Maybe because Lord William could be my real father?'

Tom nearly choked on his drink.

'What?'

A few people looked across to where we were standing.

'What?' he whispered.

'Oh, I don't know. He implied that my mother and he were lovers. It happened back in Ireland before she met my father so the timings are wrong, or so it seems. If it is true, it would certainly fit with Julian being a cuckoo and talk of changing the succession. Thing is we need more before we go to the authorities, you know we do. There has to be something else; there has to be although I don't know what, maybe a letter or document or something?'

Tom wiped some froth from his chin.

'Crake will know. In fact, Crake is the key to everything. When shall we pay him a visit?'

'I contacted his office yesterday. He's available next week. Can you stay until then?'

'Thanks, but I ought to get home. I haven't seen my folks in a while.'

'And I've still got a heap of Dad's papers to sort through. What say we meet in Hartlepool on Tuesday?'

'The fifteenth? Good idea. I'll go straight from York.'

'That's settled then. I'll wire his office to confirm.' My eyes jumped to the door. 'Hang on; we'll talk about it later.'

Jane was making a beeline over. Immediately behind her were Julian and Clifford.

'There you are Edmund. I'm sorry I've neglected you but mother was taken ill and I've been looking after her. She's asleep now thank goodness. I was beginning to worry I'd miss the rest of the dancing.'

There was barely time to answer before Julian cut rudely between us engulfing me in a waft of cigar fumes.

'I want to know what my father told you as he lay there dying in his bed, the poor sod.'

'Oh, Julian not again, I've already told you everything I know.'

I tried to walk away but Julian grabbed my lapels.

'Let me go Julian.'

The room suddenly went quiet. It was the *County* all over again.

'Not this time I won't, you lying little bum shit. What gave you the right to worm your way in there with him? I want the truth and you're either going to tell me or I'm going to drag you outside and belt the living daylights out of you.'

Tom dived between us.

'Whoa. Come on, Julian; he's already said he doesn't know anything.'

Clifford, who had been observing proceedings stepped forward from the side-lines

'Stay out of this silly boy,' he mewed as he patted my friend's cheeks. Now I had seen someone do this to Tom before and I knew he didn't like it.

'I'd be obliged if you didn't do that,' said Tom.

Julian grabbed me by the collar and lifted me half off the ground.

'Come on, what did he tell you? I'm going to count to three…'

'For goodness sake where's your dignity? You're showing yourself up in front of all your guests.'

Julian dropped me to the floor but before I could walk away he circled his enormous fat hands around my throat and began shaking me. This time I'd had enough and crashed my knee into his groin.

'Get *off* me …'

Julian immediately released his grip, his eyes on stalks as he doubled up. Some of the men jostled forward mumbling 'foul play' but I wasn't going to stand there and let him throttle me. Julian clambered to his feet and took a swing at me as Jane tried to pull him away.

'For heaven's sake Julian, stop it! stop it!'

'You, stay out of this.'

'This is ridiculous,' said Tom. 'Come on. Enough's enough.'

Clifford leaned over and began tapping my friend's face again.

'Sonny, you're playing out of your league; now be a good lad and sit down.'

Tom swatted Clifford's hands away.

'Look. I've asked you once as nicely as I can, don't do that; I shan't ask you again.'

'Is that right?' sneered Clifford. 'Or else what?'

The atmosphere suddenly turned to menace as the ladies chewed their fingers and the men shuffled forward to get a better view. Clifford, who was in his element playing to the crowd, attempted to pat Tom again but as soon as he raised his hands, quick as lightening, Tom thumped him, once, hard in the face and Clifford crumpled to the floor. Immediately, all hell broke loose. Julian attempted to head-butt Tom while myself, Jane, and others desperately tried get between them. At the same time Clifford staggered to his feet and recovering his bearings, let out a huge roar and charged into the melee whirling his arms like some kind of deranged beast. This was the cue for various other factions, would-be peacemakers and screaming women to enter the fray, and it was only a matter of time before the indecorous, blaspheming tangle of humanity bumped into the trestle tables bringing down the surviving pyramid of champagne flutes.

The crash was so loud it would have been heard in Durham itself. It was certainly heard by Sparks and his men who raced through from the hall and started pulling people away. They had a job on their hands too because it was the classic free for all with men shouting, fists and furniture flying and women howling. Eventually, and with no small effort, Sparks and his colleagues restored order although even then, Clifford had to be restrained as he desperately tried to get at Tom.

'You, you're fucking dead, do you hear? You're fucking dead!'

Tom was leaning against the fireplace smoking a cigarette. His left eye was closed where someone had thumped him but Clifford's nose was swollen and there was blood all down his front.

'You, you're fucking dead,' he shouted again, 'Do you hear?'

Tom blew a smoke ring.

'If I were you, I'd get that silk scarf of yours to the cleaners before those nasty red stains set in.'

Clifford went purple as he struggled to break free, heaving and snorting like a rhinoceros, but Sparks and his colleagues held him tightly. Sparks turned to Julian.

'It's such a shame my Lord. There's always a handful who ruin it for everyone else. What would you like us to do sir?'

'Throw them out.'

'What, this one here?'

'No, not him you fool. The one over there holding his eye and the other yob next to him.'

'That's not fair,' said Jane, running up to her brother. 'Edmund and Tom aren't to blame. You and Johnny started it.'

Julian pointed a finger at his sister.

'You, shut your mouth. I've already warned you about the company you keep.'

Jane brought her hands to her face and started to cry.

'Don't speak to her like that,' said Tom angrily.

'I'll talk to my sister how I like. Now get out of my house before I have you thrown out.'

'Don't worry about it Jane,' I said. 'We were leaving anyway.'

Julian pointed to the door.

'And don't come back in here Bullick, neither you nor that oik you brought with you, not tonight, not ever. You'll be hearing from me later but the devil himself won't rescue you from what's coming.'

'You should know all about that,' I replied.

Tom glowered at Julian. He looked set for another round until Jane cut in.

'It's all right Tom. I'll be fine. Best if you leave like he says, and I'll see you tomorrow.'

'Like hell you will,' snarled Julian.

The doormen were closing in. It was time to go. I put an arm round my friend and turned to Sparks.

'It's all right fellahs, we're leaving, we're leaving. Come on mate. Let's go home.'

CHAPTER TWENTY-ONE

'Are you ready?'
'Hang on.'

Tom reached into his jacket and pulled the stopper from a half litre of *Croizet Grande Reserve*. He took a long, deep swig then crashed the bottle on the table.

'Helped myself on the way out, didn't I?'

'Pass it here.'

I rubbed the top and wolfed a large mouthful. It felt like someone had dumped a red-hot coal down my throat. When my eyes stopped watering, I handed the bottle back and reached for the file.

It was a small folder with just a few sheets skewered through the top left-hand corner. The first was a Medicine Log but the blank page testified only to the short time my father had been treated before he expired. I flicked over to an inventory of the patient's property. It was all there; boots, trousers, a felt shirt, tweed jacket, underclothes, a leather belt, socks, riding crop, his gold watch, a leather pouch containing some loose change, his silver cross and wedding ring. So, he was wearing his watch after all? Tench must have mislaid it. I turned the sheet. There was a handwritten note in different coloured ink confirming the nurses had to cut off his boots but otherwise nothing remarkable. I turned the page. The root document was the hospital admission sheet and this time there was plenty of information. I swept my finger down the margin. Name. Gender. Date of birth. Place of birth. Occupation. Religion. Marital Status. Address. Next of kin. It was all neatly written so he must have been conscious when they brought him in. The next section was multiple choice to record the patient's mental condition upon arrival. The options were *unconscious, semi-conscious, delirious, confused, semi-lucid, anxious* and *lucid*. The word *lucid* was circled. My father had been in control of his faculties.

In the next section a précis of his injuries recorded a severe head wound, a broken left femur and a suspected broken pelvis but that much I already knew. It was the last section titled *History* that I was looking for and I nearly fainted when I read it.

Patient states Lord Cavendish has disinherited his son and is in extreme danger. Patient rode to the moor to warn him but was confronted by monks at Friars Cross and unhorsed in the storm.

Oh my God. I fumbled for the brandy and took another draught. Tom snatched the file and scrambled through the pages.

'Holy shit,' he whispered. 'This was no accident. What does it mean though, confronted by monks? And what's Friars Cross?'

'It's a fork at the top of Hamsterley Moor. The abbey there was dissolved by Henry VIII but legend has it the ruins are haunted.'

Tom took another slug of brandy.

'I don't believe in ghosts.'

'Nor I but Lord William claimed he saw them too.'

'There must be an explanation. Kids mucking around?'

'Could be. Everyone knows they've been at it for years although Lord William thought it could be Julian and Clifford even though they were in in London. Anyhow what is certain is he changed the succession. He changed it. He didn't just tell you; your father knew and this proves it. There's nothing more to be done until we see Crake next week. We have him Edmund. We have him.'

CHAPTER TWENTY-TWO

I slept like a log that night. With all the excitement and the cognac, I'd no sooner climbed between the sheets than it was morning again and Domino was baying in the hallway. I clambered out of bed and tumbled onto the landing.

'Hang on, hang on.'

The knocking continued louder than ever. I bumped down the stairs and opened the door on one of the stable lads who looked me up and down with a mixture of trepidation and bewilderment.

'Sorry to bother you Ed. Mr Fenoughty sent me to remind you the horses will be leaving shortly.'

I glanced at my watch. Quarter to eight. Damn, I'd promised I'd help with the riding out. I raced back upstairs, splashed my face with water and pulled on some clothes. Tom's sleepy voice drifted through from the next room.

'Where are you going?'

'I promised Fenoughty I'd lend a hand with the string,' I said pulling on a shirt. 'We're taking them out with the *Braes*.'

'You must be mad. I'm going back to sleep.'

'What time's your train?'

'They run at twenty past the hour. I'll catch one later this morning.'

I yanked on a pair of riding boots.

'Right, I'll leave you to it. There's a few tradesmen kicking about who'll give you a lift into town. If you get stuck call a cab.'

'But maybe not go too close to the castle hey?'

'Aye, maybe not too close although how much Julian and Clifford will want to remember about last night is open to debate.'

I grabbed a coat from the wardrobe and stuck my head round his door.

'I'll see you in Hartlepool on Tuesday. Wire me to confirm what time you're getting in.'

'Right you are,' said Tom, diving back under the blankets. 'Just make sure you keep that file safe.'

'Don't worry, I will.'

'Seriously. I mean it.'

'Goodbye Tom.'

I snatched a helmet and crop from the hall and ran over to the yard where the horses were already circulating. Fenoughty was by the trough inspecting the shoes of a large grey gelding.

'Ah, Edmund, you've decided to join us.'

'Sorry Fenoughty,' I said, catching my breath, 'bit of a late one.'

'I don't doubt it young fellah, I don't doubt it. Anyhow the less said about last night the better.'

It seemed I wasn't the only one green round the gills. Fenoughty slapped the animal on the rump and climbed off his stool.

'Edmund, I'm putting you up on *Button* here; he's a bit of a fruitcake but a sound jumper. Warm him up in the park then when you meet up with the hunt, put him through his paces.'

Fenoughty gave me a leg up and I trotted off to join the others who were clattering around the yard. There were about thirty of us in the string including two young women. I was expecting Jane but not the other. Her face was turned away from me but there was no mistaking the willowy form that first captivated me on that awful day at Saint Cuthbert's. Jane trotted over smiling broadly under her navy-blue hunting cap.

'Well hello there Edmund Bullick. And how are we feeling today?'

'Fit as a fiddle,' I lied.

Jane wheeled her charge alongside.

'I wasn't sure after last night if you'd remember you promised to join us.'

'I didn't. Fenoughty had to send one of the lads over to fish me out of bed.'

There was a brief silence as Button dipped his head and neighed impatiently. Time to test the water.

'It was a terrific party, don't you think, notwithstanding the unfortunate little episode at the end? How's your brother?'

'I don't know. He and Jonny didn't come to bed until an hour ago although I expect they'll materialise in the pub later. Where's Tom?'

'Going home. He's not seen his parents since we left college.'

Jane's horse stamped around for a moment, the crisp air blowing in and out of his nostrils.

'They were still calling him every expletive imaginable well after you left. Crazy when you think about it because it wasn't your friend's fault. Johnny can be a complete arse sometimes.'

'Tom can look after himself.'

'So it would seem. Can I tell you something in confidence?'

'Go ahead.'

'Your friend, Tom. I want to see him again although Julian's absolutely forbidden it and would go mad if he found out. Do you know when he's coming back?'

The horses were moving off. I flicked Button's reins.

'He's still at the house. If you hurry, you might just catch him.'

Jane said nothing but I could sense her mind working overtime as we trailed through the arch and into the park. Somewhere behind me Victoria was laughing but I conquered the temptation to look round.

'Where are we heading?' asked Jane. 'I thought everyone was hunting.'

'Fenoughty wants to gallop the horses across the plain first. The snow will do them good because it offers resistance and forces them to pick up their feet. It also treats any inflammation of the joints and tendons. We'll work them for twenty minutes or so and then those who want to go hunting can meet the rest at the kennels.'

We cut away from the drive and into the open meadows, the hooves of the animals falling strangely quiet as they left the gravel. The morning air was wonderfully clear and for a while the only sound was the jangle of harnesses and crunching of snow beneath us. When we were well into the park Fenoughty gave the signal and broke into a canter and then a gallop, with the rest of us following on. It was a circular course of about three furlongs taking in a couple of brushwood jumps and a long slope towards the river which turned into a challenging uphill slog on the return leg. The horses, who sensed what was coming, relished the workout and didn't seem to notice the drifts although these were quite deep in places. The exercise blew away my own cobwebs and as the wind rushed through my ears, I was glad I hadn't wasted the morning in bed.

After a couple of circuits Fenoughty called everybody over. All the flat horses and young hurdlers were to return with him to the stables, the chasers were free to join the *Braes*. If Jane went back now she would catch Tom before he left the house and sure enough, without saying anything to anyone she slipped away. I was just mulling it over when Victoria suddenly drew alongside. In my resolve to ignore her that morning I'd not been watching where she was.

'I'm off to the kennels,' she said casually. 'Are you joining us?'

I looked into those witches' eyes and could only admire her splendid form. She was dressed in a close-fitting navy-blue jacket with white hunting shirt, beige chaps and jodhpurs. She wore knee length black leather boots with silver spurs and in her gloved fingers she clasped a bone handled whip. She was straddled across a beautiful dark steeplechaser, every inch a champion with at least two hands over Button. The animal must have been one of Lord William's last acquisitions because if it had been in the stable for any length of time, I would have remembered it. I wondered how she'd managed to talk Fenoughty into putting her up. A sweep of those eyes no doubt.

'Well?' she said swishing her crop through the air a couple of times. 'You joining us?'

'What's it to you?'

Victoria patted her horse on the neck. Her complexion was surprisingly fresh. You'd never guess she had been up half the night.

'Still sulking from our little dance, are we?'

I leaned forward and scratched Button behind the ear. My father told me horses loved the sensation and it helped to build up trust between animal and rider.

'I didn't appreciate you leading me on and then insulting my family so as you ask, yes, I am angry. Wouldn't you be?'

'You've only yourself to blame. A cat may look at a queen *Horse Boy* but without money or connections he should stick to chasing mice.'

'I can't see any queen around here' I replied and trotted off to join the others. I heard Victoria click the roof of her mouth as her charge followed and moved back alongside.

'You seem to forget that it was you who came on to me; I never invited your advances. What did you expect me to do? Encourage you? Lie to you? Well?'

'Just forget it,' I said. If I could have thought of a slicker response, I would have made it although deep down I knew she was right.

'No, I won't forget it,' she said harshly. 'It was you who came on to me with your *la-dee-dahs* and when it was clear you wouldn't take no for an answer, I responded in the only way I knew that would silence you.'

'And how's that? Oh, I get it, by humiliating me in front of Faversham and the others? The slow dancing and teasing, the cow eyes and sweet whispers in the ear? The insults to my family. No doubt all part of your little game where you make up the rules as you go along. It must be so amusing talking down to people and calling them minions. Do you suppose I'm oblivious to your charms?'

'No, I supposed only to play you as you appeared. I would have expected at your age you would have had more experience of life which I concede was an error on my part. What do they teach you at that college of yours? Believe me *Horse Boy*; you have a great deal to learn about women.'

'I might lack understanding in the ways of *some* women I grant you, but heaven forbid any of my close acquaintance are so shallow as to live their life solely in pursuit of riches like you seem to.'

'Hah' she replied with a toss of her head. 'Women are all the same or hadn't you noticed? They all crave wealth or rather they covet the freedom and security that money brings. They always have and they always will. It's certainly how things are where I come from; wealth and connections are king and from one generation to the next we forge alliances to preserve and consolidate our society. It's in the genes of us all and neither you nor I can do anything to change it.'

'It's the genes of greed and unhappiness more like.'

She did not answer and for a while we rode on in silence.

'Lady Alanna thinks you're going to marry Julian,' I said presently.

'She makes no secret of it, does she? He's certainly rich enough but then so are Faversham and a few of the others. I'll probably wait and see if there are any more declarations before I make up my mind.'

'Is that all you care about? Is there no place in that shallow mind of yours for mutual respect, affection and love? What about passion and the unconditional yearning to want to look after another person and to make them happy? Is your heart so cold that you are immune to these things also?'

We had reached the kennels where the riders from the *Braes* were circling round. I remember the sudden burst of colour with all the red jackets and the black and sandy coloured hounds framed by the whiteness of the snow. Some of the riders were shouting across, urging us to hurry. A small crowd from the village had also gathered and were mingling between the horses. Victoria reached down and grabbed a drink from a passing salver.

'I'm no stranger to love and passion however, and as I thought I'd made clear last night, I don't look at you in that way. I won't deny you seem a decent enough lad but you and I are from different worlds, it's something neither of us can change and the reason we can never be together.'

Before I could answer the air was ripped by the blast of a hunting horn sending the hounds into a frenzy. As the bystanders dispersed, the Master roared something I couldn't make out, but its effect was immediate as the riders howled back in the same dialect and shuffled their mounts forward. Victoria tensed her grip on the reins. A look swept over her face I had not seen before, like a mixture of cruelty and wild excitement. She dug her spurs into the flank of her mount and turned scornfully.

'See you at the kill *Horse Boy*. That's if you ever get there on that pit pony of yours. Haaah!'

I seared with rage. If I could have reached the girl, I swear I would have throttled her but she was already away. I screamed at Button and with a furious shake of the reins we tore off in pursuit.

There must be something aboriginal to account for the thrill of hunting; perhaps it is a legacy from Neanderthal times and the lionisation of those who brought home sustenance for the community, either that or the sinister anxiety to be there at the kill. I had been brought up with the baying of hounds and always revelled in the chase although on this occasion, I was especially determined to overtake my quarry. Button was no pit pony. He may not have been as powerful as Victoria's mount, but he had a decent stride and I was able to keep tabs on her as the field strung out across the park.

We would have been galloping for about a mile when over on a small hillock to the right, a fox suddenly broke cover and made a dash for the woods.

'Halloo! Halloo!' screamed the master.

The chase was on. Suddenly all hell was let loose as to a profane discord of howling and horns Victoria and the string ahead of me swung about drawing the cruel, merciless pack in their wake.

This was my chance. I yelled at Button and pulling the reins to cut the apex, rode like fury to head the fox off before he reached the safety of the thicket. It was a close-run thing. I thought I would get there in time and very nearly did but Reynard was nothing if not cute and when I reached the boundary, it was just in time to see him look over his shoulder and slip underneath the hedge. As I cursed our luck, Victoria and the others arrived on the scene hotly pursued by the hounds who thundered through the gap and into the forest.

The Master smacked his thigh in frustration.

'The jammy rascal, I was sure we'd got him.'

Victoria rode forward and inspected the hedge, her face glowing with the exercise.

'You're not going to give up are you?' she panted. 'Come on, we have to get after them if we want to be in at the kill.'

'The privet is too high Miss,' said the Master.

'Nonsense,' cried Victoria wheeling her charge round. 'We can clear that surely?'

'Maybe we can but there's barbed wire in the hedgerow and it's too dangerous. Mr Fenoughty would not want you to risk your charge Miss. There'll be other foxes. This one's going to ground.'

'Not if we catch him first, he's not. Come on, what's wrong with you all? I'm going after him. Haaah!'

Before anyone could stop her Victoria sailed over the hedge, her gelding disappearing into the forest with a scissor kick of the hind quarters. The Master was furious.

'That bloody woman. For goodness sake someone, bring her back before she kills herself or worse still, injures the horse.'

'I'll go,' I said and swung Button round. The hedge was solid blackthorn and must have been over five feet but there was no time for second thoughts and to my immense relief we brushed through the top of the foliage before landing heavily on the other side. I pulled Button to a standstill and leaned forward to cradle his neck.

'You're a good boy,' I whispered.

Inside the forest it was strangely quiet. Somewhere far off the hounds were baying but as I broke into a trot, there was only the rustle of foliage and snapping of twigs to feather the silence. I shouted her name. Nothing. I called again, this time at the top of my voice. Nothing. Not even the palest echo. It was as if the very trees had closed ranks and sucked away every tortious syllable. I looked to the carpet of rusty bracken. A light covering of snow had somehow made its way through the crown of evergreens and a few hoof prints were visible. I patted Button's neck and followed the tracks deeper and deeper into the plantation, all the while calling her name. Suddenly, in the distance, I saw her riderless gelding standing uneasily beside the skeleton of a dead fir tree. Something had spooked it because the saddle had slipped and one of the stirrups was broken, although of the rider there was no sign. I jumped down and taking Button's reins in one hand slowly walked forward. As I drew nearer, the gelding whinnied nervously and stamped a warning.

'Whoa. Easy boy, easy now.'

I gathered the loose bridle then, having fastened both horses to the dead fir, started combing the area, all the while calling her name. This time there was a faint answer.

'Hello? Hello? I'm over here.'

'Where?'

'Down by the brook.'

I followed the contour of the land where it fell towards a small stream. Victoria was at the bottom of the bank lying face down in a tangle of driftwood, her legs half in the water, her fine clothes splattered with mud.

'Victoria. Thank the Lord. Are you alright?'

Victoria twisted onto an elbow and wiped the mud from her face.

'Hello *Horse Boy*, what are you doing here?'

'I've been sent to find you. Didn't you hear me calling?'

'I vaguely remember someone shouting but I was desperate to keep up with the hounds.'

I crouched down and took her hand.

'It's alright, just keep still for a moment. Are you injured?'

'I don't think so.'

'What happened?'

'I'm not sure. I just remember riding flat out when a pheasant sprang up and next thing I knew, I was down here.'

She was smiling now, almost laughing. She didn't appear to be injured at all.

'Are you crazy?' I said irritably. 'The Master expressly told you not to jump the hedge and you deliberately went and ignored him. Do you think he was warning you for the benefit of his health? You could have been cut to ribbons on that wire.'

A shaft of daylight poked through the trees. Victoria brought a hand up to shield her eyes.

'Pah, fiddlesticks,' she muttered.

'Is that all you can say?'

'It's only a horse, for goodness sake.'

'No, it's not. It's someone else's horse or does that not bother you either?'

'Oh, stop being so pious, it really doesn't suit you.'

I listened to the gentle trickle of water. Somewhere in the branches a lonely pigeon had seen enough and clattered away. I stared into that lovely face streaked in filth and without saying another word, leaned forward and grabbing the back of her head pulled her towards me and kissed her roughly. Our mouths met for a second or two, no more. I had barely time to savour the experience before she went berserk.

'How dare you!' she screamed lashing out wildly as she jumped to her feet. 'How fucking dare you!'

'I'm sorry Victoria, really I am; I'd never…'

'Get off! No, take your hands off me! Just who the hell do you think you are?'

'Please, don't be like that….'

She was already striding up the bank to where the horses were tethered. I ran after her catching her arm just as we reached the dead fir.

'I'm sorry. You must know I'd never do anything to offend you.'

Victoria, who was already reaching for the saddle, span round and swatted me away.

'Get your hands off me. No! How dare you?'

'Look, I've said I'm sorry and I am. Truly I am. It was a mistake. I just thought…'

Victoria grabbed the cantle and vaulting astride the horse, glared down at me, eyes burning.

'You thought *what* exactly? Let me tell you something *Horse Boy* and you listen real good. If you ever, *ever* try and touch me again I'll make you wish you'd never been born.'

'What do you expect after the way you tease me? I can't help how I feel.'

'You just don't get it do you?' she glared, horse twisting round as she stamped in vain for the broken stirrup. 'We cannot be together. Now get out of my way. I never want to see or hear from you ever again. Ever. Haaah!'

'Wait! Will you just *listen* for a moment …' but it was no use. She was already charging off into the distance and I might as well have been shouting at the trees.

Bugger.

Bugger. Bugger. *Bugger.*

CHAPTER TWENTY-THREE

The monuments stood guard on Palace Green as they must have done for over a thousand years. There was no sinology in their placement or design, the weathered slabs protruding from the snow like broken, crooked teeth, the epitaphs faded with the memory of the people they had spoken of, people like me who had once passed this way but were no more. I spared a thought for the illustrious men and women of their times who would be lying in these graves and it saddened me they were no longer mourned. What was the point of even existing? I recalled the words of Cannon Brown at my father's funeral; *Life is a temporary arrangement within which nothing is constant but change.* He was right. Whatever else the future had in store, the only pathetic certainty was oblivion at the end of it all. And yet surely, there had to be more to living than dying? I kicked the frozen slush off my boots and stepped through the great North Door.

Inside the cathedral I experienced an overwhelming sensation of stillness and calm, and from the moment I stood before the magnificent East Window I was at a loss to understand why it had taken me this long to explore such riches on my doorstep. There were few people about. It was still early and as I wandered through the cloisters, the only sound keeping me company was the quarterly peel of bells from the top of the Great Tower, that and the rolling whispers from a service taking place in one of the side chapels. I took a seat at the back and craned my neck to where the massive drum columns melted into the ribbed vault of the nave roof. How on earth did our Norman ancestors manage to do all that? I thought it an astonishing feat of engineering all the more so because it must have been accomplished using nothing but mathematics, chisels, blocks, pulleys and ropes. And faith of course. The man who has faith can move mountains. That's what it says in the bible doesn't it, not once or twice but over and over again? The man with faith, albeit the size of a mustard seed, can move mountains. I supposed the architects and masons from all those centuries ago must have been deeply religious people, for many mountains had been moved to create their monument.

Hearing footsteps I turned to catch the outline of a clergyman passing by the baptism font. I jumped out of my daydream and crossed the aisle to intercept him.

'Excuse me, I'm looking for the holy man of Jarrow?'

He was an elderly cleric who reminded me very much of Brother Wallace with his wisps of snow-white hair and twisted gait that made him shuffle rather than walk. He carried a prayer book in one hand and a walking stick in the other and when he looked at me, I noticed his eyes were milked over, although his voice was soft and clear.

'You seek the holy man of Jarrow? Of course. You will find his shrine in the Galilee Chapel at the back of the cathedral. The entrance is over there.'

He steered a finger in the direction of an enormous pipe organ to the side of which was a small archway. I thanked him for his assistance and crossed to the south aisle.

I discovered the resting place of Saint Bede among some other ancient graves at the foot of a small bank of granite steps. I have to say I was expecting something far more splendid, perhaps akin to the likes of Walsingham or Canterbury but instead my eyes rested on an unassuming marble sarcophagus adorned with nothing more imposing than a large wooden candlestick at each corner. I reached for the marble and ran my fingers over the Latin inscription. The letters had worn greatly through the ages but there was no mistaking the word 'Bede' and I knew I was gazing into history. At the foot of the tomb was a small cushion. I fell to my knees and gathered the piece of card.

Christ is the morning star, who when the night of this world is past, brings to his saints the promise of the light of life and opens everlasting day. Alleluia.

There was much to pray for. I started by asking Saint Bede to beseech God for the repose of the souls of my parents and for Lord William who throughout his life had shown my family nothing but kindness. I then prayed for the living, for my brother in his grief and to give strength to Lady Alanna and Jane. I was not intending to pray for anyone else but awkwardly aware of Christ's teaching to be reconciled with one's adversary before making any offering, I prayed for Julian and for Clifford and then at length for all those people on Palace Green and elsewhere who had no one to pray for them. Lastly, I prayed for myself.

*Oh Saint Bede in your wisdom and through the grace
of God you already know my most earnest desire yet
I shall ask it. Please, I beg you, please, please help me
for I am sick and I cannot go on any longer. I implore
you here and now with every part of my soul to make
Victoria love me, to fill her heart until it overflows
with desire for me, that she will run into my arms and
we can be together. Amen.*

I meant every syllable of every tortured word. This girl had crept so deep under my skin that I could barely think of anything or anyone else, and the more she refused me, the more I wanted her to the point I was starting to go out of my mind. Perhaps I was already insane and didn't know it? Why else would I lay my burden before a heap of ancient bones trusting the person who once lived in them could somehow answer my prayer? But then the man with faith can move mountains. According to St Mark's gospel, Jesus said that you can pray for anything, anything at all, and so long as you have faith, it would be given to you. The notion seemed absurd but what was done was done. I had asked in faith and while only myself and Saint Bede knew about it, for one fleeting moment I had believed. There was nothing more I could do. I left the cathedral feeling strangely positive and fortified with a resolve to make the most of every precious moment that had been given to me, and to leave no stone unturned in my quest for the truth about my heritage.

As for the rest, God knows.

CHAPTER TWENTY-FOUR

About a week later I was in my father's office burning the midnight oil with his journals when Domino's ears went up and he began to growl at someone in the courtyard. I listened for a moment expecting the footsteps to pass but when they reached the house, they suddenly fell silent, and there was a soft knock on the door. I racked my brains who it could be this time of night remembering only too well that the last occasion I'd been disturbed this late was with the summons to Lord William's deathbed. I knew there was no one at the castle. Jane and her mother were staying with relatives in Bath, while Julian, Johnny Clifford and their party had left for a week's shooting in Northumberland. It crossed my mind it could have been an unexpected visit from Tom, but then he'd have let me know he was coming, and anyhow we were meeting in Hartlepool in a couple of days to tackle Crake. I couldn't think of anyone else. There was another knock, much louder this time and Domino started to bark.

'All right boy, let's go see.'

I grabbed an oil lamp and trailing the dog through the hall, slid the bolt on a young woman standing alone at the bottom of the step. At first, I didn't know her for she was almost totally enfolded in her shawl, however when I raised the lantern to her face and saw the eyes, I could not help but cry out in astonishment.

'Victoria! What on earth are you doing here?'

Victoria pulled down her scarf to speak.

'Hello *Horse Boy*,' she said softly, 'are you going to ask me in?'

I looked over her shoulder and swept the courtyard. There was no one else about.

'Well?'

'Of course, of course, please, do come in; come in out of the cold.'

Victoria stepped into the hall and kicked the snow from her shoes. I bolted the door behind her.

'Here let me take your things. It must be freezing outside.'

'I'll say. I've only walked from the castle and I'm chilled to the bone.'

Victoria passed her shawl and coat and shook her long black hair.

'Please, come into the back where it's warm and let me get you something to drink.'

We passed through the house in silence. In the kitchen she leaned against the stove while I hung up her coat and pulled up a couple of chairs.

'Please, sit down and warm yourself. I only have tea in at the moment, is that all right?'

Victoria nodded. I turned to fill the kettle as my unexpected visitor gathered her skirts and sank into one of the chairs. As I ran the tap my mind was racing and I almost had to pinch myself to make sure I wasn't dreaming. Here was the girl that dominated my thoughts from the moment I woke to the moment I fell asleep, here in my father's house with me, all alone in the middle of the night. I struggled to second guess why she had called at this hour. What was she doing at Craven in the first place? She must have known she risked a scandal if anyone from the village had seen her. The flags scraped behind me as she drew closer to the stove. I lifted the cover from one of the hobs, set down the kettle then parked myself at the table beside her. Not knowing what to say, I resolved to say nothing and for a while we listened to the ticking of the clock. Victoria broke the silence.

'How are you?'

I thought it a strange question in the circumstances but answered in similar tenure.

'I'm well, thank you. I'm surprised everyone is back so soon. I understood you were guests of the Percy's until the end of next week?'

'Julian and the others are still in Northumberland. I left early because I must return to London to attend my mother who is ill.'

'I'm sorry to hear it. Your brother, is he going with you?'

'No, he would rather not, at least not at the present time. The sport on the estate is exceptional and he and the others are making the most of it, bagging pheasants in the day and drinking in the taverns at night. I don't care much for either activity, I never did and everyone else we know up there has been grounded by the weather. Alnwick may be beautiful when the daffodils are out but believe me, it is a lonely place when the streets are choking in snow.'

She must have journeyed back on her own and my heart quickened as I realised there was no one to disturb us. What was she playing at coming around to see me when she could be under no illusion as to my feelings for her? She had said she never wanted to see me again but now she was here. Why? I determined to say as little as possible and let her make the running. If she had an agenda, it would be apparent soon enough.

Victoria swept her long black mane then held her hands towards the stove.

'When I say I had to return to London it was more of a pretext so as not to offend our hosts. Don't misunderstand me. My mother is genuinely unwell, she has been ill for some time but to own the truth there is nothing so urgent in her condition that would command my immediate presence. The reality is, Northumberland, or rather your Northern weather, does not suit me and at this time of year I would rather be in Belgravia.'

I decided to cut to the quick.

'Why are you here Victoria?'

Victoria leaned back in her chair and brushed the top of her legs as if sweeping away some invisible dust.

'Alnwick to Kings Cross is too far in one trip,' she said matter-of-fact, 'and it suited me to break my journey at Craven to gather the remainder of my belongings and run some errands for Julian. I continue to London on the Pullman tomorrow evening.'

'That's not what I meant, and you know it. Why have you come to my father's house? Is your quest for amusement such that in the absence of any other you thought you would seek me out? If that's your game, I would rather you left now.'

Victoria's face softened as she drew her chair closer to mine.

'No. No, not at all. I can understand why you think that way, but nothing could be further from the truth. I walked over here tonight for two reasons. Firstly, I've come to see you because I owe you an apology for the way I have behaved towards you, and for some of the things I said, particularly when we were last together.'

I stared at her uneasily, barely able to believe what I was hearing. Her beauty and presence unnerved me and fearful of what might follow if I said the wrong thing again, I went to the stove where the kettle was whistling.

'Milk and sugar?'

'Just milk, thank you.'

I passed her a mug and sat down again without another word. Victoria seemed to take this as encouragement and reaching for my hand continued in the same fashion as before.

'I want you to know that I am utterly ashamed of the way I spoke to you, especially after you demonstrated nothing but guarded admiration and a desire for friendship. I can scarcely countenance what you must think of me for I shudder when I remember some of the things I said. I didn't mean any of it, not a word, really, I didn't. I thought I was being clever trying to show off to Faversham and the others but in reality, I was just making a fool of myself. I see only too clearly that you are an honourable man, just like your father before you, and I ask from the bottom of my heart that you forgive me for being so odious and wretchedly narrow minded. I am so sorry, truly I am.'

There followed a brief silence as those dark eyes seared into my core. I could swear there were tears in them but were they real? I leant forward and brushed her cheek.

'Hey, don't get upset, please don't, it's all right, really it is.'

'I'm so sorry,' she whispered, 'and to think I said all those things at a time you were already grieving for your father. It was utterly selfish, and I am ashamed when I think of how I behaved. Will you forgive me?'

'Of course I forgive you,' I replied adding quickly, 'believe me I've been called much worse.'

Victoria laughed, sincere and spontaneous; it was like a bird singing; beautiful, infectious.

'Thank you. Thank you so much,' she said softly. There was a short pause then she suddenly held out her hand.

'Look, I know I've done nothing to deserve it, but can I ask that you overlook what happened before and that we can start again?'

As she spoke, she looked straight at me as if reading my mind. Her words were everything and more I could have wished for and I felt myself starting to well up. She smiled again. It was not the switched-on accessory I was used to, this time her whole face was shining as she cocked her head, all the while holding my gaze.

'Friends?' she asked again.

I slipped my fingers into her outstretched hand.

'Friends,' I replied.

Victoria reached for her mug and for a while we drank our tea.

'You said you walked over for two reasons. What was the other?'

Victoria drew a tissue from her sleeve and blew her nose.

'I have a few hours to kill tomorrow before I catch my train. I've always wanted to explore the moors around Craven only I don't know the area well enough. I came to ask if you were not doing anything in the morning if you would ride out with me?'

My heart leaped at the prospect as she surely knew before she asked. It was settled in moments and we arranged to meet at the stables at nine. Victoria rose to her feet.

'Now I simply must go. It's been a really long day and I'm so tired.'

I was disappointed at this although I should not have expected anything else. In fact, I hadn't been expecting anything at all and was still reeling at her sudden appearance. I gathered her coat and shawl and walked her to the door. Victoria turned and held out her hand.

'Until tomorrow then *Horse Boy*. Goodnight.'

'Goodnight Victoria'.

For a couple of seconds we stood and looked at each other. I felt an overwhelming urge to grab her but after what happened in the forest I didn't dare, and the moment passed. When she was halfway across the courtyard I called after her.

'And the name's Edmund.'

Victoria smiled amiably over her shoulder then disappeared into the shadows.

CHAPTER TWENTY-FIVE

Needless to say I barely slept that night and by 5.00am I'd had enough and decided to get up and re-lay all the fires. While I was about it, I realised the whole house was due a good clean, so I scrubbed all the flags and swept and dusted upstairs and down, then, having changed all the beds and replenished the scuttles from the coalhouse I slumped into an armchair and tried to get my head around the sudden change in Victoria. Was this really the same girl who had screamed at me in the forest? I thought of the Galilee chapel. I would take a great deal of persuading that the road to Damascus cut through the snowdrifts of Northumberland but her unexpected friendliness and anxiety to make amends were extraordinary. I fished the key out of the Gimcrack Cup and checked the contents of the safe. The purse of gold sovereigns, my father's various bank books and statements, they were all there together with his last diary note and the file Tom and I had taken from Dryburn hospital. I checked my watch. It was 8.50am. I locked the safe then dropping the key back into the trophy, pulled on some riding clothes and made my way across to the stables.

It was a grey, overcast morning and Victoria was already there talking to Fenoughty who, to my surprise, had entrusted her with the same black gelding as before. I could only assume he didn't know of her reckless behaviour in the forest, or if he did, he chose to overlook it. Probably the latter. She had that way with men did Victoria; one smile and they would forgive her anything as I knew only too well from our conversation the previous evening. She greeted me amiably.

'Morning' said she. 'Sleep well?'

'Like the dead' I lied. 'Yourself?'

Victoria tied back her hair as she pulled on her riding hat. 'No, not really. Too much on my mind.'

She looked straight at me as she said this but before I could reply Fenoughty cut over us.

'Edmund, I'm putting you up on Button again. He's not the swiftest as you know, but he's reliable and the two of you seem to get on well.'

'Button and me, well we're like that aren't we boy?'

Button gave a little whinny as he nuzzled my palm.

'I feel like I've been cooped up for an age,' said Victoria brightly. 'Shall we get going?'

I cupped my hands to give her a leg up into the saddle. For a brief moment I took the weight of her body as it stretched out in front me and I swear my heart clanged with lust. Sensing my face changing colour and knowing what must have been written there I turned and vaulted across Button before anyone would notice. Victoria twisted into the stirrups as Fenoughty gathered both bridles and led us out of the stable, his eyes searching the sky.

'Well Edmund, the weather looks like it'll hold but there's a low cloud and your options might be limited. Where d'ye reckon on going?'

'It'll depend on the drifts but assuming the trail's clear, I'll take Miss Clifford to Friars Cross then drop down to the river and pick up the towpath.'

A look of unease swept across Fenoughty's brow. He knew we would pass close to where my father and Lord William had met their end. He appeared about to say something but then checked himself as if he understood I was resolved to make the journey and that argument would be useless. All the while Victoria was humming to herself as she adjusted her hat. I shuffled Button alongside her black gelding.

'We about ready then?'

Victoria nodded although it was Fenoughty who spoke.

'I'm sure you don't need a lecture from me young 'un' he said ruefully 'but take it steady up there and keep clear of the old workings.'

I didn't need a lecture but was glad of it just the same. There were so many mines and pits the moor was a death-trap to anyone who didn't know their way around. I assured him we would keep to the trail and return the horses well before dark. Fenoughty switched his eyes to Victoria then gave me a peculiar look before shaking his head and disappearing into the stables. I wheeled Button round and set off over the cobbles, Victoria drawing alongside as we slipped under the arch and out into the Park.

'What did Fenoughty mean by old workings?'

'There's a ruined monastery at the top of the crags about four miles from here. The community was wiped out by Henry VIII, but a number of shafts are dotted about where the monks used to source their iron and coal.'

'A monastery?' exclaimed Victoria. 'How exciting. It sounds the stuff of fairy tales. Will you take me there?'

'If you like. The trail passes right by or almost right by. There's not much of the original building left but it's only a couple of hundred yards from the fork at the top. We'll be there in an hour or so.'

'Then its settled boy, isn't it?' said Victoria leaning forward to address her horse. 'We can't wait, can we? No, we can't. Do you know I asked cook to pack us some lunch so maybe when we take a rest if there's an apple in the parcel you can have a piece? Yes you can, you know you can, you good boy. Da, da da.'

Her black gelding snorted in approval and I couldn't help but smile. I had not previously thought of Victoria as someone who regarded horses as anything other than a means of transportation, yet here she was all clucking and sweetness itself. Perhaps I had misjudged her. I tweaked Button's ears so he didn't feel left out as we followed the path of a small brook that stumbled down from the top of the fell.

'Tell me, isn't this the place where your father and Lord William had their accident?'

'The very same,' I replied. 'I knew I would have to come back here some day and when you called last night, it not only gave me the incentive to get on with it but meant I wouldn't be riding out alone. It's such a beautiful view from the top you see, and I always felt it was wasted if there was no one to share it with.'

Victoria coaxed her mount a little closer.

'I've heard so much about the beauty and solace of these fells,' she said quietly. 'Ever since I saw the landscape from my room in the castle I've wanted to ride to this place and explore its secrets.'

We followed the track as it wound in and out the contours of the fell before disappearing into the boulders altogether. A faint breeze swept down from the top where little seahorses of mist were dancing around the crags. Victoria hoisted herself up in the stirrups and stretched out her arms.

'It's so beautiful up here,' she cried. 'So wild and desolate and yet beautiful. Tell me what's that strange *peta peta peta* noise? It sounds like someone playing the castanets.'

'They're Red Grouse. The heather's full of them, so much so that I'm surprised Julian and your brother went all the way to Northumberland to shoot. Their call which you can hear is very distinctive; it's as if the birds are telling us to go-back-go-back-go-back. They are extraordinary creatures. Do you know that when they sense danger, the hen will protect her chicks by scurrying across the moor dragging a wing, as if feigning injury to divert the predator? It's not just the Red Grouse that are worth watching. There's a host of other magnificent birds on the moor, Partridge, Curlew, Lapwing and Merlin to name but some. But forgive me; I don't want to bore you with anecdotes about Mother Nature when we hail from such different worlds.'

'Oh, please don't say that. You're not boring me at all. Really, you're not. This is fascinating.'

I dipped my head and looked into her face.

'Truly?'

Victoria smiled warmly and gave a series of nods. 'Truly.'

'Well, it's not just the wild animals and birds that draw me up here. There's all manner of rare and beautiful plants that only grow on the moor. There's the heather, obviously, but also unique grasses, bilberry and a beautiful yellow bog shrub that comes out in the spring. I know it might be cold and a bit miserable today but the moor changes so much throughout the seasons, all the beautiful colours, the different fragrances, I just adore it. When Alfie and I were little my father used to bring us up here and show us all the different flowers and teach us the various calls of the birds. I suppose a part of me has remained up here ever since.'

We reached an old wooden gate. I slid down from the saddle and walked the horses through.

'You must have loved him very much,' said Victoria. 'He sounds so different from my own father who I barely saw at all when I was growing up.'

'How was that? Did he not live with you?'

Victoria leaned forward and stroked her horse behind the ear.

'In a fashion. To the outside world it appeared we were this big happy family however in reality, we were anything but. When he wasn't working at the Foreign Office, father spent most of the time at the races or playing cards at his Club and mother, Johnny and I came a poor third. Truly, he was hardly ever at home, either in the morning when I got up, or in the evening when I went to bed. He never once read me a story or asked us to ride out with him in Hyde Park although I knew he used to go there every Sunday. We never once sat down as a family, just the four of us and ate a meal together; not even at Christmas when my brother and I were consigned to a different room. Next thing I knew I was grown up and there he was, this stranger. Oh, I'm not saying I don't love him. I do love him, very much, I always did, he was always so dazzling but I can't say I know him in the same way you knew your own father, and it's at times like this that I would it had been different.'

I closed the gate and pulled myself back aboard Button.

'And your mother? I take it you are close to her?'

'I am. I saw far more of my mother when I was little and unlike my father, she was always there for me. I didn't realise it at the time, but my father's long absences must have been very difficult for her.'

Her words struck a chord as I remembered what Lord William had said about Lady Alanna rattling around the castle and how it was the beginning of the slippery slope.

'You said your mother is unwell?'

'She is. I might as well tell you this because you'll find out eventually. About six years ago my mother caught smallpox when she accompanied my father on a ministerial trip to Egypt. She became so ill she was not expected to survive and indeed for several days she lay close to death. In the event she managed to pull through, but the infection left her with terrible scars and drained what was left of her youth. It was so utterly tragic for them both. My father couldn't bear to look at her once lovely face and spent less time than ever at home, while fearful to show herself in public, my mother retreated into the family home in Belgravia where she lives like a hermit.'

'I'm so sorry,' I said, and I meant it. With all the grief and uncertainty of our own situation I hadn't stopped to consider there might be other people out there suffering, particularly a family like Victoria's who seemed to have so much going for them.

'It's why I left Northumberland,' she continued. 'Yes, there were other reasons, tedium not being the least of them, but I would still be at Alnwick if my mother had not sent for me. I don't expect you to understand because you have probably never been on your own, it's not something that young people think about, but I have seen how loneliness afflicts my mother and when she sent for me, I didn't hesitate.'

The trail was rising sharply now and the seahorses of mist that had swept the fell all morning began to close in around us. The top of the moor was shrouded completely and while there had been no rain, the horses were dripping and tiny globules of water had settled on our faces and clothes. All the while Victoria remained a most engaging companion without the faintest trace of her previous arrogance or self-regard. Her manner was easy, her conversation intelligent and amusing and, as time and distance slipped by, I found myself opening up to her. Oh, don't get me wrong, I didn't divulge anything regarding Lord William's death or what Tom and I had discovered in my father's journal, and I certainly wasn't going to tell her about our excursion to Dryburn the previous week and to be fair to her, she didn't pry, far from it. Instead, we just talked about this and that, sometimes seriously, other times laughing and joking, it was light and it was easy although I would be doing these pages a disservice if I did not also record how with every passing moment she only increased in my esteem.

At the top of the fell, the weathered stone guarding the fork to the monastery loomed into view. I drew Button to a halt and jumped down from the saddle.

'This is it. We're on foot from here.'

Victoria's gelding snorted as she pulled him alongside.

'Where exactly are we?'

'Friars Cross. The stone here marks the track that leads off to the abbey ruins. You can't see them through the mist but they're not far.'

'It doesn't look much like a cross to me,' she said lightly, 'more like a giant gatepost.'

'Many people say the same when they first come up here but it's a cross all right, or at least it started out as one before it was battered by the seasons. Evidently, it's been here for centuries, parish records testifying to its existence as far back as the Plantagenets and there were almost certainly a number of earlier wooden structures. According to legend, the cross marks the graves of one of the monks and a local farm girl who used to conduct illicit trysts here until they were discovered by the ecclesiastical courts and committed suicide rather than be parted.'

I reached for Victoria's hand as she slid down from the saddle, her leather boots splashing into the mud as she hit the ground. For a moment we looked at one another until conscious of what must be written across my face, I turned on the pretext of gathering Button lest he started to wander off. Victoria removed her hat and brushed the moisture from her sleeves.

'How awful for them yet it's a frightfully romantic notion don't you think? You know, that they still lie together after all this time?'

My heart skipped at the poignancy of her words.

'I have always thought so. It's because of the legend that the cross has always been associated with clandestine meetings, a place for lovers who have nowhere else to go. They say you only have to find *Hob Hole* to see the truth of it.'

'*Hob Hole*?'

'It's a cave somewhere at the back of the ruins where the monks used to store ice and provisions. I vaguely remember my father pointing out the entrance when I was a child although I've never had reason to go there.'

Victoria led her gelding round so we faced one another.

'*Hob Hole* sounds a bit bleak. What does it mean?'

'I suppose a literal translation would the place or the dwelling of the Hob, a short, foul, hairy creature such as a goblin or a troll. These days you only meet them in children's stories but in the less informed times of our ancestors they were real enough and blamed for everything from crop failure to the disappearance of travellers.'

'I adore spooky tales and folklore. Can you take me there?'

'If you like, that's if we can find it. If I remember correctly the hollow lies up in the rocks at the back of the ruins. It's not far but there's a bit of a ridge so stay close.'

We led the horses in single file until after a minute or so the broken stones of the monastery ghosted through the fog. Victoria gave a cry of delight and having tied her bridle to a piece of broken fence began to scale the nearest wall.

'Be careful' I said. 'You shouldn't climb on anything round here. It's not safe.'

Victoria heaved herself to the top where she lurched upright and stretched her arms to the sky.

'Woo hoo. This is amazing. If you look down from here, you can still trace the outline of the chapel and what was probably the kitchen and dormitory. And over there, that dovecote, it's still got birds in.'

'Come down Victoria.'

Victoria took no notice and began to inch her way along the ledge, her slender arms reaching out as if she were treading a tightrope.

'I'm the king of the castle and you're the dirty rascal.'

I hurried to the foot of the wall and implored her to get down.

Victoria pulled a face.

'Oh, I'm the queen of the castle and you're the dirty rascal.'

A rook clattered out of the stones beneath her. Victoria shrieked in fright displacing a shower of masonry as she lost her footing and ended with her midriff trussed across the rim of the wall. My heart skipped as I reached up and grabbed her ankles to prevent her falling off completely. Victoria looked down anxiously, her face as white as a sheet.

'Oh goodness, that was a bit close. Maybe you were right after all.'

'You're crazy,' I said irritably. 'You could have been seriously hurt.'

I eased her down from the ledge. As soon as her boots touched the ground she drew away and flapped at the dirt and dust that was now smeared over her riding coat.

'Oh, *Horse Boy*, you're such a stiff; don't you ever take a risk?'

'There's already been one tragedy up here or had you forgotten? I don't believe either of us could cope with another.'

'Fiddlesticks,' she retorted.

'You wouldn't be saying that if you'd broken your neck.'

'I was perfectly fine' she said brightly and then before I could respond, 'now never mind that, tell me, where's this *Hob Hole* place?'

Aware that admonishment would only shatter any real or imagined spell, I let it go and we walked through the ruins until the track came to an abrupt halt at the overhanging cliff. I was a child when my father had brought me here, but I recalled him telling me the cave entrance was hidden somewhere in the face at the top of an old landslide. I looked around and sure enough the giant moss-covered rocks were still there, everything in fact exactly how I remembered it from all those years ago. I hauled Victoria onto the first boulder from where we started clambering up the fall. Near the top of the stones a small fissure no more than four feet by three opened up in front us.

'Is this the hollow?' cried Victoria drawing breath. 'It doesn't look big enough to be an entrance.'

'I can't see any other so it must be. Come on, this way.'

I crouched to my haunches and squeezed through the gap, Victoria following close behind.

My first impression of the cave was a prodigious sense of forbidding, like we had no business being in there at all. It was eerie to say the least and even after my eyes had adjusted to the darkness, there remained such a tangle of shadow that it was impossible to gauge how far it extended into the ridge. The chamber itself was as cold as the tomb, cold, musty and dank and as I stood there catching my bearings the only sound was of water dripping from the roof into some invisible pool. Victoria took my arm. She was standing so close to me I could hear her breathing.

'Can you see any goblins?' she whispered mischievously. I called out into the blackness, my words clanging off the rock like a pebble bouncing on ice. Then silence.

Victoria stood on her tiptoes and whispered in my ear. 'Perhaps they've all gone out for the day.'

'Perhaps.'

I struck a match, carefully guarding the flame in cupped hands. The cavern briefly flickered to life.

253

'Look!' she cried. 'By the wall!'

'Where? I can't see anything.'

'The far side, over there, something glimmered.'

I stumbled across the jagged floor, cursing as the match burned down and seared my fingers. I waved it away and struck another, this time looking up with the flare. In the wall ahead, cut into the rock was a ledge of old drip bottles with candles of various cycle. What place was this? I made my way over and struck again, the nearest taper spitting into a flame which Victoria poured along the shelf to mate with the others. When she finished, we stood for a moment and watched as the sharp contours around us melted and the chamber came alive in a ruddy cauldron that would have done justice to the starkest depiction of the underworld in a renaissance painting. Victoria surveyed the ever-expanding vault, her voice bouncing off the rock face.

'This place is absolutely amazing. Look how huge the cavern is and I still can't tell how far back it goes. You'd never have guessed from that tiny entrance.'

As the space around us filled with light I became aware of a large amount of graffiti scratched into the walls. The writing was everywhere; names, murals, dates; some of the script stark, much of it faint, a few segments barely visible at all but every mark the testament of others who had trodden this way before. I picked up a bottle and held it to the wall suddenly understanding the common thread.

'They were lovers.'

'Who were?'

'The people here. They were all lovers. Look at all the names woven in hearts and shields, the dates and secret messages. This is astonishing.'

Victoria picked up a bottle and went to the far side of the hollow.

'So they were. Good Lord. There's dozens of them. Dozens. Some of these go back years. There's a very old one here;

Thomas and Lettice
Together forever
30 July 1778

Here's another;

Katherine and Francis
My love as always on this silent night.
24 December 1843

And here, although this one is a bit strange. It's some kind of message.'

'What does it say?'

'Hang on; I'll put the light a bit closer. It reads

Dearest Alice
At my back I always hear
Time's winged chariot hurrying near
Percival

What does he mean *Time's winged chariot*?'

'It's from a poem by Andrew Marvell' I replied. 'His sweetheart was coy with her favours and he's telling her to seize the moment before it passes forever. The *winged chariot* is time itself about to cut them down.'

'It's incredibly romantic don't you think? All those trysts here, fraught with danger, the unions no doubt as swift as they were secret?'

Victoria brought her bottle over and placed it back on the shelf as I continued to explore the graffiti. It wasn't just names either. There were sketches, diagrams, lines of verse I didn't understand, strange numbers and equations, the whole a rich testimony to generations of lovers who had been hostages to this place because there had been nowhere else for them to go. I moved the candle closer raking the wall and then suddenly the word ghosted in front of me. Derina. The name of my mother. It was intertwined with the initials WFC. Obviously not her then. Not a common name mind. Must be a coincidence. WFC? Who was WFC? Abruptly the identity of the author leaped out of the rock. William Fitzroy-Cavendish. My mother and Lord William here in this place? Surely not. There must be other girls who bore the same. But Derina? No, she was the only Derina I had ever heard of. If she had been with Lord William it would explain everything. Could it be true? I was so consumed by the discovery that I barely noticed Victoria as she gathered a stone and began scrawling on the wall.

'What are you doing?'

A finger went to her lips.

I watched as her slim hand weaved and scratched over the rock. When she had finished, I held up my light and stared at the trace.

Edmund and Victoria
lovers in this place
14 December 1914

I looked at the words again hardly taking in what was before me. I read it for a third time then switched back to the girl. Victoria dropped the stone and folded her arms around my neck until our foreheads touched, the candlelight dancing in her beautiful black eyes.

'What I have written, it's the truth,' she whispered. 'I swear it is. I've felt that way ever since I first saw you at the church.'

I was too confused and overcome with shock and desire to say anything. Victoria drew her long willowy body against mine.

'I know you feel the same way, I know you do. I can see it when you look at me.'

I had never been in this situation with a woman before let alone someone who I craved and wanted as much as she. All the time images of my mother and Lord William flashed before me. It had to be true then. They were lovers. It was what Lord William had tried to tell me on his deathbed before guilt and time ran him through. Another thought washed over me. My God had I been conceived in this place? All of a sudden, I didn't know who I was any more. Victoria traced her fingers over my lips.

'See around you. These walls do not lie.'

I looked again at what she had written and read it out loud.

Edmund and Victoria
Lovers in this place
14 December 1914

'But this sudden change, the *County*, your behaviour towards me at the ball, what you said in the forest. I don't understand. You told me we could never be together.'

'I said those things to put you off, and to try and chase you from my affections. Oh, believe me, I knew what I wanted from the moment I first saw you, but I also knew that any liaison between us would be totally repugnant to just about everyone else and it was for that reason and for that reason alone that I said what I did.'

What was this? That she had liked me from the first? The image of Lord William and my mother fornicating here in the candlelight rushed through my mind. I read Victoria's mural again. *Lovers in this place.* What kind of lovers? The thought of sex with Victoria had intoxicated me from the moment I first saw her. Did she mean it literally or was the girl a tease, like a cat playing with a mouse?

'Tell me Victoria why do people live their lives in the shadow of what others might say or think about them? If you really feel that way, then why let other people's aversion stop you? The names on the walls here, they are from different times when people who wanted to be together had no choice but to meet in secret. But that was then, and this is now. Surely times have changed?'

'It's a spirited notion but you are not being realistic. Who is to stop us you say? How about just about everyone I can think of? We are broke, Edmund. Our family is broke. My father's losses have been devastating and everyone is depending upon me to make a good marriage to restore our fortunes. Lady Alanna has thinly disguised hopes of a union whereas Julian's more rudimentary aspirations are barely disguised at all. My father and mother are desperate to conclude the match and while my brother has no plans for anyone but himself, I am as certain as I can be that you do not feature in any of them. If this wave of hostility was not enough, there's a social gulf between us, you know there is. You are a Catholic. You are without wealth or connections, it's not your fault, it's not even a fault and it's certainly not an accusation but it is a fact and from where I come from these things matter. You and I, we are poles apart and just about everyone, certainly everyone in the orbit of my life would be totally against me having any kind of relationship with you. Surely you can see this?'

'Of course I see it, but if it doesn't matter to you and it doesn't matter to me and we want to be together, then what is to stop us?'

Victoria sighed deeply and buried her head in my shoulder.

'Oh, were it that simple. What is to stop us? It is the crux that I have struggled with these last few weeks. What people will say and think, or rather what people of position and influence will say and think. It matters enormously, but then it is my life, no one else's and closing my eyes to the way I feel about you is making me ill. I am so afraid, frightened of what will happen, frightened of how my family and friends will react but most of all frightened that I don't have the courage to see this through. I knew I wanted you from the moment I first saw you. I never felt that way about anyone before and it scared me which is why I tried to put you off by making you detest me, yet the more I tried, the more I wanted to be with you, I still do. I always will. And now it's come to this as it was always going to, that very soon I shall be forced to choose between my obligation to my mother and father and what lies in my heart. I am so utterly confused between what's right and what's not that I don't know what to do.'

She was crying now, her tears wet against the side of my face. I folded my arms around her and spoke softly into her ear.

'Hey, shhh, you mustn't weep on my account, please don't for I cannot bear it.'

'You have no idea how it's been for me. Why can't we all be free to love who we choose? I want to be with you so much, you do not know the half of it but I'm so scared.'

I brought a finger to her lips and folded her trembling body into my own.

'Listen to me Victoria. At this precise moment I couldn't give a damn about anything other than what you mean to me. You are all I think about from the moment I wake up until the moment I go to sleep. I live every part of my existence dreaming and praying that I might be with you. I don't want or need anything in this life or the next other than your love. I have to tell you this because it is the truth. I am utterly yours forever, and I swear to you here and now that if you place your trust in me, I shall never let you down. I will always take care of you, I am completely and totally mad for you. I would die for you.'

Victoria reached up with both hands and grabbed the back of my head. In a moment she had pulled her mouth to mine and we were kissing violently, the tip of her tongue penetrating my lips, her grip tightening as her body rose and melted into my own.

'I love you Victoria, God, I love you, I love you.'

'Oh Edmund, I'm so sorry for hurting you. I love you too. Oh Edmund I'm so sorry.'

It was the first time she had spoken my name. A bolt of lightning ran through me and I began to pull wildly at her clothes urgently exploring her body. Victoria winced and pushed me away.

'No. No, don't,' she sobbed.

'Forgive me,' I cried catching my breath, 'forgive me for I cannot help myself.'

'No, don't apologise. I'll do it.'

Victoria removed her jacket and waistcoat and lifted the front of her shirt to reveal an ugly graze stretching across her midriff just above the navel.

'It's from the fall on the abbey ledge earlier. It's why I stopped you'.

I gazed in wonder at her hourglass figure and beautiful skin, her body radiant and irresistible in the flickering candlelight. I had never seen anything so completely and utterly captivating and that first memory was to haunt me forever. I reached down and wetting the corner of my handkerchief in a nearby pool gently dabbed the wound. Victoria flinched and cried out.

'I'm sorry; I didn't mean to hurt you.'

Victoria raked her hands through my hair, twisting and wrenching at the curls.

'Kiss me,' she whispered. 'Kiss me there, over the gouge, where it hurts, oh Edmund.'

I sank to my knees and grabbing her hips put my mouth and tongue to the porcelain skin of her belly, stroking and exploring the ridge of the graze and in and around her navel before impulsively trailing upwards probing for her breasts. Victoria began to wail, it was a cry that I had never heard from a woman before, almost like a wounded animal. In a moment she had wrestled her shirt over her head and was pulling at the buckle on my waist. The blood rushed through my ears as every sinew in my body tore in a million directions.

'I'm crazy about you. Oh my God I love you Victoria. I love you.'

'Hold still Edmund, just a moment longer.'

Victoria placed a hand on my shoulder and kicked off her boots. As she stepped out of her jodhpurs I marvelled at her beautiful long legs and wondered if the darkest craving in my heart was about to come true. Victoria placed her hands on my shoulders and looked me in the eye.

'Do you want to screw me, Edmund?'

In my shock and embarrassment, I could only mutter something about whether she felt certain it was what she wanted.

Victoria's breath was heavy, and the words came fast.

'I've never been more certain of anything in my life. I knew we would be lovers from the moment I saw you. It was as if our destiny was already written on these walls. I want to do this more than anything Edmund, now, quickly, before the world out there finds us and the moment passes forever.'

There was no inhibition as I tore off my shirt and trousers, all the while staring and burning up as Victoria removed her underclothes until she stood naked before me with her arms across her breast.

'Hold me Edmund, I am cold.'

How desperately and ardently had I longed for this moment. I drew her against me, our naked bodies trembling in the dancing shadow. It was the most intoxicating, utterly exhilarating feeling I had ever known and there was nothing else in creation that could come near it. I gave silent thanks to God and Saint Bede for the impossible moment I had dreamed about and prayed for. As we kissed, I fell deeper and deeper into those beautiful dark eyes while the boiling urgency that only lovers can understand rushed within me.

'You must know it Victoria. You must. I have never been with a woman.'

'Don't be afraid,' she whispered. 'We shall manage well enough.'

She motioned to the far end of the cave where a small shelf of rock protruded from the wall.

'I want you to sit down on that ledge and face me.'

Without asking why I seated myself on the rock and pressed my shoulders into the cold granite. Victoria followed me across with a drip bottle which she placed on the ground to the side. In the flickering light I traced her long sleek body from her beautiful hair to the brightly painted fingers and toenails. I was so mad for her I thought I would burst.

'Put your hands behind your head Edmund, close your eyes and keep perfectly still.'

I shut my eyes and sank into the rock. I heard Victoria blow out the candle and sensed her edging towards me. After what seemed an age her knees brushed mine at which she arched her torso, threw back her head and coiled her limbs around me.

CHAPTER TWENTY-SIX

Victoria did not return to London that afternoon. Instead, we ambled down the fell in silence, our spirits hostage to what had passed between us and where it would lead from here. In the evening she came over to the house and we took Domino for a walk around the gardens before cooking supper together in the kitchen. I found a bottle of claret in one of the cupboards and when we had eaten, we stretched out in front of the fire exchanging stories and singing songs as we toasted our future from the Gimcrack trophy. Later, when we went to bed, I opened my heart and told her everything starting from the dreadful news at college to what transpired at Lord William's bedside, the mystery of my father's diary and the papers Tom and I had recovered from the mortuary. It was the longest, sweetest night of my life, each savoured contour the essence of undiluted happiness as we passed the hours making love and making plans and more love and more plans until mentally and physically exhausted, I yielded to the bottomless sleep of the just. When I awoke it was midmorning and Victoria had already slipped away to catch the early Pullman. I reached for the note on the bedside cabinet.

You looked so peaceful I didn't want to wake you
Sweet dreams darling and see you next week
Love you
V x

I threw back the bedclothes ready to conquer the world, my body aching sweetly, my soul bursting into flower with all these emotions I never knew existed. Our lives had been joined. We were going to be together. I began to chant the song we had first danced to, the melody ringing around the house as I bathed and dressed.

Oh, by the light of the silvery moon,
I want to spoon, to my honey I'll croon love's tune

I opened the wardrobe and pulled out Dad's Sunday best in readiness for our appointment in Hartlepool that afternoon. The trousers were a bit baggy round the middle, but I found a pair of braces in one of the drawers and after a few adjustments I was suited and booted and ready to go. I checked my watch. Barnaby was calling round at twelve thirty to drive me to the station. I cleared away the dishes and had just finished making up my brother's bed when the horn sounded in the courtyard. I locked the front door and jumped into the automobile. Three hours later I stepped off the pavement into *The Grand Hotel* where I found Tom in a corner of the restaurant pushing around a plate of mince and dumplings.

'I thought you'd never get here. The food's awful.'

I grinned uncomfortably at a waiter folding napkins on the next table and ordered a mug of chocolate.

'How was your trip?'

'Usual hassle at Darlington waiting for a connection then it was shuffle-bump, stop-start all the way to the coast. Anyone would think there was a war on. How about you? I like the suit by the way.'

I checked the waiter had gone then leaned across the table and lowered my voice.

'Tom, you'll not believe it. Everything fits. My mother and Lord William were lovers after all. Not just back in Ireland but later in Durham after she married my father. I discovered their names side by side in *Hob Hole*. It's where they met in secret. You know what it means don't you? Lord William was almost certainly my father. You were right all along. It had to be the reason he called me when he was dying. It's what he was trying to tell me.'

Tom stopped eating and parked his knife and fork.

'Whoa slow down. What's *Hob Hole*?'

'It's a place, or rather it's a cave hidden at the top of an old rock fall on Hamsterley moor where the monks stored provisions. Lord William and my mother used to meet there in secret. I found their names on the wall with the others.'

'What others?'

'Other lovers. Dozens of them. Tom you wouldn't believe it, there are names carved into the rock going back hundreds of years. I never knew the place existed and I've lived in Durham all my life. I still can't get over it. To think that all the time my mother and Lord William were having trysts up there behind Lady Alanna and my father's backs. Only now it seems he wasn't my father at all and all this time they were deceiving me as well. Tom, what's going on? So much has happened in the last few weeks I scarcely know who I am anymore.'

My friend who had been listening intently slumped back in his chair and closed his eyes.

'Do you believe your mother was capable of having an extra-marital affair?'

It was not a comfortable thought. I was only little when she died and her unqualified love for me had always been an incorruptible shrine.

'You mean did she cheat on my father? It's the critical question, isn't it? Did they rekindle their love? Lord William claimed to have seduced her when they met in Ireland and I have no reason to doubt him. He also said he bitterly regretted the liaison on account of my mother's virtue which appears to have been a rare currency in the society in which he and Derrymore operated. There can be little doubt she was in love with him at the time.'

'I agree,' said Tom. 'The only question therefore is whether it is too far a step to believe them capable of rekindling their ardour when their paths unexpectedly met at Craven. Lady Alanna's confinements together with your father's excursions to the racetrack will have afforded them abundant opportunity but did they have the resolve? I wasn't sure about this until your discovery in the cave but now you must see it's the last piece of the jigsaw. They must have been lovers. Why else would Lord William call you to his deathbed and tell you he had altered the succession? Why else would he direct you to treat with Crake if he hadn't altered his Will in your favour? There is no other plausible explanation. It's you Edmund. It has to be you. Lord William must have made you his heir because he must have been your real father.'

It was the only logical conclusion, and I knew it. Any lingering doubts I had previously harboured vanished the moment I saw their names gouged into the granite, and I had been reeling from the shock ever since. To discover after all these years that I was not the man I thought I had been or at least not the flesh and bones of the man was heart wrenching. Had both of my fathers known all along? That I was the true blood heir to the Craven estate? The key was Crake. Everything came back to him. Crake. Crake. Crake. I swallowed the remainder of my chocolate and banged down the mug.

'Let's see what reception we get this afternoon. Crake gave nothing away at the reading and if Lord William *had* changed the succession, you would have expected him to say so then. Perhaps he has his reasons for keeping quiet, and if so, no doubt he'll tell us. However, I don't trust him even if Lord William did. We must tread carefully.'

'I agree,' said Tom. 'Who knows? He may yet surprise us with his integrity.'

'I doubt it. However, before we do battle with Crake there's something else you need to know. It happened so unexpectedly I still can't believe it myself, but it's true.'

Tom reached for the water and looked at me over the rim of his glass. It was a cracking shiner.

'That exciting hey? Do tell. I hope it's worth the sanctimonious grin on your face.'

'It most certainly is.'

'Indeed?' he retorted damping his mouth. 'Hang on. No, no. Let me guess. At long last you finally got your leg over? Am I right?'

I beamed back.

Tom slapped his thighs.

'Congratulations old man. And about time too. Who's the poor filly?'

'Victoria' I mouthed.

'What?' he mouthed back.

'Victoria. Clifford.'

Tom flicked a glance at the waiter who had returned from the kitchens and was hovering around the sideboard.

'Could I have the bill please?'

The waiter nodded and disappeared through to the back. Tom fished out a handful of change and rose to his feet.

'That should cover it. Come on, we'd better get going or we'll be late.'

The offices of *Baxter, Crake and Lockwood* were at the end of Church Street a few minutes' walk towards the railway station. As usual Tom set off at a blistering pace.

'I don't believe you by the way.'

'I tell you it's true.'

'What, you and Lucrezia Borgia? Come off it Edmund, the girl can't stand you. Anyone could see that from the way she made a complete fool of you at the party.'

We paused outside *Woods* the opticians to comb our hair. Tom lit a couple of cigarettes and passed one across. I straightened my collar and squared up to his reflection.

'You shouldn't believe everything you see. It was only a ploy on her part. She loved me from the moment she saw me at the funeral and the unpleasantness was just a screen to try and drive me from her heart because she knew the trouble that would follow if we ever got together.'

Tom snorted through a cloud of tobacco.

'Her heart? The woman has a *heart* you say? Tell me Edmund, have you been on the sauce?'

'It's true, honestly it is. She's not the madam we took her for at all. I know it's hard to believe but when you get to know her, she's absolutely delightful. Tom, I'm crazy in love and she feels the same way.'

'Don't be ridiculous, Edmund. Spoilt, self-centred brats like Victoria love nobody but themselves. The only thing they get off on is cash, cash and more cash; they need it in abundance, and she told you herself you couldn't afford her.'

We peeled away from the window and continued down the hill.

'I can understand why you think that way but you're wrong.'

'Of course I'm not wrong. It's common knowledge the Cliffords are broke. Everyone's a walking balance sheet to them and people like you and I are far too irrelevant to feature in any ledger. Good wind up though. A different girl and I might have believed it but that stuck up cow? If she ever gazed into your eyes, you'd be stone by now.'

'You can mock me all you like but Victoria and I are lovers. We slept together last night. You've got to believe me. If you don't believe me no one else will.'

'Edmund, the day you plough her I'll run stark-bollock naked down York Shambles.'

I was still trying to convince him when we reached the solicitors, but Tom was having none of it and I could see I was wasting my breath. So be it. I would explain everything later but for now we had to focus on the assignment to hand. My friend twisted his cigarette into the pavement.

'Right. This is it. Remember what we agreed and don't jump in straight away. Let the bent bugger do all the talking then when he's finished hit him right between the eyes. I'll watch closely for his reaction because those first few seconds will tell us everything we need to know.'

'Come on' I replied. 'Let's get it over with.'

We stepped into the foyer, our appearance heralded by a brass bell that tripped somewhere above the doorway. I took in our surroundings. I thought it an expensively fitted room for a reception, all oak and brass with an enduring smell of leather and polish. My eyes searched out the counter where a smart, middle-aged woman in a tweed suit looked up from behind the sweep of an electric lamp.

'Good afternoon gentlemen, may I help you?'

'Good afternoon Miss. My name's Edmund Bullick. I have an appointment with Mr Crake.'

'Oh yes, Mr Bullick. Mr Crake is expecting you. If you'd like to hang your coats on the stand over there and I'll let him know you're here. Can I ask the name of your companion?'

'This is Thomas Brentnall miss, a friend of the family.'

'Thank you. Gentlemen if you would be good enough to take a seat. I shan't be a moment.'

We removed our coats and sat in an alcove. I reached for the table and had just started flicking through a copy of *Punch* when we were hailed from the top of the stairs.

'Mr Crake will see you now gentlemen. If you'd like to follow me, please.'

Crake's office was situated at the end of a narrow, curiously lopsided corridor. It was a musty, dusty chamber with a threadbare wool carpet, distorted mahogany panelling and a fake alabaster ceiling, the latter heavily discoloured from years of detritus generated by a coal fire which even at this late hour was roaring away in the hearth. The room was illuminated by two spherical gas lights hanging down over the main desk, their effect enhanced by several reflections of the same in the windows which gave the impression of further light coming in from outside. A giant bookcase of *Halsbury's* and other periodicals stood against one of the walls while a handful of college photographs and satirical prints of red judges stared down from another. The only other fittings of note were an old 'hunting theme' grandfather clock tucked away in the corner, and a large pelt clad desk and side table, both groaning under mounds of documents some of which had splashed onto a floor where there were scattered so many other papers that it made you wonder how anyone knew where anything was. Such, then, was the ordered or more aptly the disordered chaos in the lair of Thomas Mathias Crake solicitor, the whole dominated by a large bay window that looked out over Church Street and from which vantage point the occupier slowly turned and stretched out his hand with unexpected affability.

'Good afternoon Edmund, I hope you don't mind me calling you Edmund. Please, please make yourself comfortable. And Mr Brentnall, Thomas I think it is? You are most welcome gentlemen, please sit down. Mrs Crane, can you bring me the Fitzroy-Cavendish trust papers and ask Mr Glyder to join us please? Thank you so much.'

The receptionist clucked an acknowledgement and disappeared into the corridor as the solicitor cleared a space on the desk in front of him and sat down. A few moments later, Glyder struggled into the room with a large metal strongbox and pulled up a chair to the side of his master.

'Edmund, you'll remember my clerk from the reading of the Will I'm sure. I've asked him to join us so he can bear witness to the trust deed I've drawn up in accordance with his lordships' wishes. Your friend Mr Brentnall here can be the second witness. However, before we address the business of the day the first thing I want you to know is how sorry we all were to learn about this dreadful accident. I did not have the honour of knowing your father but as the estate solicitor, I can tell you that he was greatly respected by Lord William who always spoke of him in the highest terms. I realise his untimely passing will have been a dreadful shock to your family and you must allow me to express our deepest sympathy on your loss.'

The sentiment was generous, but the words decanted easily and the lack of warmth in the eyes of the orator betrayed every hallmark of insincerity.

'I appreciate your comments Mr Crake. My father was an excellent man who served the family with honour and distinction.'

'So it would seem, so it would seem,' replied the lawyer as he sieved through a heap of documents Glyder had suddenly poured onto the desk. From where we were positioned it was impossible to clock everything, but the haul included title deeds, bank books and accounts together with a large bundle of railway and shipping debentures, an assortment of marriage and death certificates with a sheath of old photographs and a few pieces of jewellery tumbling out at the end. There followed a brief exchange between principal and employee as they checked the contents against an inventory at the conclusion of which exercise the solicitor passed everything back except for a solitary document bound in pink ribbon. Glyder returned the surplus material and snapping the lid shut, placed the strongbox on the floor by the grandfather clock and resumed his seat. I switched my attention to Crake who was unfurling an exquisitely inscribed parchment.

'Edmund, you see in front of you the form of assent that gives effect to Lord William's intentions regarding your future education. You will recall the Will directed the trustees to invest the sum of three thousand pounds in ten-year Treasury Stock, the interest thereof to be applied to the continued full-time education of your brother and yourself with the capital to vest absolutely and equally in you both when the last of you- we shall assume Alfred – completes university. If you agree, I suggest we arrange for the fund to address any fees as and when these are presented with the balance of the accumulated interest to be paid each quarter day from the firm's trustee account at William and Glyn's. Alfred, not being of full age, is unable to take the income in his own right but I deduce that if the sum is paid to you directly, you will manage it for both. I regret we didn't get the opportunity to speak at the reading or I would have explained the proposals at that time and given my personal assurance then, as I do now, that we shall be administering his lordships' bequests to you as speedily and efficiently as possible.'

'Lord William's settlement upon my brother and I is extremely generous don't you think?'

Crake looked up from his papers for a moment, his eyes razor sharp behind their thick lenses.

'Ah Edmund,' he sighed, handing over a pen, 'you will appreciate we lawyers are not engaged to form opinions on such matters. Our duty is to give effect the intentions of the deceased and no more although as I have already said, Lord William held your father in the utmost regard so the degree of his generosity might not be wholly unexpected. Now if you would care to sign the form of assent just there at the bottom of the page then I shall invite my clerk and Mr Brentnall here to witness the same and you can be on your way.'

'I'm not signing anything,' said Tom.

There was an uncomfortable silence as Crake and Glyder looked up with a mixture of surprise and incredulity. Glyder turned uneasily to his master as the latter removed his glasses and placed them on the desk in front of him.

'Excuse me?'

'He said he's not signing anything Mr Crake, and neither am I.'

Crake turned his cold grey eyes upon me, every trace of his previous attempt at civility dissolved in the moment. 'You won't sign? What, neither of you?'

I shook my head.

'Good grief. Why ever not? Can you not see that Lord William has been extraordinarily generous and that his bequest will keep you and your brother solvent for the next few years?'

I held his gaze. Glyder stopped taking notes and began fidgeting.

'I see it clearly Mr Crake, but I am not persuaded that you have disclosed the whole of Lord William's instructions.'

'Indeed? And might I enquire the basis for this inclination? I can assure you that this is Lord William's only Will; there is no other document and if my office is to make distribution according to his bidding I must insist upon your cooperation, indeed I suggest it is a matter of honour and duty to the deceased's memory that you render me nothing less.'

There was another awkward silence. I stared into the crumpled faces of the solicitor and his clerk and remember thinking Glyder's eyebrows needed a trim. A seagull hopped along the window ledge and cried a warning that brought me to my senses.

'Mr Crake, it is precisely because of my respect for Lord William's memory that I am not prepared to sign this document or any other document. I won't do it; not today or any other day and the reason I won't do it is because just before he died, Lord William called me to his deathbed and told me he had altered the succession to the estate. That's right; he confided in me that Julian had been disinherited. You seem surprised. Why do you look surprised? You know I speak the truth because only a few weeks ago Lord William himself came here to this office and gave you specific instructions regarding the matter. The document you read out with such aplomb in the library the other week, that was not the deceased's Will, or at least not his last and true Will. I know this because as he was dying, Lord William told me he had changed the succession; he also told me that you could be trusted to give effect to his revised intentions and with his very last breath he urged that I treat with you. In these circumstances I find it somewhat disingenuous that you should be lecturing me about fidelity and loyalty.'

As I spoke these words the solicitor steadily turned purple and I thought he was about to explode.

'You *dare* to come here into my office and accuse me of misfeasance and corruption?' he hissed. 'After all I have done for the estate over the years, after all my efforts to try and expedite the administration so you and your brother are not out on the street, and you *dare* to come here and speak to me in this manner?'

It was no time for faint hearts.

'Oh, I most certainly do dare it Mr Crake,' I replied, handing back the pen. 'I dare it because I know you have another document in your possession which gives effect to the true intentions of Lord William. I know this because Lord William told me so himself and it seems to me that it would save a great deal of time and trouble for everyone concerned if you abandoned this ludicrous charade and started to address your professional obligations with the degree of integrity and transparency that Lord William expected of you.'

I wondered if I had gone too far but it needed to be said. The reaction, though, was inevitable. Crake slammed his fist on the table and sprang to his feet, his face like thunder.

'How dare you? How *dare* you? I ought to have you arrested for criminal slander. Get out of my office, both of you, now. Get out before I call the police.'

'If that's your wish, sir, then we shall leave' said Tom coolly, 'but before you close the door on us, we should tell you we have evidence.'

'Evidence? Evidence?' shouted Crake as he started across the floor. 'What, the unsubstantiated, uncorroborated ramblings of a delirious dying man? You call that evidence? The poor fellow was stark raving mad at the end. Dr Addison has already given a statement to the Coroner as to his Lordship's capacity and his expert opinion is unimpeachable, or are you intending to attack the good doctor's professional integrity as well? Now get out.'

Tom and I climbed to our feet and made to leave.

'We have other evidence' I said defiantly.

Crake stood by the door and held it open.

'Oh really? Such as?'

'We have documents in our possession that substantiate Lord William's true intentions.'

'Documents? What documents? If you are referring to the file of papers you stole from the Coroner's office you can take those out of the equation straight away.'

The words didn't register at first. What did he just say? How the hell did he know that? And then the scales fell from my eyes and I nearly threw up.

'That's right Mr Bullick. You are not the only one who made provision for this interview. And as for you Brentnall, you insolent whelp; do you know the penalty for burglary?'

Tom, who must have been equally shocked by this ghastly turn of events, responded with admirable calm.

'Burglary?' he replied loftily. 'I haven't the faintest idea what you're talking about.'

'Oh, I think you *do* Mr Brentnall. My information is the two of you broke into the Dryburn mortuary only – when was it Glyder?– the week before last? Thank you, yes only the week before last. You know, right in the middle of Lord Julian's coming out party hoping no one would miss you? Surely you haven't forgotten already?'

'You can't prove a thing,' said Tom.

'Is that so? Then you've clearly never heard of fingerprint evidence, how the lines and grooves of our digits are unique personal characteristics, and that no two peoples' are the same? Our sources at Durham Constabulary assure me that following recent advances in science, any impressions left on furniture and glass surfaces can now be lifted and examined through a forensic dusting process – not dissimilar, in fact, to recovering the trace of a nib from, say, the lower page of a diary. One word from me and they will go over Sergeant

Tench's office with a toothcomb. Would you care to take that chance Mr Brentnall?'

My heart sank. Was there anything he didn't know? I stole a glance at Tom to catch an expression of utter bewilderment. We had been betrayed. It was Crake's moment of triumph and he seized it.

'Mr Bullick, I've a good mind to call the police and have you arrested here and now. What the two of you have done amounts to blatant obstruction of His Majesty's Coroner in the execution of his duty, conduct only exacerbated by the ungodly nature of the undertaking together with your total lack of remorse and impertinence to me this afternoon. Have you given any thought as to how long you'd get at the local assizes? Well, have you? Four years I'd say, maybe five with nothing to look forward to thereafter but the hopeless task of trying to rehabilitate yourself into a society that would never forgive the revolting nature of your crime. And your younger brother Alfred? In your blinkered self-serving pursuit of this crock of shit about Lord Julian being disinherited, did you ever spare a thought as to how he would manage with his only guardian and protector banged up? Well? Answer me? Did you?'

There was nothing I could say. There was no point. The game was up and all I could do was stand there and curse my own stupidity. Crake sustained his harangue, on and on he went calling us every label under the sun until after a while I ceased listening altogether. Oh, how could I have let myself fall into the trap? Damn it, damn it, damn it. Fool Bullick, fool!

Eventually, Crake fell silent as if gathering his thoughts before resuming in an unexpectedly conciliatory tone.

'Mr Bullick, I do not deny that Lord William came to see me a few weeks ago. It is no secret he was a regular visitor to the office although this is hardly surprising with his substantial maritime interests in the town. You will appreciate I am bound by client confidentiality as to the substance of our discussions, but you should understand here and now that there was never, *ever* the slightest suggestion of Lord Julian being disinherited or of his father altering the succession or any other aspect of his will. Absolutely none. When his Lordship died, he left behind only the one Will, the contents of which have already been imparted. The instrument in question was drawn up personally by me in 1905 and that there has never been any amendment or codicil to it I can appeal to the testimony of my partners, and my clerk Mr Glyder here.'

Crake was compelling and I realised if he ever took the stand in this mode, the court would swallow the lot. The man was a pillar of the establishment while Tommy and I were, well, nothing. I even started to doubt what Lord William had told me. I couldn't help it. Maybe he had been delirious after all? What was certain was that if Crake brought in the authorities we were done for. Damn it. How could I have been so blind? Regroup. We needed to regroup and realising there was no more to be achieved in the office, I caught Tom's eye and flicked my head that it was time to leave. We had reached the top of the stairs when the solicitor unexpectedly called after us.

'Wait. Come back in here and close the door.'

We followed his bidding and shuffled awkwardly in front of the desk as Crake resumed his seat and looked up with his chin resting on linked fingers. If the stakes hadn't been so high, it would have reminded me of a dressing down in the headmaster's study.

'Gentlemen, now that we understand each other I want you both to listen to me and listen well as if your very future depends upon what I am going to say, because believe me, it does. The only thing stopping me from turning the two of you over to the police right now is my desire to avoid tainting his lordship's reputation with these outrageous accusations. So let me tell you what I am prepared to do, although believe you me it is against my better judgement. The time is now- Mr Glyder? Just approaching four thirty? Thank you – just approaching four thirty on Tuesday the fifteenth. This evening I am travelling to Newcastle on business and do not expect to return until Thursday morning. Between now and then I shall leave this deed of assent open, that is until close of business tomorrow. When I return Mr Bullick, I expect to find that you have signed it – and Mr Brentnall, I expect you to have witnessed it – so that the estate can be distributed in accordance with Lord William's intentions. On the understanding you will make the necessary arrangements with my clerk here and the document is attested by you both when I get back, we shall put this unsavoury episode behind us. If you decline, I shall immediately report everything I know to the authorities and the two of you can rot in hell for all I care. You have twenty-four hours to decide. Do I make myself clear?'

Our position was hopeless. Crake held the aces, and he knew it.

'Do I have a choice?'

'I suggest not. Mr Brentnall?'

'The expression *short and curlies* springs to mind Mr Crake.'

'Indeed it does Mr Brentnall, and you and your friend here would do well to remember it.'

Crake leaned forward and rang a hand bell on the edge of his desk.

'Well gentlemen, I believe that concludes our business this afternoon. Thank you so much for your attendance. Mrs Crane will show you to the door.'

We retraced our route along the twisted passageway and through the foyer before stepping into an arctic blast filleting the length of Church Street. Tom hugged the wrap of his coat and kicked the pavement.

'I can't believe it. I can't. How the *hell* does he know all that? *How?* It isn't possible.'

There was an awkward silence. Better get it out.

'It's my fault.'

'What do you mean?'

'Victoria'.

'What? Clifford? What about her?'

'I tried to tell you.'

Tom studied me for a moment then brought his hands to his head.

'Oh no. *Please* don't tell me you took that bitch into your confidence? You didn't, did you?'

Silence.

'You did? Oh no. You *did*, didn't you? Oh Ed, I thought you were having me on.'

'I wish I was'.

Tom turned away and kicked the ground again.

'You *idiot*. You bloody idiot.'

'I know.'

'What was the last thing, *the very last thing* I said to you before we parted the other week? Make sure you keep the safe locked I said. 'Oh yes' you said 'I'll make sure' you said and now this. For pity's sake man how could you fall for it? What were you thinking of?'

Crake was peering down at us from the bow of his window. I dropped my voice so not to be overheard.

'It's easy for you to judge but it's not straightforward, believe me it's not; you didn't see the change in her. She was so, well, convincing and when she said she loved me and promised to help, I believed her. I don't expect you to understand, but at the time I thought I could trust her. In fact, I was certain of it.'

Tom kicked the pavement again, his voice rising in frustration.

'Oh, I understand completely. She was sent in there to find out what you knew. She could see your brain was in your trousers, so she told you what you wanted to hear; it's the oldest trick in the world mate and like the bloody fool that you are you fell for it. For heaven's sake man, after everything we went through, after all the risks we took to get that file and you go and chuck it away and for what? The hopeless, brainless, blinkered pursuit of an unattainable leggy cow like that? Sheesh.'

The words seared and I began to get angry.

'All right, all right you've said your piece now give it a rest. It's not as if I've lost anything I had in the first place. Yes, I misjudged her. Yes, it was a hideous mistake but there's bugger all I can do about it now and believe me, I'll pay a heavier price for my folly than you could ever understand.'

'Oh, like you love her and thought she really loved you and now it breaks your heart to discover she was lying all along? Love at first sight and all that? Yeah, right. Truth is she had your measure from the first. I told you before; self-seeking, avaricious little brats like Victoria Clifford love only themselves. And money of course. Themselves and money. I still can't believe you fell for it. What were you thinking of? You're a bloody fool mate.'

'Oh, piss off.'

Someone called out from the other side of the street. 'Hey Edmund! Ed Bullick? Is that you?'

I turned to see a clump of soldiers loitering outside the tobacconists.

'It's me, Alix, Alix Liddle' shouted one. 'You know, from the Durham train last month?'

So it was. I raised a hand in acknowledgement at which Liddle jumped between a trolley and a coal cart and ran across.

'Well, this is a turn up for the books,' said he pumping my arm. 'What brings you to Hartlepool?'

'I had some business with my father's lawyers. We've just finished and are heading to the station.'

'What? You're not going back this minute surely?' he cried motioning over to his colleagues.

'We are, actually. We have a train to catch.'

'Balls to that. Look, me and the lads over there, we've just done ten hours sentry on the cliffs and are off for a well-earned drink. Why don't you join us?'

In other circumstances I might have been tempted, but at that precise moment the thought of participating in any form of joviality was distinctly unappealing.

'Thanks for the offer Alix but I'd sooner not. To be honest things are pretty awful right now and if it's all the same to you, I'd like to get home.'

Alix unfastened his arms in supplication.

'What? Look don't give me any of that. Really, you can stop feeling sorry for yourself right now. Life is just too short to be miserable and a couple of drinks never harmed anyone. What do you say?'

'Oh, I don't know...'

'Come on man. What else are you going to do for the rest of the day? Slide into an ever-deepening gloom? You need cheering up, you know you do and while you're at it you can tell me how you got on after we parted at Durham station. Who's your friend by the way?'

'I'm so sorry Alix, this is Tommy Brentnall, a mate of mine from college. Tommy, this is Alix Liddle, the jockey on the train I told you about.'

Liddle shook hands then leaned forward to speak into Tom's ear.

'Now see here Tommy with the purple eye, never mind your friend for a moment, you look to me like a man who could do with a drink. The *Camerons* brew here is the best in the North and it would be disrespectful to leave town without oiling your neck. Also, we're a couple of blokes light for the darts match at the *Albion* later. What d'ye say?'

'I think it's an excellent idea,' said Tom unexpectedly. 'Oh, come on Ed, don't frown like that. It's been a rotten afternoon and I need a drink. Come on. It's still early and there's plenty of trains.'

I thought about it for a moment. There was no special reason to hurry back. Alfie would be home later, but I'd already arranged for Barnaby to collect him from the station. Sod it. Why not?

'Alix, we'd be delighted, but just a couple mind then we have to go home.'

CHAPTER TWENTY-SEVEN

There were six of us in our party that evening; myself, Tom, Alix, a subaltern called Hallet who played the piano and two others from the 18th DLI and needless to say it wasn't a couple of beers, it was considerably more. Those of you who drink will know the form. You go out with the best intentions of taking it steady, but unless you actually get up and leave at some point, you inevitably cross the threshold when all bets are off and any agenda goes out of the window. In my own case, I know I can handle three swift pints and just about keep to previous arrangements but any more than that and I might as well jump into a time machine. Tom says it's exactly the same with him. Three drinks -fine- but anymore and he never knows where he'll end up. Looking back, we didn't stand a chance.

We started out in the *Freemasons* and then moved on to the *Commercial* where it had been our intention to have a final pint and then leave for the station until someone – probably Tom thinking about it- bought a double round and before I knew it we'd put our departure back a couple of hours so we could play darts with the rest of them down at

The Albion. Needless to say the minute we stepped in there we crossed the Rubicon and as the drink flowed, it washed away our plans. In the sober light of day it can be difficult to understand such a rapid change of perspective, but that's drinking for you and in *The Albion* that night we ended so far in our cups that time didn't seem to matter at all. Mind you, it's also true to say that the beer was as good as we had been told, Alix and his colleagues were great company and with the pub heaving for the match it was a really good night out. I can still smell the sawdust and the hops now and see Hallet on an old, battered piano in the corner and a wall of soldiers around him trotting through the favourites including *You Made Me Love You (I didn't want to do it), Daisy Daisy* and *Oh! Oh! Antonio.* There was also the excitement of the darts match, the prize for which turned out to be a silver cup and a crate of stout for the winning team. I'd always been a handy player and quickly found my stride as I caught up with Alix who I had not seen since we had parted on that drenched night at Durham station. He told me he had been training in Otterburn with the rest of the 18th DLI when the company was suddenly posted to the town's defences on the Headland.

'It's so tedious,' he moaned. 'Like every day is the same as the one before, three hours of square-bashing followed by eight hours sentry duty on top of Parton Rocks. I mean, look at us now, fit as fighting cocks and straining for action and the CO tells us this morning 'sorry lads but we're here for another six months'. Six months? It'll be over before we get there.'

Alix's frustration was palpable although I could think of worse places to be holed up. Mind you, we didn't just talk about the conflict. In-between the singing and the darts we swapped and shared tales about horses and famous races and contemplated the future for the local tracks with the uncertainty of war. We figured York would survive and probably Ripon and Thirsk but the smaller courses such as Stockton and Catterick might have to close for the duration. Alix knew of Lord William's death and we discussed the expected appointment of Budgett and whether his training methods were likely to differ from my father's.

I was suddenly aware of Tom leaning over the table. We'd not spoken for a while, in fact the last time I'd looked up he was arm wrestling with one of the locals.

'Ready for another chaps?'

I downed my drink including as much foam as I could tip out from the bottom and banged the empty glass on the table.

'Certainly am.'

'Alix? Same again?'

Alix grabbed my empty glass and clambered to his feet. 'No, no, it's my shout. We've gone round once. What'll it be?' I scanned our team and did a quick bit of arithmetic. Good Lord, so we had.

'What's this stuff we're drinking anyway?' I asked.

'It's called Lion bitter,' he replied as he gathered up the empties.

Tom studied his empty glass. 'What, Zion bitter? Never heard of it. Is it foreign?'

'No, not *Zion* bitter, *Lion* bitter. As in L-i-o-n. It's the local Camerons brew. Wonderful stuff don't you think?'

'I'm not sure,' I replied. 'I reckon I need a few more before I make up my mind'

'Well I don't,' cried Tom. 'I love it although at this rate we'll all be roaring drunk by the end of the night. Hah! Roaring drunk? Get it? *Lion* bitter? *Roaring* drunk?'

Well, when Tom said this it was one of those moments in your life where you absolutely crease yourself laughing until you find you can't stop. We couldn't help it, and the more we looked at each other the more the tears fell until it was virtually impossible to say anything at all. Neither did the hilarity end at our table as the quip sprouted wings until the whole bar was a cacophony of roaring and other jungle type noises. It was tremendous craic; even the sour faced landlady raised a smile, although as the evening went by and people continued to roar at her it probably started to wear a bit thin. Eventually when we managed to calm down, and believe me it took a while, Tom and I stumbled off to the gents where I lit a couple of Woodbines and passed him one.

'Fabulous idea this mate,' I said clutching the cistern pipe for support. 'Don't think I've had such a laugh in ages.'

Tom was swaying at an adjacent urinal, his eyes fixed on the trough where he was clearing a dam of cigarette butts.

'Agreed *Blue*, agreed. Just what the love doctor ordered.'

'Love doctor? Bah, don't remind me. I wonder what she's doing right now. Probably making cow eyes at some other poor sod. The way we left it she was supposed to come and stay with me next week. I guess I can put a red line through that.'

Tom Buttoned his fly and turned to the washbasins.

'Edmund, there's more chance of a nine-legged lobster jumping out of that urinal and grabbing the end of your dick than of Victoria showing her face when you get back. Mind you, I'd have said the same about your chances of sleeping with her and it seems I was wrong about that.'

A heavy boot at the door announced the entry of a couple of squaddies. Time to change the subject.

'When's the last train?'

Tom shrugged his shoulders.

'Dunno. Guess it leaves when it leaves doesn't it?'

His apathy was infectious.

'True. It wouldn't be the first time I'd spent the night in a waiting room. We should ask though. Perhaps Alix or Hallet can tell us.'

We returned to the bar to catch Hallet, fag in mouth, weaving his way to the table with a tray full of drinks. The beer was already sloshing over the sides when someone bumped him and a glass rolled off and smashed on the floor. Hallet shrieked a curse and immediately flung the lot to the ground – glasses, beer, tray *et al* – just like that. It was astonishing; I'd never seen anything like it. Needless to say a huge sarcastic cheer went up at which one of the barmaids – who fortunately for Hallet didn't witness the event – came scuttling round with a mop and shovel leaving him to go back to the counter and roar for another round.

Tom took a drag of his Woodbine and exhaled a clutch of smoke rings that passed through one another like the segments of a telescope. I watched mesmerized as the hoops slowly lolled towards the ceiling where a huge moth was orbiting the solitary light bulb. Over at the piano Hallet struck up *Daddy Wouldn't Buy Me a Bow Wow* generating the usual howling and barking to add to all the roars.

'Look Ed, I didn't mean to have a go at you back there outside the office, and I'm sorry if it came across that way. I was just a bit pissed off after everything we went through to get the file.'

'Hey, its not a problem. I'd have said pretty much the same if it had been you. I've been racking my brains working out how she did it. She must have rifled the safe when she slipped away this morning, the cow. Thing is, what do we do next?'

Tom took a large gulp and wiped the froth from his mouth.

'I suppose it depends if Crake means what he says about turning us in. Do you really think he'd do it?'

'I don't see he has a choice. If we refuse to cooperate, he'll have to apply to Court where everything would come out and the judge would want to know why he hadn't acted sooner. Faced with that unpalatable option plus the delay for a listing he must go to the police now, unless he can blackmail us first which is effectively what he's doing. He knows once we sign the agreement, he'll have us where he wants us and there'll never be any comeback.'

'Seems he has us where he wants us already.'

'It rather looks that way, doesn't it?'

Alix appeared with a fresh tray just as the landlady called last orders. Tom grabbed a glass and having drained the contents in a few gulps raced off to the counter to get them in again before the shutter came down. Meanwhile someone shouted from the dartboard for Alix and me to take our place at the okey. I'd not been following the game, but it appeared it was the deciding leg, both teams were down to the bull and the first person to get it took the match.

'What time's the last train to Durham?'

Alix threw and missed.

'If that's the bell I'm afraid you're too late. They leave on the hour and the last was at 2200. Sorry Ed. I should have said something before.'

'Don't worry about it. We were coming back tomorrow anyway.'

'Have you anywhere to stay?'

There was a tap on my shoulder. Someone passed me a set of darts.

'Not yet. We'll probably take a room at *The Havelock*.'

'What, the week before Christmas?' cried Alix. 'You'll be lucky, especially rolling up this time of night with a bellyful of beer on board. Why don't you doss down with us? I'm sure we can sneak you in and it's got to be better than roughing it.'

The player in front of me missed the target and it was now my turn. I shuffled to the okey trying to focus on the board through the predictable channel of oscillating humanity. The first dart was a tracer and missed by a mile. The next struck the outer bull and bounced out. Suddenly there was a hush. Last throw. I recalled the softness of Victoria's knees in Hob Hole and thought of her black heart and summing up all the bitter sweetness inside screamed her name to myself and hurled viciously at the board. A most extraordinary thing happened. The throw was so wild the flight came away leaving the featherless arrow to cartwheel through the air, until it somehow managed to lodge itself the wrong way round just inside the wire of the bull's-eye. If I hadn't been there to see it myself, I would never have believed it was possible but I tell you, that's exactly what happened. We all gaped at the board in astonishment until realising the angle was perilous and the dart could drop at any moment, I leaped forward and recovered it at which our little posse went crazy while everyone else in the bar screamed foul. In the mayhem that followed there was the usual pushing and shoving until eventually, one of the old timers was dragged through from the Snug to mediate. There was nothing in the rules, he said, that dictated which way round the dart had to enter the board nor how long it should linger in the matting, only that the projectile should pierce the intended section and remain there entrenched until it was retrieved by the participant. The throw was therefore good he said, an adjudication promptly endorsed by the landlady who, conscious of the hour, had her own reasons for ratifying it. And that as they say was that. Fluke or not we had prevailed and as if sufficient refreshment had not already been taken, to the inebriated victors went also the spoils and it was way after eleven when we tumbled into the street. As the door bolted behind us, I sucked in the cold air and gawked at the unfamiliar landscape. Where the hell were we? I hadn't a clue. Tom must have been of the same mind for he suddenly piped up the refrain of *How Much Is That Doggy?*

'Can somebody show me to my quarters? (woof!
woof!)
I haven't a clue where to go (woof! woof!)
Can somebody show me to my quarters? (woof! woof!
Vic-tor-i-a I love you so (WOOF! WOOF!)'

'Very funny. The *woof woof* bit was spot on though. Bah, when I think about her now, d'ye know what I think?'

'Nope. What do you think?'

'Woof! Woof!!' I yelled.

Tom looked up at the moon and howled.

Alix and Hallet locking arms on the outside hadn't the faintest idea what we were on about but joined the howling anyway as we clanked down Brougham Terrace with our crate of stout. Hallet was next to burst into song, I knew the words to this one and we all followed suit.

Show me the way to go home
I'm tired and I want to go to bed
I had a little drink about an hour ago and it went
right to my head,
No matter where I roam...

A couple of policemen scowled at us from the junction of Turnbull Street.

'Hoi you lot' barked one. 'If you don't put a sock in that caterwauling, you'll be roaming the glasshouse in the morning d'ye ken?'

We *kenned* all right and apologised profusely, all the time sniggering and 'shushing' as our tangle sloped off towards the harbour. As soon as we were clear, a couple of the lads began dribbling an empty milk bottle until it smashed against a warehouse door forcing us into the shadows in case there were any other bobbies around. At the quayside we paused to relieve ourselves against an old rusty winch. The water was at high tide and all the fishing boats were bobbing up and down. On the far side a couple of destroyers were building up steam for the dawn patrol. I stared down at the trails of urine snaking over the concrete as they merged and felt their way to the harbour edge. It was like a minuscule version of the Nile Delta we had studied in Geography. I reflected on the contrast and thought it bizarre how such an oblique comparison had only manifested itself in drink.

When we reached the Headland, we slipped through some twisted railings onto the Town Moor, a large area of spiky-silver pasture that glistered in a frost that turned to dust as it measured our footprints. Ahead of us the shore battery loomed menacingly on the point where the Heugh lighthouse tirelessly swept the old town, its beam cutting across Saint Hilda's churchyard and the small city of bell tents flapping away on the clifftop. We halted to pee again, this time over a giant roller on the edge of the heath. I leant back and gazed up to the sky. It was a crisp, clear night and as the six of us watered the ground there must have been a billion stars gazing down from space. Alix and the others went ahead to square things with the guards leaving Tom and me in the company of an old donkey that stumbled of the shadows to see what was going on. I felt his muzzle searching my pockets and scratched his ears.

'Hello little fellah, what's your name then?'

The donkey gave a soft bray as he tried to draw my handkerchief with his teeth. Tom pulled out a cut of liquorish and stroked his little woolly neck.

'According to Alix he was brought here from Blackhall Colliery at the end of his working days. He'd have been put down otherwise. Now he spends his old age giving rides to the children. The lads from the battery love him and are always coming over with apples and treats.'

Alix returned from the garrison with a flashlight.

'We're sorted. We can't get you into the compound but some of the NCO's are billeted round the corner and you can crash down with them.'

What a relief. The cold air had started to hit me and I was about done in. We bade a noisy farewell at the gates then Tom and I stumbled off with one of the batmen who came out to show us the way. Five minutes later we were tucked up in an attic room at the end of Bath Terrace watching the lighthouse beam sweep across the ceiling.

'Eight and a half seconds,' declared Tom.

'What is?'

'The time it takes to do a revolution.'

'Did Jane track you down after the hunt?'

'She did.'

'And?'

'And what?'

'How did you get on?'

'Very well. I'm meeting her at New Year.'

'Julian will go nuts.'

'Suppose so.'

We listened to the tide sloshing against the sea wall.

'Tell me something Ed, how did you manage it? I mean get Victoria into bed? How did you do it?'

'You wouldn't believe me if I told you.'

'Try me.'

'You'll only laugh.'

'Like you'll laugh at me when I run naked down York Shambles?'

I snorted loudly. I'd forgotten about that.

'Let's just say I thought a man with faith could move mountains. How wrong can you be, hey?'

'Don't be consumed by bitterness. You got what you wanted didn't you?'

'I wish I'd never met her.'

'I doubt that very much'.

'I mean it.'

'Look Ed, no one enjoys being turned over, but don't tell me the pain you feel now is as awful as the yearning that went before.'

'It's worse. I love her Tom. I can't help it, even after what she's done. My life wasn't great before she crashed into it but at least it was my own. Now it's in tatters.'

'No, it's not.'

'It's true. I'll never love anyone else.'

'Yes, you will.'

I counted the revolutions, all the while agonizing who Victoria might be sleeping with right now and if her partner knew she was still warm from going to bed with me.

'You're going to sign tomorrow, aren't you?' said Tom yawning.

'I don't see we have a choice. Do you?'

Tom grunted an acknowledgement.

'We'll stop off at Crake's first thing. Might as well do it on the way to the station. What do you think? Tom?'

Tom didn't answer. He was already snoring.

CHAPTER TWENTY-EIGHT

I dreamed I was lying in a field of corn being kicked by Sparks.

'Get up! Quickly! You have to get up!'

I stirred to unfamiliar surroundings, the blows persisting as I struggled to remember where I was.

'You have to get up! Get up! Get up!'

I wiped my eyes to see Alix stride over to the window and tear back the curtains.

'You've got to get out of here lads. Now. Tom, you as well. Quickly.'

I swung to the edge of the bed and fumbled for my boots. 'Good heavens Alix, what on earth's the matter?'

'I don't know yet. I thought it was just another drill, but we've been issued live ammunition.'

'What time is it?' asked Tom yawning.

'Seven fifty. We should have been stood down ages ago. Something's not right. You have to get out of here.'

Tom and I trailed Alex into the street where one of the orderlies ran up to him.

'*HMS Doon* reports unidentified vessels six miles off the headland, sir. Colonel Robson has called *Action Stations*.'

Alix frowned. 'It's probably another drill but the CO won't take any chances. You'd better get yourselves to the station lads, quick as you can, and I'll see you when I see you.'

Alix and the orderly raced across the heath and disappeared into a foxhole on top of the dunes. It was another hour before Crake's office opened so with time to kill, we merged with a few of the locals who had come out of their homes and were lining the railings. I scanned the horizon to see what all the fuss was about, but the light was poor with visibility restricted by spray and a rolling mist. Someone yelling through a bullhorn turned my attention to the three giant guns guarding the estuary, one just behind the lighthouse with a couple more poking out of the cliff near Alix's emplacement. I traced their long grey barrels pointing menacingly over the North Sea and realised the defences were even more formidable than they had appeared when we tumbled home the previous evening.

Tom stamped around blowing into cupped palms.

'Well I can't see a thing mate. Come on. Let's get a coffee somewhere. Its bloody freezing and I'm as bad as a dog.'

I couldn't see anything either. I wiped my eyes but there was nothing; just a blank canvass of waves spattered with a few white gulls. The far-off bells of St Aiden's chimed eight o clock. The sea air filled my lungs and I suddenly felt very hungry. We'd give it a couple more minutes then head into town and find a cafe.

Just then a clamour of excitement rippled along the wall.

'Ye Gods' said an elderly man next to me.

I turned back to the horizon where about a mile from the shore an enormous grey warship ghosted out of the mist. It was the largest, most magnificent vessel I had ever seen in my life, sleek as a whippet but with tier upon tier of huge guns and rigging so tall it scraped the overhanging bank of fog.

'A White Ensign!' said the old boy. 'Three cheers for His Majesty's navy'.

'Look' said Tom, 'there's another two Dreadnaughts behind it.'

Even as he spoke a second battlecruiser and then a third glided out of the mist and lined up behind the first with all three facing the town. For a moment we gazed at them spellbound until without warning, a massive orange flash erupted on the stern of the first vessel followed by a large explosion that engulfed the whole in a dense cloud of smoke.

'It's blown up!' cried a woman behind me. 'It's blown up! The ship's just blown up!'

I was about to say something when there was the most a terrific rushing noise like the sound of the wind passing through telegraph wires.

'Oh my God they're Germans!' yelled Tom. 'They're firing on us! The bastards are firing on us! Get down! Get down!

We plunged behind the wall just as the first shell smashed on top of Alix's foxhole where in appalling slow motion, the occupants were lifted high into the air before tumbling back to earth like rag dolls with bloody, mangled limbs. Amid the pitiful screams of the wounded someone bellowed for stretcher bearers but just as help reached them, a second salvo crashed down next to the first blowing everyone and everything to kingdom come. I gaped in disbelief at the smoking pit where Alix and his companions had been. We had only been talking to him a few minutes earlier and now there was nothing.

At the seawall everyone started running for their lives, the parents shepherding the little ones into what they thought would be the safety of their homes while out in the estuary, all three cruisers joined the slaughter with the largest exchanging volleys with the shore battery while the other two poured shells into the unsuspecting town. The noise was absolutely and utterly deafening; I'd never heard anything like it, each ear-splitting crack reverberating through the terraces like thunder, rattling all the windows and scattering the gulls. I watched mesmerized as a canister skimmed off the fortifications and burst at the back of the moor where it blew away the old donkey and his little timber home. Another projectile the size of a milk churn crashed through the roof of Saint Hilda's. I screamed at Tom to make for the railway station, but he was already ahead of me and as we sprinted down Cliff Terrace, I chanced a final look over my shoulder to see the sky filling with miniscule black orbs that grew bigger and bigger until they smashed into the streets around us tearing down buildings and sending debris and fragments of scorching, twisted metal fizzing through the air.

Tom and I ran like the wind not stopping for breath until we reached the junction of Northgate and Durham Street. Everywhere we looked it was the same pitiful scene of misery and confusion as in the absence of the men who had left for work, the terrified women and children rushed into the streets, many of them only half dressed. Looking back, they would have been safer indoors but oblivious to what was happening, their instinct was to get away at all costs, not realising they risked being blown to pieces in the open, as indeed many of them were.

We tore through the docks as fast as our legs could carry us, all the while stalked by the merciless *swee swee swee* of destruction raining down from the skies, and how we were not killed that morning like so many others is a mystery that I have never been able to comprehend. All through the town, between the Headland and the railway station, buildings were being toppled like stacks of cards while in the harbour several vessels were hit including a new steamer which was struck in the hull, the shell passing in at one side and out at the other. Bizarrely, I don't remember being so much afraid as utterly overwhelmed with a sense of excitement that had neither fear nor horror in it, because it was too full of awe.

We left the quayside behind and raced by shops and houses all completely destroyed with furniture and people blown into the road and, in one case, a bloodstained bed blasted onto the roof. A tramway office between the two Hartlepools and the headquarters of the *Northern Daily Mail* was completely wrecked, a telegraph pole in front of the latter carried away in an eruption of earth and masonry as if it were matchwood. Another shell smashed into the side of the *Mill House Inn* barely seconds after we had passed, totally obliterating the frontage of the building before crashing through a party wall to bring down the house next door. Everywhere around us it was the same: nothing but destruction and misery as the westward road out of town started to choke with tearstained women and children running for their lives, many of them still in the nightclothes they were wearing when the attack began.

As we rounded the corner into Brougham Terrace we came across an upturned milk float where the still harnessed pony was struggling to get to its feet. The beautifully painted cart to which he was attached had splintered like balsa, while a shard of glass had lodged in the animal's throat from which blood was spraying over the smashed bottles and eggs. I ran across and put my fist in the wound to try and stem the flow but as I frantically looked about for a tourniquet, the animals' eyes misted over and I could only watch helplessly and cradle him as he expired.

In Dene Street a whole section of terrace had collapsed, and we could hear the most appalling cries coming from under the rubble. There was already a human chain in place and as we frantically clawed away with the others, I became aware of a small group of children standing over a bundle of rags further down the pavement. We screamed at them to get inside but they refused to move so I ran across to discover a boy rolling what looked like a side of butcher's meat with his foot. He could only have been about seven or eight and was holding hands with a young girl who cried repeatedly it was her 'da'. I looked to the ground and realised she was pointing at the top section of a man's leg with crushed bones and tattered flesh. Her brother wailed that the rest of the body 'was blown into Middleton Road'. I swept the children up and ran into the nearest house where I passed them to the occupants who were taking cover under the dining table.

The shell in Dene Street caused great execution and as I blenched at the carnage around me, I realised the device had been invented for this very purpose, to be dispatched into populated areas and there to burst and tear flesh from flesh and destroy peoples' homes. It was an utterly cowardly and inhumane thing of the Germans to do, it sickened me to the core and like many others who witnessed the slaughter, I determined to enlist as soon as I could. We had been brought up on swashbuckling tales of the Boer War, patriotism and heroics, but the bloodstained streets of Hartlepool were reality and from that moment, every glorious notion of combat with which I had been indoctrinated was vanquished forever.

When we reached the station there were so many others converging that those at the head of the crush were tumbling through the barriers and onto the track. A train was on the point of leaving and a guard was actually running down the carriages slamming the doors when a ghostly whooshing noise sent everyone scrambling for cover. I looked to the skies to see the first missile overshoot the terminal and land in the sidings where it threw a string of trucks into the air as if they were toys. A second shell headed straight for us, spinning over and over but just as I braced myself for the end, it clanged off the road and smashed through the station wall onto the platform where, incredibly, it failed to explode. I watched helplessly as through the dust and flying bricks, the terrified passengers leaped out of their carriages and ran blindly down the track. At the same time the horrified mass outside the station turned and charged back into town, panic ensuing as amid the crashing of further shells, masonry falling and glass breaking came also the petrified screams of the men, women and children.

Several areas of the town were now on fire and with the railway out of action, escape was impossible. We didn't know how long the bombardment would last, or indeed if the country was about to be invaded. The only certainty was that if we remained above ground, we were going to be killed and it was as we tore along Church Street looking for a basement that we came upon the wrecked offices of *Baxter, Crake and Lockwood*.

CHAPTER TWENTY-NINE

The damage to the lawyers' premises was so severe that it was almost impossible to equate what was left of the building to the scene of our Waterloo but a few hours before. The striking Georgian fascia had all but vanished, the remnants condensed into a stew of bricks and timber completely exposing the interior, with all the furniture within battered and broken like a dolls house on the wrong end of a child's temper tantrum. A fire was raging in one of the downstairs rooms and billows of thick black smoke were spewing into the road together with hundreds and hundreds of papers and documents, some of which were picked up by the wind and sent spiralling over the rooftops. I looked at Tom. He was totally caked in blood and filth but even as I motioned to the ruins, I knew he was of the same mind. I scanned the street. Some people at the top were trying desperately to corner a runaway horse but there was no one else in sight. It was now or never. The opportunity would not come again. I clambered into the empty fascia, Tom following on, both of us knowing that at any second what remained of the building might come crashing down and entomb us.

We groped our way through the dust and smoke until we reached the staircase. The planks and spindles were already smouldering in the heat; it was only a matter of time before they, too, caught fire but there was no other way up. Without pausing for breath, we raced to the top hurdling a section of staircase as it collapsed before us. In the lopsided corridor, the exterior wall was blown out and we were soaked by a deluge of water cascading down from the attic. Crake's office lay before us. I tried the handle. It was locked.

'We can't give up now' yelled Tom. 'Come on. Kick it down!'

We were greeted by a scene of utter devastation. All the windows were blown in, the furniture and panelling reduced to matchwood while several beams and most of the alabaster ceiling had collapsed on top of the files and documents giving the chamber the appearance of an enormous builder's skip. Attempting to locate the Fitzroy-Cavendish trust papers among such disarray would have been impossible save that incredibly, the black metal strongbox in which they were retained was still intact by the wreckage of the grandfather clock, exactly where Glyder had left it.

A few streets away there was an almighty roar as the gasworks went up blowing in the remainder of the glass. All the while the crackle of flame from downstairs grew louder.

'Hurry man!' yelled Tom. 'The whole place is about to go!'

I tipped the box and plunged into the contents, pausing at a wad of birth and death certificates which I threw over .

'Check these.'

A projectile suddenly crashed through the roof of the tobacconist on the other side of the road. There was the most tremendous explosion followed by a tidal wave of dust and debris that washed over the street engulfing the office through the void where the window had been.

'Hurry' spluttered Tom. 'We've got to get out of here. It's not worth dying for!'

'Okay Okay. I'm nearly done.'

Half choking and with eyes streaming I clawed furiously through the pile. There were now all sorts of documents blowing about and there was so much smoke and dust it was difficult to see anything. An ear-piercing howl like a passing express train heralded yet another close call as the blaze from downstairs licked the doorway. I was just about to give up when all of a sudden, the codicil I had been looking for ghosted in front of me. I blew off the dust and muck. It was dated Tuesday 20 October 1914.

'I've got it! I've got it!'

I rattled through the text. It was not a long document.

I, Lieutenant-Colonel William Surtees Fitzroy-Cavendish, 6th Marquis of Craven, CVO OBE TD DL of Craven Park in the country of Durham being of sound mind, memory and understanding do hereby make this codicil to my existing Will dated 16th day of April nineteen hundred and five...

'He changed his Will! He's changed it! Tom? Tom?'

Tom was absorbed with his own sheath of documents.

'You need to see this.'

I ignored him and leapt back to the text.

I make the following specific amendments

Clause 1

I direct that the Craven Racing Stables and Equine Stud Company shall continue to be managed after my death by the said James Michael Bullick or if he shall predecease me or otherwise be unable to accept the appointment, I direct that the said enterprise shall be offered to the said Edmund James Bullick ...

'Tom, he's chosen me to succeed as trainer!'

Another shell burst on the road bringing down the tram lines.

'Did you hear me, Tom?'

'Yes, yes! But come and look at this!'

'Hang on. Hang on.'

Clause 2

I hereby revoke clause thirty-seven of my original Will and direct that the residue of my estate including all land, livestock, buildings, shares and chattels and all other investments in Great Britain and overseas, and all other property, possessions and personal chattels, whatsoever and wheresoever ...

'He changed the succession!'

'Ed, you have to look at this!'

...together with the hereditary seat, the castle and grounds of Craven, and title of Marquis I devise and bequeath to my son...

'He changed it!' I screamed. 'We were right! He's changed it!'

Tom grabbed my shoulders and shook me violently.

'Will you shut up! Just shut up! Look at this. LOOK AT THIS!'

I snatched a birth certificate from his hand and jumped to the principals. William Fitzroy-Cavendish was one. Derina Bullick was the other. I stared at the name to the side and then back to the codicil.

Oh my God.

Alfred Michael Bullick.

THE RAVEN
AND
THE PIPE

CHAPTER ONE

A t last. North Lodge.
A ruddy pool spilled from the window of the keeper's cottage.

'This is it. Sound the horn!'

Tom leaned through from the back.

'Come on pal! The horn, the horn!'

Our driver glanced across resignedly, ash tumbling from the cigarette bobbing in the corner of his mouth. Looking back, I felt a bit sorry for the guy. We'd been on his case since we'd flagged him down at Durham station.

A couple of toots brought out old Amos who shuffled across the gravel and raised his flashlight. I pulled down the window.

'It's me, Amos. Open the gates! We have to get back to the house!'

The old man stared at the mask of dust and filth.

'Mister Edmund? Good grief lad. You look dreadful.'

'We've just come from Hartlepool. We were on the front this morning when the Germans shelled the town. There could be an invasion!'

'So, it's true then?'

'Aye, it's true. I'll tell you about it later but please, we have to get back to the house.'

Amos fished for his keys and unravelled the heavy shackle. As soon as the gap was wide enough the driver crunched into gear and we shot beneath the old stone arch and into the estate.

'It's another mile yet. Put your foot down.'

'You got it bonnie lad.'

We tore through the park scattering deer and clouds of rooks that had nestled in the treetops for the night. Curls of mist rolled over the trout lakes as in the half-light, the murky skeleton of Craven Castle rose slowly out of the ground.

'Please hurry. There's no time to lose.'

The familiar *woof* of the cattle grid announced our arrival as we swung into the stable courtyard and drew up outside my father's house. I leaped from the vehicle. My brother, who had been looking out from the window, was already halfway down the path with Domino, Dad's old black lab stumbling along behind. Alfie's little body trembled as he threw his arms around me.

'Edmund?' he shrieked and then backed away as he took in the sludge and filth. I'd forgotten I was still caked in blood from the milkman's pony.

'Are you hurt? Oh, my goodness. Is it really you? I've been beside myself! And Tom? I thought you'd been killed! I thought you were dead!'

I raked the yard. There was no one else about.

'Hey, don't cry. Come on now. It's all right; we're a bit roughed up but we're fine.'

'I thought you weren't coming back' he sobbed. 'I'd given up. I thought you were dead.'

'No, we're not dead' I whispered. 'We're very much alive but God only knows how. Are you on your own?'

'Yes, but Barnaby's been down here looking for you. He says he needs to speak to you urgently, but he won't say what it's about. We've also had a burglary in Dad's office, everything's smashed up and then this afternoon the police were here looking for you. I've been so worried. I didn't know what to do. I explained you were at the lawyers in Hartlepool, but I couldn't tell them anything else. I didn't think you were coming back. I thought you'd been killed.'

I reached for Alfie's shoulders.

'Whoa stop. Stop. You're going too quickly. Now take a deep breath, start again and tell me what happened.'

Alfie nodded as he wiped his eyes.

'Good. Now tell me about the police first. Who's been here you say? PC Ball from the village?'

'No, not him. Two plain clothes men from Durham I've never seen before. They were horrible Edmund. They kept asking questions about where you and Tom were on the night of Julian's party. I told them I didn't know as I was away at school, but they kept asking. They waited for over an hour and said they'd be back. Hang on, one of them left his card. Here it is.'

I stared at the print.

Inspector Mark Honeyman
Criminal Investigation Department
City of Durham Constabulary

I didn't like the look of this at all.

'Apparently they want to speak to you about a burglary at Dryburn Hospital a couple of weeks ago.'

My heart sank.

The police were on to us.

But how?

Crake. It had to be Crake, the bent solicitor. Apart from Victoria who will have tipped him off, no one else knew what we'd done. And there he was only yesterday promising to wipe the slate if I signed the agreement. What a serpent.

'Did they say anything else?'

'Yes. You are to report to Old Elvet police station as soon as you return. Why do they want to see you Edmund and what's this about Dryburn? You're not in any trouble, are you?'

'It's obviously some kind of mistake'.

'They were most insistent' said Alfie inquiringly.

'What? Like the *Keystone Cops*?'

We laughed. I studied the card again and slipped it in my pocket.

'Look, it's clearly a misunderstanding. I'll go and see - what's he called - Honeyman? I'll go and see Inspector Honeyman when I'm next in town and find out what he wants.'

My brother's head tilted at the unexpected lack of urgency.

'I'll deal with it, Alfie. There's nothing to worry about, really.'

'Well, I'm glad for it because I didn't care for the chap at all. He might be a policeman but what a creep. Horrible. Anyhow, enough about him. Tell me about Hartlepool this morning? What on earth happened? It might be twenty miles away but as soon as we heard the crash of gunfire, everyone ran outside wondering what was going on. Harry

Sample said it must be the Royal Navy practising but later in the morning old Mr Cobb cycled up from the post office and told us German battleships were shelling the town. Is it true? We couldn't believe it at first then I remembered you and Tom were seeing Mr Crake and when you didn't come home, I thought you'd been killed!'

'How we got out I'll never know. Many others were not so fortunate. Alfie, it was terrible. There were dozens- scores more like- simply blown to bits in the street. Blood and guts everywhere. Dead people and body parts strewn all over the place, most of them women and children. I've never seen anything so awful. Houses flattened, buildings smashed like matchwood. It was dreadful, truly dreadful, the deliberate cold-blooded murder of innocent people going about their everyday lives. We were incredibly lucky to have escaped but look, I'll tell you more later. Right now, I need to settle up with the driver. Also, we've had nothing to eat or drink all day and I'm dying for a cup of tea. Can you go into the kitchen and put the kettle on? I'll be through in a minute.'

Tom was by the taxi smoking a cigarette with the driver. I beckoned him over.

'The police know about Dryburn.'

'What?'

'They were here this afternoon grilling Alfie.'

My friend took a long drag as he processed the unwelcome news.

'Crake must have told them' he said at length. 'After all the assurances he gave as well. Thank goodness you didn't sign the assent.'

'My thoughts exactly although I never imagined we'd be grateful to the Germans for anything. Problem is, what are we going to do now? The police could be back at any moment. We need to think, and we need to think fast.'

Tom took another deep draw.

'There's no choice' he said. 'You have to get Alfie out of here as quickly as possible'.

He was right.

'Look. Go and hold the cab. Ask the driver if he wants a cup of tea or something and I'll see you in the house.'

My brother was filling the kettle.

'Alfie, are any of the family in residence? I need to know.'

'Why? What's the matter?'

'Just tell me Alfie. Who's at the castle?'

'Just Barnaby and the staff. Julian is in Alnwick shooting with the Percys. Lady Alanna and Jane are still in Belgravia.'

They weren't back. Thank the Lord for that. We had time. Not much time, but it should be enough.

'I don't understand all this urgency' my brother continued 'but before you go on, as I said, we've been burgled. While you were away someone broke into the office.'

'What? Show me.'

In the corner of my father's study the heavy iron door to the safe was sloping on a single hinge. Books and documents were scattered all over the carpet. A crowbar I recognised from the tool shed lay nearby.

'It must have been a rushed job' said Alfie. 'Either that or the thieves were disturbed.'

Or they knew what they were looking for…

'I found it like this when I returned from Ampleforth last night' he continued. 'Dad's only been dead a couple of weeks. You wonder what kind of person could do something like this?'

My heart ached as I surveyed the chaos. My father's private papers were strewn all over the floor together with boxes of shotgun cartridges and tranquilisers for the horses. The only thing missing was his little purse of gold sovereigns. That and the Coroner's file Tom and I had gone to such lengths to extricate from Dryburn mortuary. And the deciphered page from my father's journal where he had tried to warn us about Julian. These were missing too although I'd known that much as soon as Crake sprung his trap. What I didn't understand was why Victoria should smash the place up when she'd had free run of the house? I mean, I'd been dead to the world when she'd let herself out the previous morning and if she were going to steal anything, surely that was her opportunity? And to use a crowbar? She wasn't strong enough unless there was someone helping her. But then why force the safe at all when she knew where I kept the key?

I rushed to the sideboard and dipped inside the Gimcrack Cup. The key was still there. A peculiar feeling swept over me. Maybe Victoria wasn't responsible after all and not for the first time I'd misjudged her. But then someone must have told Crake we burgled the mortuary and if it wasn't her, then who else could it have been? My mind was racing as Alfie led us through the scullery and pointed to the back door.

'As you can see, they smashed their way in here. We're going to need a new door and probably a new frame by the look of it.'

I surveyed the damage. A large panel was fractured, and I could see right through into the vegetable garden at the back.

'This is dreadful. What did the police say? I assume you showed Inspector Honeyman the damage?'

'I did, but he wasn't interested. He said you would have to attend the station and make a formal complaint.'

'Incredible. There's been a burglary, a safe is forced, money and documents stolen and he doesn't want to know?'

Alfie stepped into the void and poked his head back through the splintered hole.

'I was surprised as well but not his department apparently. Do you know, you hear about property being ransacked when the owner dies but I never dreamt it could happen to us. Look at the damage. I hope we're insured. We'd better let Mr Crake know. I don't suppose with the German attack you managed to sort out Lord William's legacy?'

Tom peered up from his haunches from where he was trying to piece together some of the larger fragments.

'Actually, your brother and I met with Mr Crake yesterday afternoon but I'm afraid he wasn't very helpful.'

Alfie swept the dust from his jacket as he clambered through from outside.

'Really? I thought you said you were impressed with him at the reading of the Will?'

'I *was* impressed' I answered. 'Lord William's solicitor is an impressive man but I'm afraid he doesn't have our family's interests at heart. In the end- although it was no thanks to Mr Crake- we left his office with everything we could have hoped for and more, but we have a bit of a problem.'

'A problem with what? You make it sound as if you are in some sort of trouble.'

'I wouldn't call it trouble exactly but while we were in Hartlepool, Tom and I discovered something which we need to bring to the attention of the authorities.'

There was a hiss as Alfie placed the kettle on the stove.

'What do you mean?'

'I mean that while we were in the solicitor's office, we discovered that just before he died, Lord William disinherited Julian and made another Will.'

Alfie looked at me in astonishment.

'Disinherited Julian? Their only son? My goodness. They kept that quiet.'

'They did more than keep it quiet. They tried to keep it a secret but there can be no mistake. We took the new Will away with us. I have it here in this envelope.'

'Did Mr Crake give it to you? If it was supposed to be a secret, I'm surprised he handed it over.'

'He didn't' said Tom. 'We discovered it in in his office when we took shelter there during the bombardment.'

'But that's stealing. He's certain to find out. What if he goes to the police?'

'He won't' I replied. 'His office burned down in the raid and he'll assume these documents went up with everything else. By the time he realises they didn't it'll be too late for him to do anything about it.'

'Why? What are you going to do with them?'

'*We're* not going to do anything. We'll simply take the papers and what we know to the authorities and let them deal with it. We just need to find someone around here that we can trust.'

Alfie emerged from the larder clutching a bottle of milk.

'Why not give them to Inspector Honeyman when you go to the police station? You could report the burglary while you're down there.'

'I'd thought of that but we can't involve Durham police at the moment. The city coroner, Lockwood, is Crake's business partner and I don't trust him. No, we'll have to take this out of the area but until we decide who to, we need to keep the documents somewhere safe. We also need to get out of Durham for a while. It wouldn't be for long, just until things settle down.'

My brother looked at me in bewilderment.

'Go away? But where to? You've only just come back and its Christmas next week.'

'I'm taking you to Ireland' I replied. 'We'll spend Christmas with the O'Hares.'

'What, Fergus O'Hare?'

'That's right. He invited us over at Dad's funeral if you remember?'

'But I want to stay here.'

'I wish we could but it's too risky. Look Alfie, you asked me a minute ago if we were in any trouble. The answer is we could be and if the police are on the warpath, you can bet your last farthing they'll be back and I'm damned if I'm going to get locked up leaving you at Craven on your own. We head for Tipperary first thing tomorrow. I'll square things with Inspector Honeyman later.'

Alfie poured the tea in silence regarding me with a mixture of alarm and anticipation.

'You scare me when you talk like this Edmund. I'm worried what you and Tom have got yourselves into. Worried, but sort of excited at the same time.'

'It's nothing we can't handle but we want you somewhere safe before we take action. Now look, there's not a moment to lose. Take your drink upstairs and start packing your things while I sort the taxi out. I'll join you in a minute and we'll talk some more over supper. Promise.'

Alfie looked at me uncertainly.

'If you're sure it's for the best then I'll do as you say. What about Domino?'

'I'll leave a note for Sample. He'll look after him at the Smithy.'

'And Barnaby? Will you see him before we depart?'

'No. I'll leave him a note as well although I won't say where we're going. Just that we're staying with friends for a while.'

Tom kept quiet until Alfie's footsteps were thumping overhead.

'Ireland is a sound plan. The police will never look for you over there. But what about the codicil and birth certificate? If they fall into the wrong hands we'll never see them again.'

'You're right of course. I was going to lock them in Dad's vault but that's clearly out of the question. There's nowhere else secure here and the papers are too precious to carry around.'

'What about Barnaby?' asked Tom. 'He seems pretty straight. You said yourself he's the nearest thing to family you have left.'

'No. As head steward his first loyalty is to his employer who with the death of Lord William, is now Julian. If we confide in him, he's bound to be conflicted. Suppose we took a chance and he spills the beans? You remember what Crake said. We're already looking at five years for the Dryburn break-in. Five years! Heck Tom, if we get five years for that, what do you suppose we'd get for looting the solicitor's office during the bombardment?'

My friend took another deep drag and furred his brow.

'Indeed. We could expect little mercy and I'm not sure how close Barnaby is to Lady Alanna. You must have seen them dancing together at Julian's party? Lord William and your father barely in their graves as well. She came across like one of those African lionesses you read about, you know, who go and mate again the instant the old king is dead. *Weird.*'

I recalled the awkward way Lady Alanna had addressed me that same evening. Had she been involved with my father? Was she involved with Barnaby? Perhaps. Whatever the truth the mere possibility ruled him out and we had to find someone else. I racked my brain. Who else we could trust? Damn it. There had to be someone. But who? Who? And then suddenly it came to me.

'Conway!' I exclaimed. 'We'll give the papers to Conway. He can be trusted; you know he can. We won't need to tell him what's in the sachet either, just that documents are vitally important, and he must look after them until we get back.'

Tom exhaled through a cloud of smoke.

'Of course. *One-way Conway.* Just the man. He'll be working in his father's taxi office this very evening I shouldn't wonder?'

'He's bound to be. Oh, why didn't we think of this before? Look, it's what? Four fifty? Right. Here's what we do. You take the taxi now and get yourself back to Durham. There's just enough time to square things with Conway and catch the last train home. Alfie and I will head for Liverpool in the morning. I'll wire O'Hare first thing to let him know.'

Tom twisted his cigarette into the gravel.

'I'll go to it now. I need to catch up with my folks who'll be worrying what's become of me. How long do you suppose you'll be away?'

'I'll see Christmas through then get the ferry back. Alfie will stay on until we've delivered Crake to the authorities. Seven, ten days maybe? What say we meet back in Durham on New Year's Eve?'

'New Year's Eve it is' replied Tom before continuing mischievously 'I'm seeing Jane that night and who knows? We might even run into the enchanting Victoria.'

Victoria. The very word thrilled me as I remembered the scent of her perfume. The whisper of her breath. The warmth of her skin. Victoria. Even though she had betrayed me I wanted nothing more than to see her again. What was happening to me? Is this what it's like to be in love? Is this how love is supposed to be?

'Edmund?'

I snapped back to reality.

'Sorry. You were saying?'

'I said you, Jane and I could go out on New Year's Eve and who knows, we might even run into Victoria.'

'Hardly. She'll be long gone, back to the city lights from whence she came. And d'you know what? The really galling thing is that when she slipped off yesterday, she actually left a note to say she'd be back next week. Imagine that, hey? Lady Muck consorting with the *hoi polloi*? I don't know what rips me up more Tom, her leading me down the garden path or me allowing myself to be led. I'm such a fool. How could I be so blind?'

'I don't think you were blind. Dazzled maybe, and yes, she tricked you. But blind? No. And anyway having seen that mess in your father's office, I'm not so sure she was responsible.'

'Of course it was her. Who else knew we took the Coroner's file let alone where to find it?'

'True. But a crowbar? And all that damage? Hardly the work of the fairer sex.'

'There must have been someone with her. But never mind Victoria. Let's get back to New Year's Eve. By my reckoning that's two weeks tonight. Where shall we meet?

We were at the vehicle. I motioned to the driver who climbed into the cab and pulled at the passenger door. Tom whispered softly.

'Not here. If the police are onto us this is the first place they'll look. No. It had better be somewhere in town. How about *The Shakespeare* on North Bailey? I'm on good terms with the landlord there.'

'Fair enough. *The Shakespeare* it is. Shall we say New Years' Eve 4pm?'

Tom buried the sachet of papers deep inside his coat.

'4pm it is.'

The driver started the engine.

We shook hands.

'And Merry Christmas!' I yelled after the vehicle, although it was already rattling over the grid and I don't suppose he heard me.

CHAPTER TWO

Alfie and I slipped away in the early hours. I'd secured the services of the driver from the previous evening but wary of being traced, I devised a story about a tending a sick relative and asked to be taken to Chester-Le-Street market. As soon as the taxi was out of sight we walked down to the station and boarded the first train to Liverpool. I thought we would never get there. Every coach was packed with soldiers and we spent the whole journey rammed up against the toilet door. I don't think I can ever remember being so cold. There was no heating where the carriages connected and as the wind whipped up the snowflakes outside, we huddled under my greatcoat to try and keep warm.

It was dark when we finally drew into Lime Street. A Salvation Army band was playing carols under an enormous Christmas tree and I recall how Alfie, who had never been to Liverpool, craned his neck to the cathedral like proportions of the terminal. There was no blackout in those early days of the war. Most people had never heard of a Zeppelin let alone seen one. We fought our way through the crowds and steam and purchased two tickets for the overnight ferry to Dublin.

The tram to Pier Head was also crammed with everyone staring vacuously out of the window as they gripped the infrastructure to ride the contours of the track. It was only a few days before Christmas and with so many scheduled and unscheduled halts in the crowded streets, it would probably have been quicker to walk. After what seemed an age, we alighted at the City of Dublin Steam Packet terminal and joined the queue threading their way aboard *RMS Leinster*. Little did we know it but the vessel would be torpedoed later in the war with the loss of hundreds of passengers just like ourselves. However, this was December 1914 and the unrestricted U Boat campaign that so nearly broke the country was- like the Zeppelins - a terror of the future and as everyone settled down that night, the possibility we might be attacked didn't even cross our mind.

We slipped into Dublin in the early hours and caught the train to Thurles where the tiny figure of O'Hare was waiting outside the station with a horse and trap.

'Lads, lads, welcome to Tipperary!' he cried excitedly as he strode towards us 'I received yer telegram this morning and am delighted you could make it, so I am. How was yer crossing?'

O'Hare was a good friend of my father in the 1880's when they were apprentice riders in Kilkenny. When Dad grew too tall for the job and moved to England to train for Lord William, O'Hare continued riding eventually becoming stable jockey for the Earl of Shannon for whom he won two Irish Derbies. When he finally lost his battle against weight and injury, he had enough put away to retire to the family farm near the village of Holycross where he now trained a small string of his own.

The suspension of the trap dipped as O'Hare clambered aboard and pulled me and Alfie onto the bench beside him.

'Now, Edmund me lad, as I said to yer at yer father's funeral, Judy and I couldn't bear the thought of sitting down to Christmas dinner knowing that on the other side of the watter, you and yer brother were by yerselfs.'

'I can't thank you enough, Mr O'Hare. It's been awful with Dad dying and we're so glad to get out of Durham, if only for a while.'

'Ha. Say nothing of the kind lad' he answered cracking his whip. 'It's our pleasure. And call me Fergus. Yer father Jimmy was a very good friend to me when I was starting out and having yer both to stay is the very least I can do. Morgan is making up your room and it should be ready by the time we get back. But tell me, what made you come early? Don't get me wrong lad, I'm overwhelmed to see yer both and yer welcome to stay as long as yer like but we wasn't expecting yers until next week.'

'I had to get away' I replied. 'I was in Hartlepool yesterday morning when the Germans shelled the town. There's talk of an invasion. You must have heard?'

'Aye, news reached the village last night. The bastards pounded Whitby and Scarborough an' all you know? We could scarcely believe it, the murdering scumbags. And you say you were actually there?'

'I was. Purely by chance a friend and I were in town to see the family solicitor. We should have gone home the night before, but we bumped into some pals and decided to stay over. Early next morning we were making our way to the station when the Germans appeared on the horizon and started firing.'

'What? Just like that?

'It was unbelievable. These three massive battleships loomed out of the fog and began pouring shells into the town. I tell you Fergus, you had to see it to believe it. It was like an abattoir. The terrified people -mostly women and children because the men were at work- they stood no chance and were literally blown to pieces when they ran out of their homes to see what was going on.'

A watery sun peeked through the clouds and lit the frosted pasture. It took O'Hare by surprise and he brought his hand to his forehead as we rattled over a small stone bridge and headed into the open country.

'So it's true then? The swine. I blame that bloody Kaiser of theirs. He aint right in the head, you know. War mad he is- so long as it's not him doing the fighting of course. His cousin, that Russian Tsar fellow, he's just as bad. It's what happens to families when there's no thinning of the blood. They aint balanced proper. You see it with horses. Interbreed them and you never break them in. How did you get away?'

'Pure luck. The killing was that indiscriminate. As we ran through the streets people around us were blasted clean off their feet, right up into the air and then landing like rag dolls. If our name had been on any one of those shells, we would have been done for as well. As it was, we took refuge in a burned out building but when it began to crumble around us, I swore at that moment that if the good Lord spared us, I would go straight home, gather Alfie and we'd get the hell out of it.'

O'Hare whistled softly and shook his head.

'Holy mother of God! I ask yer, what sort of war is it when the women and bairns are on the front line? The lads in the village, they were talking about it in the pub last night. Many have family in England and are joining up.'

'I've a mind to do the same. I'm supposed to go to Cambridge in the New Year but having witnessed what I saw yesterday, I don't see how I can.'

O'Hare slowed as we cut through a string of about a dozen horses. The riders were known to him and he exchanged a few words with the lad at the front. When they filed through, he flicked the reins and we broke back into a trot.

'Well Edmund me boy' he said brightly 'Have you and yer brother had anything to eat?'

I confessed we had not.

'You'll be famished then' he continued. 'Judy and I thought as much. 'Do you know Fergus', she said to me when I left, 'those poor lads will be half starving after the crossing. You go and fetch them while I put the breakfast on.'

'I'm so hungry I could eat a scabby donkey' said Alfie.

O'Hare laughed. 'I think we can do better than that young 'un. Anyhow you'll soon see because we're nearly there.'

He was true to his word. Holycross was only a short ride from the station and after a few minutes we arrived at the farm. I was in for a shock. Even though I was used to the splendour of the training facilities at Craven, I knew a rundown establishment when I saw one. The first sign was several boarded-up windows in the main house and bits and pieces of old farm machinery left to rust where they had broken down. There was a decent sized ménage to exercise the horses, but the sand was overgrown, and the modest row of boxes had tiles missing from the roof with tufts of yellowy grass poking out of the gutters. The access road too was in obvious disrepair and as we bumped over the potholes, I couldn't help noticing several old, rather scraggy looking horses standing around in the front field.

We drew up outside the porch. O'Hare jumped down and threw the bridle to a waiting groom.

'Welcome to *Suirbanks* lads. Now please, before we go in, I want you to promise me you'll treat this place just like you would your own home.'

'Thank so much' I replied casting a final look over the field. 'Tell me Fergus, are they your horses?'

O'Hare reached for the door.

'The ones at the front are all retired or long term injured. Its Morgan you see, she can't help it, she keeps taking in everyone else's worn out animals. She can't bear the thought of them going to the hounds at the local hunt.'

'It can be a difficult decision. We all have our favourites.'

'We do indeed' sighed Fergus 'but taking so many will be the ruin of us I shouldn't wonder.'

'The horses we passed on the road. There were some good-looking animals among them. Are they all National Hunt?'

'They are lad. We've a couple of entries at Thurles on Boxing Day and we're getting as much roadwork into them as we can.'

'You do right. Dad was the same with the Craven horses when the fields were too icy or muddy. He always said roadwork was good because the change of scenery kept the horses interested while getting them used to different types of footing.'

'Aye, true enough. The only problem is with the recent bad weather most of ours are short of work. There's nothing wrong with them but it's less than a week until Thurles and we're desperate to get them ready. I know it's not why I invited yer but can I ask yer, while yer here, would the two of yer mind mucking in a bit with the lads?'

O'Hare's entreaty was music to our ears. There was nothing we could have wished for more and our collaboration was settled in a moment.

'I never doubted it fellahs' laughed O'Hare 'but I thought I'd ask just the same. Yer father Jimmy always said you were grand little riders. In fact, Edmund, he told me that if you weren't so determined on becoming a vet, you were in line for stable jockey.'

'I wouldn't take too much notice of that. My father tended to exaggerate.'

'That he did, but he was always earnest when he spoke about his boys. He was very proud of you, you know.'

O'Hare's wife Judy, a short, well-built woman with a ruddy complexion fluttered around us like a mother hen.

'Boys! Boys! I'm so pleased to see you' she squealed. 'How was your journey? Are you warm enough? Here Fergus darlin', throw a shovel of coal on the fire. You poor things, crossing over on a day like this. You must be frozen and half starving. Please, please, sit yourselves down and I'll cook breakfast while Morgan takes your bags. Morgan? Oh, where's Morgan when I need her? Ah, Morgan sweetheart, come over here and meet Edmund and Alfie who have come to stay for a while. The boys are sons of your father's old friend Jimmy Bullick – you'll remember Dad travelled to England for his funeral last month?'

Morgan couldn't have been more than eighteen and when she held out her hand, she fixed us with striking pale green eyes that reminded me of a cat. Her skin was also surprisingly soft and I thought her unusually pretty with a cascade of auburn hair that nearly reached the floor. She looked at us shyly then without speaking a word, grabbed our cases and scuttled off upstairs. Fergus exchanged a knowing glance with his wife.

'Don't be put off boys' he laughed. 'We don't get many strangers here.'

Breakfast consisted of boiled ham, poached eggs and freshly made bread lifted from the hearth, the sum washed down with several large mugs of tea and I don't think I'd ever tasted a more welcome meal. Afterwards Morgan reappeared and we followed her in silence to a small bedroom fashioned into the loft which was to be our home for the next few weeks. The window had a commanding view over the river and through the haze I could just make out the Knockmealdown Mountains. However, it was the walls that interested me. They hung with a multitude of rosettes, jockeys' silks and in the corner a grainy photograph of O'Hare in his younger days and a small boy, the two standing either side of a dapple pony. All three were looking straight into the camera, the horses' ears pricked and O'Hare and the lad both smiling. The boy clutched a small silver trophy and I wondered who he was because I understood from my father the O'Hare's only had the one daughter.

Downstairs the master of the house was waiting in the hall.

'Right lads put these boots on, and I'll give you a tour of the stables. The facilities may not be as grand as Craven but at the end of the day, a racehorse is a racehorse and who knows? You may find we do a few things different and learn a trick or two.'

Suirbanks was not a large complex and after a tour of the boxes we spent the remainder of the day mucking out stalls, preparing feed, cleaning tack and bandaging equine legs. It was hard work, but Alfie and I were used to it and the stable lads, no doubt glad of the extra assistance, were more than welcoming. The next day was pretty much the same only in the afternoon we joined the string out on the roads. Alfie took one of the hacks while I was presented with an unraced five-year-old called *Spartacus*, a scraggy, fractious chestnut who started bucking and squealing as soon as I threw the saddle over his back.

Fergus spoke softly as he gave me a leg up.

'He's our little star this one but be careful. He's a scally and needs a strong ride.'

I grabbed the horn of the saddle and vaulted aboard.

'I'll manage' I replied loftily. 'There's worse back in Durham.'

I was wrong though. There wasn't worse back in Durham. *Spartacus* was a complete sod. I was no sooner flexing for the stirrups when he reared violently, and the stable went spinning. I looked up from the wet slabs. Knowles, the stable jockey, and one of the other lads nudged each other and sniggered. Fergus surveyed me hand on hips.

'I did tell yer' he said with a wink.

I clambered to my feet and shook off the muck. I wasn't hurt but my pride was stung. Serves me right I suppose. I reached for the saddle again but *Spartacus* was having none of it and stamped a warning as he skewered away. Everyone was now watching. I was damned if I was going to be thrown again in front of this lot. I made my way round to the front and yanked the bridle.

'What do you think you're doing?' I shouted.

A peculiar crease appeared above his long lashes.

'You heard me. I said what do you think you're doing?'

A swivel of the ears.

I pulled him close and met his eye.

'Now you listen to me, you bugger. You can either stay here on your own or go out with the rest of the string. The choice is yours but I'm telling you now, you do that again and you go straight back to your box. Do we understand each other? Do we, hey?'

A flick of the tail suggested we probably did.

'Right. Now stop mucking around and do as you're told.'

This time I managed to stay in the saddle and after a few more arguments over who was in charge, *Spartacus* settled and we latched onto the rest of the string. I remember it was a cold afternoon and as we clip clopped through the countryside, the tarmac glittered with the first signs of frost. *Spartacus* continued his antics; he was a spirited animal for sure but as the miles slipped by, we gradually found the measure of each other. As we headed back to the stables Fergus drew alongside.

'I want to congratulate you on a fine afternoon's work young man. He's a demanding ride.'

'He's incredibly strong' I replied, drawing in the reins. 'He'll make a decent chaser one day if you can channel all that aggression. Do you have any plans for him?'

'We do. We don't get many good ones here but *Spartacus* has the potential. He's in the bumper at Thurles on Boxing Day but whether he takes his chance depends upon what work we can get into him beforehand. He's not without sufficient ability to do well but as you can see, he's a bit crazy and not yet ready for the track. You seemed to hit it off with him though. A little unconventional maybe but yer father used to talk to them like that.'

'He did indeed. He used to say there were no philosophers in the world who understood us better than horses and dogs.'

The days slipped by in similar routine and we quickly settled into it. Alfie and I rose early, fed the horses, mucked out the stables then spent the afternoon exercising *Spartacus* and the rest of the string. Sometimes Morgan joined us and we took them way out into the countryside trudging through ploughed fields to get them used to the heavy going. It was hard, tiring work but it was second nature to us both and for a while, the troubles at home seemed a long way away. I wondered how Tom's meeting with Conway had gone and if the precious documents were safe. Surely they were or he'd have wired to let me know? In any event it had been the right decision coming over. Alfie and I also found that with the exercise and fresh air we felt better and slept better than we had in a long time.

On Christmas Day we finished early and the five of us settled down for dinner. When everything was cleared away Fergus produced a set of pipes and after a few sea shanties, called on Morgan to sing. She had the loveliest voice, soft but clear and I needed no knowledge of Gaelic to capture the mood as she stole the occasional glimpse only to quickly look away. When she finished, Fergus moved to the fireplace and tapped his pipe on the hearth.

'I've decided to let *Spartacus* take his place in the bumper tomorrow. He's really come on in the last week and the ground will be right. We should give him a go.'

Morgan's green eyes lit up.

'Does he have any chance Dad?'

Fergus refilled his pipe as he turned from the fire.

'There's a large field. Some of the others have racing experience and he meets them at level weights. He'll get the trip mind and has a good engine.'

'Who will you put up?' I asked.

'Davy Knowles. He's a bit gobby but he's the best we have and knows his way around the track.'

We sang a few more songs and talked well into the night until one by one, the others slipped away until there was just the two of us. Fergus pulled his chair to the dying embers and knocked his pipe against the hearth.

'Now then lad ' said he. 'I'm not one for prying, you know I'm not, but I get the feeling you are in some sort of trouble back home. Do you want to tell me about it?'

And so I did. I explained everything right from that first ghastly day when I was pulled out of lectures. I told him about Lord William's deathbed confession, identifying my father's remains, breaking into the mortuary, the coroner's file, Victoria's trickery and the duplicitous Crake. I told him the lot. Absolutely everything. Fergus threw in the occasional question but otherwise listened intently. When at last I had finished, he sank back into his chair and refilled his pipe.

'What a tale' he said at length. 'What a tale.'

'It's all true. Every word. The documents are safe with Conway, at least for the present they are, but thing is, what next?'

Fergus reached for his matches.

'You must do the right thing. You have to go back. You realise that don't you lad?'

'I know. I'm just worried about Alfie.'

'Don't be. Your brother will be safe here. Judy and I will take care of him as long as necessary.'

'I was so hoping you would say that.'

'Think nothing of it' replied Fergus through a cloud of tobacco. 'It will be a pleasure to have a lad about the house again.'

I asked about the grainy photograph in our room.

'That's Liam, our son' answered Fergus with a watery eye. 'The picture was taken when he won the children's Gymkhana. He died in an accident six years ago.'

'I'm so sorry Fergus. I don't know what to say.'

'I'll confess it's not been easy' said he blowing his nose. 'We're still trying to get used to it but know we never will. He'd be about Alfie's age now.'

My heart went out to him. The poor man. Poor Judy and Morgan.

'Tell me' said Fergus breaking the silence. 'Is there anything you need? Do you have enough money?'

I replied that we had. When I thought about it, I was reasonably well off, at least on paper if Lord William's codicil ever made the light of day.

Fergus poured two glasses of Scotch.

'When do you leave?'

'I'll take the ferry next week. I'm meeting Tom in Durham on New Year's Eve.'

'We'll miss you, lad. Morgan will miss you. You probably didn't catch the look on her face when you were playing chess the other night, but her mother and I saw it.'

I'd seen it all right. I couldn't fail to.

'Morgan is wonderful. You must be very proud of her.'

Fergus smiled knowingly.

'Take care, Edmund Bullick She's like her mother. She knows her mind.'

And that's how we left it. I would return home, square up with the police and come back for Alfie when it was safe to do so.

'Onwards and forwards then' said Fergus draining his glass.

'Time for bed'.

CHAPTER THREE

The following morning, we loaded *Spartacus* and his stablemate on the short train ride to Thurles. The course was just beyond the town and reminded me of Sedgefield with its oval track and sharp uphill finish. It was another cold day but this time, there wasn't a cloud in the sky and a low auburn sun had chased the frost out of the ground. It was perfect national hunt weather, and a large Boxing Day crowd was out to enjoy the sport.

The afternoon started badly. The stable's first runner, of whom there were also high hopes, crashed out at the second and bolted off towards the town. When we eventually caught him, the horse was unharmed, but Knowles had dislocated a collarbone and was promptly stood down by the stewards. Fergus spent the next hour desperately trying to find a replacement, but *Spartacus* was an unknown quality and with the principal jockeys already booked there were no takers.

Fergus threw his cap to the floor in frustration.

'Damn and blast. You spend months getting an animal to peak condition then just when he's ready to do the business this happens. Of all the cursed luck. We're going to have to pull him.'

Alfie broke the silence.

'Can Edmund not ride him?'

'I'd thought of that but your brother isn't registered with the Irish Turf Club.'

'I may not be registered over here but I'm a member of the Jockey Club at home. Does that not qualify me?'

'You don't have the experience' said Fergus.

'Maybe not in Ireland but I've won loads of point to points back home. Also, this is a bumper flat race, and it can't be much different to the gallops at Middleham. Look. I know I can do this. I know I can. I've been riding him out all week.'

The old man furred his brow as he weighed up the options.

Judy was next to speak.

'We've got to at least try darlin'. It took us so long to get him ready. Why don't you see the clerk to the course and run it by him?'

A few minutes later Fergus was back from the steward's office.

'They've agreed' he said quietly. 'They've bloomin' agreed! Not only that but as an amateur you can claim seven pounds. That'll put him right in the mix.'

The bumper was the last race on the card, and I watched with a mixture of unease and anticipation as the list of runners and riders was hoisted above the crowd. There it was in fresh, slightly smudged chalk. I wished my father was here to see it.

No 14 Mr E Bullick (7)

I emerged from the jockeys changing room to a discord of hooves on tarmac, jingling harnesses and the general hubbub of a bank holiday crowd. I scanned the parade ring. At the far end Morgan was leading *Spartacus* round with the other horses. He was yanking his head a bit as he took in his surroundings but appeared reasonably settled. Thank goodness for that. A sea of unfamiliar faces stared back from the rails. It was late in the day and many of them were in their cups.

'Don't fancy yours much' called one.

'Hey lanky lad! Lanky lad! What a donkey!' sniped another.

A couple of the other jockeys nudged and whispered as we trooped into the middle of the paddock. There'd been a few comments in the changing room but I ignored them all and went over to join Fergus.

'Now remember lad, this is a marathon not a sprint. Some of the inexperienced horses will go scorching off in front, they always do but don't be tempted or you'll burn yourself out. It's like cement out there so bade your time. Take it from me, he's fit and well, he goes on the ground and will stay every yard. However, it's vital you play a waiting game. Vital.'

Earlier, I'd noticed Fergus deep in conversation with a bunch of slightly shifty looking people who had since melted away. I had to ask.

'What odds are we?'

'Opened at nine's but going right out. He looks well enough, but Davy Knowles was expected to ride him. No one's ever heard of you.'

'Are you having a tilt at the ring?'

The setting sun poured like molten gold over the canvas tents and lit the happy faces in the throng. Fergus shielded his eyes as he surveyed the line of bookmakers then addressed the cloudless sky.

'There's seventeen runners but half of them are rags and many will be schooling. That leaves the favourite and three or four others who will be trying but the ground will catch most of them out. We'll never have ours this ready again and with a seven-pound claimer up he has to be there or thereabouts. He has to be.'

There or thereabouts? From the mouth of the trainer? I knew what that meant. I'd heard it before on the Knavesmire.

'Alfie, how much money do we have?'

My brother parted the front of his coat and buried his head.

'Thirty-three pounds. And some loose change.'

'Go and put a tenner each way on *Spartacus*'

'No' said Fergus. 'No, no. Too much. You'll let the cat out the bag. Lads, if you must have a bet give the money to me and the boys will spread it nice and thin with the rest.'

Alfie reached for his coat again, but Fergus tapped his arm.

'No lad, not yet. Too many folk around. Wait until the horses are going down.'

At that moment, the bell jangled for jockeys to mount.

Fergus cupped his hands and launched me into the saddle.

'Now remember' he whispered. 'Don't worry about the others, just settle at the back and hunt them up until the second circuit. When you round the last corner, when you see that hill stretching out in front of you, press the button.

The ground may be treacle but he loves it and the hares will come back soon enough.'

'I understand.'

Alfie gave a thumbs up as Morgan embraced *Spartacus* a final time.

'Good luck' she smiled. 'Do it for Dad'.

Do it for Dad? Whose Dad? Her's or ours? It mattered not. I would ride my heart out for both.

After a couple of circuits of the paddock, we filed onto the track and joined the rest of the horses making their way down to the two-mile start. This turned out to be on the far side of the course which I was glad of because it gave me the chance to break into a canter and warm *Spartacus* up. All the way I reassured him in short, raspy breaths.

'Now look here fellah. I know we haven't always seen eye to eye but Fergus is counting on us today, and we mustn't let him down. He and Judy are as poor as church mice but they believe in you and while they don't have much of it, they've gone and laid their money down. Now what are we going to do about it? We're going to give it everything we have. That's what.'

We were in the last clump to reach the post where the starting tape was drawn sealing off the rest of the course. I wheeled *Spartacus* round and shuffled to a standstill at the back of the field. This was it. I had ridden in amateur races and point to points at home, but Thurles on Boxing Day was something else and as the starter climbed his rostrum, I thought my insides would dissolve.

'Wait jockeys. Wait. Get in line. I'm not going to give the signal until you form a line. No. Wait. Wait. I said wait! Bloody hell jockeys! Take another turn! Take another turn!'

I thought I was going to be sick. I'd just got the horse settled. It was like bracing yourself for a tooth extraction only to have it deferred. The horses swung round again, several more than once until slowly, but surely, we assembled in some kind of order. This time the starter brought down his flag and up went the tape.

Fergus was right. Immediately, six or seven of the field went tearing off in front and when they reached the first bend we were already ten lengths down. By the second bend the distance between us had doubled. The going was as heavy as I had known, particularly at the bottom of the slope where puddles had formed across the track and even before the winning post loomed for the first time, I was completely spattered with mud. It was a strange sensation passing the grandstand. I had never ridden in front of such a large crowd and while I was conscious of all the shouting, it was like being underwater at the swimming baths and I couldn't make any of it out. It crossed my mind to look up for Fergus but I knew the importance of keeping the horse balanced so I forced my eyes to the front and concentrated on going the shortest way around. Ahead of me the leaders were already galloping out into the countryside. It was plenty enough ground to make up but I could sense *Spartacus* finding his stride and resisted the temptation to shovel on the coal. I kept on repeating my instructions. *Take your time. He'll stay but you have to take your time.*

On the far side of the course, it was strangely silent with only a few cattle looking quizzically on as *Spartacus* began picking them off. At the penultimate turn it was clear most of the others were struggling in the going and some were starting to pull up. The leaders were also coming back- just as Fergus had predicted - and when we reached the foot of the slope for the second and final time there were only five or six ahead of me. I remembered my instructions.

When you round the last corner, when you see that hill stretching out in front of you, hit the button.

I strained forward and dug my heels into his belly.

'Now boy! Now!' I yelled. 'Come on! Come on!'

Spartacus was surprised but the reaction was immediate and he seemed to find an extra gear as we dourly chopped and snorted through the bottomless ground. I was not used to riding in such conditions and as I furiously paddled away, I could feel my legs turning to jelly. I stole a look ahead. At the top of the hill the winning post ghosted into view. Suddenly a narrow gap opened to the side of the wall of horses in front of me. It was now or never. I pulled *Spartacus* to the rail then with the wind rushing through my ears, drew on the last of my reserves and rode for all my worth. Halfway up the slope there were still three ahead of us but the ground was taking its toll and I knew I was gaining. *Spartacus* pricked his ears at the clamour of the crowd.

'Çome on you bugger!' I screamed. 'Come on! Come on!'

Spartacus didn't speed up anymore but he didn't need to. He already had the momentum and there were still twenty yards to the post when he flew past the leaders and won going away.

I slumped forward and wrapped myself round his neck. I was totally and utterly drained but we'd done it. We'd done it. As I recovered my breath, one or two of the other jockeys rode over and touched gloves and when I swung round, it was to be met by the wonderful sight of Fergus, Judy, Morgan and the lads strung out like washing as they squealed and panted up the slope. Fergus, who had been nearest, was first to reach us. He'd lost his cap halfway up the hill but didn't seem to care.

'Well done lad! Well done!' he yelled.

'It wasn't me, it was the horse' I gasped. 'You were right. He loves the ground.'

'He won Daddy! He won! He won!' screamed Morgan as she and her father embraced in a little dance.

Judy was last to arrive, huffing and puffing.

'Oh, my dear boy!' she gasped over and over again as she flapped around inanely. 'Oh, my dear, dear boy!'

I had won a few point to points for connections in Durham but never witnessed such undiluted joy as howls of elation, handshakes and high fives followed us all way back to the grandstand. It clearly meant the world to the family and it gave me enormous satisfaction to have played my part in it. I almost had to pinch myself to make sure I wasn't dreaming. We had won!

It was without doubt the happiest moment in my life.

The rest of the afternoon passed in a dream. It had been the final race and with most of the crowd peeling off into town, there were not many left to cheer as Morgan led our happy little group into the winner's enclosure. I didn't care though. We had won. As I dismounted, I could see Fergus and a few of his pals scuttling off to the bookies who were already packing up their boards and orange boxes. He rejoined us just in time for the presentation. His pockets were absolutely stuffed with cash and he had the widest grin on his face.

'Well done lad! Well done!' he kept saying.

I asked him how much.

'Later lad, later. We'll be having a hell of a party when we get back, so we will.'

He was right. After a quick tot with the stewards, it was straight home then onto the local pub where the celebrations began in earnest. I knew the Irish could celebrate but I tell you, I'd never seen anything like it. The whole village must have turned out (including the parish priest) and I could only watch in astonishment at the amount of liquor they were putting away. It seemed everyone had backed the horse and as the hours slipped by, raucous congratulation followed raucous congratulation as we drank our fill and sang ourselves hoarse, each taking their turn to relive the race which everyone did, over and over again. It was getting late when I spied Fergus approach the bar and procure a gigantic bottle of whiskey however, I knew I'd had enough. I could barely stand up. Time to slip away.

Outside, it was the kind of clear, twinkling night you see on a Christmas card. It must have been bitterly cold, but I didn't feel a thing and as I made my way through the empty streets, it seemed like I was gliding on rails. I decided on a quick detour to the stables where *Spartacus* was lying down in his box. As soon as he saw me, he clambered to his feet and nudged me through the top part of the door. I fed him a large handful of oats.

'You're a good boy, you are' I whispered softly.

Spartacus gave a little whinny as he munched away.

'Good boy' I repeated.

Suddenly, there were footsteps and I turned to find Morgan fixing me with those pale green eyes.

'I wondered where you'd disappeared' she said. 'How is the hero of the hour?'

'If you're referring to the horse, as you can see, he's recovered from his exertions and is eating up. If you mean me, I'm afraid I'm plastered.'

Morgan threw back a waterfall of chestnut hair.

'So you should be' she laughed. 'The whole village is drunk. Totally drunk. Mum says she hasn't seen anything like it since old Lord Kildare's wake.'

We both laughed this time.

'It was a very fine thing you did this afternoon' she said. 'This horse is Dad's pride and joy. It would have broken his heart let alone his wallet if we'd had to pull him.'

'His wallet?'

Morgan reached up and brushed *Spartacus* behind the ears.

'My father is a proud man. He won't have said anything, but I might as well tell you. We're months behind with the rent and other creditors are closing in. *Spartacus* was our last chance to stave them off and Dad laid him out especially for this afternoon. If he hadn't won, we faced being evicted.'

Suddenly, it all made sense. The broken-down buildings and worn saddles and tack. Poor Fergus. And there he was only last night asking me if I had enough money? I shuddered to think of the strain he must have been under. Thank goodness I didn't know before the race.

'Morgan, it was a steering job. Any of the lads could have done it.'

'Actually, that's not right. They all tried to school him these last few weeks but he was too unruly. Davy could manage but he's rarely available and until you came along, we'd despaired of getting him ready.'

'You're embarrassing me now.'

'No, really. It's true.'

Morgan fed *Spartacus* another palm of oats. For a while we stood in silence.

'When do you return to England?'

'In a few days.'

'So soon?'

'Alfie will stay on for a month or so but Í have to get back.'

Morgan's face fell.

'Can't you stay a little longer?'

'I can't.'

'Not only for a little while?'

'Not only for a little while.'

'It would mean so much to my mother and father. It would mean so much to us all.'

'I have to get back.'

'I don't want you to go.'

'I don't particularly want to go either but I must.'

'Keep still. There's something in the corner of your eye.'

I did as bidden. All of a sudden, her arms were around my neck and I felt the sweetness of her lips.

'Please stay, Edmund' she whispered.

We kissed again, longer this time. I sensed the heat of her body against my own and drew away.

'What's the matter?' she said. 'Don't you like me?'

'It's late. We ought to go home.'

'Don't you like me?' she repeated.

'I like you very much Morgan. You know I do but it's difficult at the moment. I have to get back to Durham. There's something I have to do.'

'No. Please' she countered 'Don't say anything more. You don't need to explain.'

'Morgan…'

'It's alright. Really. I understand. All I can say is she's a very lucky girl. I only hope she deserves you, whoever she is.'

How the hell do women know these things? I'd never said a word. She was right though. Victoria herself was standing between us. Victoria who was worthy of nothing and no one. Victoria who cared only for herself. Victoria who had made such a fool out of me. And yet still I wanted her. Is this what loving someone does to you? I'd always supposed being in love was happy and exhilarating. Not like this. Fool Edmund, fool. Morgan is amazing. She is beautiful, kind and caring- everything that the other is not. She would never betray you. Not her. Never. The moment was about to pass. It might not come again. I was so confused and conflicted. What the hell was wrong with me? But even as I cursed inside, I knew the answer. Victoria was like a drug and I was utterly possessed. I would have traded the rest of my life to sleep with her again and as long as her memory consumed me thus, I knew I could never be with anyone else.

The following morning a green looking Fergus appeared at the breakfast table with a huge pile of cash.

'Nine-twenty, twenty-five, thirty…'

'Good grief Fergus, how much have you got there?'

'Shhh, hang on lad…nine forty-five, nine fifty-five…we were friendless in the market. Nine-sixty, sixty-five… t'horse didn't know what price he was and the more he went out, the more we shovelled on. We got sixteens' for your tenner each way ….shhh.. nine-eighty, eighty-five…right, there you go lads. That's two hundred and ten quid for you, oh, plus your stake back less five for the stable lads. That's two-fifteen. It's all yours fellahs.'

I had never seen so much money in one go. It was a king's ransom. I gave Alfie twenty to go back in his wallet. I would bank the rest at home.

The remaining days in Holycross passed as before. Alfie and I would rise early, school the horses, muck out the stables and then after supper we'd all play cards or quietly read. I wasn't alone with Morgan again although on the final morning she accompanied us to the station.

'I don't know what I'll do when you're gone' said she.

'Please don't cry. I'll be back in a few weeks to collect Alfie.'

We embraced lightly.

'God love you, Edmund.'

She didn't need to say anything else. There was nothing to be said.

Fergus was next, shaking my cheeks.

'It's been wonderful having yer to stay lad. Just wonderful. Now don't you worry about Alfie. We'll look after him. Just mind how yer go and we'll see yer when we see yer.'

Alfie was the last to say goodbye. I could see the tears welling up in his eyes and pulled him close.

'Don't you start crying as well Alfie. Don't. You'll set me off.'

'I'm frightened Edmund.'

'Don't be. I know what I'm doing. Just promise me that you'll stay here until I come and get you. Promise?'

'I promise.'

'Good lad. If in the unlikely event anything *does* happen to me wait for Tom, he knows what to do. Promise?'

'I will. I promise.'

'I know you will. Now be good and make sure you do as Fergus says.'

It was a lonely trip back to England and I spent most of it lost in thought. The train was even more rammed than on the journey out with everyone in high spirits as they made their way to wherever they were going to celebrate the New Year. After what seemed an eternity, we finally trundled into Durham. Home at last. I pulled my case from the rack and stepped wearily onto the platform. In the distance two policemen were manning the barrier. I didn't give it a second thought until I presented my ticket and one of them stretched out an arm.

'Just a minute sir. Can I have your name and address please?'

'Edmund Bullick from The Stable Lodge on the Craven Estate. My late father trained for Lord William.'

The officer conferred briefly with his colleague.

'Mr Bullick, we have a warrant here for your arrest.'

'What? There must be some mistake.'

'There's no mistake sir. You are to come with us.'

The crowd immediately parted as if I was carrying the plague.

'There's some mistake' I repeated. 'There has to be.'

'Come quietly please sir. We don't want any trouble.'

I was still protesting when my arms were yanked behind my back and on went the handcuffs. I thought about struggling but there was nothing I could do and as I was carted away, my last memory was of shocked bystanders pointing and murmuring. Oh, the shame of it. I wished the ground would open and swallow me up.

CHAPTER FOUR

At Old Elvet Police Station a craggy faced sergeant reared up from behind the counter.

'Well, what have we got here lads? Bit early for the drunks isn't it?'

'Edmund Bullick sarge. There's a warrant out for his arrest.'

'Indeed, there is. So, you're Bullick are you? We've been looking for you all over son. Put him in the back. We'll top and tail him later.'

I was shepherded into a grilled enclosure where another unfortunate lay face down on a dirty mattress in the corner. I didn't recognise him at first then he sat up and greeted me.

'Ah, Edmund. Just in time for dinner. I had in mind something from the *a la carte.*'

'Tom? How long have you been here?'

'Couple of hours. Picked up at the station. You?'

The turnkey gave a self-satisfied sneer as he locked the gate and shuffled back through to the office.

'Same. Pulled at the barrier.'

Tom looked around to make sure we were not being overheard.

'How was Ireland?'

'All good. Alfie is safe and will remain where he is until we go back for him. What about Conway?'

'Sorted. He'll keep the papers secure until they're needed. I only just caught him though. He signed up with the Royal Medical Corps to drive ambulances at the front.'

At the back of the cell, high up on the wall was a small, grated window. I jumped up to catch a glimpse of the cathedral and streets full of revellers. New Year's Eve. My friend was dressed elegantly, no doubt in anticipation of our meeting with Jane. Victoria would also be in town. I had to find her. We had to get out of here.

'This wasn't in the script. What happens now?'

Tom looked towards the office.

'I suspect we're about to find out.'

At that moment footsteps heralded the appearance of an unusually tall, thin man in a tweed suit. For a while he circled the enclosure rattling his truncheon along the bars.

'Well good evening lads' said he at length. 'My name is Inspector Honeyman of the criminal investigation department, and this is my colleague, Sergeant Crisp. I imagine you know why we're here?'

A second person joined us. He was about my age and height but appeared small next to his colleague. He carried a notebook but was content to stand quietly while the other did the talking. Tom and I also remained silent, neither of us knowing where this was leading. Honeyman fished into his pocket and lit a cigarette.

'No?' said he exhaling a flurry of blue smoke. 'We've been wanting to talk to you two gentlemen for some time. You've been naughty boys. Very naughty.'

'Inspector' I replied. 'I haven't the faintest idea what you're on about or why I have been detained. I insist you release me immediately.'

Honeyman pulled on his cigarette.

'Did you hear that Crisp? Your man here insists we release him immediately.'

'I'm afraid that's not possible Mr Bullick' replied the other. 'You are to be detained for questioning.'

'Questioning? About what? Look, I don't know if this is some kind of joke or just a mistake, but I can assure you I haven't a clue what I'm doing here. If you will not release me now, I demand to speak to your superior.'

Honeyman skewered his cigarette into the ground and pressed his face through the bars.

'Now you listen to me you little turd' he hissed. 'Earlier this month, someone broke into the Dryburn mortuary and ransacked the office, and we have reliable intelligence that the two of you were responsible. What do you say about that?'

My heart sank.

'Well. I'm listening.'

'You're having a laugh' said Tom dryly.

Honeyman turned angrily.

'Oh, a laugh is it?' he shouted, his face reddening. 'A laugh? Well, we'll see how funny you find it this time tomorrow.'

'What?' I retorted. 'You're not going to leave us here? Its New Year's Eve for goodness sake. We have plans for the evening.'

'We have plans for the evening, we have plans for the evening' echoed Honeyman sarcastically. 'Thing is sunshine, me and the sergeant here, we have plans for the evening as well so if you want to talk to us, I suggest you get on with it. We can go to my office now, you can tell us what you did and if you're straight with us, we might let you out.'

Shit. How much did they know? How much could they prove? They could be bluffing. Play for time. Play for time.

'Inspector, you have to believe me. I haven't a clue what you're on about. Honestly, I don't.'

'Honestly, I don't' he mimicked. 'How about you Brentnall? Are you able to assist us with our enquiries?'

'I doubt it' said Tom.

'Proper little comedian, aren't we?'

'Not really. It's just that I haven't the faintest idea what you're on about either.'

'Well *fuck* you lads; it's no skin off my nose. You can stay here and stew in your own juice. The desk sergeant will be through later to take your fingerprints. Sleep tight. We'll see you tomorrow. Come on Crisp.'

The detectives' footsteps dwindled down the corridor. There followed what sounded like a seasonal exchange at the front desk, then silence. We were alone.

Tom rattled the gate as if to make sure it was locked.

'I don't like the sound of this fingerprints business' he said. 'I'd never heard of it until Crake warned us. Do you think it's actually possible? You know, taking smudges off someone's hands then seeing if they match others left at the scene of a crime?'

'I do think it's possible, yes. What's more I fear our prints will be all over the mortuary. On the skylight, on the doors, on the furniture. Everywhere. If they haven't looked already the police are sure to find them now.'

Tom kicked the wall in frustration.

'This is not good. If they can place us in the mortuary, we can hardly say we don't know anything about it.'

'So what do we do? Tell them the truth?'

'I don't see we have a choice' he replied. 'We're going to have to explain what we were doing there and hope they believe us. It will be easy enough for them to check if the coroner's papers are missing. It's not as if we took anything else.'

We discussed the options for a while but there was nothing else for it. We would have to come clean. We would make no reference to Lord William's deathbed confession and obviously nothing about finding his codicil and my brother's birth certificate in the charred ruins of Crake's office. That could wait. We were in enough trouble as it was. No, for now we would restrict our account to the irrational refusal of Tench to disclose what was in my father's file and our resolve to uncover the truth.

It was a long night. As we stamped about the holding area to keep warm, I thought Tom was unusually subdued. He had arranged to meet Jane on Framwellgate Bridge and now she would think he'd stood her up. On the other side of our grated window the cathedral bells chimed down the hours. When they struck midnight, I pictured the crowds on Palace Green and wished we were up there with them. 1915. Another year. What would it bring? My thoughts strayed to Victoria. I couldn't help it. The memory of being with her utterly consumed me. I wondered who was with her right now and if she was sleeping with him.

Tom and I were alone when we were locked up but as the evening wore on an assortment of drunks and the usual misfits of society were shovelled into the cage with us. One of them vomited all over the floor and when another knocked over the stained bucket that served as the communal toilet, I nearly threw up myself. I thought of all the people in town who would be making merry and wondered what I was doing here. 1am. 2am. Time crept. I closed my eyes and imagined I was in *The County* with my back to a coal fire, glass of punch in hand. How did the rhyme go?

We'll take a cup of kindness yet
for auld lang syne?

We'll take cup of kindness yet? Perhaps. But it wouldn't be this New Years' Eve. Damn it. How long were they going to keep us here? As I shivered in that cold cell, I couldn't wish the time away quickly enough.

Honeyman and Crisp returned the following afternoon and took us away for questioning. It was clear they were a double act with Honeyman even more obnoxious than before while Crisp masqueraded as some kind of friend with only our best interests at heart. We were not taken in by either and stuck to what was agreed until I was questioned a second time and the interview took a worrying turn.

'You say you broke into the mortuary to steal your father's papers?'

'That's right. We recovered them from one of the cabinets in the office. They weren't difficult to locate. Everything was filed alphabetically.'

'Burglary is a serious business. What did you think you were going to accomplish by it?'

'We were searching for the truth. We didn't believe Sergeant Tench when he claimed there was nothing important in the file. It was blatantly obvious he was lying. In the event our reservations were justified because the papers included a contemporaneous note of my father's last words.'

'Last words, hey? Saying what, exactly?'

'When he was brought into the hospital, my father told the staff that Lord William had changed the succession and was in great danger. He explained how he had ridden out to the moor to warn him but was challenged by monks at Friars Cross and unhorsed in the storm.'

Honeyman lit a cigarette.

'Hang on a minute' he said through a cloud of smoke. 'I just want to be sure I'm hearing this right. You say Cavendish was in danger because he changed his will and when your father rode up to the moor to warn him, he was - what? - attacked by monks?'

'That's correct. Challenged by monks.'

'Are you for real son?'

'I can only tell you what was recorded in the file.'

Honeyman hammered his fist on the table.

'For fuck's sake man. You don't expect us to believe *that* do you?'

'You can believe what you like but I tell you it's true.'

Honeyman took another long pull.

'So, this file you took away. Where is it now?'

'It was stolen from the safe when my father's office was burgled. You know this much to be true. Alfie showed you the damage when you came looking for me just before Christmas.'

'I was going to ask you about your brother. He must be wondering what's become of you. Where is he by the way?'

'Alfie is at home.'

'No, he's not. We checked the house every day for the last two weeks and there's been no sight or sound of either of you. Where is he?'

Silence.

'Proper man of mystery, aren't you?'

'Inspector, has it occurred to you that I might actually be telling the truth?'

Honeyman held my eye for a few seconds. I could almost hear the cogs rattling. Finally, he stubbed out his cigarette and went to the door.

'Watch him Crisp'.

Half an hour later he was back.

'I've just spoken to Sergeant Tench. We've also checked the cabinet. Your father's file is still there.'

I couldn't believe what I was hearing.

'That's not possible'.

'Furthermore, there is nothing in it about Cavendish, monks, storms, or anything else.'

'I tell you I had that file. I took it away myself and locked it in our safe. It can't be back in the mortuary. That's not possible. It can't be. Unless…'

'Unless what? No, no, let me guess. Unless you really *did* steal the file only for that marvellous, magical Mister Nobody to steal it from you and then pull out a page or two before slipping it back in the cabinet? Is that what you're saying?'

It sounded absurd but it was the only plausible explanation.

'I tell you Inspector; I had that file. We had that file. Tommy Brentnall and I took it together and we read it together. We realised how explosive the contents were which is why we locked it in my father's safe. If it is somehow back in the mortuary it can only have been replaced by the same person or persons who took it from us.'

Honeyman suddenly leaned forward and grabbed my hair. I was too shocked to do anything but howl in pain.

'You cretin' he hissed drawing his face to mine. 'What is it with you posh kids? Do you take me for a fool? Do you? Do you think you're so fucking superior that the law doesn't apply to you? Well, do you?'

'I've told you the truth now let *go* of me you dick!'

The other released his grip and climbed to his feet.

'D'ye know what son?' said he lighting another cigarette. 'That's it. I'm through. You've had your chance. You and your chum can rot in here until next New Years' Day for all I care. Crisp?'

'Come on Edmund' supposed the other. 'This is ridiculous. I know the inspector can go over the top sometimes – yes, you can Mark – but all we are trying to do is get to the truth. We don't want to keep you locked up in this dreadful place any more than you want to be here. You must have friends outside wondering where you are and what about your brother? It seems to us you're in some kind of trouble. We only want to help you sort it out. However, we can't help you unless you want to help yourself. Now, come on, once and for all. What were the two of you *really* doing in there?'

'I've already told you. We went to recover the coroner's file and that's it.'

'You need to try again son' barked Honeyman. 'I don't think you and your chum here realise how much bother you're in. The evidence of Sergeant Tench is that whoever 'went in', as you put it, not only ransacked the place but stole money and items of value belonging to the deceased. What do you have to say about that?'

'No way. The only thing we removed was my father's file. We didn't take anything else. We didn't want anything else. We didn't look for anything else.'

'That's not what Sergeant Tench says.'

'I'm telling you the truth.'

'So, Sergeant Tench is making the whole thing up?'

'If any other property is missing, we certainly didn't take it. As for the file, yes, Sergeant Tench is making it up. We took that file. Sergeant Tench knows that. I just don't understand why he is lying about it.'

'When picked up at the station you had almost two hundred pounds in assorted notes on you. Now where did a little tow-rag like you get that kind of dough? Win it on a horse I suppose?'

There was nothing to be said. He wouldn't believe me and to impart the truth would only betray my brother's whereabouts.

Honeyman gathered his cigarettes and matches.

'Do you know what son?' said he with a scrape of his chair. 'I've been doing this job for over twenty years and in all that time I've never heard such a load of complete and utter *shite*. The two of you will be charged with burglary and put before court tomorrow morning. Take them back to the cells, Crisp.'

CHAPTER FIVE

The inspector himself presented the Crown's case to the magistrates. I recognised the chairman, Colonel Walford, as one of the stewards at Hexham but there was not a flicker of empathy as he listened in stony silence to the allegations. Neither did Honeyman spare the detail. As feared, our prints were all over the mortuary. Items of value were missing from the office. Gold rings, money and jewellery. We had subsequently left the area. A large amount of cash was discovered in my possession together with a ticket stub from Liverpool. The burglary had every hallmark of a professional operation and the public interest could only be served by remanding us both in custody. When Honeyman eventually sat down things could hardly look bleaker.

Walford addressed us in a clipped military tone.

'Gentlemen. You don't need me to tell you these are serious allegations. Do you have anything to say about them?'

Tom cleared his throat.

'Your honour…'

'Stand up when addressing the chairman!' barked a tiny figure crouched like a weasel in front of the bench. It was

Gibbon the court clerk. I'd almost forgotten he was there. His only previous input had been to read out our names when we were brought in.

Tom cleared his throat again.

'Your honour, I do not - we do not - deny that we entered the mortuary, but we were only looking for the coroner's file. We didn't take anything else.'

'That's not what the police are saying. Mr Bullick?'

'What my friend has told you is true. That's the only reason. We wouldn't have gone there at all if the Sergeant Tench had shared the information.'

Walford deliberated with his colleagues.

'Gentlemen. It occurs to us that you are in need of legal advice. Madam Usher, are there any solicitors available?'

'There's Mr Nixon and Mr Hill your worships, but they are both engaged with prisoners.'

'Will they be long?'

'It would appear so, sir. We have a large number in custody.'

'Anyone else?'

The usher looked up from her clipboard.

'Mr Latimer is in the building somewhere.'

Gibbon stopped writing and swung round to the bench.

'Your worships, it may not be wise to involve Mr Latimer.'

'I am only too aware of Mr Latimer's idiosyncrasies' said Walford 'but my colleagues and I have a long list to get through this morning and we intend to make progress. Mr Bullick. Mr Brentnall. We are going to stand this matter down for you to take legal advice. Madam Usher, please inform Mr Latimer of the position then ask the bridewell to send up the next prisoner.'

We were taken back to the cells where we were joined by a third person who I initially took to be another detainee, such was his state of dishevelment. He was about fifty, rotund with matted white hair and whiskers and an old-fashioned tweed suit which, like its owner, had seen better days. He carried a small reef of papers and a fountain pen that had leaked over his tobacco-stained fingers and onto his frayed cuff. He introduced himself in a waft of stale alcohol.

'Ah, good morning to you gentlemen, good morning. Gilbert Latimer, senior partner at Latimer and Latimer of Durham City at your service. The magistrates have requested that I speak to you regarding your case and I am happy to do this. I understand from Inspector Honeyman that you are charged with the burglary of money and property, value as yet unknown, from Dryburn mortuary. This is a most unusual allegation. Do you know anything about it?'

'We've already told the police what we know.'

'Ah yes, so I s-see' he answered consulting his notes. 'You admit to breaking into the building but not, I-I understand, to stealing anything? Is this correct?'

'Not quite. We took one of the coroner's files from the office.'

I peered into Latimer's rugged face as he subconsciously mouthed back what we were saying to him. His eyes were watery and bloodshot, and I sensed a certain sorrow in them.

'Ah yes Mr Bullick. This being the file relating to your late f-father. Is that all you took? Nothing else?'

'Nothing else.'

Latimer put down his notes and removed his glasses.

'Now there we have a bit of a problem, gentlemen. The police don't believe you and I'm afraid to say, neither will the court. The difficulty we have is that most people know nothing about mortuaries because in the ordinary course of events, most people don't visit them. There is a t-taboo about these places and as with many taboos, they are regarded as something between the sinister and sacrosanct. I'm afraid it doesn't matter what you took away with you. I fear the fact you broke into such a building will excite n-nothing but distaste.'

I watched the lawyer closely as he spoke to us. You didn't need to smell the drink to know it was his master. His attire and general lack of cleanliness gave it away and one could understand the clerk's reluctance to involve him in the proceedings. And yet when I looked beyond his condition and stutter and listened to what he was actually saying, the man was clearly erudite and I sensed that if caught on a good day, he would probably be as sharp as any other lawyer in the building. I hoped we had caught him on a good day.

'I'm confident we can persuade the court we are telling the truth' said Tom brightly. 'What other motive can we have had? No one's going to believe we went in there to rob the dead!'

'You will certainly have the opportunity to explain yourselves' replied Latimer 'b-but this will not arrive until you appear before the Crown Court on a date to be determined. The only issue for the justices this morning is bail.'

'What's that?' asked Tom.

'Bail is a legal t-term but essentially it concerns where the two of you spend the time between now and your trial. Tell me, do either of you have a cigarette on you?'

I replied that all of our property had been confiscated when we were arrested. Latimer left the room for a couple of minutes then returned puffing away.

'Where were we? Ah y-yes, bail. Inspector Honeyman is very much against your release. The charges are serious and he will s-suggest that if the court allow bail, you will only abscond. Neither is our situation helped by Mr Gibbon being the court clerk today. His role is supposed to be administrative but I'm afraid he is very prosecution orientated. Tell me, do either of you young men have access to any money or someone – a friend or relative perhaps- who will stand surety for you?'

There followed a discussion on these lines. Tom's father had attended the hearing from York and would presumably stand surety for him but I had no one. The legacy I had been left by Lord William was tied up in Crake's office which was now a smoking ruin. The cash in my father's safe had been stolen and the winnings from *Spartacus* were being held by the police. Perhaps Barnaby or Lady Alanna could be prevailed upon but there was nobody from the estate at court. Latimer left the room briefly to speak to Tom's father but we were still reviewing our options when the case was suddenly called back on.

Walford opened the dialogue in his customary clipped tone.

'Yes. Mr Latimer?'

'Your worships, I have taken instructions from these two y-young men. They deny the offence, or the greater part of it and unusually for an allegation of this nature they are not known to the police or these courts. They both have settled addresses and in all the circumstances I invite you to grant them bail this morning to appear before Durham Assizes when their c-case is listed for disposal. Now while I understand the police are against their release today…'

'They are sir' said Gibbon over his shoulder to the chairman. 'The police position is that if admitted to bail, the prisoners would abscond.'

Latimer's face creased at the interruption. It was obvious he and Gibbon didn't care for one another but to his credit Latimer ignored the sleight and continued.

'…er as I was saying I invite the court to release these young men to a settled address. Mr Brentnall's father has attended court and instructs me that he will stand surety in any reasonable sum for b-both. In addition, and to address the Inspector's concerns about absconding, you could also direct that the prisoners reside with Mr Brentnall senior at his home in York and report to the local police station twice a day…'

'How can you say that?' interrupted Gibbon. 'These men broke into the city mortuary causing a huge amount of damage and then stole property and valuables belonging to people who had died. It is an outrageous crime that will attract a substantial custodial sentence, these defendants well know it and if they are not remanded in custody until the next assizes, in all probability they will simply disappear again.'

Latimer lost his patience.

'Do you mind sir?' he snapped. 'I was addressing the organ grinder.'

The court fell silent. A ghost of a smile crossed Walford's face as Gibbon slowly turned purple.

'How dare you speak to me like that?' he whispered. 'How *dare* you?'

'You forget yourself Mr Gibbon. These young men are entitled make submissions through me without you constantly b-butting in.'

'It is my duty to intervene when such nonsense is aired before the justices. You of all people should know that Mr Latimer.'

'Y-your duty is to advise the justices on matters of law and nothing else. The way you conduct yourself I'm only surprised the police felt it necessary to have a representative here at all.'

'Gentleman' cried Walford. 'Genn-tell-mennn! Thank you, gentlemen. That will do. My colleagues and I have heard sufficient from you both and will now withdraw to consider this matter. Mr Gibbon, will you allow us a few minutes then join us in the retiring room?'

'Court rise' said the usher from the back.

When the magistrates adjourned the spat resumed.

'How dare you speak to me in that manner in front of the justices Latimer? How *dare* you?'

'Oh, I dare, and I don't have any compunction about it. You're supposed to be the court clerk. You're supposed to be impartial. What right do you have interrupting advocates when they are on their f-feet?'

'I have every right' snapped Gibbon. 'I am the clerk to the court, and it is my duty to ensure the efficient administration of justice in this town. I will not tolerate timewasters. *You* are a timewaster. *You* have always been a timewaster.'

'And you, sir, are nothing but a self-serving, obsequious little p-prick.'

Latimer had spoken under his breath. The clerk didn't quite catch it but everyone else did and the court erupted into hoots of laughter.

'What did you say? What did you say? You have not heard the end of this Latimer. I shall be lodging a formal complaint about your behaviour with the Law Society.'

'Go ahead. I couldn't care less. You might ask them to enrol you on a course for common sense while you're at it.'

(laughter)

The exchange continued in similar fashion as the clerk gathered his papers and made his way to the dividing door.

'Oh, go and have another drink Latimer.'

'What an excellent idea. That's the first s-sensible thing you've said all morning.' (laughter)

The magistrates were back within minutes.

'Court stand.'

Walford gravely resumed his seat and addressed the assembly.

'These proceedings will be committed to Durham Crown Court for disposal on a date to be fixed. My colleagues and I have listened carefully to the submissions of Inspector Honeyman for the police and Mr Latimer for the prisoners. In the case of Mr Brentnall bail is granted on a surety of fifty guineas together with conditions of residence at his home address in York and daily reporting to the local police station. In the case of you, Mr Bullick, bail is refused and the direction of the court is that you be remanded in custody until the next assizes. That is all. Take him down.'

My heart sank. As the jailers closed in I ignored the smug look on the faces of Honeyman and Gibbon and motioned to Tom.

'Find Conway. Find Conway and get those documents.'

Tom nodded.

'Leave it with me.'

'Silence in the dock' barked Gibbon.

Even as he spoke the handcuffs were fastened and I was led off down the stairs.

CHAPTER SIX

Durham Jail lay half a mile across town and I had the ignominy of being conveyed there in a secure wagon with the rest of the morning's harvest. It was to be the first of many humiliations. Immediately upon arrival I was examined by a surgeon then after a freezing shower, my head was shaved. To add insult to injury, as I quivered in the waiting area a few of the other prisoners, sensing my discomfort, took it in turns to goad me. Was it that obvious I was a fish out of water? I reasoned it must be. It crossed my mind to tell them to go to the devil however I was in enough trouble as it was so merely gritted my chattering teeth and waited my turn.

'Edmund Bullick? Step forward Bullick.'

My induction was delivered by a short, fleshy prison officer with foul breath who looked up from his clipboard and pointed to a large notice on the wall.

'Bullick, you have been remanded in custody until the next assizes at Durham Crown Court. Between now and then we have certain rules which you are expected to follow.'

'I've seen them'.

'Don't get clever with me bonnie lad. There aint many here who can read and so we don't get any misunderstanding later on, you're going to listen carefully to what I am about to tell you because I won't be repeating myself.

One. You will obey members of His Majesty's prison staff at all times and abstain from preventing anyone who works in the prison from getting to where they need to go for example by erecting a barricade to stop someone entering your cell.

Two. You must not fight or conduct yourself in any way that could offend, threaten, frighten or hurt someone else.

Three. You are forbidden to escape from prison or from attempting to escape. This includes running away or trying to run away from a prison escort.

Four. You are forbidden to drink alcohol or gain access to alcohol.

Five. You are forbidden to cause damage to the prison or any part of the prison or to set fire to any part of the building or anything in it.

Six. You are forbidden to put anything on the walls of the prison or write or draw anything that could upset, threaten or frighten anyone.

Seven. You are forbidden to take or steal anything that is not yours from another person or from the prison.

Eight. If you are directed to do work, you must do that work. If you do not do it properly or at all, if you do not follow an order or a rule that you should follow or if you break any of the prison rules or try to help someone else to do so you will be punished.

Nine. Punishments include the immediate withdrawal of privileges including visiting rights, the receipt and sending of mail and any association with other prisoners. Serious cases will warrant solitary confinement for a period of thirty days. Have I made myself clear?'

I replied that he had.

'One final thing Bullick. It's not on the wall or in the manual here but there's another prison rule and it goes something like this: anyone behaving like a dick can expect a good hiding. Again, have I made myself clear?'

'Very officer.'

'Right. Follow me.'

I was escorted to the laundry where my clothes were exchanged for the standard garb of two pairs of pants, two pairs of socks, a pair of pelt sandals, a pair of flannel trousers (that reeked of mothballs) and two collarless shirts. I assumed the latter would be covered in arrows like you see in caricatures, but the ones issued to me were grey with thin black stripes. They were incredibly itchy at first but there was nothing else to wear and I quickly became used to them.

My induction concluded at lunchtime just when all the prisoners were filing out of their cells into the refectory. The din was tremendous. Yelling and shouting. Whistles blowing. Heavy doors slamming. The clatter of trolleys. The rattle of cutlery. The hobnail tramp of the screws. Above all else, the foul, sickly stench of misery which totally engulfed that vast hive of battleship grey. I had never encountered anything like it (either before or since). It was like a blend of testosterone, stale urine and rotten cabbage and the stink remained in my nostrils for years.

We left the cacophony behind and made our way deep into the complex. At the end of a long corridor my escort halted and fished for his keys.

'Your suite, sir' he announced sarcastically. 'We're bunking you in with McMash who will show you the ropes.'

I stood in silence as the door opened on a small, whitewashed vault about the size of one of the birthing boxes at the stables. It reminded me of a segment of a tunnel, dimly lit and humid with the unmistakable aroma of soap and warm shit. In one corner a basin, a small table and two tiny stools were bolted to the floor. In the other was a large bucket. A narrow timber bench ran down one of the walls and opposite that, a wooden bunk bed from where the occupant of the lower tier raised his head over a copy of *John Bull*.

'Who the fuck are you?'

'Good afternoon Mr McMash' said the escort with a surprising degree of reverence. 'This is B313 Bullick who was remanded in custody this morning.'

'Not with me he isn't. I thought I'd made myself clear. No more cellmates. Or have you forgotten what happened last time?'

Last time? What did he mean, 'last time'? I didn't like the sound of 'last time'.

'Apologies Mr McMash. Governor's orders. The prison is at bursting point and we need every available space.'

'Not this available space you don't. Now piss off and take that skinny twat with you.'

'You know I can't do that'.

McMash threw down his magazine and rolled to his feet. 'Are you deaf pal?'

The warder ignored him and locked the door.

'I'll, er, leave you two gentlemen to get acquainted' said he before adding 'Just shout if you need anything Bullick.'

I raced to the grill but he was already halfway down the corridor. Just shout if you need anything? How about 'help'?

I turned round and looked at McMash. He was an absolute giant of a fellow and when he stepped forward my bowels almost liquefied.

'Who the *fuck* are you?'

Keep calm. Show no fear. Keep calm. Oh God, help me.

'Hi, I'm Edmund. I'm sorry to intrude. I had nothing to do with this placement, I assure you. I really don't want to be here at all.'

McMash swatted my outstretched hand as he looked me up and down.

'Don't want to be here? What do you mean you don't want to be here? Is there something wrong with me?'

Cripes. How do you answer that? The fellow was obviously looking for trouble. Think Edmund, think.

'I wasn't suggesting anything of the kind Mr McMash. It's just I heard what you said to the warder and I want you to know I'm not here by choice.'

'Too fucking right, I don't want any more cell mates. Do you know what happened to the last fairy they put in here?

'I'm afraid I don't. Infirmary perhaps?'

McMash burst out laughing covering me with a spray of saliva.

'No. He went to Dryburn. Dryburn Hospital. I put him there because he was a twat. *You* look like a twat. Would you like to join him?'

'I've already been to Dryburn. I was at the mortuary a few weeks ago to identify my father.'

McMash turned and walked to the window.

'You don't seem very afraid of me. You should be. Do you realise who you're talking to?'

'I'm sorry I don't. I've only just arrived.'

'Well let me tell you. My name is M184 McMash. M-A-S-H only I'm better known on this wing as *Masher*. *Masher* by name and *Masher* by nature. What do you think about that?'

Think Bullick. You've tried humour.

'What you expect me to say? I don't want any trouble but if you're determined to have a go there's not a great deal I *can* say.'

McMash regarded me for a moment as if trying to weigh me up.

'You don't sound like you're from these parts. Bit of a posh lad, are we?'

'Excuse me?'

'I said you sound like a bit of a posh lad. What's a posh lad like you doing in Durham jail?'

'I was locked up by the magistrates this morning.'

'What for?'

'Burglary. How about yourself?'

'Grievous bodily harm. With intent. A bit like this…'

I didn't see it coming. Everything happened so quickly. All I remember was this flash and next thing I was on the floor clutching my face.

McMash surveyed his handiwork.

'That'll teach you not to get clever with me, you twat.'

The room was spinning. It was as if I had been smacked between the eyes with a fairground mallet. I struggled to my haunches gazing at the blood running through my fingers and dripping onto the flags. I didn't need to look in the mirror. The head-butt had shattered my nose. I'd broken it once before in a point to point. I felt a wave of nausea and thought I was going to be sick. I had a sudden yearning for home, for my father and brother.

'Posh twat' he repeated.

I clambered to my feet stumbling against the wall as my assailant returned to his bunk and resumed his journal. I looked at his huge carcass bending into the mattress. The man was a bully. Not only that but a cowardly bully of the very worst kind. I had always detested bullying. I had seen enough of it at college to know if I didn't stand up to him now, McMash would be back for more. I was no hero. I certainly wasn't brave. I was a coward at heart but there are some occasions in life where you have to put aside your fear and stand up for yourself. Now was such a time. Having taken the decision to fight back, I didn't utter a word. Instead, I made a move towards the table then at the last second span round and belted my assailant in the face as hard as I could. The blow landed square in the mouth and I knew he felt it because I cracked a knuckle on his teeth.

McMash sprang up from his bed and flew at me like a deranged animal.

'I'm gonna kill you for that' he screamed. 'I'm gonna kill you! I'm gonna fucking kill you!'

Now McMash may have been a Colossus, but he was a slow Colossus while I was fit from riding and used to boxing with the stable lads. As he tried to grab me, I danced to one side and struck him again. This made him wilder but even as I repeated the process, I knew there could only be one outcome. It was a tiny arena and with nowhere to run I was quickly forced into a corner whereupon McMash threw me to the ground, kicked me a few times then before I could recover, flung his giant frame over and straddled me. I bucked wildly but it was no use. I could scarcely breathe let alone move. I looked up at this enormous moon face staring down at me. I remember thinking his trunk-like thighs were soft and warm and that his trousers smelt of cobalt and urine.

'Time to say goodnight posh boy.'

'You don't scare me, you wanker.'

'Any last requests?'

'Yeah. Go fuck yourself. And my name is not posh boy. I am Edmund Bullick of Craven Stables.'

McMash raised his enormous fists. I screwed my eyes for the *coup de grace*. I once heard that just before the end of your life, the whole of it flashes before you and I tell you, it's true, because at that moment my life flashed in front of me. The child sitting on my father's shoulders in the unsaddling ring at Thirsk. The mother I never knew. The stables at Craven. *Stornoway* winning the Gimcrack Cup. Lord William's ghastly deathbed confession. Tommy Brentnall laying out Clifford. The horror of the mortuary. The merciless bombardment of Hartlepool. The blood and guts in the street. Alfie waiting for me in Ireland. The O'Hare's. *Spartacus*. Victoria. Victoria. Victoria. The warmth of her skin. Her breath in my ear. God, how I loved her. I thought of the man I could have been. Be near me Lord Jesus.

The blow never came.

I waited and waited then opened my eyes. McMash was still gawking down at me, but a peculiar look had swept across his face.

'What did you say your name was?'

'Edmund Bullick of Craven Stables.'

'What? 'Bullick' as in Jimmy Bullick the racehorse trainer?'

'He was my father.'

McMash rose to his feet and pulled at my arm.

'Get up. Come on. Get up. Why the hell didn't you say so? Jimmy Bullick is legend in these parts. Any son of his is a friend of mine.'

I rose and collapsed across the table. McMash had hurt me badly. Blood was pouring down my face and over my clothes. It ran down the back of my throat. It was spattered on the whitewashed walls.

'I don't understand' I mumbled. 'Did you know my father?'

'No. I never had the honour, but Jimmy Bullick was a master of his profession. No finer trainer in the County. Nor as straight. Never known to pull a horse so when the stable turned one out, you knew it would try its best. Me and the lads made a killing when *Stornoway* won the Gimcrack. An absolute killing. That little Aussie Franky Wooten was up and you could see two furlongs out he had it in the bag.'

'You were at the Knavesmire?'

McMash threw me a towel.

'I was. I used to work the doors in the *Hat and Feather*. The stable lads drink there so we knew he was flying. I tell you half the pub went to the York that day and when it won, we all got so pissed we took the wrong train back and ended up in Skipton. You must know the *Hat and Feather*? It's at the bottom of Market Place.'

'I don't feel well' I groaned. 'I have to lie down.'

McMash came across and helped me to my bunk. As he pulled a rug over me his voice was surprisingly gentle.

'You rest easy lad. We'll talk some more later.'

The frame shuddered as McMash returned to his journal.

'You'll be fine in a few days' said he from below. 'I didn't want to hurt you but you are a cocky twat.'

I supposed that was as close to an apology as I was going to get. The room was still spinning. I closed my eyes and drifted away. So McMash was a racing man. Perhaps now he would leave me alone.

CHAPTER SEVEN

I quickly settled into the prison routine. Yes, it was January and yes, it was lonely and bitterly cold but I had been at boarding school for most of my life and adjusted with surprising ease. Each day was the same. It would start around 5am as I lay on the top bunk listening to the cathedral bells. This is when I used to say a few quick prayers thanking God for being alive and asking Him to guide me through whatever lay ahead. At 6am I would jump down for the morning ritual of washing my face and brushing my teeth and then read quietly at the table as we waited for the guard to unlock the door and escort me to the kitchens. I had volunteered for the work. It not only relieved the boredom, but I had been constantly hungry for the first few days and the assignment brought much needed titbits and scraps. The remainder of the morning was spent in the cells then it was back to the kitchens to prepare lunch. When everything was washed and cleared away, we filed into the exercise yard and walked round and round for an hour before being locked up again.

There was little organised interaction between prisoners. McMash said there used to be a general association before supper but when this was seized upon to beat someone up or attack another group of people, the concession was withdrawn. Showers, while infrequent, were especially perilous, the wardens turning a blind eye to beatings and rapes which became so commonplace that I didn't dare go in there on my own. In fact, everywhere I looked there was danger although it was the night I dreaded the most because of all the time it gave me to think. How I used to hate it, those forsaken hours lying on my bunk with nothing to do but dream and remember as I waited for the next peel of bells. It was always the same. At 6pm sharp we were locked back in our cells where I would sit and read until we were suddenly plunged into darkness. I had been caught out by this on my first night when the solitary bulb flashed once and then went out a few minutes later, although I followed the signal thereafter.

I rapidly learned there was a strict pecking order among prisoners. At the top of the tree was an inmate called Hayward who was standing trial for the murder of an Easington postman and his wife. He'd apparently shot them both in a robbery that went wrong and word among the prisoners was he'd hang at the next assizes. Hayward was kept in solitary confinement in the next wing so I never came across him although I understood from McMash this was no bad thing as the man was truly evil and everyone, including the warders, was terrified of him.

'Steer well clear kid' he would say. 'Hayward is an animal. He would just as soon put his thumbs into your eyes as look at you.'

So far as the rest of the prisoners were concerned, McMash was well placed in the hierarchy and could gain access to almost anything- writing paper, stamps, tobacco, chocolate, even whisky and gin. Heaven knows where it all came from. The prison was a like a fortress with its thick, sooty walls crowned with a forest of barbed wire and the only way in or out was through a multi gated entrance which was closely watched and guarded at all times. All visitors without exception were methodically searched (both on their way in and on their way out) and there were notices all over the place warning of immediate imprisonment for anyone caught smuggling contraband. And yet here was McMash with an abundance of luxury goods. Where did he get them from? I reasoned it must be the guards, or some of the guards. They would not be paid a great deal, say a guinea or two a week? What were a couple of guineas when you could earn twice as much for bringing in the odd bottle or simply looking the other way?

McMash was also the prison bookie and I quickly became of use to him with information about various trainers and the peculiarities of the local courses. Henry Budgett was earmarked to take over from my father at Craven. Colonel Troy's novice chasers were always well schooled. Danny Baskerville's hurdlers were ex-flat and normally fit on debut. The jockeys Globe and Sewell were alcoholics and underperformed at weekends. Charlie Martin was heavily in debt and took bungs to throw races although he usually tried in the more valuable ones. High Gosforth Park was poorly drained and suited horses that went in heavy going. Sedgefield had a steep uphill finish favouring the low weights. Hexham was always blustery and the course dried out quickly. The Irish raiders flourished at Ayr and Liverpool and so on.

McMash not only laid horses but ran a *Crown and Anchor* board on which he would take bets in the chapel. It was surprisingly easy to do this because unlike other jails such as Lincoln (where there were apparently separate booths for individual prayer) the chapel at Durham was open and prisoners conversed easily without interference or where discretion was needed, they communicated by mouthing. It was the same in the cells where messages travelled along the corridors by a system of raps to such effect that it was possible to send an instruction from one end of the prison to the other faster than it could be carried. This ingenuity of the inmates to address the basic human desire to interact totally amazed me, fostering as it did a feeling of common identity that separated us from the warders.

I had been in custody for about a fortnight when early one morning there was a jangle of keys at the door.

'Bullick? Someone to see you. Follow me please.'

I was escorted down a labyrinth of corridors until we reached the visitor's area. The hall was absolutely rammed but there was no mistaking the solitary figure leaning back at the appointed table smoking a cigarette.

'Crikey Ed, your whole face is black and purple. What the hell happened?'

'Let's just say it was a local greeting.'

'And your hair? What have they done to your hair?'

'It'll grow. But never mind that. Tell me, what news? Have you spoken to Conway?'

'Unfortunately not but I know where to find him.'

'What do you mean?'

'You'll remember he volunteered for the Royal Army Medical Core immediately after the bombardment? Well, he's been posted to St Albans to train on the ambulances.'

'St Albans? But that's the other end of the country. When is he expected back?'

'He isn't. I made enquiries and they're going to the front. I've sent a message to his CO asking him to get in touch urgently but I'm afraid I haven't heard anything yet. It seems any contact with home is discouraged until they find their feet.'

'When are the next assizes?'

'Latimer says our trial is listed the week before Easter. That's Tuesday 30 March to Thursday 1 April.'

'It doesn't give us long. You have to find Conway and recover those papers. Have you said anything to Latimer?'

'About taking the Will and birth certificate from Crake's office? Heavens, no. I've only seen him a couple of times since I was released. He wrote last week asking for 300 guineas on account of costs before his firm did anything else.'

'300 guineas? How on earth are we going to find that kind of money? We need to borrow it from somewhere. What's the mood like at Craven?'

'Grim. I went to see Barnaby yesterday, but he made it clear Lady Alanna and the family want nothing to do with us. It seems Julian tipped poison in her ear and everyone in the village is only too ready to believe the worst.'

'Everyone? What about Jane?'

'I'm in touch with Jane. We met secretly last Tuesday in the cathedral library. She will help if she can but Lady Alanna and Julian have forbidden her to contact us and are watching her closely.'

'Damn it. There has to be a way. There's some money in Dad's savings account but I can hardly get at it from here. Likewise the funds left to me by Lord William under the first Will. They're as good as locked as well. It all comes back to Conway. Tom, you've got to find him and recover those documents.'

'I know, I know. I'll keep trying. If I have to, I'll go to St Albans myself. In the meantime, my father will stand the legal fees. He's not a wealthy man but says there's enough to pay Latimer and a barrister to take on the case.'

'How do you find Latimer? Do you think he can be trusted?'

'I've only met him twice and he stank of liquor on both occasions. However, he assures me he knows what he is doing and for what it's worth, I believe him. His mind may be fuddled by drink, but he seems honest enough.'

'What about Alfie's birth certificate? Is there not a copy somewhere?'

'One should have been lodged with the Somerset House Registry in London but I've made enquiries and they can't find anything.'

'What about Saint Cuthbert's parish records?'

'I've checked that too. The baptism entry records your father and mother as Alfie's parents. There is no mention of Lord William, not that I expected there to be.'

'And Victoria? Is there any news of her?'

Tom lit two cigarettes and passed me one.

'I knew this question was coming. Victoria was a guest of the family over New Year and her engagement to Julian was announced last week. I'm sorry Ed but its better you know now rather than clutching at straws.'

My heart sank. Engaged to Julian? How could she? She didn't even like him.

'I'm also sorry about not believing you before' continued Tom. 'I now realise she slept with you for information, and

I don't blame you for feeling the way you do. However, Victoria is a nothing other than a selfish, self-serving cow and you must see it is because of her that we are in this terrible trouble.'

So, Victoria had travelled to Durham for New Year after all, just like she said she would and now she was engaged to Julian. How could she do it after the night we spent together? Had she been lying when she said all those things to me? Was she really that calculating? The evidence was overwhelming yet still I could not accept it. I wondered if she had slipped down to the house to try and find me or if I had even crossed her mind?

I was woken from my daydream by the sudden blast of a whistle.

'Time's up ladies and gentlemen. Prisoners will assemble for escort back to cells.'

There was a slow scrape of furniture and not a few sorry cries of farewell. I passed Tom a letter for Alfie and we shook hands.

'Look, thanks for coming. You don't know what it means to see a friendly face round here.'

'I'll be back soon. In the meantime, you just hang on in there. We're going to get through this.'

'You've got to find Conway.'

'I know. I'll also see what Jane can do about getting hold of some money.'

Another shrill whistle. Tom rose to his feet and headed for the exit. At the last moment he smiled and gave me the thumbs up. I returned the gesture but I was utterly devastated and for the first time I began to have doubts that all would be well. If things were not grim enough already, Victoria was now engaged to someone else while we were abandoned by almost everyone, with only Tom's father and an alcoholic lawyer standing between us both and years in this hell hole.

There was a thunderstorm over Durham that afternoon and with the kitchens flooded, there was nothing for it but to lie on my bunk and stare at the ceiling while the rain crashed down on the prison roof and spewed through unseen gullies onto the flags below. Little did I think it would come to this. As I plunged the depths of despair, I had never imagined life could be so completely and utterly dire.

CHAPTER EIGHT

And so the days turned into weeks as with the passing of time, each morning broke that little bit sooner. I always rose early and while McMash snored and farted through oblivion, I read at the table as on the other side of our rusty grill, the city woke from its own slumber. Horses on the cobblestones. Footsteps on the street. Children making their way to school. A solitary tweet from a blackbird before one or two others replied and then the host as if to confirm that beyond these filthy granite walls, life for everyone else was going on as usual. It was not always the blackbird. Occasionally gulls would cry out as they wheeled high over the prison. Perhaps there was a storm at sea, or they were scavenging the refuse bins at the back of the kitchens.

Sometimes I would haul myself up to the grill and gaze out longingly although the view of the town was obstructed by another wall and there was not much to see apart from a protruding overflow pipe that was visited several times a day by an enormous raven. In my boredom I used to wait for ages for this bird and when he appeared, I could only marvel at his agility as he twisted, croaked and flapped while sipping his fill. I wish I were as free as you are, my friend.

Each Thursday Tom and Latimer came to the prison and we slowly constructed our defence. The prosecution case was now framed in an indictment alleging we had entered Dryburn Mortuary as trespassers and therein stole cash, jewellery and other items of value belonging to the deceased and their families. The principal witness for the Crown was Sergeant Tench whose evidence would include our initial meeting (when I had attended the mortuary to identify my father) and who had apparently drawn up a schedule of missing property. The case was fortified by the discovery of our fingerprints all over Tench's office and the fact of my immediate disappearance after the event and subsequent inability to account for my whereabouts and the large sum of money in my possession when I was detained.

We decided there was nothing for it but tell the truth and hope the jury believed us. We would run the defence on the lines of what we told Inspector Honeyman namely that while we admit breaking into the mortuary, we took nothing other than the coroner's file. Although this was the truth it would involve challenging Tench's evidence and we had to decide upon what basis. Tench was either mistaken about all this property going missing or he was lying. Which was it? We reasoned that the schedule was too long and detailed for there to have been any mistake so Tench must be telling the truth; the property on that list had gone missing. The next question was if we hadn't taken it, then who did? And where was my father's gold watch? We talked this round and round before reaching the only logical conclusion. Tench himself must be the thief. He was the only person with unsupervised access to the office and had already lied to us about the contents of my father's file. We would go for Tench.

Which other witnesses were we likely to face? The prosecution would have to explain how we came under suspicion in the first place. This would mean calling Crake, and, presumably, whoever imparted details of our involvement. This must have been Victoria. We could think of no one else. There was no one else. No one else had known. Would Victoria be prepared to give evidence? Latimer reckoned that if it *was* her who betrayed us, then she would have no choice. The problem, therefore, was not whether Crake or Victoria would give evidence against us, but how on earth were we to discredit them when they did?

The solicitor let out a heavy sigh.

'They will be totally against you, you realise that? Mr Crake is the deputy coroner and a pillar of the establishment and the judge will be very much on his side. I also expect Lady Clifford to tell the court you admitted stealing all of this property, presumably in the misguided belief it would go no further.'

'Well at least that much is true' I said blandly. 'I did confide in Victoria. You might as well know Mr Latimer; Victoria Clifford and I were lovers. I told her about the burglary when we were in bed together. I thought I could trust her.'

The solicitor immediately stopped writing and looked up from his notes. 'What?' he whispered incredulously. 'What?' he repeated as he looked around furtively to ensure we were not being overheard. 'You and Lady Clifford were *lovers*? As in sleeping together? As in carnal relations and all that?'

'It's true. Oh, I realise now she was under instructions from Julian to find out what Lord William told me on his deathbed. I see that now, but I was utterly besotted with the girl and like a fool I told her everything. She used me Mr Latimer. She used me although I doubt if even Julian's nasty mind could have foreseen the relish with which she pursued her assignment.'

Latimer gawked at me as if trying to make sense of what he had just heard. Eventually he picked up his pen and buried his head back in his notes.

'Do you *seriously* expect the jury to believe that? Edmund, you must see the very notion is absurd. Quite absurd. That someone of her background and position in s-society would consort with -pardon the contrast but I have to draw it- would have sexual relations with the impecunious son of the local horse trainer?'

'Thank you very much. And I love you too, Mr Latimer. However, it is the truth. Victoria and I slept together. She told me she loved me. She can't deny it.'

Latimer shook his head.

'Of course she is going to deny it! The mere suggestion will be regarded as nothing other than a scurrilous falsehood and as your solicitor I would be failing in my duty if I did not suggest you would be out of your mind to make it.'

'But it's true. I tell you it's true. She can't deny it. She can't. I kept the hand-written love note she left when she slipped away after our night together. It's under the mattress in my room.'

Latimer continued scribbling for a while then slowly laid down his papers.

'So that's your defence, is it?' said he despairingly. 'That everyone else is lying? That Mr Crake is lying. That Sergeant Tench is lying, no, not only lying but that he, Sergeant Tench, is actually the thief? And then to cap it all, Lady Victoria

Clifford, the illustrious daughter of a peer of the realm took *you*, Edmund Bullick, a penniless Oxbridge scholar to her bed and that, yes members of the jury, she is lying as well? D-do you realise how utterly implausible this all sounds? Well, do you?'

'Implausible or not it is the truth and I want you to run with it.'

Latimer folded his arms and shook his head.

'No. No, no. This is most unwise. I tell you Edmund, I have been the champion of many lost causes but let me c-caution you in the strongest possible terms; if you pursue this line of defence you will find yourself in unfathomable trouble. It will destroy you.'

'It's a risk I am prepared to take. I don't have a choice.'

'Yes, you do. You could plead guilty. Oh, don't look at me like that. You're an intelligent f-fellow. You must see the evidence against you is overwhelming?'

'What? Plead guilty to something we didn't do? Mr Crake reckoned we would get five years. I'm not pleading to that.'

'Five years? Five years? Believe me young man if you are convicted after making such wild accusations you can expect nearer eight. Do you not see the judge will hammer you? I urge you to think very carefully about your situation and how we might limit the damage. That you broke into the mortuary is not an issue. The only measure between the Crown and ourselves is what was taken. My advice is you mitigate your position while you can and throw yourself at the mercy of the court. With the death of your father and previous good character you might even get away with three years.'

'Absolutely not.'

'Please, will you at least consider it?'

'I already have and my answer is the same. I will not plead guilty to something I didn't do.'

'But think of your brother, your future, your…'

'Mr Latimer' said Tom 'We have made our decision. These are our instructions.'

Latimer closed his notebook and reached for his briefcase.

'Very well' he sighed wearily. 'But on your own heads be it gentlemen, on your own heads be it.'

CHAPTER NINE

About a week later I received an unexpected visit from Tom. Even as he weaved through the tables I sensed something was horribly wrong.

'What is it?'

My friend removed his coat, drew up a chair, lit a couple of cigarettes then passed one across.

'Conway has been killed.'

'*Killed?* How? When?'

Tom's hands were shaking. He took a several deep drags then stubbed out the remainder.

'He fell at Ypres ten days ago.'

I froze as if I had been bitten by a snake.

'But are you sure? How do you know? Is it certain?'

'Yes, quite certain. I was with his father this morning. The family received a telegram from the War Office followed by a letter of condolence from his commanding officer. It appears they were in a convoy transferring wounded down the Menin Road when Conway's ambulance was hit by a stray shell. Everyone on board died instantly. The only consolation is he wouldn't have known anything about it.'

I struggled for words, but none came. Conway dead? Like gone forever? Gone as in no more? But gone where? No. Not Conway. Of all people, not him. It couldn't be true. But then it had to be. I looked into Tom's blenched face.

'I'm so sorry' said he.

Conway dead? I thought I was going to be sick. A thousand images flashed across my mind. School rugby teams. Cricket matches. Conway perennially gathering cups and prizes. Always praying in the chapel. Always immersed in puzzles and crosswords. We had grown up with him. He was ubiquitous. He was indestructible. And now he was gone for eternity and with him the key to our liberty and my brother's destiny.

'Shit.'

'Quite. Shit.'

'Did his father say anything else?'

Tom pulled up his stool so we wouldn't be overheard.

'Regarding the documents? In spite of the anguish of the situation I obviously raised it but his parents know nothing. When I explained a little more, they suggested we searched Conway's room together. As you can imagine I didn't relish the prospect but they were most insistent. Oh, how I wish I'd declined and left there and then. It was absolutely unbearable going through all his things. The cupboards and draws. His personal letters and files. We even looked behind the pictures and photographs on the walls. His mother was crying throughout and in the midst of such betrayal I half expected the man himself to burst in and ask me what the hell I was doing?'

'Conway would have understood, I'm sure of it.'

'No. I don't think so. I was there, you were not. I tell you it was awful. Bloody awful. I felt like some kind of ghoul intruding on their misery. I so wish I hadn't gone around.'

'I don't see you had a choice. I would have done exactly the same. Conway might not have liked it, but he was utterly straight, he hated injustice and would have approved still less of us being sent to prison for something we didn't do. Now you listen to me. His death is shocking, yes, but there will be time enough to grieve when we get through this. Right now, we have to concentrate on what on earth we are going to do without those papers. How did you leave it?'

'They said they'd keep looking but Conway must have taken everything with him. Actually, when I think about it, I made him promise he would never let the documents out of his sight. They must have been with him. We can only hope they turn up.'

'Did they say anything else? Anything at all?'

'Only that it was comforting to know their son had so many friends and asked that I would keep in touch with them. I promised to visit often, and when this dreadful business is over, I intend to.'

'You and me both, that's if I ever get out of this hole. Talking of which our trial is only a couple of weeks away. Have you seen anything of Latimer? The last time he was here he tried to persuade us to plead guilty.'

'My father went to his office this morning and made the closing payment on account of his fees. That's 300 guineas in all. He had to take a debenture on the shop to raise it but at least that side is dealt with.'

'I'll pay him back later. What about Latimer though? Did he say which barrister he's instructing?'

'No. Just that he was on to it and we'll have a conference shortly.'

At that moment the bell rang to mark the end of visiting. Tom climbed to his feet and pulled on his coat.

'Before you leave, I meant to ask. Did you find Victoria's letter?'

'Heavens, I almost forgot. Yes, I did. Jane sneaked up to the house and recovered it from under the mattress like you said.'

'Well at least we have something although without those papers we're a sitting duck.'

'We mustn't despair. Conway's death is a blow but we're not finished yet. Now look. I'll be back next week with counsel. Until then, for the sake of us both, you have to stay positive and keep your nerve. Do you understand?'

Keep your nerve. It was easier said than done. Conway's demise so soon after my father's was devastating. In a way it was worse than dad's because while news of both struck from the clouds, Conway's was even closer to home. I had only been with him a few weeks ago. He was so young with so much to live for and now he was gone. As I lay on my bunk that night, I tried in vain to get my head round it. He was gone. Gone. Where had he gone? His poor parents. I pictured that awful scene, his mother in tears as they trawled through his possessions. He had been their only child, their pride and joy. What was left for them now but to step into a never-ending desert of misery?

CHAPTER TEN

A few days later I was working in the kitchens when one of the screws poked his head round the door and shouted there was someone to see me. It was way past visiting hours, but any prospect of our overdue legal conference quickly vanished when I was escorted into a side office and the presence of a young army Captain.

'Are you Edmund Bullick?' said he.

I replied that I was.

'Hugo Poskitt. Royal Army Medical Corps, 33 Field Hospital. How do you do?'

I surveyed my companion. He would be a few years older than me, tall, polished and immaculately turned out in his neatly pressed khaki and dark blue beret. I wondered what he was doing here and what he could possibly want with me. I did not have long to wait. As soon we were alone, he pointed to the empty chair, sat down himself and reached for his briefcase.

'Good God man' he said crisply. 'You took some finding'.

'It's a long story' I replied.

'I would I had time to hear it but there is none. I return to France tomorrow and I have a train to catch. I will therefore get straight to the point. I had the honour of being Lieutenant Conway's commanding officer. I believe he was a friend of yours?'

'He was. We were at Ampleforth together.'

'So I understand. You will therefore know he was killed in action?'

'I heard a few days ago. I still can't believe it. His poor parents.'

'His poor parents indeed' exhaled Poskitt. 'I was with them this morning which is how I learned of your incarceration.'

A brief silence ensued as my unexpected visitor looked at me oddly as if trying to make sense of our predicament.

'What can I do for you Captain?'

Poskitt snapped back to reality and fished inside his case.

'When Lieutenant Conway was killed' he said gravely 'I was given the sorry task of disposing of his personal effects. Among his belongings were a number of private letters he wished to be distributed in the event of his demise. One such communication is addressed to yourself. Here. Take it. Take it.'

I stared at the small, pencil written envelope. The reverse side was endorsed with red crayon and various official looking stamps but there was no mistaking the extravagant hand on the front.

Edmund Bullick Esq Durham

'The script has been vetted by intelligence' continued Poskitt. 'I must caution you it's quite heart rendering, almost prophetic as if he knew he would not be coming back. There's also some gobbledygook at the end we couldn't make sense of. Perhaps you will have better luck.'

I gaped at the envelope again, completely lost for words.

Poskitt was already on his feet.

'Lieutenant Conway was not with us for long' said he pulling on his greatcoat 'but your friend was a very brave, young officer. Please accept His Majesty's deepest condolences on your loss.'

'Hang on. Please wait. There must have been something more? Did he leave any other message? Anything at all?'

'No. I don't think so, or if he did, it never reached my ears. Now if you will excuse me, I really must take my leave.'

I took his outstretched hand.

'I want to thank you for taking the time and trouble to find me.'

'It is no more than my duty Bullick. It only remains for me to wish you well in whatever mess you appear to have got yourself into. Good day to you.'

I was promptly escorted back to my cell, all the while Conway's letter burning a hole in my pocket. McMash looked up from his bunk.

'Where've you been?'

'Legal visit' I said casually although my heart was thumping as I sat down at the table and unfastened the envelope.

St Pancras, London
28 December 1914

Dear Edmund,

I remember how you and Tom would tease me for my methodical approach to life and for spending so much

403

*time in the chapel however tomorrow we sail for Le
Havre and I am taking the precaution of settling my
affairs.*

*When I joined up, I discounted the possibility of
anything happening to an irrelevant ambulance
driver but in my few days in London, I have seen
so many wretched wounded pouring into the city
bringing such horrendous tales from the front that
I realise it would be foolhardy to regard myself as
somehow invulnerable.*

*I know we didn't always see eye to eye but looking
back, I now understand that any previous discord
between us was spawned from envy on my part.
Although you could be flippant, the truth is I admired
you enormously and the way you made friends so
effortlessly which I always found difficult. You and
Tom, Edmund, are the kind of people I always aspired
to be and as we became close in these last few weeks,
I want you to know how much your friendship meant
to me.*

*It is strange, but even as I write this you may never
know of my regard because if I do come through
whatever awaits me, I'll probably never find the right
moment. However, in the event that you do read this
letter, it will mean I am not coming back in which
case it is fitting that these final words are the truest
that have passed between us.*

*Farewell Edmund, my friend. I ask that you
remember me and pray for me and that God will bless*

you and deliver you and yours safely through this
dreadful time.

Yours ever,
Albert

PS The papers are in a secure luggage cabinet. There's
no one else I can trust so I have left the key with
Veronica at St Pancras Station. Seek and ye shall find.

PPS John 19:16

CHAPTER ELEVEN

Tom slumped at the table and shook his head. His eyes were bloodshot, and he was plainly haggard from his exertions.

'Nothing I'm afraid. Ab-so-lute-lee nothing.'

'What? *Nothing*?'

'Nothing.'

'I don't believe you.'

Tom lit two cigarettes and passed me one.

'Complete dead end. I'm sorry.'

My heart sank. I was expecting so much.

'That's all we need. But are you quite certain?'

'No, not totally, but we're as certain as we can be. Oh, don't look at me like that Ed, I'm gutted too but Dad and I combed the place from top to bottom and I'm telling you now, there's no one of that name at St Pancras.'

I fished out Conway's letter for the umpteenth time and read the postscript.

...I have left the key with Veronica at St Pancras Station...

'He couldn't be any plainer, you must be mistaken.'

Tom took a deep drag.

'Nope.'

'But I don't understand. I don't. Conway is so exact in what he says here and he wasn't the type to get these things wrong. Are you absolutely *sure* you checked? Did you see any lockers? Are you certain you asked around thoroughly?'

'Oh, there's a mountain of left luggage lockers. Scores and scores of them but as for Veronica with the key, I tell you, she's not there. She can't be. We spent two days making enquiries. That's two whole days starting from seven in the morning until seven at night and I tell you, there's not a trace. Not a single lead. No. We must have been looking in the wrong place. Now think Edmund. Think. There has to be something else between the lines of that note. What about the reference at the end?'

'*John 19:16*? It's a passage from the New Testament. I looked it up in the chapel; it says '*Finally Pilate handed him over to them to be crucified.*'

'Is that all?'

'That's all.'

Tom shook his head.

'Poor Conway. It's like he knew he was also condemned. Any other ideas?

'*Seek and ye shall find.*' He says that as well.'

'Seek and ye shall find? I tell you Edmund, we 'seeked' this woman everywhere and must have knocked on a hundred doors in that massive basilica. Honestly, a hundred bloody doors. Not a single stone unturned. Not one. We scoured the offices, the shopping arcades, the flower stands and newspaper kiosks. We questioned the Salvation Army, the recruiting offices and trawled every cafe, teashop, bar and pub not just in St Pancras but at Kings Cross as well. We put up notices appealing for information, we asked the porters, the police, the taxi drivers, even the tramps and toilet attendants but no one has ever heard of her. No one. She's not there Edmund, unless she's been and gone but even then, we asked so many people that if there is or had ever been anyone of that name anywhere near the station, I tell you, somebody, somewhere would have said something.'

'What about the lockers? Could you not access them anyway?'

'Not a chance. We pleaded with the station master but there's just too many. He said if we knew the number, he might be able to do something otherwise we would have to go to the police and get a warrant.'

'As if they'd lift a finger to help us.'

'Quite.'

Everything had depended on recovering those papers. How I wished I'd never parted with them in the first place. We went through the options over and over again, but the conclusion was inescapable. We were caught on a sandbank and with the hearing imminent, our situation was now desperate. Where on earth were they? Where had he put them? Where?

Worse was to follow. There had been no sign of Latimer. It was as if he had vanished off the face of the earth. I sent letters and messages and Tom repeatedly called at his office but no one knew where he was, or if they did, they weren't saying. It was not until the day before our trial that he finally materialised, and we discovered what the problem was.

'I'm sorry gentlemen, the money's gone.'

It was the first thing he said. The very first thing.

'What do you mean it's gone?' I replied ominously. 'We've given you 300 guineas. Are you saying you want some more?'

'No. I'm not saying that.'

'Then where's our barrister? We need a conference urgently, like straight away. Who have you instructed?'

'I haven't instructed anybody'.

'What? Mr Latimer, you were supposed to engage our brief weeks ago. Weeks ago. What do you mean you haven't instructed anybody? You assured us everything was in hand. You promised us faithfully.'

'I'm sorry. I've let you down.'

I stared through the odour of liquor and tobacco into Latimer's gaunt, unshaven face. The subject gazed back pathetically where behind the greasy lenses I met the jaundiced eyes of a sick man. Tom slammed his fist on the table.

'But the money?' he shouted. 'For fuck's sake Latimer! What have you done with the money?'

The eyes of the hall were suddenly upon us.

'Keep it down Tom.'

'Bugger that. Where's our money?' he demanded. 'What have you done with our money?'

'I've spent it' came the weary reply. 'I'm so sorry.'

Tom sprang across the table and grabbed Latimer by the throat.

'Now you look here you little prick…'

He got no further. The words had barely left his mouth before one of the screws raced over and flung him back into his chair.

'Is there a problem here Mr Latimer?'

The solicitor waved him away.

'No, not at all. Just a minor difference of opinion. We're fine officer. Really.'

'Are you sure Mr Latimer?'

'Yes, quite sure. Thank you.'

'Well, if you say so sir' he grunted before pointing his baton at Tom. 'You. Watch it. Any more trouble and you'll be banged up with the rest. Do I make myself clear?'

'Perfectly officer. My most profound apologies.'

The warden glowered at Tom for a moment then turned and shuffled back to the door. Latimer waited until he had resumed his post then took a deep breath before continuing.

'I wasn't going to come to the prison today' he said wearily. 'I really didn't want to because I know what I have done is inexcusable. However, I can see you are decent lads and I owe you an explanation.'

'I'm all ears' said Tom sarcastically.

'The money you gave me. I've spent it.'

'But how?' I asked 'It's such a large sum. Where on earth did it go?'

Latimer shifted uneasily.

'I really don't know where to start' he said. 'I don't expect you to understand.'

'Try me,' said Tom.

The solicitor took another deep breath then leaned forward so as not to be overheard. I winced at the smell of sour booze.

'Let me say before I begin that it was always my intention to do the very best I could for you both. Always. You see, when we met at the magistrates court, I believed you straight away when you insisted you hadn't taken anything other than Jimmy Bullick's file. My colleagues and I have long suspected the coroner's assistant was on the take and I believed with a good barrister and a favourable jury, we might finally expose him. However, and I don't expect you to understand this, I have demons of my own, and when the money for your defence fell into my lap, I began dipping into it. My practice was in trouble. There were creditors. I have a son at boarding school...'

'Oh, come on man, don't blame your kids' said Tom angrily.

'As I say, I don't expect you to understand, how could you? At first, I only took a small amount here and there with every intention of putting it back. However slowly but steadily, a little became a little more, a little more became much more then before I knew it, half of the money was gone. It was at that point, realising the hopelessness of my position and seeking to recover what I had spent, that I took what was left to Gosforth Park and ventured the lot on a short-priced favourite which, I'm sorry to say, was turned over.'

Tom put his head in his hands.

'I don't believe I'm hearing this.'

'What? *All* of it?' I asked incredulously. 'You staked the *lot*? Are you saying there's nothing left?'

'I'm so sorry.'

'But that money was to pay for our defence. Tom's father mortgaged his business to raise it.'

'I know. I'm so sorry.'

'I don't understand Mr Latimer. Why do it? Why?'

'I was desperate.'

'And Gosforth?' I whispered disbelievingly. 'What on earth made you risk anything at Gosforth? If you knew how many punters had done their money on that treacle run-in, you wouldn't have gone near the place.'

Latimer shook his head miserably.

'I realise that now. However, and please believe me, the information came from an impeccable source. I was assured the horse could not be beaten.'

'Mr Latimer, if I had a shilling for every time I heard someone say that, I'd be as rich as the Agha Khan himself.'

'I'm so sorry lads' he repeated.

'So that's your explanation is it?' growled Tom. 'You intended to look after us but when it came down to it, you decided to get drunk instead and throw the lot away?'

'But it wasn't like that. Really, it wasn't. I'm a slave to alcohol, that much is true, but I rarely gamble. However, I was desperate. The information was sound, it was a chance I had to take and if it had come off, we would not be sitting here talking about it. Unfortunately, however, the horse didn't win. It was beaten. Only by a whisker, but it lost just the same. And now I am finished.'

I looked despairingly at Latimer. I'd seen it all before. I'd been brought up on the track and were it not for our own predicament, I might even have felt sorry for him.

'But why risk it?' I said. 'I don't understand. Why? We could at least have salvaged something with what was left. Why didn't you say you were in trouble?'

'I wish I could tell you, however if you haven't been there yourself, the utter wretchedness of my addiction is impossible to describe.'

'Oh, don't come that' said Tom irately. 'I enjoy a good drink as much as the next bloke but it would never cross my mind to steal from anybody.'

'You really don't understand, do you?' sighed Latimer. 'You may get drunk now and then but you're not an alcoholic or believe me, you would know. When you are in as deep as I am, the addiction is absolute; it sacrifices all reason and accountability to the blind, blinkered pursuit of the next fix to the point where absolutely nothing else matters, nothing at all. This is how it is with me. This is what I am or rather what I have become. Let me put it another way. It's as if my tortured life is akin to the existence of one of the crane operators on Gateshead Quay. There I am, looking down from the top of my little world, the master of all I survey. I carefully manoeuvre this cargo here and lower that cargo there, everything is in order. Then as soon as I have a drink, it's as if this stranger suddenly enters the cabin, taps me on the shoulder and says he'll take over. Of course, I readily agree and leave him to it however once I sober up and return to the controls, I look around to discover to my horror that everything is chaos and all that was dear to me now smashed and broken.'

It was a sorry tale and for a while no one spoke. Tom lit two cigarettes then after deliberating for a moment, struck a third and passed them around.

'That's all very well' said he at length 'but if you knew how it would be, what were you doing taking us on in the first place?'

'I know. I should never have agreed. However, I believed in your cause- I still do - and I was determined to secure an acquittal and with it, redeem something of my reputation.'

413

'Do you realise what you have done?' said Tom angrily. 'Well, do you? My father mortgaged his business to raise the money for our defence. What am I to say to him now?'

Latimer could only stare at the floor.

'You know we are going to have to report this to the police' I said.

'I understand. I deserve nothing less. I realise I am finished.'

'You're finished? *You're* finished?' I whispered. 'What about us? We're in court tomorrow. What would you have us say to the judge?'

'There's nothing for it' he replied. 'You must explain your predicament and seek an adjournment'.

'An adjournment? I've already spent over three months in this hell hole. There must be another way.'

'I fear there may not be. I'm so sorry.'

'Sorry?' I shouted at him. 'You're sorry? For goodness sake man, is that all you can say? 'Sorry'? Tell me, have you any idea what it's like in here? Really, have you any idea? Cooped up for twenty-three hours a day in a stinking cell next to a stinking drum of shit, sharing sod all with the dregs of society, continually watching your back in the showers bracing yourself for the next good hiding or even worse?'

'There has to be another way' said Tom. 'Please Mr Latimer. You must know someone who can represent us.'

The bell clanged for the end of legal visits.

The solicitor rose to his feet.

'I cannot help you. I am so sorry. I am so sorry' he repeated and headed for the door.

'Wait Mr Latimer' I shouted after him. 'Please. You cannot leave us like this.'

But he did. At the sound of raised voices, the hostile gaze of the warden was once more upon us and all we could do was stare helplessly towards the exit where the solicitor joined the queue and melted away. We never saw him again.

That afternoon, Hayward hanged himself in the showers and in the subsequent riot, twenty or so prisoners barricaded themselves into E Wing with some managing to access the roof from where they rained slates onto the passers-by. It took several hours for the jailers to gather reinforcements and restore order during which time everyone else was locked in their cells. As I lay on my bunk listening to the crash of debris and screams of mayhem, I had never felt so dejected in my life. I thought of my brother, far away in Ireland. I wondered what he was doing now and if I would ever see him again? And my father. He would have known what to do. Oh, how I longed for his advice, even the smallest word of comfort. But then I pictured him as he would be now, lying in the eternal silence of his casket deep under the soil of St Oswald's. No. My father had his own cup of sorrow when he was with us. At least he would be spared mine. I drifted back to when I was a boy and the crisp April mornings riding the buttercup gallops of Middleham tan. The scent of leather and grass. The jangle of buckles. The clip clop of the horses ringing off the cobbles as the string made its way through the village. And Victoria, always Victoria. Her long black hair splayed over the pillow. Her pale limbs wrapped around me. Her breath in my ear. And now I was abandoned. I was completely and utterly alone. I turned my face into the mattress and wept bitterly.

CHAPTER TWELVE

The following morning our trial opened at Durham Assizes. It was Tuesday 30 March 1915 and as long as I live, I shall never forget it. The ring of hobnails in the corridor. The familiar jangle of keys. The empty expressions of the warders as they clunked on the handcuffs and steered me to the door.

McMash lay on his bunk surveying events over the rim of *John Bull*.

'Good luck kid and remember, tell the truth. It makes the porridge easier when they find you guilty.'

'Ever the optimist, hey?'

'Realist more like. You're toast.'

'I'll visit when I get out.'

'No you won't. I've opened a book on you going down so don't disappoint me.'

'Cheers mate.'

I was marched in silence through a labyrinth of passages until we reached a flight of stone steps at the top of which was a wooden door, half open. The jailers yanked my handcuffs to check they were fast.

'Right Bullick, listen to me' said one. 'You are about to enter the Crown Court where you will shortly be identified and where you are to remain seated at all times and not speak unless you are spoken to. Do you understand?'

'Yes sir.'

'Good - because, believe me, if you give us any shit in there- any shit at all- me and the lads will be down your cell this evening to tuck you in.'

We climbed from the underworld into a torrent of sunshine that seared down from a window somewhere high up in the wall. As I adjusted to the light I slowly took in my surroundings. The lofty, majestically carved ceiling and richly panelled walls. The rows of benches sloping down to the pit. The barristers and officials drifting through towers of documents as they waited for the business of the day. To their right was an enclosed wooden lectern not unlike a church pulpit which I took to be the witness stand. Immediately opposite to this, on the left side of the court, was a railed area securing two wooden benches from which vantage point the twelve members of the jury, already assembled, were craning their necks for a first look at the wretches upon whom they would shortly be invited to pass judgement. On a bench at the back, a solitary barrister was scribbling away while high above him, a crammed public gallery looked down from under an enormous clock that marked each passing minute with a soon-to-be-familiar 'clunk'. I raked the string of faces. They were all there. Julian leering smugly, Lady Alana looking vacant, Barnaby, Sample, Cobb, Fenoughty- in fact half the village had congregated for the entertainment in Court Number 2 where over the next few days, our very future would be decided.

The unmistakable focus of the arena was an elegant teak altar at the far end of the court directly facing the dock. It was set higher than everything else- deliberately so - and in the middle of it rested the empty throne from which the trial judge, Lord Horridge, would shortly oversee proceedings. On the wall above him, the intertwined lion and unicorn looked silently over the assembly. *Dieu et mon droit. God and my right.* Was all this really for us?

It was so bizarre. Surely someone else must be the focus of the dark looks and I was just another bystander. But no one was. My heart thumped wildly. Oh, be near me Lord Jesus.

Tom was already in place. I thought he was impeccably dressed, his collar and tie in sharp contrast to my festering prison garb. He looked up and gave me a thin smile.

'Fingers crossed mate.'

'No talking in the dock.'

I had just settled between the two guards with a third at the end boxing us in when three sharp raps emanated from the judge's connecting door.

'Court rise.'

Horridge swept in and stood for a moment at the back of his chair.

'Let all persons having business before His Majesty's court draw near and give their attention.'

The assembly bowed deferentially. Horridge responded in similar fashion then took his seat.

'Yes?'

The entreaty was answered by a red-faced man shaped like a rugby ball who was sat immediately below the judge and who I took to be the court clerk. He was a plump, serious looking fellow with a salami head poking out of the remainder of his body which looked as if it might burst from his robes at any moment.

'My Lord' he puffed 'I call the case of the Crown versus Brentnall and Bullick. The prisoners will stand. Are you Thomas Brentnall?'

'I am'.

'Are you Edmund Bullick?

'Yes.'

'Sit down.'

Horridge peered over the rim of his spectacles.

'Yes. Mr Jackson-Fagg?'

The prosecutor climbed to his feet.

'My Lord, I am instructed by the Crown in these proceedings. The defendants are represented by I know not who.'

'Indeed?' said the judge.

'I regret I am unable to assist. I have made enquiry with my colleagues but to no avail.'

'Very well. Learned clerk?'

Sausage-head twisted his portly frame.

'There is no one on the court record, judge.'

'I see. The prisoners will stand. Mr Brentnall, Mr Bullick. Who is representing you in this matter?'

'There is no one your honour' I replied.

Horridge removed his spectacles.

'What? No one? No one at all? But this case was listed weeks ago. Are you telling the court that in all that time you did nothing to arrange your defence?'

'We instructed Mr Latimer, a local solicitor' answered Tom. 'Unfortunately, he withdrew at the last minute and we have no choice but to ask for an adjournment.'

'Out of the question' said the judge.

'But we have no one to defend us' I said. 'We need time to instruct someone else'.

'Absolutely not' barked Horridge. 'Do either of you have any idea how much it costs the exchequer to administer these courts? The judiciary has enough difficulty balancing its books without squandering precious resources on prisoners who will not help themselves.'

'But it wasn't our fault' I pleaded. 'Really it wasn't. We paid for counsel in advance, but the solicitor spent all our money.'

Horridge folded his arms.

'This is ridiculous. Mr Jackson-Fagg. What say the Crown?'

'We oppose any adjournment. Our witnesses are here and we look to proceed.'

'Quite.'

'But what my friend has told you is true' said Tom. 'The solicitor let us down. He was paid up front to engage counsel but disappeared with all our money.'

Horridge removed his spectacles and placed them on the bench.

'This is absurd' he mumbled. 'Utterly absurd.'

The silence was broken by a crisp voice from the back of the court.

'Perhaps I might be of assistance, my Lord?'

We all turned round. The solitary barrister who had been scribbling earlier was now on his feet.

'And you are, sir?'

'My name is Hall, my Lord. Edward Hall. As your lordship may know I was instructed for the defence in Court Number

1 but unfortunately, my client passed away yesterday and I am, as the saying goes, at a bit of a loose end.'

'So you are Edward Hall?' said the judge with a surprising degree of veneration. 'A very warm welcome to Durham, Mr Hall. The court is aware of events at Durham prison yesterday. Shocking business.'

'Indeed, my Lord.'

It was only then I noticed that all the barristers and staff were gawking at Hall as if they were in the presence of some kind of royalty. Tom looked at me quizzically and shrugged his shoulders. I hadn't the faintest idea who he was either. Hall? Edward Hall? I'd heard the name before. Where? Where? Then it came to me. Could it be Edward *Marshall* Hall? Good grief, it was. The man himself. *The Great Defender*. I'd read about his exploits at college and how he saved Wood, the Camden Town murderer from the gallows.

'And you say you might be of assistance in this matter?'

'I do. I could not but help overhearing your Lordship's exchange with these two gentlemen and in the circumstances, I am more than willing to volunteer my services. I have already made arrangements to be in town for a few days and there is nothing else to occupy me.'

Horridge was impressed.

'The court is indebted to you Mr Hall' he clucked. 'How much time do you need?'

Hall fished for his watch.

'Well' said he snapping back the cover 'I must take instructions from the prisoners and liaise with my clerk. However, if your lordship was prepared to stand the case down for the remainder of the day, I would expect to be in a position to proceed first thing in the morning.'

'I have in mind reconvening this afternoon' said the judge.

'I would be afforded a little longer, my Lord.'

'No, Mr Hall. This trial was listed weeks ago. I will not have it delayed any longer.'

'But my Lord..'

'Mr Hall, I have made my decision. The issues in this matter are not complicated. You may have until this afternoon.'

Hall bowed.

'If it pleases your Lordship'.

'It does' said the judge gathering his papers. 'The court will resume at two pm.'

'All rise.'

We were escorted down the stairs into a small conference room where twenty minutes later, we were joined by Hall who promptly sat down at the table and shook off his wig.

'You may leave us' said he addressing the warden.

'But sir, my instructions are to remain with the prisoners at all times.'

'You will take your instructions from me, officer. Now please wait outside. I will call if I need you.'

Hall was not the sort to argue with. If the warden was about to respond he thought the better of it and duly stood sentry in the passage with his back to the glass pane of the door.

I surveyed our visitor. Hall would be in his mid-fifties, tall and stout with a razor-sharp eye. He held out his hand in an unexpectedly friendly manner.

'Good morning gentlemen. Now we have very little time so rather than waste any of it on unnecessary small talk I will get straight to the point. I have discussed your case with Mr Jackson-Fagg and it appears to me the two of you are in a spot of bother. The offence of burglary is serious enough but to steal from a mortuary in the dead of night? What on earth were you thinking?'

'But we didn't steal anything' answered Tom.

'The police suggest otherwise. Are you saying you didn't do it?'

'We broke in, it's true' I replied 'but all we removed was the coroner's file on my late father. We didn't take anything else. You have to believe us.'

Hall sighed wearily.

'Mr Bullick, what I may or may not believe is immaterial. It's what the jury make of your behaviour that counts. Tell me this gentlemen; have either of you been in trouble with the police before?'

'No.'

'Mr Brentnall?'

'Never.'

Hall looked through his notes then scribbled a few more.

'Gentlemen, I want you to tell me more about this file. You appear to have gone to extraordinary lengths to recover it? I want to know why.'

'The coroner's file held crucial information relating to my father's death in a riding accident including details of how he came by his injuries and what he said to the staff when he was brought into Dryburn hospital. The coroner's officer, Sergeant Tench, would not allow me to see this information when I went to identify my father's body. I knew he was hiding something, and then back at the office when I went through my father's journal, I discovered a note he left for me although the original page had been torn out and we had to decipher the trace from the one below...'

'Stop.' said Hall. 'Stop right there. Mr Bullick, your dialogue is like a bucket of water being poured over my head and if you address the court in this manner, you will be very quickly silenced by the judge. Now look, if I am to represent you, I need some *structure* to your account. Do you understand?'

'I'm sorry, Mr Hall. There's just so much on my mind and we have been at a loss to find someone who will listen to us.'

'You have no need to apologise, young man. I am at your disposal, but time is short and we must use what we have wisely. Now start again, but I want you to go slowly, to be precise and leave nothing out. Even the tiniest detail, though it may appear irrelevant to you, you must tell me. Above all, if I ask either of you a question, I want your word that you will answer me promptly and above all, truthfully. Have I made myself clear?'

We replied that he had.

'I must warn you Mr Hall' said Tom 'we don't have any money.'

'So I understand.'

'We cannot pay you' I added. 'Our solicitor took everything we had.'

'My fees are not important. The cost of your defence has been guaranteed by a third party.'

'Good Lord' said Tom. 'Who on earth by?'

'I am not at liberty to disclose their identity. It is sufficient you know the matter has been taken care of.'

A secret benefactor? Well, well. Perhaps our luck was turning.

Hall clasped his hands behind his neck and leaned back on his chair.

'Right gentleman, to business. I am all ears...'

CHAPTER THIRTEEN

Tench, the first prosecution witness to take the stand trotted out an impressive history. Yes, he had served in the regulars during the Second Boar War and was wounded at the defence of Kimberley for which heroics he was awarded the Queen's South Africa medal and clasp. On his return to England, he had joined Durham Constabulary where he was duly promoted to sergeant in which latter capacity he had been the personal assistant to the county coroner for the last seven years. His duties included the day-to-day administration of the mortuary and acting as liaison officer between the relatives of the deceased and the coroner himself.

Horridge peered over his glasses.

'Liaison officer for the coroner you say? It must be a position of some delicacy?'

'It can be your honour' replied Tench deferentially. 'Very often the relatives are so upset that explaining the legal procedure requires a considerable amount of discretion and tact. I always regard it as a balancing exercise. Yes, there's a job to be done but at the same time I try and put myself in the shoes of the bereaved and explain the measures we take with the deceased as discreetly as possible.'

'Your circumspection does you credit, I'm sure Sergeant. Continue please Mr Jackson-Fagg.'

Tench went on to describe our first meeting on that awful day I attended the mortuary to identify the body of my father. I had appeared an agreeable, polite young man and at the time he had no misgivings about leaving me alone in his office while he went to fetch my father's papers. What was kept in the office? Mostly archives of previous inquests, an array of medical records, pathologist gowns, notes and instruments, that kind of thing. The office also retained the personal belongings of the deceased which were methodically indexed and stowed away for eventual distribution in accordance with any last wishes. What kind of property? Money, watches, rings and any other chattels which had been in the deceased's possession when they were admitted.

'Now these young men' supposed Jackson-Fagg pointing at the dock 'are charged with stealing from your office. I don't believe it is a matter of dispute that they entered the building in the middle of the night, however I would like you to assist the jury with what you discovered after the premises were broken into?'

Tench reached for his handkerchief and blew his nose loudly. He wiped his mouth and continued.

'Your honour, I have a room at the hospital where I sometimes stay over. I don't always use it but I had been working late that evening. The first I knew of any break-in was when I was woken in the middle of the night by a commotion in the asylum ward.'

'The asylum ward?' enquired Horridge.

'It's a secure area of the hospital where the county lunatics and mental defectives are treated your honour. The ward adjoins the mortuary office and when I heard the racket, I obviously went down to investigate.'

'And what did you find Sergeant?'

Tench wiped his nose and continued.

'Chaos, utter chaos. The patients had broken free of their shackles and were running about wildly, screaming and shouting. All of them were in considerable distress with several injured as if they had been fighting.'

A low murmur rippled across the courtroom.

Jackson-Fagg shook his head gravely.

'And when you came upon this scene, what did you do Sergeant?'

'I immediately blew my whistle for assistance and was promptly joined by the porter and then eventually by some of my colleagues. It took a while- we had to draw truncheons- but eventually we managed to restore order and secure the patients. However, it was a most frightening experience.'

'I don't doubt it Sergeant. And the break in? What can you tell the jury about that?'

'I didn't realise there had been a break in. Not at first, anyway. It was only when I went to check the office that I discovered someone had been in there.'

'How so?'

'To put it bluntly, the place was wrecked. Totally wrecked. It was as if a hurricane had passed through it. All the cabinets were forced open with papers strewn across the floor. It was then I realised it must have been an intruder or intruders who set the patients off. I just couldn't work out how they had got in there.'

'And how did they gain access?'

'From the mortuary sir. It transpired they had forced a skylight and entered the office through a connecting door. The mortuary was also in disarray I would add.'

Jackson-Fagg paused for a moment until he had the attention of the jury.

'Let us be quite clear about this Sergeant. Are you saying the intruders entered your office having forced a skylight in the mortuary?'

'That's correct sir.'

A low hum rippled through the court. Jackson-Fagg waited until it subsided then continued.

'And tell me Sergeant, were there any deceased resting in the mortuary at that time.'

'Yes sir. There were seven.'

A more audible murmur rippled across the court. I sensed the eyes of every member of the jury fixed on us with a mixture of bewilderment and abhorrence.

Jackson-Fagg paused again, milking the drama.

'And what did you do next sergeant?'

'I obviously secured the ward as best I could then returned to the office and started to tidy up. It was then that I noticed the locker containing the deceased's' personal effects had been wrenched open.'

So far Tench had told the truth but now he was lying. We hadn't touched any locker. We didn't even know it was there. I felt an overwhelming urge to shout out but felt Tom's hand on my arm.

'And was anything taken?'

'Yes sir. Everything of value had been removed.'

Another audible gasp rippled through the court. This time I couldn't hold back.

'That's not true' I shouted. 'He's lying. We only went for my father's file! We didn't take anything else!'

The judge smacked down his gavel.

'Mr Bullick. In due course you and Mr Brentnall will have ample opportunity to impart your version of events to the jury however right now, the prosecution is making its case and until Mr Jackson-Fagg and his witnesses are through with their evidence, I will not have these proceedings interrupted from the dock. Do I make myself clear? Thank you. Please continue, Mr Jackson-Fagg.'

'I am obliged my Lord. Sergeant, you explained to the jury a moment ago that everything of value had been removed from the locker. Can you be more specific?'

Tench wiped his muzzle and peered into his notebook.

'I can sir. I immediately checked the inventory and the following personal effects were missing;

Two gold pocket watches.
Three wrist watches, one gold, two silver, one with a leather strap.
One antique rolled gold necklace with jewel cluster.
Three gold wedding rings.
Four assorted dress rings.
Four pairs of earrings, one gold, three silver.
A silver tie pin.
One silver chain and crucifix.
A leather purse containing nine gold sovereigns.
Twenty-six-pounds ten shillings in notes.
Four pounds, six shillings and threepence ha'penny in assorted change.'

The lying bugger. A ripple of disgust swept through the court and I wished the ground would swallow us up. Jackson-Fagg was pleased with what he had heard.

'Thank you for your evidence Sergeant' said he, beaming at the jury. 'Please wait there and answer any questions from my friend for the defence.'

Hall scribbled a few notes then rose to his feet.

'Why did you refuse to allow Mr Bullick to see his father's file?'

'How do you mean sir?'

'You say you left Mr Bullick alone in your office while you went to fetch his father's papers?'

'That's correct sir.'

'When you returned, he asked to see those papers but you would not let him. Why not?'

'The coroner's papers are classified.'

'Classified? How so?'

'The files have confidential information in them sir. It is not our policy to allow the public to view them.'

'Confidential information? Such as what? Circumstances of admission? Medical information? Last words? That kind of thing?'

'I suppose so sir, yes.'

'Mr Bullick will tell the court he asked to see the file because he was anxious for information, any information, as to how his father, the racehorse trainer James Bullick, met his end. Are you saying his request was unreasonable?'

Tench blew his nose again.

'That's not for me to decide sir. All I know is the rules do not allow it.'

'Really Sergeant? I suggest his entreaty was perfectly rational and you snubbed it - not because the papers were 'classified' as you put it - but because there was information in that file that you did not want him to see.'

'No sir. It's just not our policy…'

'That file' clipped Hall 'contained a dying statement from James Bullick that Lord William Surtees had changed his will, didn't it?'

Gasps of astonishment swept the courtroom.

'Silence please' said Horridge.

Tench shuffled uncomfortably.

'No sir, it did not.'

'That file' repeated Hall 'contained a dying statement from James Bullick that Lord William Surtees had disinherited his son Julian, did it not?'

This time there was uproar as the reporters suddenly woke from their daydream and began to scribble furiously.

'That's a lie!' bawled Julian from the gallery behind us.

'Members of the public' cried Horridge. 'Members of the public, I must ask you to refrain from shouting out while this witness gives his evidence. I will not have these proceedings interrupted.'

Hall paused while the clamour abated.

'Well Sergeant, can we have your answer?'

'No sir.'

'And it was because of your intransigence that the defendant, exasperated to discover how his father died, returned to your office and removed the file.'

'But the file wasn't taken sir. We still have it.'

'You do now, yes. However, I suggest it was most certainly taken away and when subsequently recovered, it was filleted by you and placed back in the cabinet for the purpose of these proceedings.'

The hammer had struck the nail. Just for a moment Tench hesitated.

'Well Sergeant?'

'No sir. That's not correct.'

Jackson-Fagg leaped to his feet.

'My Lord, this line of cross-examination is preposterous.'

'I am against you Mr Jackson-Fagg. Your opponent can put whatever questions he chooses to this witness. The jury will determine whether they are preposterous or not.'

'I am obliged My Lord' said Hall. 'Now, Sergeant, I would like you to assist the court with this schedule of property. You say you discovered the items were missing when you checked the office on the night of the break in?'

'I did sir. Directly I went in there.'

'And did you call the attention of your superiors to the fact?'

Tench wiped his nose.

'No, I don't believe I did.'

'Why not?'

'It may have slipped my memory.'

'Do you mean by that you *did* consider reporting the theft to your superiors, but forgot to do so?'

'At the time I never thought to tell them of it.'

'Remarkable. This morning you have described in great detail the property you say was stolen, yet on the night in question you failed to mention it. Are you certain each and every one of the items you declared was removed?'

'To the best of my recollection they were sir.'

'To the best of your recollection. Is your recollection good enough to swear that they were?'

'To the best of my recollection.'(laughter)

It was a classic example of the law having its educated fun at the expense of an uneducated witness, but Hall was not done.

'Do you recall making a statement to the magistrates regarding this incident?'

'I do sir.'

'Was not your evidence at that time that there had simply been a break in, with nothing said about anything being stolen?'

'I cannot say.'

'You cannot say. Did you or did you not omit the detail?'

'I may have done.'

'You may have done' he repeated softly. 'Tell me, can you assist the court with this Sergeant? If you did omit the items in your evidence to the magistrates, how are you in a position to impart the meticulous detail you have just given to the court?'

'It may have slipped my memory to make a list at the time, but I completed one later.'

'Later you say? When, precisely, was later?'

'I'm not exactly sure sir.'

Hall glanced at the jury then back to the witness.

'Oh come, come Sergeant. These proceedings turn on what property was removed from your office and yet you are telling the court that having immediately discovered the theft, you discarded not one, but two opportunities to report the details to your superiors?'

'As I say, it may have slipped my memory.'

'Clearly, Sergeant Tench, clearly. Which is it to be then?'

'How do you mean sir?'

'I mean do you now stick to your initial understanding that items may have been missing or are we to admit the detailed schedule you told the court about a minute ago?'

'That is it sir. The detailed schedule.'

'Remarkable. You understand you are on oath Sergeant?'

'I am telling the truth.'

'The truth?' repeated Hall throwing his arms in the air. 'The *truth*? And what exactly is the truth? The jury may wish to know how, having previously failed to mention any theft, you are suddenly in a position to roll out a long and detailed schedule?'

The colour drained from the witness, his previous self-assurance dissolving by the moment.

'I-I'm telling you' he blustered 'I'm telling you all, every single item I have described, every single item was stolen that night.'

'Might it be the case that the property was removed by a colleague without your knowledge?'

'No, sir. That's not possible. I am in sole charge of the office. I have the only key.'

'I don't doubt it Sergeant in which case I suggest the property you referred to this morning was not stolen by these young men. I suggest it was stolen by you.'

This time there was pandemonium. Jackson-Fagg leaped to his feet.

'My Lord, this is an outrageous suggestion!'

'I don't disagree with my friend' said Hall coolly. 'The suggestion is outrageous. But it is also true.'

'My Lord' fumed Jackson-Fagg 'My Lord, this is most improper. I urge you to put an end to this line of cross-examination.'

If Horridge was as surprised as everyone else by the turn of events he gave no sign of it.

'I am against you Mr Jackson-Fagg' he replied. 'As I have already ruled it is for Mr Hall to conduct the case for the defence as he sees fits. The jury will make of it what they will. You may continue Mr Hall.'

'Well Sergeant. What is your answer?'

Tench was rattled

'It's not true' he blustered. 'I swear it's not true. I didn't steal anything. I swear it on my grandbairn's life.'

'No, you don't Sergeant' countered the judge.

'Your honour?'

'Your grandchild's life has no place in these proceedings. Let your *nays be nays* Sergeant. Mr Hall?'

'Is it not the case, Sergeant, that my clients' actions that night presented you with a perfect opportunity to help yourself to the contents of that locker and you took it?'

'No! I didn't! I didn't! I never took anything! I swear it! I swear it!

'I have no further questions of this witness' said Hall and resumed his seat.

'Mr Jackson-Fagg?'

'No re-examination, your honour.'

'Very well' said the judge gathering his papers. 'Sergeant Tench, you may stand down although I give you the same warning as I shall give to all witnesses in this trial namely that you are not to discuss this case with any other person when you leave the building.'

'Ladies and gentlemen, time is marching on and rather than call any further witness this late in the day I shall now rise and reconverse tomorrow morning.'

'Court stand.'

CHAPTER FOURTEEN

At 10.30am precisely three sharp knocks thumped on the connecting door.

'Let all persons having business before His Majesty's court draw near and give their attention.'

Horridge ghosted to his chair, exchanged bows with the assembly then sat down.

'Yes. Mr Jackson-Fagg?'

Jackson-Fagg climbed to his feet.

'Your honour, the Crown calls Lady Victoria Clifford.'

The name tumbled down unseen corridors. I thought I was going to faint.

'Victoria Clifford. Call Victoria Clifford'.

Victoria entered the court with an usher and made her way to the witness stand. She was dressed completely in black with a curtain of speckled netting covering the top part of her face. Every eye was fixed upon her slim frame. I had never seen her look more beautiful.

'Take the bible in your right hand and repeat after me. I swear by almighty God...'

As she took the oath, I trained my eyes upon her, willing her to look at me, but she did not.

'You are Lady Victoria Wyndham Clifford of Petworth House, Sussex?'

'I am.'

'Lady Clifford, my name is Jackson-Fagg. I represent the Crown in these proceedings in which capacity I will shortly ask you some questions. The gentleman to my right is Mr Hall who appears for the defence and who may also have some questions for you. Now, this is a large courtroom so could I ask that when you give your answers, you keep your voice up so everyone can hear what you have to say? Do you understand?'

'I understand.'

'Lady Clifford, I want to begin by asking if you know the two gentlemen sitting over there in the dock?'

Victoria turned her head and just for a second her eyes met mine. God, she was so lovely. I tried to hold her gaze, but she turned away.

'I recognise Edmund Bullick who is known to me vaguely. The other gentleman I do not know.'

'I see. And can you explain to the ladies and gentlemen of the jury how you know Mr Bullick?'

'Yes. He is the son of James Bullick, the late racehorse trainer at the Craven estate. I made his acquaintance when I was a guest of the Surtees family at the end of last year. Mr Bullick was working in the stables at the time.'

'I see. And can you tell the members of the jury in what circumstances you made his acquaintance?'

'Of course. We met in November at a ball to celebrate Lord Julian's majority. Mr Bullick came up to me, said I was the most beautiful woman he had ever seen and asked if I would dance with him. I declined. We had not been formally introduced and I could see he had been drinking, however he was most insistent and eventually, to placate him, I agreed. I wish now I had not.'

'And why is that?'

Victoria reached for a glass of water.

'Mr Bullick did not know the steps and constantly trod on my feet. I had the bruises for weeks.' (laughter)

'I believe your paths crossed again?'

'They did. Twice more. We conversed briefly the following day at the Old Raby hunt. I remember Mr Bullick drew alongside, apologised for his behaviour the previous evening and asked if we could start again. I made it clear I was not interested.'

The lying cow.

'And the second occasion?'

Victoria took another sip of water. I stole a glance at the judge, then the jury, the barristers, the reporters and craned my head over to the packed gallery. Every eye was fixed upon her.

'A few days later I went down to the stables and asked Fenoughty, the head lad, if he could spare someone to escort me on the moor. I usually ride alone but I was not familiar with the area and there are some abandoned mine workings up there. Mr Bullick overheard our conversation and volunteered to accompany me.'

'Did you accept his offer?'

'I did. Eventually. I was a bit wary at first but Fenoughty assured me Mr Bullick was utterly reliable. He was also local and would know his way around.'

'What happened next?'

'We saddled the horses and went up to the moor. I remember it was a very misty day and we had to keep close to the bridle path. Mr Bullick was pleasant and engaging. It was clear he knew a great deal about the history of the area pointing out various landmarks as we went along. His company was agreeable, at least at first it was.'

'How do you mean?'

'How do I mean? Well, when we set out Mr Bullick was polite and attentive, and we made the usual small talk. However, as time went by the conversation changed and he started bragging about being the best rider on the estate and how one day, he was going to take over the string. I could see he was trying to impress me and dismissed it all as bluster until he started to tell me things I really didn't want to know.'

'Things you didn't want to know? Such as what?'

Victoria took another sip of water.

'He explained that his father had been killed and that he was desperate to find out what happened and what did I think he should do? I didn't know what to say. I mean, what could I say? I had obviously heard about the accident and told him how sorry I was for his loss. It was at that point Mr Bullick claimed the coroner's office was keeping the circumstances of his father's death from him. I said he must be mistaken but he assured me it was so. He said that when he attended the mortuary to identify his father's body, the coroner's assistant, a Sergeant Trent - or 'Tent' or something like that- was being evasive so he and a friend went back in the middle of the night to see what they could find out.'

'Quiet please' said the judge.

'Are you quite certain this is what he said?'

'Oh yes. He was very open about it. He described how they forced their way into the mortuary through a skylight and how they were nearly caught on the way out when some mental patients in an adjacent ward raised the alarm. I couldn't believe what I was hearing to be honest. The whole thing sounded so outrageous I thought he was joking, at least at first I did, but then it wasn't a joking matter and it suddenly dawned on me he was being serious.'

'Did he tell you anything else?'

'Yes. He described how having broken into the mortuary the two of them ransacked the office.'

'Ransacked the office?' said Jackson-Fagg stealing a glance at the jury. 'Did he mention if they took anything away? Any personal property for instance?'

'I don't know. I cannot recall.'

'Are you *certain* about that Miss Clifford?'

'I cannot recall. He may have done.'

The lying cow.

'He may have done' repeated Jackson-Fagg softly. 'And tell me Miss Clifford, what was your reaction when you heard all of this?'

Victoria took another sip of water and looked up at the judge.

'I was shocked your honour. It was all so incredible, the thought of the two of them creeping around the mortuary in the dead of night. It was scary. *I* was scared. I began to wonder what sort of person I was riding out with. You have to remember there was just the two of us out there alone on the moor.'

I had heard enough.

'Judge, your honour, your honour, this is not true! Victoria, why are you lying? Why? You know as well as I do ...'

A smack of the gavel and the court fell silent

'Edmund Bullick. Stand up.'

Everyone turned and I felt the eyes of the assembly upon me. The blood filled my cheeks but I couldn't let her get away with it.

'Mr Bullick. I will not tolerate interruptions from the dock while witnesses are delivering their evidence. This is the second warning I have given you. There will not be another. If there are any more outbursts you will both be confined to the cells and I shall direct these proceedings continue in your absence. Have I made myself clear? Very well. Carry on please, Mr Jackson-Fagg.'

'Lady Clifford. You were explaining to the jury how Mr Bullick's conversation made you feel - what? - uncomfortable?'

'It did. I was appalled. I'm not easily scared but the matter-of-fact way he described the mortuary chamber and dead people and lunatics screaming frightened me and I couldn't wait to get back to the stables. Mr Bullick sought to engage me further on what they had done but I replied it was not something that I wished to talk about and promptly changed the subject. However, as soon as we returned, I went straight into Durham to find Mr Lockwood and report what had been said to me.'

'Mr Lockwood, he being the city coroner?'

'That's correct. I already knew Mr Lockwood. His partner Mr Crake is the attorney to the late Lord William's estate. It seemed the right thing to do.'

'Indeed Miss Clifford, indeed. And have you seen Mr Bullick since this time?'

Victoria paused, turned her head to the dock and looked straight through me.

'No sir. I have not.'

I was about to spring up but felt Tom's hand on my arm.

'Thank you for your answers Miss Clifford. I have no more questions for this witness at the present time my Lord.'

'Mr Hall?'

Hall finished scribbling and rose to his feet.

'Lady Clifford. You explained to the jury how after you met Mr Bullick at a ball last November and then again at the Raby Hunt, your paths crossed a third time at the stables. I believe you said he volunteered to accompany you to the moor?'

'That's correct.'

'I suggest that's not correct. I suggest that when you encountered my client on the third occasion, it was because *you* went his home late one evening where it was *you* who asked *him* to accompany *you* to the moor?'

'No sir. I would not do anything like that.'

'Really, Miss Clifford? I suggest that is exactly what you did do. I also suggest that the purpose of you going to his home that night was because you intended to engage my client on the very subject, which a moment ago, you claimed to have found so disturbing.'

'No sir. No, that's not right.'

'And' continued Hall 'I suggest that when you rode up to the moor the following afternoon, far from finding my client in any way disagreeable, you flourished in his company and encouraged his attentions.'

'I did not.'

'Lady Clifford, you have already told the jury that my client found you attractive.'

'He may have done. I cannot say.'

'Oh, don't be so *coy* Miss Clifford. Your evidence to my learned friend a moment ago was that Mr Bullick approached you at the ball and said you were the most beautiful girl he had ever seen. Do you remember saying that?'

Victoria was silent.

'Miss Clifford, you knew my client admired you did you not?'

Victoria was silent.

'Come, come Miss Clifford. It's a simple enough question.'

'In retrospect, I suppose I did.'

'In retrospect you suppose you did' repeated Hall. 'In which case knowing that he admired you, what was your purpose in riding out to the moor alone with him?'

'As I have already explained, I was not familiar with the area and I needed a guide.'

'The moor is a remote place is it not?'

'I cannot say. I had not been there before.'

'You would be unlikely to encounter anyone else?'

'My Lord' interrupted Jackson-Fagg 'I canvas the relevance of this line of cross examination?'

'I agree Mr Jackson-Fagg' said the judge. 'Mr Hall, where is all this leading?'

'My Lord, I ask that you bear with me. The focus of my questions will become apparent to the court - as I am sure they are already apparent to the witness.'

'Very well but make your point. We haven't got all day.'

Hall ignored the slight and continued.

'Miss Clifford. I suggest you went out of your way to engineer a situation where you knew you would be alone with my client.'

'No. What possible reason could I have for doing that?'

'For *information* Miss Clifford. You wanted information about the late Lord William and you knew my client had it.'

Victoria shook her head.

'I haven't the faintest idea what you are driving at.'

'Oh, I think you *do* Miss Clifford. You knew Edmund Bullick was the only person present at Lord William's deathbed and you were determined to get him on his own and find out what had passed between them.'

'That is an absurd suggestion. I needed a guide. I had no other purpose.'

'I suggest you wanted information from Mr Bullick and you were prepared to go to any lengths in order to obtain it.'

'No. I did not want information. I wanted a guide.'

'Tell me Miss Clifford. Do the words *Hob Hole* mean anything to you?'

Victoria flushed. Just for a moment she hesitated.

'Well Miss Clifford?'

'Hob Hole?' said she bringing a hand to her temple. 'Let me think. Yes, I remember, it's a cave, yes, that's right; I believe it is a cave up on the crags near the ruined monastery?'

'You don't sound very sure.'

'I remember now. It's an old cavern on the moor. The monks used to store ice and provisions in there before the Dissolution. Mr Bullick pointed it out to me.'

'I suggest he did more than point it out to you. I suggest you and he spent several hours alone in there.'

Jackson-Fagg jumped to his feet.

'My Lord, I object. That is an outrageous suggestion!'

Horridge was having none of it.

'I am against you Mr Jackson-Fagg. Your opponent has his instructions. The jury will make of them what they will'.

'Miss Clifford' continued Hall 'Did you or did you not spend several hours alone in that cave with my client?'

'I did not!'

'So, if the members of the jury inspected the cave for themselves, they would not discover your name and his scrawled on the wall under the names of others who had once met there?'

Victoria was rattled.

'I-I cannot say. All I do know is I have never been in there. What you are insinuating disgusts me.'

'You entered that cave with my client and spent several hours alone in there with him, did you not?'

Jackson-Fagg leaped to his feet.

'Mr Hall' said the judge waving Jackson-Fagg down. 'That will do Mr Hall. This witness has answered your question. I rule her response to be final. Move on please.'

Hall bowed reverently and continued.

'Miss Clifford, do you recall meeting my client on a fourth occasion?'

'No sir. I did not meet Mr Bullick again.'

'Come, come Miss Clifford, surely you remember going back to his home that same evening?'

'No, my Lord.'

'Where you spent the night alone with him?'

Victoria went crimson. The hammer had struck the nail and the uproar was immediate. Horridge looked up from his notes as if he couldn't quite take in what had just been said. Shouts and jeers came from the public gallery. Lawyers whispered while reporters scribbled furiously and the jurors exchanged uneasy glances. Jackson-Fagg was incandescent jumping up and down at the end of the bar straining to be heard above the noise and confusion.

'My Lord, this is outrageous! My Lord...My Lord... My friend seriously oversteps the mark. This is utterly outrageous I say! These questions are a disgrace... I urge you My Lord... (clamour, shouts)...I urge you ...' but still he could not be heard and it took several smacks of the gavel before any semblance of order was restored.

'SILENCE! SI....LENCE!'

As abruptly as it had broken out the clamour subsided. Horridge waited until the court was hushed.

'Ladies and gentlemen. May I remind you -all of you- that this is not a public tavern or some kind of football match. This is a court of law within which hallowed stones it is the responsibility of each one of us to discharge our duty in pursuit of the King's justice. I say again I will not tolerate these proceedings being interrupted while witnesses are giving their evidence. I ask you all - every one of you - to remember who you are and where you are. Mr Hall?'

'Lady Clifford. I suggest that after you returned from the moor, you accompanied my client back to his home?'

'I did not' sobbed Victoria.

'And there spent the night alone with him?'

Jackson-Fagg leaped to his feet, but the judge waved him down.

'I will save you the trouble, Mr Jackson-Fagg' then to Hall 'Mr Hall. Do your clients understand the likely consequence of this line of questioning if the jury reject their account?'

'They do my Lord.'

'And that in such event they can expect equal measure from the court?'

'I will put the defence case, my Lord.'

'So be it, Mr Hall. Proceed, if you must.'

Hall removed his glasses and slowly turned to the witness. Every eye in the room was fixed upon him and you could have heard a pin drop.

'Lady Clifford' said he quietly 'I suggest you were desperate for information from my client..'

'I was not...'

'...so much so that you were prepared to sleep with him for it and duly did. That's what happened isn't it?'

'No! No! How *dare* you? That's not true. I swear it. I swear it' wept Victoria.

'And...' continued Hall ..'it was during what is colloquially called 'pillow talk' that he explained why they had removed his father's file from the mortuary and told you where it was kept in the house.'

'No' wailed Victoria. 'That's not true. It's not true. I cannot believe I am hearing this.'

'And very early the next morning' continued Hall 'when my client was dead to the world, you sneaked off taking the file with you on the way out?'

Every word was spot on but rather than answer the question, Victoria sobbed and sobbed and shook her head. To look at her weeping so forlornly you would think butter wouldn't melt in her mouth. It was a compelling performance.

'Lady Clifford' continued Hall 'I have a document here I would like you to examine.'

'What document is this?' exclaimed Jackson-Fagg. 'What document is this?' he repeated. 'The Crown have no knowledge of any document!"

Hall reached across to his opponent who snatched the note then stared at Hall in disbelief.

'Absolutely not my Lord. Absolutely not. The Crown objects most strenuously to the admission of this document. The very notion is out-rage-ous!'

'I will not be deterred from putting my client's case' said Hall coolly.

'Pass it here' said the judge.

Horridge scanned Victoria's note then peered over his glasses.

'Mr Jackson-Fagg?'

'My Lord' pleaded he. 'My Lord, you cannot allow this. It is the prisoners who are on trial, not the witness!'

'I don't disagree Mr Jackson-Fagg. However, with the jury now knowing of the existence of this document I must ask myself how justice can be seen to be done if its contents are kept from them. This note- whatever its origins- also goes to the credit of the witness. Mr Hall. I am minded to rule in your favour however before I make my determination I must ask again, do your clients understand the consequences of this line of attack if the jury dismiss their version of events?'

'They do.'

'So be it. You may proceed Mr Hall, but you are playing with fire.'

The note was gathered by an usher who made her way to the stand and passed it to the witness.

'Miss Clifford. Do you recognise this handwriting?'

Victoria stared at the note, then around the courtroom then imploringly at the judge.

'My Lord.....'

'You must answer the question, Miss Clifford.'

Victoria pulled a handkerchief from her sleeve and wiped her eyes.

'I recognise it ' she said quietly.

'The handwriting is yours, is it not Miss Clifford?'

The witness was silent.

'My apologies, Miss Clifford. I didn't quite catch your reply.'

'It is mine' she whispered.

'The ladies and gentlemen of the jury will wish to know what is in that note. Will you read it to them please?'

Victoria looked despairingly at the judge.

'But this is a private letter' she wailed. 'It is personal correspondence. It is nobody's business but my own.'

Horridge was having none of it.

'You must oblige, Miss Clifford,' said he.

Victoria took a sip of water. Every eye was riveted on her as she unfolded the note and slowly read the contents.

'You looked so peaceful I didn't want to wake you.
Sweet dreams darling and see you next week.
Love you.
V '

Hall waited for the murmuring to subside.

'All of it if you will, please, Miss Clifford.'

'I have read all of it.'

'I think not, Miss Clifford. You omitted a digit at the end. Can you tell the jury what it is?'

Victoria read the note again.

'If you mean the letter 'x', the note concludes with a small letter 'x' at the end.'

'Indeed it does Miss Clifford. A small letter 'x'. After the words 'Love you.' Is that not so?'

Victoria shuffled uncomfortably.

'Now Miss Clifford, I suggest that the note you have just read to the jury is the same note that you left for Mr Bullick when you crept out of his bed early that morning.'

'No. No, no, no. I cannot believe I am listening to this.'

'But surely you remember? You have already told the jury it is your handwriting.'

'I did not write the note for Mr Bullick' she sniffed.

'Come, come Miss Clifford. That note was left by you for my client was it not? You know, just before you sneaked off that morning helping yourself to the coroner's file on the way out?'

Victoria gathered her wits.

'All right. All right' she repeated. 'I'll tell you. I don't know how or in what circumstances you came across this note and to my eternal embarrassment, yes, that is my handwriting, and I did pen it. However, it was not written for Mr Bullick. It was written for someone else.'

'Oh really, Miss Clifford? Such as who?'

Jackson-Fagg sprang to his feet.

'My Lord, this is preposterous. It is the defendants who are on trial here, not the private life of this witness.'

'I'm inclined to agree Mr Jackson-Fagg' said the judge. 'Mr Hall, this line of questioning has run its course. Move on please.'

Hall bowed then raising his voice spoke directly to the witness.

'Miss Clifford. I suggest that you were sufficiently determined to illicit information from my client that you were prepared to sleep with him for it, and duly did so. That's the truth, isn't it?'

'No. That's a lie.'

'I also suggest that having engineered your way into his affections and ascertained why he and his friend broke into the mortuary, you then slipped into his father's office and removed the coroner's file on the way out?'

'I did not' she wailed.

'You know very well they took nothing but the coroner's file from the mortuary office, don't you?'

'I don't know that at all. All I know is that Mr Bullick boasted how he and his friend had broken in there and when he told me, I did what any reasonable person would have done and went to the authorities.'

'And..' continued Hall '...you have come here today and told the jury nothing but a pack of lies.'

'No. I am speaking the truth.'

'The truth Miss Clifford?' said Hall slapping his papers on the bench. 'The truth? I suggest the only connection between yourself and the truth is that you are strangers to one another.'

Victoria reached for her handkerchief and blew her nose.

'Your accusations disgust me' she sobbed. 'I am not a liar. I am telling you the truth. The Clifford name itself is my bond. We are descended from one of the noblest Scottish families.'

'And so was Lady Macbeth' quipped Hall. (laughter)

Jackson-Fagg leapt to his feet.

'My Lord, I object to that remark. My colleague conducts himself reprehensibly.'

'I agree, Mr Jackson-Fagg. Mr Hall, that was an odious suggestion to make to the witness. You will withdraw the statement immediately.'

Hall bowed.

'As it pleases your Lordship' he beamed. 'I have no further questions.'

The damage had been done. There was no re-examination from Jackson-Fagg and Victoria was released. She was not finished though. As she made her way from the stand she suddenly dipped into the assembly of lawyers and jettisoned a tumbler of water over Hall.

'That will do Lady Clifford' piped the judge with a surprising degree of reserve. 'Now please leave the building before I find you in contempt.'

Victoria stamped out of court. All eyes followed her until from the shelter of the corridor she suddenly stopped and looked at me over her shoulder.

'I'm sorry' she mouthed.

Then she was gone.

I couldn't believe it.

In the bowl of the pit Hall wiped himself down.

'My profound apologies Mr Hall' said the judge drolly. 'These things are sent to try us.'

'It is of little consequence my Lord' answered Hall. 'I usually take some refreshment at this hour of day. A tad early perhaps...' (laughter)

'Mr Jackson-Fagg, Mr Hall. This seems an appropriate time to break for the day. I will now rise and reconvene at, say, 10.30 tomorrow?'

'Court stand.'

CHAPTER FIFTEEN

Crake marched confidently to the witness box and took the oath. Do you know how sometimes in your life you come across these people who possess such an air about them that before they even say anything, you just know they are a class act? Crake was one such individual. Even as he brushed down his immaculate tails, I sensed we were in trouble.

Jackson-Fagg took the witness through an impressive resume of qualifications and quasi-judicial appointments. The jury were quickly under his spell and to my consternation, so also was Horridge, who made little attempt to disguise his esteem as he pumped his head up and down with each accolade.

'I am suitably grateful, sir' said the prosecutor. 'Now would you be good enough to explain to the jury how you come to know these two defendants?'

Crake dipped his thumbs and turned to the jury. 'Of course. Ladies and gentlemen, I am the executor of the estate of Lord William Surtees, lately of Craven Castle. Mr Bullick was awarded a legacy under the deceased's will. He attended my office in connection with the matter in December last year.'

'And Mr Brentnall?'

'Mr Brentnall is an associate of Mr Bullick and accompanied him to the appointment. However, he is not a beneficiary under the Will and took no active part in the business of the day.'

'I see. And what was the legacy to Edmund Bullick?'

'Lord William bequeathed the sum of three thousand pounds, in trust, to be applied for the university education of Mr Bullick and his younger brother, Alfred. He directed that the interest should meet the fees of each as and when these arose with the Bullick brothers to take the remainder of the fund absolutely when their education was completed.'

'Thank you. It would appear a generous bequest?'

'Indeed. Most generous. However, the Bullick family were held in some regard by the deceased and to remember them among the beneficiaries was typical of Lord William's generosity. There should be no misunderstanding about his. The Bullick brothers were extremely well provided for - a state of affairs that makes the subsequent conduct of Edmund Bullick all the more reprehensible.'

'I object to that remark' said Hall.

'I quite agree' answered the judge. 'Members of the jury, you will ignore that last comment. Mr Crake, please restrict your evidence to the facts.'

'I apologise my Lord' said Crake. 'I meant nothing untoward in what I said.'

'I doubt it' muttered Hall.

Jackson-Fagg smirked and bashed on.

'Can I take you back to the occasion when you say Mr Bullick and Mr Brentnall attended your office?'

'Of course. It was the afternoon of Tuesday, 15 December,

the day before the town was shelled by the German navy. I had written to Mr Bullick asking him to come in so we could formally set up the account and nominate the trustees. However, immediately before the appointment I learned from my partner, Joshua Lockwood, that Mr Bullick was wanted for questioning in Durham regarding a burglary at the hospital there. When I imparted this information to Mr Bullick, he said it was none of my business and insisted we proceeded with the business of the day. It was clear he wanted to get his hands on the money as soon as possible and asked me for an advance. I was most uncomfortable with this and refused. I said before we went any further with the legacy, he should return home and surrender himself to the police.'

'Sound enough advice. And what was Mr Bullick's response?'

'He was indignant. Most indignant. He said it was my duty to give him his money and refused to leave until I had done so. I recall his friend, Mr Brentnall, was particularly impertinent. I replied that I would not be lectured on professional ethics by either of them and when they persisted in their demands, I had to ask my clerk, Mr Glyder, to show them the door.'

Whaaaaaat? What did he just say? I couldn't believe it. I was expecting a tall tale but nothing like this. The worst of it was he sounded so plausible. I glanced at the jury who were lapping it up. Tom was already on his feet.

'That's a lie Crake! You know very well that...'

'Silence in the dock!' barked Horridge.

'But it's all *lies* judge' shouted Tom 'I can't believe I'm listening to this!'

'Mr Brentnall, one more outburst and I assure you, you won't be. You have already been warned not to interrupt while witnesses are giving their evidence.'

'But judge...'

'SIT DOWN MR BRENTNALL!'

Silence fell on the assembly.

'Mr Hall' snapped Horridge 'I am at the end of my tether with this perpetual heckling from the dock.'

'I do apologise my Lord.'

'I have a trial to conduct. How can I possibly be expected to get through it with your clients constantly barracking the Crown's witnesses? No. Enough is enough. They will be confined downstairs until the conclusion of the prosecution case.'

'I'm sure that won't be necessary my Lord. Might I have a few minutes with them?'

Horridge pinched his lip.

'I think not. Mr Jackson-Fagg?'

'The Crown endorse your Lordship's concerns. These proceedings are overrunning as it is'

'Quite.'

'My Lord' interjected Hall. 'My Lord, it is long established in these courts that the defendants in a criminal trial have the right to hear witnesses who would speak ill against them.'

'I don't disagree Mr Hall - but at what cost to the integrity of the King's justice? You know as well as I that there comes a point where that right is forfeit.'

'I would be given the opportunity my Lord.'

The judge frowned.

'I would be given the opportunity' repeated Hall. Horridge pushed back his chair.

'Very well' he snorted. 'You have five minutes, Mr Hall. Use them wisely before I change my mind.'

'Court rise.'

Hall's pale knuckles gripped the smudged bronze rail of the dock. He spoke in a low voice so as not to be overheard. 'I'm afraid he means it gentlemen. One more squeak and he'll send you down.'

'It's all very well for you' whispered Tom 'but you're not the one he's lying about. How can we be expected to just sit here while he talks such complete and utter *bollocks*?'

Hall was annoyed.

'Now you listen to me young man. I have enough on my plate as it is. The judge is already against you and the jury are not far behind.'

'But Crake is lying through his teeth' said Tom 'and as for that Jackson-Fagg bloke, he's a complete jerk.'

'I don't care for him either Mr Brentnall. However – and unfortunately for you both – he is very good at his job and at the moment you are playing right into his hands. Now look. If I am to make any headway with your defence, I *must* be left to my devices without constantly worrying that the two of you are going to butt in. I cannot be dealing with it. I cannot. If there are any more outbursts, you will not only find yourselves locked up downstairs, you will find yourselves without a defence barrister. Have I made myself clear?'

We replied that he had. Hall was not the sort to argue with.

'Look' he whispered. 'I did not have to take on your trial. I could have caught the next train back to London. I do not need the work, I assure you. The only reason I'm still here is because, for what it's worth, I actually believe you. However, ring of truth or not to your instructions, if I am to continue as your advocate, it will be on my terms and my terms are that from now onwards, you sit quietly through the remainder of the case and say nothing - absolutely nothing- until you are called upon to give evidence. Do you understand?'

'I'm sorry Mr Hall'.

'I don't want your apologies, Mr Brentnall. Just your silence. Now please gentlemen, let us have no more of this nonsense. I shall deal with Mr Crake.'

The court reconvened and difficult though it was, we sat on our hands as counsel for the Crown led the witness through the remainder of his evidence, our hearts sinking as each measured exchange slowly tightened the strings of the prosecution case.

'There remains a final matter I would like you to assist the jury with please, Mr Crake. It is this. When interviewed by the police, the defendants claimed that shortly before he died, Lord William attended your office and changed his Will. Are you in a position to comment?'

'Absolutely. The suggestion is nonsense. Lord Surtees made but the one Will, the substance of which I have already imparted to the court.'

'Indeed' said the prosecutor leafing through his papers. 'Mr Crake, you have been most helpful. Please remain where you are and answer any questions that might be put to you by my friend.'

'Your witness Mr Hall?'

Hall was buried in his notes.

'Mr Hall?' repeated the judge.

Hall waited until he had the attention of the assembly then climbed to his feet.

'Mr Crake. You explained to the jury a moment ago that you are the executor of the estate of Lord William Surtees?'

'That's correct.'

'When did he make his last testimony?'

Crake reached for a pile of documents and untied the ribbon. 'Unfortunately, the original Will was destroyed in the fire at my office' said he 'however I have brought the grant of probate. Bear with me a moment...ah, here we are. The Will was executed on the sixteenth of April 1905.'

'I am not interested in the original Will' said Hall sharply. 'I was referring to his *last* testimony.'

'The 1905 Will was his last testimony. There exists no other, I assure you.'

'Now that's not correct, is it?'

Hall was on to him. Just for a moment Crake hesitated.

'I don't follow you sir. Not correct as to what? The date? The details are very clearly recorded. The Will was executed on the 16 April 1905. I distinctly remember the occasion because it was a Sunday when Lord William was in town sailing. We opened the office especially.'

'I don't doubt it Mr Crake. However, he came to see you again, didn't he?'

All eyes switched back to the witness.

'I don't understand what you are driving at'.

'Very well. Can you explain to the jury what is meant by a 'codicil'?'

Crake stopped in his tracks. You could almost hear the spinning of cogs.

'It's a simple enough question, sir.'

'A codicil?' he replied, regaining his composure. 'A codicil is a formal document, usually attached to an existing Will that makes a change to it.'

'Indeed. Now I suggest to you that shortly before he died, Lord William attended your office and made a codicil to his Will. That's right, isn't it?'

All colour slowly drained from the witness.

'No. No, my Lord. Absolutely not.'

'Your evidence to the court a moment ago was that you distinctly recall Lord William coming to see you one Sunday in 1905 to execute his Will. Do you remember saying that?'

'Of course.'

Crake shuffled uneasily as he took guard for what might be coming next.

'Then you will surely remember last autumn when he came to see you again?'

'No.'

'No? Do you mean 'no' as in he did not come to see you last autumn or 'no' as in you are unable to recollect if he did?'

The self-assured flow had dried up. Instead of answering the question Crake simply stared back at Hall.

'Well? Which is it to be?'

'I mean 'no'; he did not attend my office last autumn.'

'Really? Then allow me refresh your memory. I put it to you that on Tuesday 20 October last year Lord William attended your Hartlepool office and made a codicil to his 2005 Will...'

'No. Absolutely not...'

'...and his purpose in so doing was to disinherit Lord Julian Surtees in favour of Alfred Bullick.'

The impact was immediate. Jackson-Fagg span round to Honeyman and Crisp as gasps from overhead confirmed the public had tuned into this unexpected line of attack. Horridge looked over his spectacles.

'Silence in the gallery.'

'May I have your answer please?'

'The supposition is ridiculous.'

'Really? My clients will tell the court there was most certainly a codicil which you concealed in your office together with Alfred Bullick's birth certificate.'

The witness stared at Hall as if he had seen a ghost.

'Well, Mr Crake?'

'No. Absolutely not. As I have already explained there was no other Will and no codicil.'

'And Alfred Bullick's birth certificate? You hid that away as well, didn't you?'

Silence.

'Didn't you?'

Crake gathered his wits.

'I haven't the faintest idea what you are talking about.'

'You are on oath sir. Is the court to take that as your final response?'

Crake turned to the judge in supplication.

'My Lord, there was no codicil in favour of Alfred Bullick or anyone else and no birth certificate. The suggestion is ridiculous. Indeed, the investigating officers would be more than welcome to search our records for themselves had these not been destroyed in the German bombardment.'

Horridge put down his pen.

'Your office was damaged in the raid?'

'Very much so' answered Crake, seizing the distraction. 'Our building is in King Street, an area of the town that was particularly hard hit. The premises were gutted and it will be several months before we can even think about reopening.'

'I am sorry to hear this' said the judge.

'It is a most difficult time' continued the witness, drawing out the exchange. 'The damage is immense, and the practice has been set back dreadfully.'

Jackson-Fagg was now on his feet.

'My learned friend makes quite extraordinary suppositions to this witness. In fact, the thrust of the cross examination of all the witnesses is at such variance with the prosecution case, I must canvas if the defence are calling any evidence to back up these outrageous allegations?'

'I was fast reaching the same conclusion myself' said the judge. 'Mr Hall, I trust you are in a position to substantiate these assertions?'

'Certainly, my Lord.'

'I hope so Mr Hall - because right now, I am at a loss to understand where all this is leading. It is as if I am being asked to try two entirely different causes.'

Hall overlooked the remark and batted on.

'Mr Crake. Returning to the issue of a codicil; now, a moment ago, you told the court...'

'Mr Hall' interrupted the judge. 'Mr Hall, this witness has already stated his position regarding the codicil. He told you there wasn't one. He could not have been more explicit in which circumstances if you were proposing to mine the seam further, allow me to save you the trouble.'

'It is no trouble, my Lord.'

'So you say, Mr Hall, however I must ask myself what impact this tedious line of questioning will have on the attention span of the jury.'

'That is entirely a matter of conjecture, my Lord.'

'No it is not, Mr Hall' replied the judge sharply. 'It is a matter of common sense. The witness has already dealt -

most capably I would add- with your suppositions regarding the possibility of a codicil. Any fool can see he is not going to change his response however you clothe your attack.'

'I am not persuaded your Lordship speaks subjectively.' (laughter)

'Mr Hall, you will withdraw that remark immediately.'

'My profound apologies, my Lord. I meant no sleight on your Lordship's office. I was simply reminding myself not to try and gainsay the stance of the jury who, as your Lordship knows, have a habit of seeing things very differently from the rest of us.'

Horridge, stung by the first rebuke was now purple with indignation.

'You exceed your remit, sir' said he, barely able to contain himself. 'In all my years on the bench I have never been so affronted. Never.'

'Your Lordship has misunderstood me. No offence was intended, I assure you. If any was taken, again, I offer my unreserved apology.'

'Your apology is not accepted, Mr Hall. You knew perfectly well what you were saying, and you can take it I shall be referring your remarks to the Bar Council.'

Hall rolled his eyes. 'It grieves me that your Lordship takes offence where none was intended. I strive only for the latitude to complete my cross-examination.'

'No, Mr Hall. It seems to me that if left to your devices, you would labour the same point all day. My ruling on this matter is final. I shall entertain no further investigation about a supposed codicil.'

'How can I be expected to illicit the truth from this witness if your Lordship chains me thus?'

'The only chains are those of your making, Mr Hall.'

'But your Lordship, my questions regarding the codicil go to the heart of...'

'No, Mr Hall' said the judge cutting him dead. 'My mind is made up. I will admit no more questions on the issue. Now, if there are any other aspects of this witness's evidence to be explored, then by all means continue although it appears to me you have an uphill struggle.'

'If I am to be silenced as well as misunderstood, I see little point in continuing' said Hall.

'That is entirely a matter for you' said the judge sharply. 'With respect, it will be a matter for your Lordship when I return - because I shall' said Hall and promptly sat down.

Jackson-Fagg, crouched quietly throughout, took obvious delight at the quarrel. It marked the high water of the allegations against us and counsel for the Crown knew it. There was no re-examination and when Crake was released, Jackson-Fagg closed the prosecution case.

CHAPTER SIXTEEN

Hall took me through my evidence-in-chief beginning with that dreadful afternoon when I was called out of lectures. I explained how upon my return home I was summonsed to Lord William's deathbed and told the jury word-for-word exactly what was imparted to me there. I described my visit to Dryburn Mortuary to identify my father's remains and how following an exasperating exchange with Sergeant Tench, we resolved to go back at night and recover Dad's file for ourselves. I told the jury what was in the file and how we intended to deliver it to the authorities only to be thwarted by Victoria who, to my eternal regret, I had taken into my confidence.

'What was the nature of your relationship with Lady Clifford?' said Hall.

'Victoria and I were very close. We were lovers. She intoxicated me and I could not refuse her. I told her everything I knew. I believed I could trust her, confide in her. I was mistaken.'

The question about Victoria was always coming and when I answered it, I had expected uproar. However, there was none. Instead, the court, transfixed on what I was saying, listened in total silence. Looking back, it must have sounded incredible although every word was true.

Hall moved on to our meeting at the solicitor's office. I explained how Crake, tipped off that we had broken into the mortuary attempted to use the information to blackmail us.

'To *blackmail* you?' whispered Hall. 'How so?'

'Mr Crake said that unless we endorsed the original Will, he would bring in the police and we would go to prison for five years. However, if we did as he asked, he was prepared to overlook the matter. The choice was ours.'

'Did you do as he bid?'

'No, not straight away. Mr Crake gave us twenty-four hours to consider the matter. We obviously didn't want to sign but he had us over a barrel, and it seemed we had little choice. We were actually on our way back to his office the next morning when the German navy loomed out of the fog and began shelling the town.'

'Did you see Mr Crake again?'

'No. At least not until this afternoon.'

'Now, returning to the night in the mortuary. Your evidence to the court is that the two of you took nothing other than the coroner's file of papers relating to your father's demise. Do you stand by this account?'

'I do. Tom and I are not thieves. We only sought the truth about my father.'

'Thank you, Mr Bullick. I have no more questions at this time my Lord.'

Jackson-Fagg sprang up like a jack-in-the-box.

'Not thieves you say? You heard the evidence of Sergeant Tench. He told the court that when he went to clear up the mess you and your friend left behind, he discovered a large amount of jewellery and cash missing from one of the draws. Are you saying he is lying about the matter?'

'I am not saying that at all. I only know we didn't take anything apart from my father's file.'

'Oh really? What do you suppose happened to all this property then? Vanish into thin air did it?'

'We only took the coroner's file.'

'Your fingerprints were discovered all over the place. Are you saying someone else was responsible?'

'If property was missing then clearly, someone must have removed it. I only know it was not us.'

'What do you mean *if* property was missing? You heard the schedule that was read out to the court. Sergeant Tench was very precise about it. Are you saying he is making the whole thing up?'

'He could be. He had already lied to me once when I attended the mortuary to identify my father.'

'What utter drivel. The reality, Mr Bullick, is that you and your friend stole this property, and it is *you* who is lying to the court.'

'No.'

Jackson-Fagg leafed through his papers shaking his head. 'The police found a large quantity of cash in your possession when you were detained at the railway station. Where did you get it from?'

'I was not aware that carrying money was a criminal offence, my Lord' said Hall.

'You are perfectly right' answered the judge 'however the implication of possessing such a sum is obvious and your opponent would be failing in his duty if he did not make it.'

'Well, Mr Bullick? Where did you get it from?'

'The money was mine- rather it belonged to me and my father. I was not comfortable carrying it around but the safe in our office was damaged and I had no choice.'

'Why not put it in the bank?'

'My father's account was frozen when he died. I am unable to open one of my own until I attain my majority.'

Jackson-Fagg tried a different approach.

'What were you doing in Liverpool?'

'Our family have friends in the area. My brother and I were invited to stay there over Christmas. Alfred is still with them.'

'Oh really?' sneered Jackson-Fagg.

'Really.'

'What nonsense. I suggest you were in Liverpool to dispose of your ill-gotten gains!'

'No, we were there for Christmas.'

Jackson-Fagg conferred with Honeyman.

'I wish to return to your appointment with Mr Crake. Now he made it quite clear that before he dealt with your legacy under the Will, you should first go back to Durham and surrender yourself to the police?'

'Mr Crake said no such thing. He tried to blackmail us into signing the assent as I have already explained. He very nearly succeeded.'

'So Mr Crake is lying as well is he?'

'He is.'

'I see. And the supposed codicil referred to by your counsel? And your brother's birth certificate?'

'Lord William attended Mr Crake's office on 20 October last year and changed his Will in favour of my brother.

However, Mr Crake kept the meeting a secret and hid the codicil away in his office together with my brother's birth certificate.'

'You sound very sure about the matter?' sneered counsel.

'I am sure. I saw the documents. We both did.' 'Remarkable. I suppose Mr Crake pulled them out of his desk and handed them over did he?'

'They were not kept in his desk. They were kept in a strongbox by the grandfather clock.'

'Let you rummage through his office, did he? Like you rummaged through Sergeant Tench's, hey?'

'No. We came across the documents by chance when we took shelter in the premises during the bombardment.'

'What? Pardon me for being so blunt Mr Bullick but do you seriously expect the court to believe any of this?'

'With respect sir, I was there. You were not. I can only tell you what happened and what we discovered.'

Horridge stopped writing and laid down his glasses.

'Mr Bullick, these are the most extraordinary allegations. I must ask again, do you understand the likely consequences to you and your friend if the jury reject your account?'

'I can only say how it was your honour.'

Jackson-Fagg shook his head.

'These documents you found' supposed he with a sigh. 'The codicil and birth certificate you recovered during the bombardment. Pray, where are they now? Have you brought them to court with you?'

'No. They were passed to a friend for safekeeping while we decided what to do next.'

'What?' said Jackson-Fagg incredulously. 'Hold on, Mr Bullick, let's get this straight. Are you seriously asking the court to accept that having stumbled upon all this crucial information, you gave it away it to a *friend*?'

'That's correct sir.'

'But why didn't you go to the police? You knew they were looking for you. Why not surrender yourself as Mr Crake had suggested and pass everything over to them?'

'I wish now that we had. However, at the time we felt we could not trust the police to do the right thing, or at least we could not trust the local office in Durham'.

Jackson-Fagg stretched out his arms as if he were juggling.

'So are the jury to add Durham police to your gallery of rogues?'

'We had good reason to be wary of them. You have to look at it from our point of view. Victoria Clifford had already taken one set of documents. We did not know who we could trust.'

'I see. And this friend of yours? What is his name?'

I had to keep him out. Conway was not in a position to defend himself and his parents were going through enough as it was.

'Well, Mr Bullick?'

'I'd rather not say.'

'You'd rather not say' repeated the prosecutor mockingly. 'Tell me Mr Bullick, this friend you have no name for, is *he* bringing the documents to court today?'

'Unfortunately not. He was killed at Ypres a few weeks ago and we don't know where he put them.'

'Oh, how *very* convenient!' said counsel glancing at the jury. 'Tell me this Mr Bullick. When the Germans shelled the town, did you receive a bump on the head? It's just that I am trying to fathom how your recollection of events differs so markedly to everyone else's.'

'I'm telling you the truth.'

'No Mr Bullick, you are not. I suggest you are in an impossible predicament, the evidence against you is overwhelming and instead of acknowledging your misconduct, you have come here today and told nothing but a pack of lies.'

'No. I am telling you exactly what happened.'

Jackson-Fagg shook his head as he reached for a glass of water. 'I do not propose to spend much time on this next point my Lord, however I would be failing in my duty if I did not revisit the evidence of this witness regarding Lady Clifford.'

'I agree Mr Jackson-Fagg. Please continue.'

'Mr Bullick, you will need no reminding that your account of your relationship with Victoria Clifford is markedly different to her own. You were never lovers! She couldn't stand you - as was patently obvious from her evidence!'

'You are wrong sir. Victoria and I were lovers. We slept together in *Hob Hole* and later that day when she came back with me to my father's house. She knows it and I know it. She said she loved me and like a fool I was completely taken in and showed her where I kept the key to my father's safe.'

'You *dare* to come to court casting these atrocious slurs on the character of a thoroughly decent young woman doing no more than her civic duty? Your conduct disgusts me Mr Bullick. You are a disgrace sir' said he angrily and sat down.

Tom's evidence was consistent with my own and he would not be shaken. Jackson-Fagg went at him hammer and tong for much of the afternoon but to no avail.

'I am at a loss to convey my utter contempt for you'

said the latter concluding his cross-examination. 'You are a scoundrel of the very worst kind.'

'I have only told you the truth, sir. We both have.'

'The truth? Do you *seriously* expect the jury to believe such a cock and bull story? You are nothing but a despicable liar Mr Brentnall. In fact, I am at a loss to find words to sufficiently convey your wickedness.'

'So it would seem' piped Hall. 'You've been repeating yourself for the last twenty minutes.' (laughter)

Jackson-Fagg turned angrily on his opponent.

'Do you know, when you first entered the profession, somebody ought to have said 'hush', you know, just the once. You really think you're something, don't you?'

'I've forgotten more law than you'll ever know' countered Hall 'but take heart, I've not forgotten much.' (laughter)

'Oh, *what* a wag my friend is!' said Jackson-Fagg turning to the jury. 'No, seriously ladies and gentlemen, such exquisite oratory is quite wasted here. He's like a stand-up comic. In fact he should be on the stage! Much Ado About Nothing sort-of-thing, you understand?' (laughter)

'I don't care what you think about me' answered Hall. 'I don't think about you at all.' (laughter)

'That's quite enough' said Horridge. 'This is not a revue or some kind of sketch. Mr Jackson-Fagg, you represent the King. Mr Hall, you stand between your clients and their liberty. Be valiant gentlemen. Your fencing has no place here.'

The closing speeches followed similar vein. Jackson-Fagg went through the evidence focussing the attention of the jury on the extraordinary measure between the prosecution position and our own.

'Members of the jury' said he at length 'for all that you have heard these last three days, when you retire, there is but one question for you to determine and it is this: Who is telling you the truth? We may not be able to step into the minds of those who were set before the court, however I suggest there are signposts that will assist you with your deliberations. Take the evidence of Sergeant Tench for instance. This witness is a decorated war hero with more than fifteen years exemplary service in His Majesty's police force. I ask you, ladies and gentlemen, is it plausible that such a person would tell you that a large amount of property was stolen from his office were it not so?

If you are with me thus far, you must then ask yourselves whether it is credible that an officer of Sergeant Tench's standing would take the property for himself, as suggested by my learned friend? Well? Is it credible? No, ladies and gentlemen, I don't think so.

The stark reality is each and every item described by Sergeant Tench was stolen by these two men. Consider the evidence. They admit to breaking into the office. Their fingerprints were all over the furniture. They claim they only removed the file on Mr Bullick's father however Sergeant Tench told the court that the file is still there. If the file was not taken, then what exactly *were* they up to? The inescapable conclusion, ladies and gentlemen, is that these two men forced their way into the office for one purpose and one purpose only. They were there to plunder the belongings of the deceased and duly did so. Think about it. Edmund Bullick had ample opportunity to poke around the office when he first met Sergeant Tench. He only needed an accomplice to help him force the skylight, apparently no mean feat but into which void stepped Thomas Brentnall. If you need any more convincing, reflect upon the testimony of Victoria Clifford. She told you Mr Bullick actually *boasted* about what they had done, one assumes in the mistaken belief that it would go no further. Consider also the evidence of Mr Crake, again, an individual you may consider of the highest calibre. He told you that when he learned of the break-in, he urged the defendants to return to Durham and surrender themselves to the police. Think about it. If there was a *grain* of truth, the slightest grain, in their account then was that not the logical thing for them to have done? Report the fraud that they claim to have discovered and leave the authorities get to the bottom of it? But no. *Oh* no. These men had other plans. As soon as they learned from Mr Crake that the game was up they bolted and were it not for the vigilance of the railway police, I venture they would still be out there spending their ill-gotten gains. And as for their defence? Sergeant Tench is making the whole thing up don't you know? Victoria Clifford is lying too, not only about Mr Bullick's confession when they went riding together but also regarding a supposed sexual relationship she had with him. Members of the jury I suggest the very notion of such a connection is as scurrilous as it is untrue. As if!

And Mr Crake? Well of course he is lying as well, not only lying but he tried to *blackmail* them don't you know? Oh really? What complete and utter nonsense. I could go on members of the jury, but you will have my drift. The prosecution witnesses have given their evidence in the clearest possible terms and as judges of fact, you will shortly be invited to assess the plausibility of what they have told you. However, when you retire, ask yourselves this: is it really credible that each and every one of the witnesses called for the Crown is in his or her turn lying to the court? Well, are they? Hmm? No, ladies and gentlemen, of course they are not lying. They have simply told you exactly what happened, and the inescapable conclusion of their evidence is that these two men did it. They did it. They are guilty. They are guilty as charged and *that*, I suggest, is the only possible verdict with which you can return.'

Counsel for the Crown resumed his seat to self-satisfied murmurs and pats on the shoulder from Honeyman and Crisp. The prosecution team were entitled to be pleased with themselves. Hall warned us he knew his stuff and I didn't have to look up to sense the glare of the jury. Heck, things were bleak.

'Mr Hall?'

Hall finished scribbling and rose to his feet.

'Ladies and gentlemen of the jury' said he. 'You may recall that earlier in these proceedings, his Lordship commented upon the extraordinary measure between the prosecution position and our own. In fact, I believe his words were, it seemed as though he was trying two completely different causes. On the face of it, his assessment was well founded. There is a *gulf* between the accounts given by the prosecution witnesses and what you have heard from these two young men. They are simply poles apart- poles apart - in which circumstances, when you retire, you would be forgiven for asking one another how on earth do you even begin to unravel what everyone has said?

Members of the jury, you must watch the ball here, watch the ball. Mr Bullick is not on trial for boasting that he was the finest rider at the stables. Neither is he on trial for enjoying strong drink or for the quality of his ballroom dancing nor, indeed, regarding any other aspect of his relationship –whatever this may have been - with Victoria Clifford. He is certainly not on trial for accusing Mr Crake of blackmail any more than Mr Brentnall answers for the derogatory comments he is alleged to have made at the same interview. Neither, ladies and gentlemen, are these men on trial for causing damage to the mortuary skylight- although perhaps they should be. No, members of the jury, what falls for you to determine is not- as my friend suggested- who is telling you the truth in all of this, but rather where the truth lies with regard to the solitary accusation that forms the prosecution case. These two men are here today to answer one allegation and one allegation only: namely that on the night of 20 November 1914 they entered the mortuary of Dryburn Hospital as trespassers and removed specific items of property belonging to the deceased. That is the only charge that has been brought against them and whether they must answer for it is the one and only matter for you to determine.

Now, ladies and gentlemen, somewhat unusually in this type of case there is actually an abundance of common ground between my learned friend and myself, so much so that you can narrow the issue still further. It is not denied these young men entered the coroner's office. They readily admit to it, only they say it was not to steal any valuables but for the sole purpose of recovering the police file relating to the death of Jimmy Bullick, the father of one of the accused. I suggest this explanation is entirely plausible. You heard Sergeant Tench concede under cross examination that he had refused to allow my client to inspect the coroner's file in which circumstances, if you were Mr Bullick, what would *you* have done? Think about it ladies and gentlemen, just imagine for a moment if *your* father had died in suspicious circumstances and the authorities had refused point blank to engage with *you*? How would *you* feel about it? I venture that far from being deterred in your quest for the truth, like Mr Bullick, you would stop at nothing in order to uncover it. The case therefore turns on what happened in the mortuary office that night which leads me to the evidence of Sergeant Tench.

Let me refresh your memory regarding what he claimed was removed. I have the schedule, here it is;

Two gold pocket watches.
Three wrist watches, one gold, two silver, one with a leather strap.
One antique rolled gold necklace with jewel cluster.
Three gold wedding rings.
Four assorted dress rings.
Four pairs of earrings, one gold, three silver.
A silver tie pin.
One silver chain and crucifix.
A leather purse containing nine gold sovereigns.
Twenty-six-pounds ten shillings in notes.
Four pounds, six shillings and three pence ha'penny in assorted change.

A long and most detailed list, is it not ladies and gentlemen? Further, if one were to suppose- because there is no evidence to the contrary - that it represents *all* of the property in the office that evening and that nothing remained, would you not expect the sergeant to have immediately reported the theft to his superiors? That he omitted to do so on the first available occasion is cause for concern in itself, but that he made no reference to the matter for several days is, I suggest, quite extraordinary. Bear in mind the witness was in singular charge of that office - no one else had access to it- surely, then, in those circumstances and in the knowledge there had been an offence of such gravity, was it not his duty to go straight to the authorities? And yet he failed to do so. He failed to do so ladies and gentlemen and you must ask yourselves why? *Why?* What possible reason could he have had for overlooking the matter? I submit the only plausible explanation is that- contrary to what Sergeant Tench would have you believe- the property was *not* taken from his office on that evening; rather, if any property were removed at all, it was taken by another or others and on a later occasion.

Members of the jury, there are other matters you may wish to consider. It will have not escaped your attention that none of this property has been recovered notwithstanding the array of such distinctive artefacts. Where, then, did it all go? Nothing was found in the possession of the defendants when they were detained nor was anything turned up when the police searched their homes. Durham is a small town, there are only so many outlets through which- if you pardon the expression- 'hot' property might be channelled yet notwithstanding the intelligence the police receive from the underworld on such matters, again, not a single lead which in a case like this is extraordinary. My learned friend knows the current whereabouts of the property is a weakness in the prosecution case and seeks to persuade you that Mr Bullick must have travelled to Liverpool to dispose of it. Really? I venture that to have such illicit contacts at one's disposal on the other side of the country bears the hallmark of a seasoned criminal gang rather than an Oxbridge scholar. Is it not more plausible that Mr Bullick and his brother went to Liverpool – as he told you – at the invitation of friends of their father who took pity on the prospect of the two of them spending Christmas in that large house on their own?

Members of the jury, you must also consider the character of these two men. My learned friend places great store on what he says are the impeccable qualities of the witnesses for the Crown but I ask you, are not the defendants similarly divested? They are both from excellent families. Edmund Bullick is the son of a highly esteemed racehorse trainer. Thomas Brentnall hails from an eminent family of chemists in York. Neither has any previous history with the police - rather they are both studious, thoroughly decent young men who having excelled at one of the finest Colleges in the land are now on the point of entering university to advance their education. Ask yourselves this ladies and gentleman; is it credible that either of them are the kind of people who would stoop so low as to steal possessions belonging to people who have died? Well, is it credible? No. I suggest it is not.

Ladies and gentlemen, in this country it has long been established that citizens who appear before the criminal courts are presumed to be innocent until the contrary is proven. In fact, throughout the complex web of the whole legal system, this presumption of innocence is so sacrosanct it has been described as the one, golden thread - and rightly so. Think about it ladies and gentlemen. The one, golden thread. What this means is that the prosecution must *prove* the allegation they are making- they have to prove it - and if, at the end of the case, there exists a reasonable doubt that they have done so, the accused are entitled to be acquitted.

It matters not the allegation or where the trial, the principle is the same- it is for the prosecution to establish the guilt of the accused beyond all reasonable doubt and there can be no attempt to whittle this duty down. Reflect upon what this means for a moment if you would. Reflect upon it. It is not for these two young men to convince you that they are innocent. They don't have to prove anything. No, ladies and gentlemen, it is for the *prosecution* to satisfy *you* beyond *all reasonable doubt* (Hall thumped the bench with each syllable) that they are guilty. In other words, the obligation lies with my learned friend not only to substantiate this allegation, but to *prove* it to you to the extent that before you come back with the verdict he is asking for, each and every one of you is satisfied so that you are all *sure* that these two men stole this property. Well, are you *sure*? Can you be *sure*?'

Hall paused to take a drink of water. As he replaced the jug every eye in the room was upon him.

'If you seek any further guidance with your deliberations' he continued 'I can do no more than remind you of the gravity of the oath that each one of you took at the beginning of this case. You *swore* to Almighty God that you would well and truly try these young men and give a true verdict according to the evidence. According to the *evidence*, ladies and gentlemen. The *evidence*. The word is quite deliberately included in the oath that you took because the word is the very key to unlocking these proceedings. *Evidence*, ladies and gentlemen. The currency of this court is *evidence* and in order for you to return the verdict requested by my friend, you must be satisfied *on the evidence* so that you are *sure* that these two men are guilty as charged. It is not enough for you to be persuaded that they *might* have been responsible.

It is not enough for you to conclude that they probably *were* responsible. No, ladies and gentlemen, before you return a verdict of guilty, you must be satisfied so that you are all sure. You have to be sure.'

Hall paused and took another sip of water.

'I have little more to say other than to remind you that the responsibility is yours now, and not mine. If you are satisfied beyond all reasonable doubt that these young men stole all this property, though it breaks your hearts to do it, you must find them guilty and send them into the abyss. But, if, when making up your minds for yourselves upon this matter, if you feel you cannot truthfully and consciously say you are satisfied that the prosecution has proved its case, then surely, it is your duty, as it must be your pleasure, to conclude that they have not? Ladies and gentlemen, the very future of these young lads is in your hands and you have to get this right. This whole case turns- absolutely turns- upon the evidence of Sergeant Tench and I say to you his account of what became of this property is not only a shambles, but as *evidence* placed before this court, is woefully insufficient upon which to convict these men. It must follow therefore, ladies and gentlemen, that the only proper verdict in these proceedings is one of *not* guilty, and *that* is the finding with which I invite you to return.'

Hall resumed his seat. The court was utterly spellbound, and you could have heard a pin drop. It was left to Horridge to break the silence.

'Thank you, Mr Hall. Ladies and gentlemen, it is now four thirty; it has been a long afternoon and I propose to suspend proceedings for the day. The courts do not sit over Easter so could I ask you all to return, please, at 10.00am on Tuesday when I shall deliver my summing up.'

'Might I address you on the question of bail my Lord?'

'My apologies, Mr Hall. Bail for Mr Brentnall will be extended on the same terms as before.'

'I am instructed to make an application for Mr Bullick.' Horridge was surprised.

'Indeed? Mr Jackson-Fagg? What say the Crown?'

'We oppose bail. Your Lordship will recall that when detained at the railway station, the accused was in possession of a ticket from Liverpool. If released today, there must be every prospect he will simply disappear again.'

'I agree, Mr Jackson-Fagg. Bail is refused.'

'My Lord' said Hall. 'Mr Bullick has been in custody since December. That is a very long time for anyone to be remanded, let alone a young man who is a complete outsider to the prison system. He seeks only a small window to set his affairs in order. He would obviously comply with any conditions imposed by your Lordship.'

Horridge drummed his fingers.

'Four months is a long time. Mr Jackson-Fagg? Your opponent suggests conditions. Are you still against?'

'We object to bail for the reasons previously stated. This man cannot be relied upon to return. If you are against me, my Lord, then I urge you to impose only restrictions of the most rigorous type.'

'What would you suggest?'

Jackson-Fagg conferred with the police. 'At the very least we would expect a condition of residence somewhere other than the stables at Craven - and a large surety.'

'Do you have a sum in mind?'

'Two hundred and fifty pounds would not seem unreasonable, my Lord.'

What? Two hundred and fifty pounds? Where would I find that kind of money? Jackson-Fagg knew I didn't have it.

Horridge pondered for a moment.

'Stand up Mr Bullick. Mr Bullick, I have in mind granting bail on condition that you reside with the Brentnall family, that you report at 10.00am daily to York police office, that you remain at all times within three miles of York Cathedral and that you do not interfere, communicate or attempt to communicate with any of the prosecution witnesses. I also direct that a surety of two hundred and fifty pounds is deposited with the court before you are released. Do you have anyone who will stand you in this sum?'

'All I possess is the money that was taken from me by the police.'

'That must remain with the authorities pending the conclusion of this case' said the judge. 'Is there anyone- a family member or friend- who will come forward and pledge the sum on the understanding it will be forfeit if you fail to surrender next week? '

I replied there was not.

'So be it Mr Bullick' said Horridge gathering his papers. 'You will be remanded in custody until Tuesday.'

'Court rise'.

McMash glanced up from his magazine.

'How was it then?'

'Awful. Crake did us good and proper.'

'Excellent. I'll cash up the book then, shall I?'

I kicked off my sandals.

'You're so funny.'

'You mean you're not finished?'

'No. Stood down over Easter. You'll have to wait.'

'How was Marshall Hall?'

'Did his best but he reckons we've had it too. The judge is prosecution orientated and will finish us off in his summing up.'

'Ah well, never mind. Worse things happen at sea.'

'I doubt it' I replied sinking into my bunk.

I must have dozed off because the next thing I remember was the rattle of keys in the lock and someone shouting my name.

'Bullick? Get your things.'

'What?'

'You're being released.'

'Released?' I cried disbelievingly.

'Order of the judge. Now hurry up.'

I wasn't going to argue although McMash couldn't understand it either.

'You jammy get. How did you manage that?'

I shrugged my shoulders.

'Don't ask me. I'm as much in the dark as you are.'

'Well, well, wonders never cease. Bring me forty *Navy Cut* when you get back would you?'

I was taken to a small office. Hall was sitting at a table smoking a cheroot.

'Leave us'.

The warden locked the door and stood sentry in the passage. I turned to Hall.

'What's going on?'

'You have been granted bail until Tuesday morning.'

'Granted bail? But how? I'm broke!'

Hall leaned back in his chair and blew a smoke ring. 'I'm not.'

'I don't understand.'

'I'll be straight with you Mr Bullick. If I have learned one thing at the bar, it is that people who get sucked into the justice system do not usually end up there by chance. They are habitually the dregs of society- thieves, killers, rapists, extortionists - delinquents of the foulest kind each of them more than worthy of their place in the dock, or on the trapdoor. You and Tommy Brentnall have no business at all being here and while the jury may not give you the benefit of the doubt, I am prepared to.'

'Did you stand surety?'

'I did.'

'But why, Mr Hall? I mean, don't think I'm ungrateful but you don't owe me anything.'

Hall pulled on his cheroot.

'I owe you nothing personally, it's true, however I don't get many opportunities to put something back into the profession that made my fortune. Such times that have arisen, when I could have done the right thing, I failed to act and to my eternal regret the moment passed. I will not make the same mistake today.'

'I don't know how to thank you.'

'There is no need' said Hall passing me the list of conditions. 'Just promise me two things. First, whatever happens, make damn sure you are back here at ten o clock on Tuesday morning.'

'You can count on it. And the second?'

Hall stubbed out his cheroot.

'You must find those documents, Mr Bullick. Find them.'

CHAPTER SEVENTEEN

And so it was after nearly four months detention I stepped from the squalor of Durham jail into the cool, spring air. Oh, to be outdoors. To quit the misery and filth of that vilest of places and walk the streets again. To be free.

Tom and his father were waiting outside and as we strolled through the cobbled lanes I cherished once more the everyday clamour and shades of that beautiful city. The Minster bells calling over the valley. The pale scent of blossom. Carts rattling down Whinney Hill. The newsboy howling on Framwellgate Bridge. The swans on the river. Looking back, everything was so utterly ordinary, but it had been the ordinary things in life that I had yearned for most when they had been taken away from me.

We jumped on the first train to York then walked the half mile or so to the Brentnall's house which lay in the shadow of Micklegate Bar. I was still in my prison apparel which brought some strange looks and when we arrived, Tom's mother had to find me some clothes while I had my first bath for months. Oh, such bliss. I could have wallowed there for eternity. The ordinary things in life, you see?

After dinner, we settled in front of the fire with a bottle of Scotch. There was only one topic of conversation. Where, oh where, had Conway put the key to the left luggage box? Where had he put it? Who was this Veronica woman? Where was she? Conway's letter could not have been clearer – St Pancras Station he had said- but Tom and his father had already turned the place upside down to no avail. We simply had to find her. We had to. But where? We trawled endlessly through the possibilities getting more and more drunk until next thing I knew, it was gone midnight and we were still no further forward. Tom's father polished off the bottle.

'Bugger this lads' said he and promptly fell asleep in his armchair.

The following morning Tom and I reported to the police station in Silver Street. It was Good Friday and with the city closed down, the avenues were oddly quiet. We made our way to Deans Park and finding the old Minster Library open, pulled out some reference books and began thumbing through the pages.

Saint Pancras (Latin: Sanctus Pancratius) Roman martyr beheaded aged fourteen during the persecution of Christians under the Emperor Diocletian c304. Name thought to be Greek (Παγκράτιος) meaning "the one that holds everything". Patron saint of children.

Fourteen? The poor kid. I skimmed through his little life but finding no mention of a Veronica moved swiftly down the page. *St Pancras Avenue, St Pancras Church, St Pancras Diocese, St Pancras Fields…*

St Pancras Infirmary. Camden, London. Served as
hospital for the St Pancras Workhouse from 1848
and constructed within the original 18th century
building. After St Pancras North Hospital opened in
Highgate in 1869, building renamed St Pancras South
Infirmary.

Nothing there. Move on. *St Pancras House, St Pancras*
Library, St Pancras Road, St Pancras Road, hang on, here we
are...

Saint Pancras Station. Euston Road, London. Opened
1868 by Midland Railway Company to connect the
capital to other major cities. Extravagant Baroque
magnum opus of Victorian Gothic architecture
considered to be one of the most sophisticated
terminals in the world. Later extended over supposed
burial place of Irish and French Catholic refugees who
died in London...

All very interesting but nothing about Veronica. Damn
it. The answer was there somewhere, it had to be- in all
likelihood it was staring us in the face, but where?

Veronica (Veronika, Verónica, Weronika) female
name, Latin translation of Greek name Berenice,
Βερενίκη, derived from Macedonian Φερενίκη,
Phereníkē, or Φερονίκη, Pheroníkē, from φέρειν,
phérein, to bring, and νίκη, níkê, "victory", i.e. "she
who brings victory". Name propagated throughout
Eastern Mediterranean including Ptolemies of Egypt
and the Seleucids of the Levant. Status enhanced in
medieval mythology via Christian endorsement of

the veil of Saint Veronica. See also <u>Veronica Franco</u>
(1546–1591), Venetian poet and concubine <u>Veronica</u>
<u>Giuliani</u> (1660–1727), Italian mystic <u>Veronika Gut</u>
(1757-1829), Swiss insurgent

And so it went on for there was nothing we could do but persevere. 'Seek and ye shall find' said Conway but as the hours slipped by, our frustration only grew with the turn of each silent stone.

'This is hopeless' said Tom eventually.

'You're telling me.'

'Sod it mate, I need a break.'

We had a mug of ale in *The Golden Fleece* then sat on the riverbank with a couple of newspapers. The headlines were all about the war although further in was a grainy photograph of some posh aristocrat or other who denied sleeping with a member of staff. It all looked very interesting until I read on and realised the girl in the picture was Victoria and the scoundrel of the piece was me. It was so unreal I couldn't believe it, how someone I didn't know and had never met could write such trash about me and with such authority. I glanced around anxiously. Others were reading the same paper and I couldn't help wondering if they were talking about me and what they were saying. At the time I was shocked and deeply upset at the reports. They were inaccurate and slanted although looking back, this was only to be expected with the salacious details of our trial and the involvement of Hall who the press tended to follow around.

In Duncombe Place a queue of parishioners were filing into the church of St Wilfrid's. I had forgotten it was a holy day of obligation.

'Perhaps we should consult the Almighty?' said Tom.

I shrugged my shoulders.

'Perhaps we should. We've tried everything else.'

We settled in a pew at the back and braced ourselves for the really long mass we used to get at Ampleforth at this time of year. Many of you will understand what I mean- you know, the Good Friday service where the effigies and clerics are swathed in purple and the gospel account of the passion of Christ takes nearly an hour on its own. To be honest I wasn't fond of it because it was usually the last day of the Easter term when we had packed and were straining to get home. However any fears on that score were quickly dispelled when the parish priest glided in from a side door, genuflected to the tabernacle then turned to face the congregation.

'Welcome to St Wilfrid's' ladies and gentlemen. We have gathered this afternoon to commemorate *The Stations of the Cross*, also known as *The Way of Sorrows*, in which we recall the suffering of Our Lord Jesus Christ on the day of his crucifixion.'

The priest was attended by five altar boys, one who clutched a tall shaft with a cross on the top followed by the others staring vacantly through the flames of their plump candles. After a few prayers, the assembly shuffled to the back of the church until they stood before the first of a line of wooden carvings that were spaced out along the wall. The priest made the sign of the cross then began.

'The First Station; *Jesus is condemned to death*. Now consider for a moment the humiliation of our saviour who having endured the night being spat upon and beaten up was now dragged before Pilate to be thrashed and then put to death. Jesus well knew what was in store for him.

Tacitus, the Roman historian, described crucifixion as 'the most miserable of deaths' not only on account of the extreme suffering but also because the ordeal took hours and sometimes days as the victim slowly died of thirst, asphyxiation and heat exhaustion...'

I recalled the reference in Conway's letter about Pilate handing Jesus over to the soldiers to be crucified and suddenly understood it was his way of telling us he knew he was going to die. Poor Conway. Like Jesus, he must have been so frightened.

'We now say the act of contrition. *O my God, my Redeemer, behold me here at Thy feet. From the bottom of my heart I am sorry for all my wrongs, because by them I have offended Thee, who art infinitely good. I firmly resolve that with the help of Your grace I will never offend Thee again and carefully avoid the occasions of sin. Amen*'

The service advanced down the line of stations, the priest commenting on the significance of each before revisiting the Act of Contrition.

Jesus takes up his Cross ('I often wondered if this was a single timber bar or an 'actual T-shape' like you see in the murals?').

Jesus falls for the first time ('He must have been so weak from his scourging and loss of blood')

Jesus meets his Mother ('Can you imagine the overwhelming sorrow of them both?')

Simon of Cyrene helps Jesus carry the Cross ('Had he been a disciple of Christ who offered his support or was he a bystander dragooned into it?')

'The Fifth Station: *Veronica wipes the face of Jesus*. Now in this selfless act of human decency...'

I didn't hear any more. I didn't need to. It was like the sky had opened. Tom wrenched my sleeve.

'Veronica!' he cried. 'Veronica!'

'Shhh' said someone.

'Are you thinking what I'm thinking?'

'Shhh.'

We bolted out of church and tore back to the library where the reference books lay open on the table, exactly where we had left them.

St Pancras Church, Chichester, St Pancras Church, Exeter, St Pancras Church, Ipswich, St Pancras Old Church, London …

St Pancras Old Church is an ancient place of worship in Somers Town, Central London dedicated to the child martyr Pancras. Considered to be one of the earliest Christian sites in England. The church is situated on Pancras Road in the Borough of Camden, and lends its name to the surrounding district and nearby railway station.

'That's it!' cried Tom. 'It's not the railway station. It's the church! It's the church!'

CHAPTER EIGHTEEN

The overnight Pullman slipped into Kings Cross just after dawn. We knew we were breaching bail and the alarm would be raised when we failed to report, but it was the final throw of the dice and we might as well get hung for a sheep as a lamb.

We quickly found St Pancras Old Church. It was only a short walk from the railway station but when we tried the door, it was locked and there was nothing for it but to loiter in the graveyard until someone turned up. We did not have long to wait. The board at the entrance said the first service was at 8am and sure enough, at twenty to the hour the parish priest arrived with the key and we followed him inside.

'You're a bit early lads' said he switching on the lights.

'We have much to pray for' answered Tom.

'Well, you've come to the right place' said the cleric and promptly disappeared into the sacristy.

St Pancras was now eerily quiet, the silence thwarted only by the ricochet of footsteps as we made our way towards the south aisle. I raised my eyes to the walls. The Stations of the Cross were there. All fourteen hallowed carvings running anti-clockwise around the church. We walked down the pews and stopped beneath the fifth mural. And there she was. *Veronica wipes the face of Jesus.* Veronica herself, the fabled woman who, moved by pity for Christ's suffering, wiped his brow, then found her cloth imprinted with the image of His face.

I reached up and gently shook the figure. As I did so a small shiny object fell from the back and pinged onto the cold stone floor. It was the key to the left luggage safe. We had found it.

CHAPTER NINETEEN

'Ladies and gentlemen of the jury, over the last week you have heard a number of accounts from ...yes, Mr Hall? What is it?'

'An important matter of evidence has arisen since the court last convened. It is an issue that requires clarification and upon which I seek leave to address your Lordship.'

'Really, Mr Hall? I understood I heard you on Thursday.'

'I don't think your Lordship did hear me.'

'I beg your pardon Mr Hall?'

'I said, I don't think your Lordship did hear me.'

Horridge stared back in disbelief.

'You have no right to say such a thing' said he angrily. 'It is a most improper observation for you to make. I cannot allow it.'

'I did not mean anything bellicose, I'm sure' said Hall wearily.

'I am not persuaded that is so' snapped the judge. 'You meant to be offensive, and you must not be offensive.'

'Your Lordship has misunderstood me; I did not mean to be offensive in what I said.'

'It struck me so. You were quite deliberately impertinent.'
'I am sure your Lordship will withdraw that observation.'
'I will not indeed; I am quite satisfied about it. I am also satisfied that the defence submissions were concluded last week, and you can have nothing further to say.'

Hall stood his ground.

'It is but a minor point. I expect it will take but little of your Lordship's time.'

Horridge removed his glasses, struggling to hide his irritation. 'This is most irregular. How many more speeches am I to receive? Mr Jackson-Fagg?'

'I understood my learned friend made his closing address on Thursday. I was expecting your Lordship would now sum up.'

'Indeed, Mr Jackson-Fagg, indeed. And so I shall. Please be seated Mr Hall.'

Hall remained on his feet.

'I would be heard your Lordship' said he gravely.

'No, Mr Hall. This trial is already overrunning. You had every opportunity to make your case in cross examination and again in your closing submissions. You can have nothing further to add. Ladies and gentlemen of the jury, as I was saying...'

'My Lord, I *will* be heard.'

'This is preposterous' said the judge. 'Mr Hall, you do realise your manner throughout these proceedings is unlikely to escape the attention of the jury?'

'I would hope not.'

'And that the members of the jury in reaching their verdict will consider not only the evidence, but also the stance of the advocates?'

'I would expect nothing less my Lord.'

'Nothing less' repeated Horridge through a sigh. 'So be it then, Mr Hall. Proceed if you must but I expect you to be brief.'

Hall reached for his notes and started peeling through the sheets as if searching for a particular passage. After what seemed an age but was probably no more than a few seconds, he raised his head. 'The defence wish to recall Thomas Mathias Crake.'

A low murmur rippled across the court.

'Mr Crake completed his evidence last week' said the judge flatly. 'The jury will have formed a view on what he told them although it appeared to me he was abundantly clear.'

'There remains an outstanding issue and I submit the defence be given the opportunity to explore it.'

'This is highly irregular Mr Hall' answered the judge. 'If there was anything to be clarified regarding the testimony of this witness, you should have raised the matter when you had the opportunity.'

Hall creased his arms in defiance.

'I would be given the opportunity your Lordship.'

'I think not. Mr Jackson-Fagg?'

'I object. My learned friend had the floor on Thursday. It would be wholly inappropriate to recall any of the prosecution witnesses, as your Lordship has already observed.'

'Mr Hall, I am against you.'

Hall slapped down his notes.

'My Lord, I canvas upon what basis am I to be silenced?'

'On the basis of the rules' sniffed Horridge 'as you well know.'

'The established order of cross examination is but a framework,' said Hall. 'There are exceptions to the rule where the interests of justice warrant it and I submit this is one such occasion.'

Horridge was unimpressed.

'Mr Hall, I cannot comment on how things are done at the Old Bailey but in this town, we adhere to the recognised procedure. You have already cross-examined this witness, indeed at considerable length. You can have nothing further to put. Please resume your seat.'

The court was now hushed, every eye fixed on Hall who slowly leaned over the bench as if to get nearer to the judge.

'My Lord' said he quietly. 'My Lord, from the very conception of the judicial system in this country it has been recognised that the purpose of the criminal courts is to get to the truth. It therefore goes without saying that establishing the truth is at the heart of this trial, particularly where the liberty of fellow citizens is at stake.'

'I don't disagree, Mr Hall. What's your point?'

Hall adjusted his spectacles and though still addressing the judge, twisted his lean frame to the jury.

'Your Lordship, my point is that the twelve ordinary men and women charged with discerning guilt or innocence in this case will expect - and are entitled to expect- that this Court will properly discharge its obligation to the King to discover where the truth in these proceedings lies. Thomas Mathias Crake is a vital witness in the case, and I say to you that the defence have not finished their questioning of him. And for all his bluster' continued Hall stretching an arm to his opponent 'for all his bluster, it is quite disingenuous of my friend to suggest that recalling Thomas Mathias Crake might somehow cause prejudice to the Crown when the consequences of denying the defence the opportunity to re-examine him, once lost, will be lost forever. It is down to the fundamental question of what is *fair*, an issue that is so sacrosanct to these proceedings that there can be no price too high to protect it. In appealing to the court's sense of impartiality, I invite your Lordship to direct that the remote possibility of prejudice to the prosecution case is not even a price, let alone one that could even begin to justify denying these young men a proper opportunity to defend themselves.'

I was no lawyer but I knew a masterful address when I heard one. It also chimed with the jury who nodded and clucked in approval. Hall said later the one thing judges detest is the ignominy of being turned over at the Court of Appeal on a point of law. Hall would have the connection to see it through and this must have been on the judge's mind when he relented.

'So be it, Mr Hall' said he begrudgingly 'I am persuaded. No, sit down Mr Jackson-Fagg. Learned clerk, please enquire as to the whereabouts of Mr Crake and bring him to court as soon as possible.'

'Mr Crake is in the witness room with the others, my Lord.'

So, Crake had returned? Probably didn't want to miss the kill, or so he thought. A few minutes later he was back in the stand.

'You sent for me judge?'

'Yes, Mr Crake. There is a minor point of your evidence the defence wish to clarify. Please answer any questions that are put to you by Mr Hall. You do not need to take the oath again but consider yourself still bound.'

'I understand.'

Hall rose to his feet.

'Good morning Mr Crake. There is a pen and notepad in front of you. Would you pick them up please and sign your name?'

The witness shrugged his shoulders but did as he was asked.

'Thank you. Now would you write down the postal address of your Hartlepool office?'

The witness complied. If he smelt a rat, he gave no sign of it.

'Thank you. Finally, will you write '20th October 1914' and then give the notepad to me.'

The trap was sprung. Crake faltered for a moment but the eyes of the court were upon him and it was too late to back out. When he was done the usher reached up and passed the jotter to Hall.

'Thank you' said he. 'Mr Crake, there is a manuscript here that I would like you to inspect.'

The witness must have known what was coming but before he could respond Jackson-Fagg shot to his feet.

'Manuscript? What manuscript? I understood there were a few questions for this witness. You said nothing about a manuscript!'

'My most profound apologies' sighed Hall shunting the codicil along the bench. Counsel for the Crown looked back suspiciously then untied the ribbon.

'Good Grief' he whispered and twisted to Honeyman sitting behind him. We did not catch all of the exchange but there was much shaking of heads and the words 'can't be' and 'don't understand' were in among it all.

The judge saw their discomfort.

'Whatever you have there, pass it to me please'.

The usher obliged and I watched Horridge closely as he scanned the document. When he was finished, he flipped it over a few times as if cross referencing the date. To my surprise his expression did not waver.

'Ladies and gentlemen of the jury' said he with astonishing understatement 'a minor legal point has arisen which I need to discuss with counsel in private. It will not take long, and this appears as good a moment as any for a short break.'

The jury and gallery filed away to the usual hubbub and scraping of furniture. When the last door closed, only the advocates, the police officers, Crake and ourselves were left. Horridge cut the silence.

'Mr Crake. Please return to the witness room and remain there until you are called for.'

The solicitor, horrified at the unexpected turn of events, looked beseechingly at the judge.

'Now please, Mr Crake'.

Crake must have known he was finished. He was about to say something but there was nothing to be said and all he could do was shuffle uneasily towards the exit. I met his eye on the way out. Serves you right, you bastard.

'Mr Jackson-Fagg' said the judge gravely 'this is a most extraordinary development. If this instrument is genuine- as it appears to be - I must canvas if the Crown is minded to review their position?'

'A moment please, My Lord.'

Jackson-Fagg conferred with Honeyman. Surely they would throw in the towel?

'I am instructed to continue with the prosecution.'

I couldn't believe it. He had seen the codicil. He knew we were telling the truth. How could he? Hall turned angrily on his opponent.

'You what?' he cried. 'That document blows your case to smithereens. You cannot possibly continue.'

Jackson-Fagg ignored him and addressed the judge.

'I am instructed to proceed, my Lord' said he flatly. 'I also object to the introduction of any new material at this late stage of the trial together with any attempt by my friend to put the same to the witness or before the jury.'

Hall smacked his down his papers. 'What the devil's wrong with you man? These lads are clearly innocent. Have you taken leave of your senses?'

'I have my instructions Hall. You know or ought to know better than to speak to me in that tone of voice.'

'My Lord' said Hall 'This is absurd. I implore you to put an end to this trial immediately!'

'Upon what basis Mr Hall? The police are resolved to see the matter through. It is not for me to interfere whatever my thoughts on the matter.'

'You have an inherent power to act in the interests of justice.'

'I will not intervene, Mr Hall.'

Hall was smoking.

'So be it then, my Lord. Recall the witness. Recall the witness and we'll see what the jury make of it all.'

Horridge creased his arms.

'You are too late, Mr Hall. I don't know how or in what circumstances the defence came by this document, but it should have been brought to the jury's attention when your clients gave evidence. It is a matter of record that the defence submissions were concluded on Thursday and Mr Jackson-Fagg is correct; the court rules prohibit the introduction of any new material at this late stage of proceedings.'

'You have an overriding discretion to admit the document in the interests of justice' retorted Hall. 'Its existence goes to the integrity of a critical witness against my clients and I insist that the jury are made aware of it.'

'The evidence of Mr Crake is not central to the charge of burglary, Mr Hall. You said yourself the case boils down to what the jury make of the testimony of the coroner's assistant and I am inclined to agree with you.'

'But how can you possibly keep this from the jury? How can you? Your Lordship has a duty to oversee this prosecution fairly and impartially.'

'My overriding obligation is to try the case according to the established rules of evidence' snapped the judge. 'I am not prepared to break them, even for you, Mr Hall.'

Hall was furious.

'I urge you to reconsider my Lord. You must see that the position of the Crown is as toxic as it is inexcusable.'

'I have made my decision Mr Hall. The document is clearly inadmissible and that is an end to the matter.'

'This is insanity!' fumed Hall. 'It is patently obvious that the Crown's decision to continue is driven by malice. That my learned friend conducts himself thus is deplorable, but that a highly respected and experienced judge of these courts would turn Nelson's eye to such malevolence is an affront to every concept of fairness.'

Horridge was now angry.

'You have said quite enough Mr Hall' he growled. 'This is not the first time you have overstepped the mark and I will not be lectured on judicial values by the likes of yourself. The rules are there for a purpose and I intend to apply them. The document is inadmissible. Now if you have any misgivings about it or any other aspect regarding the manner in which I have conducted this trial, you are at liberty to take it up elsewhere.'

'Is that your final ruling, my Lord?'

'It is.'

Hall shook his head.

'Will you at least comment on the extraordinary decision of the Crown to continue?'

'I will not.'

'Really? Am I to take it your Lordship has no views on the matter?'

'The incentive of those who oppose your clients is not my remit, Mr Hall.'

'I urge you to reconsider, my Lord.'

'No, Mr Hall. These men have made serious accusations against Sergeant Tench and to halt the trial now would leave an indelible stain on the integrity of the whole of Durham Constabulary.'

Hall exhaled in frustration.

'May I have a moment with the prisoners my Lord?'

'So be it.'

Hall approached the dock.

'Well, I tried my best gentleman' said he peeping over the rails. 'Strictly speaking I fear the judge is right, but the man's an arse'

Horridge had heard him.

'What did you just say Mr Hall?'

Hall turned to the judge.

'Pardon me, my Lord?'

'I heard that. What did you just call me?'

'I didn't call you anything.'

'Yes you did. I distinctly heard you say, 'the judge is right but the man's an arse' (muffled snorts)

'Your Lordship has misunderstood me' answered Hall, cool as a cucumber. 'I said only that 'the judge is right but what a farce.'

Horridge glared back like an owl in labour. He knew he could not be certain. Hall tilted his head innocuously and the moment passed.

'Recall the witness' snapped the judge.

Crake shuffled gingerly to the stand and braced himself.

'Mr Crake' said the judge. 'You are no longer required in these proceedings and I am discharging you.'

The witness could scarcely believe his ears.

'You mean, I'm free to go?'

'You are- however I give you the same warning I give to all witnesses namely that when you leave the building, you must not discuss this case with any other person. Do you understand?'

Crake stared incredulously at the judge.

'Do you understand, Mr Crake?'

'Yes. Yes, I do' mumbled the latter and promptly scuttled off. Talk about a reprieve. Hall would have shredded him and Crake knew it. No matter though. He would be paid out later. What was less certain was whether Tom I would be around to see it when he was.

Horridge peered over his glasses.

'Madam Usher, would you bring back the jury?'

Now you may have thought our prospects had been improved by the discovery of the codicil but any hope this might colour the judge's summing up rapidly vanished as the latter took the jury coldly and cynically through the evidence. While he was careful not to dwell on anything Crake had said, Horridge's approach with Victoria was strikingly different and the jury were left in no doubt of his views on that score, such was the manner in which he piled into me. Latimer was right - the Establishment protects the Establishment to the last and all I could do was wince as Horridge delivered his skewered assessment of what he believed had passed between us. If that wasn't bad enough, the crucial witness- Tench - was praised to the skies with the judge discarding the obvious inconsistencies in his evidence in favour of sieving our own account through a filter of derision and disbelief. All in all, the summing up was a humiliation, its opinionated slant treating the jury to nothing other than a rehashed version of Jackson-Fagg's submissions the previous week. Hall, as troubled about it as we were, sat throughout with a face like thunder but there was nothing he could do.

'And so, ladies and gentlemen' said the judge winding down 'there you have it, the issue for you to determine is abundantly clear. There is one allegation against these men and one allegation only, namely that on the night of 21 November 1914 they forced their way into the morgue at Dryburn Hospital and removed those articles that were so meticulously recorded by Sergeant Tench. The witnesses for the Crown have given their evidence and it is now for you to resolve if they have spoken the truth or whether, in suggesting they have not, the prisoners are trying to pull the wool over your eyes. In a moment I will ask you to proceed to the retiring room to commence your deliberations. However, before you are released, there are two matters I would like you to bear in mind. The first is that before you find the accused guilty as charged, you must first be satisfied beyond all reasonable doubt that the Crown has proved its case. The second is that when you do return, I can only accept a decision upon which all of you are agreed.'

The jury had only been out for ten minutes when we were suddenly called back. A verdict already? Surely not. We clambered from the underworld to find everyone back in their place except the judge who swept in through his connecting door. The portly clerk turned to the jury.

'Will the foreman please stand?'

A short stocky fellow in a crumpled suit rose to his feet. 'Answer yes or no. Have you reached a verdict upon which you are all agreed?'

'No.'

'No?' cried Horridge. 'I thought I made it clear that you were not to return until you had reached a decision. Is there a problem?'

'We have a question for the court' said the foreman. 'Indeed?'

'Yes sir. We would like to know what those documents were that Mr Hall gave you.'

I'll give Horridge his due. He was a cool customer and if he was as surprised as we were by the development, as usual, he gave nothing away.

'A perfectly reasonable question' said he brightly 'and I understand exactly where you are coming from. In retrospect, perhaps I should have dealt with the matter in my summing up, however, permit me to allay your concerns now. The document that was passed up to me has no bearing on the issues in this case. If it were otherwise or if it were evidence that ought to have been admitted, you can be certain it would have been disclosed to you. Does that answer your question?'

The foreman looked to his colleagues. Some of them nodded. One or two seemed puzzled. Others shrugged their shoulders.

'If you say so' he answered and sat down.

A few minutes later they were back again. What was it now? Another question? Porky climbed to his feet.

'Will the foreman please stand?' he puffed 'Answer yes or no. Have you reached a verdict upon which you are all agreed?

'We have.'

I nearly threw up. A verdict? So soon? But there hadn't been time to boil the kettle. Every eye was suddenly upon us as Tom snatched my hands and the court fell silent for the moment of truth.

'In the case of Thomas Brentnall, do you find the defendant Guilty or Not Guilty?'

'Not Guilty!' said the foreman.

'In the case of Edmund Bullick, do you find the defendant Guilty or Not Guilty?'

'Not Guilty!' said the foreman.

The court erupted. Absolutely erupted. I never heard anything like it, either before or since. Tom and I leaped in the air and pirouetted around the dock scarcely able to take it in. *Not guilty! Not guilty! Yesssssssss! Yesssssss!* In the bowl of the court Hall turned and smiled as Jackson-Fagg reached across to shake his hand. The jury were also on their feet applauding and with astonishing indifference to the judge, gave a thumbs up to the gallery who hollered back in approval. I strained the ranks from Craven. There was no sign of Julian which was disappointing although Lady Alanna gathered her coat and quietly slipped away. The judge repeatedly smacked his gavel, but no one appeared to hear it. The noise was simply deafening even before the cacophony swept through the hall and onto the green outside where a large crowd had gathered for the verdict.

Horridge finally restored order. 'Mr Brentnall, Mr Bullick, stand up. Mr Brentnall, Mr Bullick, the jury have found you *not* guilty of the matters before court and you are free to leave the building.' (More cheering).

CHAPTER TWENTY

After a few drinks in the *Hat and Feather*, I left Hall, Tom and the others to it and caught a taxi to the stables where much had changed since that cold December morning when Alfie and I had fled to Ireland. My father's house and the Smithy were boarded up and the yard and boxes were empty. There wasn't a soul about – not a soul – which could only mean one thing; the army had taken the horses for the war and there would be no racing for a very long time. It was a bitter anti-climax. In my elation at the verdict, I simply assumed I'd be able to go home and pick up where I left off. I hadn't given much thought as to what might happen next. Yes, I'd travel to Liverpool on the 'morrow to bring Alfie home but then what? It was only now I realised that nothing at Craven was the same. It never would be. A few lights blinked in the castle, but no one stirred as I pulled off the boards and went inside.

I found the house stripped of fixtures and fittings leaving just a solitary armchair under a dust sheet in the office, a splintered mirror above the fireplace and a couple of dismantled beds stacked up on the landing. Everything else was gone. The Gimcrack Cup, my father's other mementos and treasured racing prints, his binoculars, going sticks and rosettes - everything, right down to the saddles, oilskins and riding boots- they were all gone. I could have wept. I made a fire with the planks from the door and when the stove was revved up, filled the kettle and gathered the scattered tiles of mail in the hallway. It seemed the usual rubbish – bills, circulars and more bills - until I shuffled the pack and found a letter from Fitzwilliam College informing me I was accepted to read Veterinary Medicine. Good grief. I was in. I was just thinking how proud it would have made my father when all of a sudden, there was a knock at the door. Tom probably got hammered and missed the last train. I placed the letters on the side and went to investigate.

'Hello Edmund'.

And there she was, rocking on the step, just like before only this time, she had a bottle under her arm. I nearly died.

'It's raining. Are you going to ask me in?'

I was so shaken all I could do was stare at her.

'Please, *Blue.*'

I held the door open in silence. As she squeezed past, I caught a whiff of the fragrance that had haunted me for so long.

'I need a drink' said she, passing her coat. 'Glasses still in the dresser?'

I followed her through to the kitchen.

'You've got a nerve showing your face here.'

Victoria pulled at the draws.

'Corkscrew? Corkscrew? Ah, here we are.'

'You bitch, Victoria. I spent four months in jail because of you.'

Victoria heaved the stopper.

'Château La Fete Rothschild '87 don't you know? Fresh from Lord William's cellar, or should I say Lord Alfie's cellar?'

'I trusted you.'

Victoria handed me a glass.

'How could you have stolen those papers? I trusted you.'

'I didn't take the coroner's file.'

'I don't believe you.'

Victoria downed her drink and poured another.

'Honestly, I didn't. That was Julian. I hadn't the faintest idea what your brief was on about when he started accusing me.'

Was I being played again? I didn't know what to believe although it would account for the safe being forced.

'Sent you round to test the water, did he?'

'Hardly' said she with a toss of her head. 'Julian is in Dryburn. He had an accident yesterday.'

'Nothing trivial I hope.'

'It's no laughing matter. He came to grief on the moor. It seems he fell down an old mineshaft.'

'The *moor*? What the devil was he doing on the moor?'

'Scrubbing the walls of *Hob Hole*. He rode up there last night. I tried to put him off, but he was convinced Horridge would send the jury out to inspect them.'

So that's why he wasn't in court. Well, well.

'It's all a bit sketchy' continued Victoria. 'We only realised something was wrong when his horse came back alone. Barnaby found him in the end.'

'Is he badly hurt?'

'I've just come from the hospital now. It's awful. His

ankles are shattered and it looks like his back is broken. The surgeon says he may never walk again.'

'Are you having me on?'

Victoria downed her drink. Her hands were trembling. 'If only I was. Oh Edmund, it's terrible. I barely recognised him.'

I stared into that beautiful face. Good grief. She was serious.

'He was no friend of mine but I'm sorry just the same.'

'There's something else' said Victoria refilling her glass. 'He's completely off his rocker spouting a load of nonsense about ghosts and monks. Oh, I know, it's probably the morphine but to see him bubbling at the mouth and wailing like a madman was horrifying. I couldn't get away quickly enough. Alanna is still with him, but he doesn't recognise her either.'

Monks on the moor again? Poor Julian, but the irony.

'There's no such thing as ghosts.'

'Your father and Lord William probably thought the same but look what happened to them?'

I reached for my glass.

'It was kids.'

'Well, whatever it was, I'm out. I return to London tomorrow.'

'Tomorrow? But what about Julian?'

'Julian and I are no more. I'm releasing him from our engagement.'

'I see. In sickness and in health and all that?'

Victoria shrugged her shoulders.

'What do you expect me to do? Hang around Durham wasting my bloom hoping he'll recover? And for what? He's not even Lord Craven now.'

'Have you told him?'

'Not yet. I'll leave it a while then write.'

'You don't muck about, do you?'

Victoria poured herself another drink.

'Life is too short to muck about, Edmund. *Time's winged chariot*, remember?'

I supposed that much was true.

Victoria raised her glass and chinked my own. 'Anyway, many congratulations darling. I always knew you would come through the in the end.'

'No thanks to you. How could you betray us like that?'

'I'm sorry. I really am. I didn't want to, but I had no choice.'

'Yes, you did. You could have refused to get involved.'

'Hardly. I told Julian about Tench and the burglary, it's true, but I didn't think he would be that bothered about it. When he insisted we went to Lockwood, I had no option. I was already in too deep.'

'But why give evidence?'

'Julian already suspected us. If I refused, I risked losing him altogether.'

'But Tom and I could have been sent down for years.'

'You would have been too if Crake had his way. He gave me a list of the missing property and told me to say that you boasted about stealing it all, but I wouldn't do it. If I had, I doubt if even that Hall bloke could have saved you.'

A roll of thunder boomed over the courtyard rattling the windows and crockery.

'But why all the lies?'

'Oh get real, Edmund. I was hardly going to admit we slept together.'

'I'm not talking about the trial. You lied to me, Victoria.'

'No, I didn't.'

'You said you loved me, and like a fool I believed you.' Victoria fumbled for a cigarette.

'I wasn't lying about that, Edmund. I do love you, in my own way. I loved you from the moment I saw you.'

Ugh-ugh. Fool me once, shame on you. Fool me twice?

'You only slept with me for information. You don't need to pretend any more you know.'

'I was dispatched by Julian to find out what his father had said but screwing you wasn't part of the arrangement. I did it because I wanted to.'

'Do you seriously expect me to believe that?'

'You can believe what you like but I do love you. I always did.'

'Hell fire Victoria. If that's how you treat someone you love, God help the poor sod who ever crosses you.'

Victoria struck a match. Her face lit up in the glow.

'You poor, poor boy' said she exhaling. 'You still don't get it, do you?'

'Get what exactly? Believe me, I get you. I might be love-struck and perhaps it is because I am so besotted that it took me longer than it should have to figure it out. Have you any idea what you put me through? Have you any idea what it was like in that prison? Really, have you? I could have died in there.'

Victoria stubbed out her cigarette.

'Look, I'll leave now if you like. Do you want me to leave?'

As she spoke her coal eyes seared into my own and I was helpless.

Victoria walked to the window.

'Edmund' said she staring out at the rain 'I didn't lie that day when I said I loved you, I do love you, but don't you understand that sometimes, loving somebody is not always enough?'

'It's enough for me.'

Victoria ran a finger down the pane. 'You say that now, but I could never make you happy.'

'You could try.'

'I could, but I won't. I'm not the one for you, Edmund.'

'But you were prepared to marry Julian. How could you agree to marry an oaf like him? After everything that passed between us, how could you?'

Victoria shrugged her shoulders.

'You know very well how I could. He's rich or I thought he was rich. He would have looked after us and I was prepared to take a chance on the rest.'

'There you go again. Money. Why must everything with you people always revolve around money?'

'Because at the end of the day, everything always does.'

'You're so wrong. Don't you understand that the more money you have the more you want - and for what? To buy things you don't need to impress people you don't even *like*? You can have all the money in the world, but it won't guarantee you happiness.'

'It would guarantee our family name and that would make me happy.'

Unbelievable.

'Look Victoria, *I* can make you happy. I may not have much money, at least not yet, but when this wretched war is over and Alfie is Lord Craven, I'll train the string like my father before me.'

'I don't doubt it' said she.

'Then *stay*, Victoria. Stay here with me. We can rebuild the yard together; I promise you'll never regret it.'

'I need more than that, much more.'

'*More?*' I cried stamping around the kitchen. 'What more can you possibly want? I'm offering you a home, a future, a family ...'

'It's not enough, you know it's not. My parents are depending upon me.'

I threw up my arms in frustration.

'Is that all you can say? *My parents are depending on me, My parents are depending on me.* For heaven's sake Victoria, you don't owe them the rest of your life.'

She was sobbing now.

'But that's the crux isn't it? Oh, Edmund, can't you see it was not just our estates that were mortgaged to feed my father's addiction?'

'You don't owe them the rest of your life.'

'But I do! I *do*! I could never be happy with anyone if my father were ruined. It would break the family and if it broke them, it would break me. Julian could have restored our fortunes, or so I thought. There's nothing for me in Durham now.'

I booted the stove in frustration.

'Damn it Victoria, what do you want me to say? Do I have to beg?'

'I'm not the one for you, Edmund.'

'Then why are you here then, hey? Why have you come round when you know how I feel about you? Is it to torture me some more?'

'I want you to know that I'm sorry for what I did to you. I've also come to say goodbye.'

'Well go on then, sod off' I shouted and went through to the office. Victoria called after me.

'It doesn't have to be like this.'

I flung a couple of planks on the blaze and gripped the mantelpiece. Victoria followed me into the room, her jagged loveliness tormenting me from behind the glass. I stared into the flames.

'Please Victoria, I'm asking you to stay.'

'No. I am not your destiny, Edmund.'

I turned to face her.

'But if you truly care for me, like you say you do, and I love you then surely, nothing else matters?'

Victoria slipped her arms around my neck and buried her head in my shoulder. I pulled her close screwing my eyes in the anguish of the moment.

'Oh dear, sweet Edmund' she whispered. 'You think you love me, but you are green, green, green like a green apple. This is not just about my father. It's what's right for us both. You have so much more to discover about the world- about women- and when you do, I know my love could never hold you.'

'Please don't say that. People spend a lifetime searching in vain for the opportunity we have now.'

'I'll take the risk.'

'Please, just give me a chance.'

'No Edmund. I cannot commit myself. It would be utter folly.'

'You'll regret it.'

'All my boyfriends have said that.'

'But you slept with me. Are you saying it meant nothing to you?'

'It meant a great deal, but you are confusing sex with commitment. Sex is easy. People do it all the time. It's the long game that's hard.'

'Not for me it's not. I'd do anything for you.'

Victoria shook her head.

'Edmund. You and I, it would never work; we are chalk and cheese and I don't belong in Durham for the rest of my life shovelling horseshit thank you very much. You may not realise it now but in time you will see I was right.'

The fire snapped and hissed. I fought for something to say but what was the point? There were no more cards. Her mind was made up and there was nothing I could do. I pushed her away choking back the tears.

'I'll never love anyone else.'

'Yes, you will.'

'But I don't want anyone else. I want you. I love *you*.'

'A bird may love a fish, Edmund, but where will they build their home?'

In the yard the deluge was torrential, a thousand million beads patting the cobbles like grains of rice spilling on brown paper. So that was it. *Finito*. All of the hopes and dreams that had kept me sane through those long months in captivity, they were all gone. I could not imagine a future without her. Oh God, what would become of me now? I never felt so completely and utterly wretched in my life.

'I'm so sorry' she said.

I went to the window, desperately trying to pull myself together.

'Well, you can't go home in this' I swallowed. 'If you wait until the rain stops, I'll walk you back over.'

'I don't have to go anywhere just yet.'

'There might be an umbrella under the stairs.'

'My train doesn't leave until morning'.

I turned and looked into that beautiful face.

'This is the last occasion I shall come to Durham, Edmund. I will not return. Now, you can either sulk thinking about me on my own at the castle or I can stay a while longer. It's up to you but I know how I would like to say goodbye.'

'What do you mean?'

'Oh Edmund, do I have to spell it out? We can never be together but I will stay a while longer, that's if you want me to.'

I should have chucked her out there and then. It crossed my mind but only for a moment for we both knew I could never bring myself to do it. My heart quickened. God, she was so adorable. Suddenly, we were kissing and the blood rushed through my ears. Oh, the bitter, bitter sweetness of that single moment in time.

'Victoria, you must know…'

'Shut up Edmund. Just shut up and take me to bed.'

'I don't have a bed. They're stacked up on the landing or hadn't you noticed?'

Victoria laughed.

'Well then' said she unfurling the dustsheet 'we will spend the night here. Now turn around and face the hearth.'

I struggled for words, but they sank in confusion and desire.

'Face the hearth, Edmund.'

I turned to the mirror and stared dumfounded as Victoria kicked off her shoes then slowly undressed until she stood naked in the firelight with her back arched and hands clinched behind her head. A surge of unadulterated lust engulfed me, and I thought I was going to faint.

'Now, take off your clothes.'

I needed no second invitation, Victoria watching me intently as I hopped around the fireside wrenching them off.

'I won't leave a note this time' said she laughing.

'Oh my God Victoria, what have you done to me?'

Victoria knelt on the cushion and seized the back of the chair. I thought I would burst.

'What have you done to me?'

Silence.

I reached for her waist.

'You alley cat Victoria.'

Victoria glanced over her shoulder.

'What does that make you?'

CHAPTER TWENTY-ONE

In Saint Oswald's Churchyard the blackbirds chased each other through the first dusty blossoms of spring, just as Nathaniel had predicted. It was too soon for a headstone - the mound had not settled - but my father's name gazed tenderly back from a small wooden cross poking out of the soil. I laid the clump of bluebells I had picked from his garden that morning.

'Do you think he knows we're here?' said Tom.

'I'm sure he does.'

'I thought you didn't believe in spirits?'

'I don't believe they come back and haunt us, but the dead are out there somewhere. You cannot create or destroy matter. First law of science.'

'True. Makes you wonder where they all go though.'

It was the eternal question. Where do we all go? All the people that lived before us. All those living now or waiting to be born. Where do we all go? Jesus said His father's house had many mansions. How many mansions were 'many'? I could not say. All I knew is my own father was up there in one of them and I would see him again.

'Well, when I die mate, I'm joining Dad in heaven. I couldn't possibly counter anything else.'

'I applaud your conviction' said Tom.

I whispered a final prayer and turned for the entrance.

'It's more hope than conviction. Life is utterly meaningless without hope. I'm not one to argue with Saint Paul but if love really *is* the greatest virtue, there needs to be a steward's enquiry.'

Tom laughed.

'Talking of spirits, did the police find anything at *Hob Hole*?'

'Not a single monk - although it wasn't for lack of effort. They scoured the heath for days with a team of bloodhounds.'

The gate clattered behind us as we set off down the hill.

'Do you think it was kids from the village?'

'Maybe. Everyone knows they've been at it for years, but the strange thing is, when the usual suspects were pulled in, they all swore blind they were nowhere near the place.'

'They were hardly likely to admit it.'

'The police thought so too but each and every one of them had alibis and they all checked out.'

'It doesn't make sense. Something must have spooked Julian.'

'I agree, although the moor is forbidding at night and he was pretty screwed up in the first place.'

Tom shook his head.

'Well, whatever it was, you won't catch me near *Hob Hole* anytime soon.'

I had no wish to return either. I had a ghost of my own up there.

'How is he getting on anyway?'

'Julian? In a wheelchair according to Barnaby. He's also had a nervous breakdown and they've transferred him to the secure ward.'

Tom gave a low whistle.

'The poor bugger.'

'I know. I couldn't stand the guy either, but I'd never have wished that upon him.'

We shuffled through the crowd on Elvet Bridge.

'What did they say at Fitzwilliam?'

'They're holding my place until September. The war should be over by then. How about you?'

'When I told Dad, he obviously tried to talk me out of it. He said I was doing just as much for King and Country running the business, but I couldn't sit behind a desk while my pals were in France dying somewhere. In the end I just said my mind was made up and I was going with you.'

'How did Jane take it?'

'I promised to write. It's too soon to get involved, she knows that.'

I'd said as much to Morgan. It was pointless making any plans at the moment.

We paused on the bridge for a final glimpse of the river and the deep wooded gorge. So much history. So many memories. I wondered when we would return to this enchanting place or if we would return at all? From a mound dripping with primroses the castle walls grinned knowingly across the city. On the towpath below, small children fed the ducks as a pair of lovers walked by hand in hand. Everything was so incredibly still and peaceful, like it was the calm before the storm that was about to overtake us. I thought of Victoria and wondered what she was doing right now.

'Never mind Ed' said Tom, perceptive as ever. 'We've still got each other'.

I laughed. 'True. True.'

'It is true. Look, I realize things are difficult right now, but you've got to let her go.'

'Easier said than done.'

'I didn't say it would be easy, but you've got to man up. If she wants you, she'll be back.'

'Do you think so?'

'Do I think she'll be back? No, I don't actually. While everyone is haunted by someone - even her – you're chasing a rainbow, you know you are.'

In Saddler Street, we lined the walls to let through a column of soldiers.

'You're right of course but it's the lousiest feeling in the world.'

'What is?'

'Wanting someone so badly who doesn't want you back.'

'Well' said Tom 'I can't help you there but there's a young girl waiting in Ireland who might be able to.'

In Durham Market Place the square was decked with bunting and a Colliery band was thumping away by the statue of the Marquess of Londonderry. I searched the happy faces where Fenoughty and the rest of the lads were milling around in the throng. On seeing us he yelled across.

'We thought you'd never get here! Come on! You don't want to miss the Hun-bashing do you?'

I had no intention of missing it although as we joined the line of volunteers snaking into the Guildhall, I wondered if he would be quite as eager if he, too, had witnessed the carnage in Hartlepool or just spent the morning with Conway's mother and father.

EPILOGUE

My brother returned to Ampleforth, his unexpected elevation exciting him considerably less than the prospect of seeing all his friends again. His indifference was wonderfully touching but he was still young, and the implications of his heritage would dawn upon him soon enough.

We had been right about Tench. He was the magpie all along. In the inquiry following our acquittal the missing property was recovered from his loft including my father's watch and a hoard of other personal belongings carefully squirreled away during his time in office. In a sorry conclusion to such an exemplary career, he was jailed for six years.

Latimer, shamed and penniless, was expelled from the profession, the Law Society taking over his practice while he saw out his days in a bedsit. We considered pressing charges but what was the point? He could never repay us (the estate reimbursed Tom's father) and his frail constitution would never have coped with the rigours of prison life. You have to let the odd one go.

Crake's reputation was also in tatters and he was promptly charged with perjury and embezzlement. In the inevitable scrutiny of his business it transpired that he and Julian had been plundering the Craven estate for years. Realising he was finished and slippery to the last, he waited until a week before his trial then emptied the client account and took a steamer to Australia. He was never heard of again.

In an effort to distance himself from his partner's disgrace, Lockwood – the eternal *Vicar of Bray*- threw his hat into the ring to administer Lord William's estate during Alfie's minority. I thought he couldn't possibly be serious but when he started crowing on about his longstanding connection to the family it was clear he expected to be appointed. There wasn't a cat's chance in hell though, and I could only marvel at the front of the man whose card was marked that December afternoon when I called at his office and he pretended to be out- and that was before he replaced the coroner's file back in the mortuary, because it must have been him. No, it was time for a new broom and in the weeks that followed, a fresh board of trustees was appointed including some of the governors at Ampleforth, Jane and Seaton.

Lady Alanna was utterly broken by the discovery of Alfie's paternity and immediately withdrew into an isolated wing of the castle with her vodka and Dachshund. While she was well provided for under the Will and didn't want for anything material, it was a wretched existence and my heart went out to her because although Jane visited regularly, there was no sight or sign of her former friends. I frequently tried to engage with her, but it was a hopeless task and as the months slipped by, she became more and more of a recluse.

Ten months after the trial she died broken and alone after a bad fall. It was a tragic end to a tragic life.

Far from being damaged by events at Durham Crown Court, Victoria's stock flourished as the press, looking for any distraction from the horrors of Flanders relentlessly pursued this enigmatic *femme fatale* of society. I remember seeing her photograph gazing from the cover of *Tattler* under the eye-catching headline '*Victoria: The truth?*' Other periodicals followed with a stream of so-called 'exclusives' and endorsements of everything from shoes to shampoo. I could only admire Victoria for milking the intrigue while she could and the way she fashioned herself into the first of the 'It Girls'. Everyone but no one wanted a slice of the cake although the lady herself, wily as ever, played her hand shrewdly parting with little of substance but always just enough to keep the sails turning. Although she was right about us, she haunted me in E minor and I never got her totally out of my plasma aching each time she reared up from the gossip columns on the arm of some Duke or other. A few months after we parted, she became engaged to Buster Keaton although that relationship quickly fizzled out and the last I heard of her, it was in the usual fanfare of publicity when she joined the Voluntary Aid Detachment to nurse soldiers at the front.

Hall's reputation was only enhanced by our acquittal and as his achievements racked up in other sensational cases, he became very famous. I used to follow his career closely and took great delight reading about his endless spats with judges and fellow advocates. The perception he was a more accomplished orator than lawyer might explain why he was never appointed to the judiciary himself, although having seen him in action, I suspect it was because he spoke his mind too often and stepped on too many toes. He never divulged the identity of our benefactor though, and as time went by, I supposed that maybe there hadn't been one after all and it was to the *Great Defender* himself that we were indebted.

AUTHOR'S NOTE

I always wanted to be a writer. It must be something in the DNA because I started keeping a journal when I was ten – something I have maintained for over fifty years. In the decade while the children were growing up, I managed 750,000 words of my own experiences and our family history. I did this because while I remember three of my grandparents, I never knew much about their parents or those who went before. I thought 'if only someone a hundred years ago had taken the time to set it all out for future generations?' but alas, no one did and like most people, I am left to interpret the past through a handful of grainy photographs, not knowing who any of them were.

I wrote all this history for our children and theirs who follow. I also wrote it for my old age. You know, Samuel Pepys commented that a diarist lives his life three times over. He first lives it when he has the experience; he lives it a second time when he writes about the experience and then a third time (fourth, fifth) when he reads what he has written. Most of my encounters were penned in the late 1990's and early 2000's when the events were still fresh in my mind. Where the life history ends the threads are taken up by over a score of hard copy annual diaries which at the moment are gathering dust in the attic. In 2017 I began to keep the journals electronically and still do, and the text, like the hard copies, are out there for posterity if anyone happens to stumble upon them.

And so to penning *Hob Hole/Raven*? I knew I had a book or two in me but kept putting it off until one poignant evening it suddenly dawned on me that if I didn't hurry up and crack on, I'd never get it done. Time is so of the essence. On Harold Wilson's headstone in the Scilly Isles are the words *Tempus Imperator Rerum*. Time is the ruler of everything. It most certainly is and in the knowledge that one is a long time dead, I decided that instead of talking about writing a novel, I would get on with it while I could- no 'ifs' or 'buts'- and duly started by making use of the long hours hanging around Crown Court waiting for jury verdicts.

Having decided to write a novel, my next challenge was whether to voice it in the first or the third person. I thought long and hard about this and eventually settled on the first person because this is what I am used to having taken and studied thousands of witness statements at work. Next challenge. What am I going to write about? While I had in mind sketching characters at a funeral and was inspired by the wretched state of Henry VIII when Anne Boleyn first rejected his advances, I drew mainly on my own legal and other experiences. Love and gambling seemed an obvious mix then throw in alcoholism, religion, sex, a ghost or two and a Crown Court trial and I knew I had the basics. I chose to open the novel in a lecture hall where proceedings are interrupted by the headmaster who wanted a word in private. This actually happened to a mate of mine when we were in Sixth Form at Mount St Mary's College and I shall never forget it. One minute he was happy and bursting with life, the next his whole world fell apart but that is a tale for another day. Suffice to say I had my starting point; I would open *Hob Hole* in a laboratory at Ampleforth College (where we sometimes used to play rugby) then keep writing and see where it took me.

The scenes in court reflect some of the more memorable episodes I witnessed in my time as an advocate, the material fortified by adapted transcripts of famous trials, one or two including Hall himself. I appreciate the layman might find some of the dialect verbose, but the exchanges and submissions are true to life and reflect the extraordinary oratory at the command of the elite few who rise to the top of the profession. Edward Marshall Hall KC, one such individual, was the most illustrious barrister of his day and something of his aura lingers still. Standing six feet three inches, strikingly handsome and possessed of a great and remarkable personality, he was egotistical and hot-tempered yet extraordinarily sympathetic and warm-hearted. While I have been unable to discover if this champion of lost causes ever graced Durham Crown Court, I would like to think he did because standing between a villain like Hayward and the gallows was typical of the instructions he used to take on. Edmund and Tom were certainly fortunate to secure his services, Hall's appearance in the narrative akin to an unexpected cameo from someone like David Beckham that rescued the village football team. Like Hall, Lord Justice Horridge was also a real person and the caustic one-liners and various spats between the advocates are authentic as are the conditions in Durham prison at the beginning of the twentieth century.

Craven and the stable complex are modelled on Raby Castle and Witton Castle, the latter situated a few miles from Hamsterley Forest. The peaks beyond the Hamsterley plantation include a remote area of heath known as *Monksmoor* where legend has it that the crags on the summit are indeed haunted by ghostly apparitions.

The bombardment of Hartlepool on 16 December 1914 actually happened and the scenes described by Bullick (including the death of Alix Liddle) are taken from the contemporaneous accounts of those who survived. Hailing from Teesside, I grew up knowing all about that dreadful day and it surprised me when *Hob Hole* was published how few readers knew about it. The attack was real enough though. The loss of civilian life was truly appalling, the even greater tragedy being the fate of the thousands of local men who immediately enlisted only to perish in similar fashion at the front.

Having completed my novel, the greatest challenge was to find a publisher. Ever the optimist I dispatched specimen chapters to over fifty different agents but only three of them responded with a standard rejection letter. Researching the problem informed me that publishers have what is known as a 'slush pile' where they chuck all unsolicited manuscripts, and the odds of securing a writing contract in this manner are one in two thousand. What? I'm normally first in the queue for a tilt at the ring but 2000/1? Sod that. I have precious little time left as it is, so I decided to appoint my own publisher and release the book myself. I studied the field and dodging the charlatans and vanity press finally opted for York Publishing Services who I have to say were terrific – they still are. The cost? All in all, about the same as a few season tickets watching the Boro at *The Riverside* and I never parted with such a sum more happily.

Positives of writing *Hob Hole/Raven*? Too many to mention but first and foremost I managed it. The satisfaction of having set out to write a novel and finally completing and publishing it was a reward in itself. It still is and always will be. It makes all those months slaving away and scratching my head so meaningful and while this humble contribution to English literature may never sprout wings, if I were run over by a truck tomorrow, at least I would depart this world knowing that I did what I could while I could.

Regrets? Not many although I wish I hadn't stopped at 90,000 words in the first book and continued the sequel there and then, however I researched this aspect too and the common advice was to stop before 100,000 or you would tire your reader. 'They say...' and all that – whoever 'they' are.

My main regret, however, is I did not include an author's note at the end of the first edition of *Hob Hole*, you know, a few paragraphs similar to this to tell the reader a little about the author and the route I took to get where I finally ended up. Anyhow, I've put that right now.

Thank you again for reading my tale. It was the very best I could do, and at the end of the day, all you can do is what you can do. If you enjoyed it, I hope you will pass the book on to someone else, and, if you can spare a moment, maybe *like* our Facebook page and post a review on Amazon, *Goodreads* or one of the other literary sites?

And that's it, author's note completed. Again, thank you for your time because I know it is precious.

With every good wish wherever you are
yours truly
simon.catterall@mail.com